NU

Bermuda sounds like paradise, and Staff Nurse Cora Jordan means to take full advantage of living and working in such a climate. But Dr Darryl Delaney has other ideas about Cora's suitability for the job . . .

NURSE IN BERMUDA

BY

HELEN UPSHALL

MILLS & BOON LIMITED
London · Sydney · Toronto

First published in Great Britain 1984
by Mills & Boon Limited, 15–16 Brook's Mews,
London W1A 1DR

ISBN 0 263 74542 2

Set in 11 on 12 pt Linotron Times
03/0184

Photoset by Rowland Phototypesetting Ltd
Bury St Edmunds, Suffolk
Made and printed in Great Britain by
Richard Clay (The Chaucer Press) Ltd
Bungay, Suffolk

CHAPTER ONE

IT ISN'T supposed to do this in Bermuda, Cora thought crossly as she stood inside the porchway of Zenobia's Hospital and shook her umbrella outside. She had gone off duty for the afternoon aware of, but trying not to notice the wind increasing to violent proportions. The storm had finally swept across the islands, shaking and drenching palm trees and shrubs until everything looked as if it had been put through the washing machine.

Thank goodness the worst of it had passed and now a steady silent rain was falling. It would be all over by nightfall, she'd been assured.

She folded her umbrella and walked briskly through the corridor to the Casualty department. She'd come in the main entrance because it happened to be closer to the nurses' home and she guessed by the sound of the ambulance siren whining to a halt that the other entrance would be blocked by the emergency team.

After putting her wet umbrella in a corner of the locker room she checked in the mirror that her cap was on straight and only the right amount of tawny hair was showing, gave her apron a pull to tidy it round her trim waist and went to report to Sister Kenmore.

'I heard the ambulance, Sister,' she said. 'Coronary?'

Sister Sara Kenmore nodded. 'They're working on him now so it's just you and me, and young Tod Freeman, holding the fort; *and* there's a few in the waiting area. Tod's in the treatment room so perhaps you'd go along to assist him.'

Cora left Sister Kenmore drawing up an injection, and went to the treatment room where in one of the cubicles a young girl was sitting on the couch. She looked pale, but was trying to be brave as Tod Freeman, the youngest and most junior of the housemen in Casualty was busy with catgut and needle.

'Thank goodness you're back,' he said glancing over his shoulder. 'At least one more pair of hands.'

'Having a busy time by the sounds of things,' Cora said, then smiling at the little girl asked: 'And what have you been up to?'

'Fell through a glass door,' she managed in a frightened whisper.

'How on earth did you do that?' Cora pursued, hoping to keep the child's attention from what Tod was doing.

'I was running, trying to get in before the storm came,' she said.

Cora raised an eyebrow and made a face, and the girl's expression changed, a huge, beaming smile appearing, albeit briefly.

Cora looked at the notes and saw that her name was Karen Fall.

'Well, Karen,' she said jovially, 'I hope you don't live up to your name too often.'

Cora also noticed that Karen was only nine years

old, but she was a well-built girl with sparkling eyes and a ready smile, chubby cheeks which accentuated her happy disposition.

As was usual in such cases the mother looked more anxious than the patient, while Tod did the best he could with the torn, jagged flesh of Karen's knee. Cora learned that they were in Bermuda for two weeks' holiday from Bournemouth, England.

'I only arrived from England a few days ago myself,' she said. 'I'm from Cheshire orginally, but I've worked in London for the past two years.'

Tod straightened up and moved the trolley aside.

'Right,' he said, 'nearly as good as your mum's sewing, honey. I'll leave you to give her a tetanus injection, Staff Nurse, then she can go, and we'll see her again in five days' time.'

Tod moved on to the next cubicle and Cora bandaged the injured knee before going away to prepare the injection.

She heard footsteps approaching and a deep-toned male voice sounded impatiently at the door.

'Staff Nurse, I'll check through everyone now that I'm here.'

Cora couldn't identify the tremor which passed through her, though as she turned to face the owner of the voice she realised it was fear crossed with recognition and intense dislike.

What was *he* doing here at Zenobia's! She stared vacantly at him, unnerved by his size and the handsome darkness of him. He spoke perfect English but by the tanned skin, fierce dark eyes, hooded by thick black brows, and sleek ebony hair she guessed there was a hint of Latin American blood in his veins.

'Well, come along, girl, or have you been struck by lightning?' he barked.

Cora licked her lips which had gone horribly dry. He didn't recognise her, thank goodness for that.

'Sister's around somewhere,' she said. 'I was just preparing a tetanus injection.'

'Then we'll start with that patient,' he said brusquely.

She was glad the syringe was already lying in the kidney dish. He walked towards her and she knew her whole body was trembling in awe of this man.

Cora led the way into the cubicle where Karen Fall and her mother were still waiting. She handed the card to Mr Delaney while she gave Karen the prepared injection. As she rubbed her arm with the cotton wool swab she was aware of the man behind her impatiently looking about him.

'X-rays, Staff Nurse?'

Cora added the swab to the dish containing the disposable syringe and turned to look with him.

'Where are they?' he demanded shortly.

'I . . . I . . . they don't appear to be here,' she mumbled. 'I've only just come on duty,' she excused.

His fiery black eyes surveyed her briefly, then with a smile he turned to Karen's mother.

'Your daughter has been X-rayed, Mrs—um—Fall?'

Mrs Fall shook her head. 'No,' she said. 'After taking all Karen's particulars they put us in this cubicle, cleaned the wound and that other young doctor stitched her knee up.'

The next thing Cora knew was having the folder thrust rudely against the bib of her white apron. As he filled in an X-ray form Mr Delaney snarled: 'X-rays at once, Staff Nurse.'

At the door he paused. 'Don't leave until I tell you, Mrs Fall.'

Then with decisive footsteps he could be heard moving around looking in each cubicle.

'I'm sorry, Mrs Fall,' Cora apologised. 'I assumed you'd already been to the X-ray department. I'll just fetch a wheelchair to take Karen along there.'

Farther along the corridor she bumped straight into Mr Delaney.

'Who's responsible for this?' he asked gruffly. 'Surely you know by now that if a patient has fallen through the glass panel of a door, X-rays should be taken *before* the wound is stitched?'

'I told you I've only just come on duty, Mr Delaney. Dr Freeman was already stitching when Sister asked me to help.'

'Freeman,' he echoed with bitterness, 'I might have known.'

Cora was glad to escape to the adjoining X-ray department for a while. She explained to the technician in charge that Karen had been at the hospital for over two hours, so they rearranged the scheduled list to take immediate pictures of the injury. When the result was examined Cora was dismayed, but she pushed Karen back to the cubicle without comment and went in search of Sister Kenmore.

As she passed the office door she heard voices

and saw Tod Freeman in discussion with Mr Darryl Delaney. *His* name had left an indelible imprint on her mind over the past few weeks. She cringed from him, remembering how the beautiful day, now over two months ago, had suddenly blacked out for her.

Coming to Bermuda, the little-known group of volcanic islands out in mid-Atlantic, had been the start of a new life. Not that she had any particular reason for leaving the London hospital where she had trained, but her friend had been hit by the wanderlust bug soon after qualifying, and now nearly a year later Cora had been enticed to the enchanting island in the sun. Well, the sun shone most days, but it was still on the fringe of spring at present. Two months ago she had come to spend Christmas with Mandy who had persuaded her to apply for a post at Zenobia's. She had obtained special permission to stay at the nurses' home as Mandy's guest for a nominal sum which had enabled her to plan a stay of ten days, and once she had got the interviews out of the way she had hired a moped in order to explore the island. Traffic was supposed to keep to a maximum of twenty miles per hour and she knew all about keeping to the left-hand side of the road, being British, but the idiot careering round the one and only roundabout on the island must have been travelling at over forty miles per hour. She never knew quite what happened, but she found herself in a small private room at Zenobia's suffering from concussion. She got to know some of the staff which had helped considerably now that she was here to work, but Mr Darryl Delaney had visited her only once, at first showing some concern for her, and then, realising that she was not badly hurt he had informed her that he would be prosecuting her for dangerous driving.

'But you must have been exceeding the speed limit,' Cora had counter-accused in utter astonishment.

'Permissible, Miss Jordan, because I was on my way to visit a very sick patient,' he had replied curtly and left.

No one had told Cora that he was on the staff at Zenobia's. She had assumed that he was in general practice. She'd have something to say to Mandy Rawson when they met up at supper time. At least he didn't recognise her now and she hoped he had forgotten the name of his accident victim.

At the moment he had his back to her. His size was formidable, his white coat emphasising the broadness of his shoulders. He must have sensed her presence, or had been quick to notice Tod's silent acknowledgement. He turned, glowering, affording her a momentary glance from his pitch black eyes, before grasping the X-rays from her hand.

Cora remained silent as he held them up to the light then, casting a scornful look at Tod, he strode to the nearest wall screen.

Should she go or stay? she wondered, but before she could move he waved an angry hand towards the screen, including her as well as Tod in his condemning assertion that there was glass in the wound of Karen Fall's knee.

'Take a good look at that screen,' he thundered,

'and both of you feel proud of what you've put that poor child through.'

He spun round and strode off shouting, 'Nurse, prepare the trolley.'

Tod looked at Cora wearily. She guessed he'd been on duty far too long. The ferocity of the storm had caused havoc on the island with several casualties.

As she quickened her steps to follow Mr Delaney she tried to convince herself that he was a GP helping out rather than being on the permanent staff at Zenobia's.

When Cora caught up with him he was already apologising to Mrs Fall. She took it well, no doubt influenced by the doctor's handsome good looks and charming manner.

He set to work personally removing the stitching Tod had done, then carefully extracted the fragments of glass before more X-rays, and finally re-stitching the wound.

When he at last lifted his face he looked intently into Cora's eyes a moment too long. She prayed that he wasn't remembering. He couldn't possibly recognise her after only one brief meeting, but then he lowered his gaze to her name brooch.

'Staff Nurse Jordan,' he said in a significant tone, 'I'll leave you to replace the bandage and we'll see Karen again shortly.' With profuse apologies to Mrs Fall once more he went away and Cora inwardly breathed a sigh of relief.

There was no let up for the remaining working hours, except for the storm which quietened and becalmed the evening, though Cora was thankful that Sara Kenmore dutifully assisted Darryl Delaney. Even patients stopped arriving by late evening so the waiting cuts and bruises were dealt with and Tod went off duty feeling less than confident.

Cora tidied the cubicles and prepared trolleys in readiness for the night staff and when she went to say goodnight to Sara she found her in her office, Darryl Delaney perched on the corner of her desk in deep and what seemed intimate conversation.

'All right to go, Sister?' Cora enquired, anxious to put as much distance as possible between herself and the fearsome doctor.

Sara, a firm favourite with Cora and a much idolised Junior Sister by everyone, smiled in acknowledgement, and as Cora turned to leave Darryl Delaney slid to his feet and followed Cora.

'Tell me it can't be,' he said in a pleading tone.

Cora felt as if someone had caught her in a snare. She turned. It was no use trying to ignore him, she'd have to face him and at least here in the empty waiting hall there was no one around to witness the confrontation.

'Can't be what?' Cora questioned primly, knowing that her eyes were burning uncomfortably and the blood had rushed into her cheeks. She felt like Alice-in-Wonderland, getting smaller and smaller. Was he going to change into the Incredible Hulk at any minute and squeeze her into pulp? It wouldn't be difficult with his superior strength pitted against her mere five feet four inches of small bones and delicate flesh. At this minute she wished she was several inches taller with firm muscles, well-developed and a lot of aggression to go with the reddish streaks in her brownish coloured hair. At least she could manage a few electric sparks from her blue eyes in self-defence should the need arise.

He took a step nearer, bearing down on her, and like a magnet she was drawn to look up into his face.

'Jordan,' he said slowly, 'Cora Jordan, the whizz-kid of mopeds?'

Was he going to be nice about it after all? But how did she answer such a question?

'I . . . you . . .' she stammered, 'you did knock me off my moped.'

She wished she hadn't reminded him. His lips parted, his eyes narrowed, he seemed to expand before her eyes.

'I did no such thing, Miss Cora Jordan,' he exploded. 'You fell off your machine right in front of me.'

'Of course I didn't,' she argued hotly. 'What an absurd suggestion. You were travelling too fast.'

'It's time they banned holiday-makers from hiring mopeds just the same as they have cars. You're a menace to people who need to get around in the course of their work.'

'Drivers who exceed the speed limit of twenty miles per hour are the menace,' Cora retorted, 'but we shall soon find out who the guilty party was when it goes to court. I hope you realise that you might have killed me.'

She thought the corners of his mouth upturned a fraction, almost as if he was going to smile. Why was the thought of killing her amusing? she wondered.

'Well, I didn't, did I?' His tone was less arrogant. 'I just hope you're a better nurse than you are moped rider, though why you had to inflict your capabilities on Bermuda, much less Zenobia's, God only knows.' He lifted his hands in a gesture of despair and strode off through the corridor, removing his white coat as he went.

Cora retraced her steps to Sister's office.

'Sara,' she began, 'he . . . he's hateful.'

Sara glanced up, eyes twinkling and with a sympathetic look said: 'Go on to supper, Cora. He's all right, you'll soon get used to his funny ways and you'll love him the same as everyone does.'

'Never!' Cora responded with indignation. She went on to explain to Sara the circumstances in which they'd met before.

Sara smiled. 'I knew he was involved in an accident but I didn't connect it with you, but then I was off duty when you were brought in and it wasn't until later that Darryl told me about it.'

Cora decided it was no use trying to get Sara on her side: She was a devotee of the handsome doctor.

'I'll go to supper,' she murmured and went on her way.

In the staff canteen she poured herself some coffee and decided to spoil herself with a freshly baked waffle with ice-cream and maple syrup. While she was waiting for it she went to the table where her friend Mandy had reserved a place for her.

'Had a good day, Cora?' her friend asked cheerfully.

'*Had*—yes—until this past hour when I had my second brush with a certain Darryl Delaney. *I* thought he was a GP, and you didn't see fit to correct me,' she accused petulantly.

'I didn't realise that you didn't know he was on the staff here,' Mandy replied, her mischievous green eyes glinting beneath her fair lashes.

'Tell me the worst,' Cora pleaded, 'is he permanently in Casualty?'

Mandy laughed at Cora's despondency. 'He's Senior Surgical Registrar so I'm afraid I can't promise you that your paths won't cross quite frequently.'

'Cross seems inevitable,' Cora groaned. She sipped her black coffee and stared miserably into it, seeing only Darryl Delaney's taunting eyes.

A few moments later Prue, the cook, called that her waffle was ready and as she ate she gave Mandy a graphic description of the last hour or so of duty.

'Casualty in any hospital tends to be chaotic. Poor Tod,' Mandy sympathised, 'that was an unfortunate blunder to make.'

Cora sighed. 'Suppose I'm going to be on the receiving end of all Mr Delaney's bad temper. I think it was grossly unjust to suggest that my professional capabilities are as inferior as riding a moped, besides,' she added crossly, 'I wasn't in the wrong. I'm going to need a good lawyer.'

'I should wait until you hear something more definite than his accusations. Now he knows you're a colleague I'm sure he won't take it any farther,' Mandy consoled.

'If you saw the look on his face you'd have no

doubts that he means to prosecute,' Cora insisted. 'By the way, is there anything between Sara Kenmore and "Sir"?'

Mandy laughed. 'Lucky Sara if there is! Sara's married anyway, to the dishiest of policemen. He got posted here for five years, so she was able to get a job here too. You might have to watch out for Sister Longford though.'

'Mm,' Cora demurred, 'so far we've got on okay together. She's very efficient, and runs the department on well-oiled wheels. She's very experienced, of course, and has been around a fair bit.'

'Around a long time too. She must be past forty.'

'That's not old; in ten years time we shall be heading towards forty,' Cora warned. 'Do you mean that she and Mr Delaney—?'

'She'd like to think so,' Mandy divulged, 'but he's only about thirty-six.'

'So, perhaps he likes older women.'

'Could be,' Mandy acknowledged, raising an eyebrow. 'He's the most talked about doctor in the whole hospital, but, for me, Tod Freeman will do.'

Mandy was by nature a chatterbox and the conversation drifted away to the kind of day she had endured on Women's Surgical ward where she hoped to be in the running for post as Junior Sister eventually.

They took their time finishing supper and darkness had descended by the time they strolled back to the nurses' home.

The air smelled sweet after the storm and although puddles spattered the roads and pave-

ments it had stopped raining and a few stars brightened the otherwise gloomy sky. But as always in
Bermuda the evening air was tuneful with the
singing of tree-frogs.

Cora felt less depressed now and responding
eagerly to the whistling frogs she stopped by some
trees at the entrance to the hospital buildings and
peered into the bark hoping for a glimpse of one
even though she knew there was no chance.

They shone torches around the base of the tree
hopefully.

'I'll have to bring a magnifying glass,' Cora said.
'It just isn't fair of them to hide so cleverly.'

'They *are* only a half an inch long,' Mandy reminded her.

'And to think they make all this noise.'

A nearby car revved up and was about to swing
away from the hospital, but it stopped with a skid
and from the driver's seat a man's voice echoed
scornfully in the night.

'When you find one, Staff Nurse, treat it kindly
and maybe it'll turn into a Prince and carry you off.'

With a screech of tyres Darryl Delaney sped
away.

Cora's cheeks burned with indignation.

'How dare he!' she snapped angrily. 'I hate him!'

Mandy laughed. 'What a nice suggestion though.
Find a frog and he'll change into the handsomest of
men.'

'If only it were that easy,' Cora moaned.

'That's just the point. First catch your frog,'
Mandy laughed.

'All I come up with is a bad-tempered bull-frog.'

'But, oh, what a handsome one—and he really is pretty nice,' Mandy said solemnly. 'It's unfortunate that you've started off on the wrong foot. Perhaps by the time you see him next he'll have forgotten about mopeds.' Cora doubted it, but she tried to put the doctor and his sarcasm out of her mind. She'd met arrogant, conceited men like him before and they were best ignored, she decided.

This wasn't easy where Darryl Delaney was concerned, with half the hospital doting on him. But for the next few days Cora didn't see him and was thankful that work in Casualty was less hectic than on the night of the storm.

Cora was on duty when Karen Fall visited Casualty again. She undid the bandage and carefully examined the wound, then realised from the notes that Mr Delaney had requested to be informed when Karen next attended Casualty.

Cora decided to try to pass this one on to Sister Longford, it being Sara Kenmore's day off.

'This is the little girl who had glass in her knee,' she said. 'Mr Delaney wanted to be notified.'

'Then notify him, Staff Nurse,' Sister Longford said impatiently. 'Bleep him, and if he doesn't respond you'll have to personally go to the doctors' sitting room and drag him away. He's probably having coffee. It's not his theatre day.'

Cora alerted the switchboard but the minutes ticked by and eventually the telephone operator suggested that he must have switched off his bleeper.

She could send one of the junior nurses, she supposed, but Sister Longford might question that as she had them all at her beck and call, and she wasn't in too good a mood.

Cora braced herself and hoped the long trek through corridors and up three flights of stairs would increase her confidence. She hesitated outside the doctors' room where the door was slightly ajar and a low murmur of masculine voices could be heard.

She knocked and when no one answered she pushed open the door.

'Is Mr Delaney here?' she asked in a commanding voice.

A hush descended on the company, and the several young men who were there all looked in the direction of an armchair in the corner where Darryl Delaney was relaxing comfortably, one leg resting across the other knee with an open folder balanced on it while he sipped from a cup of coffee. He looked up lazily, and recognising Cora jerked his head as if demanding an explanation.

'Karen Fall is in Casualty, Mr Delaney. You wished to be notified, I believe.'

'Ah—yes—' he drawled. 'One of Tod's little misdemeanours. Just one moment, Staff Nurse.'

He drained his cup, closed the folder, and stood up. Gosh, there was so much of him, she thought, and then in a lighter vein she had to suppress a giggle. Imagine getting all of him inside the skin of a minute whistling tree-frog! No, somehow she couldn't imagine him whistling or singing, or being the least bit musically romantic.

'Lead on, Staff Nurse,' he said, and even managed the shadow of a smile.

Cora hadn't imagined how they were going to find anything of mutual interest to talk about as they moved side by side down the narrow passageway. She tried to lengthen her stride to match his, but was in danger of being left behind until he suddenly turned and paused so that she could catch up. As they neared a junction of corridors and stairs they collided with two nursing sisters and Cora found herself descending the stairs alone. Should she continue, or wait for him if he was bent on chatting up the nursing staff!

'Why walk when you can ride, Cora?' She glanced back and saw him on the landing, a real devilishly handsome Latin-American smile transforming his features. It was the cleft in his nicely rounded chin that made her falter. She wanted to turn and escape while the going was good but somehow she managed to pull herself up straight by the time she reached him. Even then she guessed that only the tip of her white starched cap was level with his shoulder. A lift stood open and he ushered her into it. In confusion Cora hurriedly stretched out her fingers to press the button for the ground floor, and Darryl Delaney's fingers reached it at the same time so he held hers prisoner.

The rotten swine, he knew he was unnerving her, and to make matters worse the lift's movement made her feel as if she had left her stomach behind on the top floor. His smile widened as she closed her eyes briefly, but he still held her fingers in his.

'I wouldn't like you to press the alarm bell by mistake,' he excused and she knew by the tone of his voice that he was getting in another dig about the moped accident and her supposed inefficiencies. She felt herself getting hotter from her toes up, or was it from her scalp down? She was in danger of losing control—and all because he had called her by her Christian name!

The lift stopped. Cora was at a disadvantage standing so close to the doors and nowhere to hold on to, but then she felt Darryl's other hand at her waist steadying her. It seemed as if the lift doors must be stuck they took so long to start gliding apart, and by now she was burning uncomfortably.

He released his pressure from her hand just enough for her to drop her arm but his fingers remained firmly round hers and she had to tug frantically to get free as they were confronted by colleagues waiting to go up in the lift. She tried to hurry along, but he was quickly at her side. She hoped she didn't look as flustered as she felt but she knew she must by the second glances some of the staff gave her as they passed through Outpatients.

It seemed as if she would never reach the cubicle where she had left Karen Fall—she was Alice again, going through a never-ending tunnel . . .

Thankfully, Sister Longford was waiting. She gave Cora a withering look, one which dismissed her as easily as if she had spoken the words, but Cora was glad to retreat and she went to the desk, picked up the next card and called the patient by name.

It was several patients later before she managed to cool off. She could hear strains of some jollification coming from Karen's cubicle and she guessed

Darryl Delaney was expert at putting young patients at ease. Perhaps Sister Longford would be sweeter tempered too, which she was until she went off duty in the early evening, leaving Cora to assist Neil Endicott, the more senior casualty officer who was in charge.

There were the usual minor injuries to deal with, and a case of renal colic. After a fractured arm had been plastered there seemed to be a lull, which Cora hoped would last until she went off duty. She was tidying the treatment room, making sure everything was left neat and tidy for the night staff, when she heard footsteps pass the door. A pause and then they returned and Cora with a pounding heart looked up to find Darryl Delaney coming towards her.

'Survived another day, Staff Nurse Jordan?'

She had already fore-armed herself against some sarcasm, or snide remark, but he looked less fierce and his smile appeared to be a natural one with a merry sparkle in his eyes. He'd gone back to using her surname, she noticed, and by his tone it seemed as if he had to keep reminding himself of who she was. Was he storing it all up in readiness for the court case, she wondered? Cora did not allow his show of benevolence to influence her. She continued laying up the dressings trolley after smiling briefly in acknowledgement.

She presumed he was going off duty too as she had taken in by her swift glance that he was wearing a pale green short-sleeved shirt, darker green tie, quite plain to match dark green trousers. From the corner of her eye she saw that he was standing, hands on hips, only inches behind her.

'It occurs to me, Cora, that I ought to enquire how you intend to get around on these islands,' he said pointedly.

She stalled for a few minutes. Would she kindle his wrath by telling him that she intended to buy a bicycle so that she and Mandy could go places together?

'Most people find taxis quite cheap, or there is an excellent bus service. Were you here at Christmas to interview for this job?' he pursued.

So many questions, all in the same breath.

'I'm aware of all the public services, Mr Delaney,' she said with stony indifference, 'and yes, I did come to Bermuda to spend Christmas with my friend, and to interview for this post.'

'Friend?' He sounded surprised, as if he didn't expect her to have any of those.

'Staff Nurse Mandy Rawson,' Cora divulged crisply.

'Mandy Rawson, the cuddly blonde?' There was a hint of familiarity in his voice. 'I couldn't imagine why you might have left England. Not that many English come here, you know, most of the staff are Canadian or American.'

'You're English?' she determined.

'Oh, you did notice? Like most people notice that there's foreign blood in my veins too?'

The conceit of the man, Cora thought, bristling inwardly.

'How long have you been qualified?' he asked when she didn't make any further comment.

'Just over two years,' Cora replied, wondering

how much of this was to be taken down and used in evidence against her.

'Mm—that makes you about twenty-three,' he speculated.

'Twenty-four, in fact, and Mandy's just twenty-five, but she's lucky she'll never look her age.'

'So you're both after Sister's posts?'

'We can wait.'

'Why Bermuda?'

'Why not?'

He suddenly and without warning swung her round away from the trolley.

'All right, Cora Jordan, I was making an effort to be friendly since you're new here, and since we shall be working together on occasion, but if that's how you feel . . .'

'*I* feel!' Cora exploded. 'I can't forget that you caused me to lose out on several days' holiday, and yet you're not man enough to take the blame.'

'I don't consider I was to blame,' he snapped, angry now at her accusations. 'But never let it be said that I didn't try to make amends. I'll see to it personally that you're compensated for the days of holiday which you spent in hospital.'

'Three days that was,' she reaffirmed hotly, 'and then I was flown home two days earlier than planned, making five in all. That's half of the ten-day holiday I came to Bermuda to enjoy.'

'But you really came on business,' he reminded her, 'to apply for a nursing job here.'

'I could have applied by post,' she argued, defiantly tossing her head. 'It's frequently done where overseas appointments prove too expensive to go flying back and forth. As I had holiday due to me I came to spend it with Mandy and to see if I liked it here.'

'And you *could* have remained here to convalesce after the accident. We would have looked after you quite competently. Rushing off back to England and not showing up until now, two months later, suggests admission of guilt. I suppose you thought I'd have forgotten you and your blasted moped by now?'

'I didn't know you were connected with Zenobia's,' she admitted.

'If you had you might have turned down the job?'

'Of course not,' she retorted, 'it was just a bit of a surprise to find I would be working with you. I had to go home to work out my notice and settle my affairs in London, but nothing you can do or say makes up for the loss of my holiday. On the other hand,' she added confidently, 'if you're so eager to compensate for what happened doesn't *that* smack of *your* guilt?'

'Certainly *not!*' he said adamantly. 'I could still sue you whether you're here or in England but it'll be much easier with you right here at hand. Suing you though is a matter for the authorities, compensating you for loss of pleasurable activities a private matter between the two of us.'

He grinned fiendishly, gloating over his triumph. Then he inclined his head saying: 'You're not vulnerable to a little attention? A little flattery perhaps? Latin-American lovers, my dear Cora, are of the highest order, and they don't take no for an answer. Shall we agree to settle out of court, after all?'

Cora felt decidedly peculiar. She didn't understand what he was suggesting so she had no alternative but to reply quickly: 'No—no! I mean, it's in the hands of the authorities.'

'It is?' He was being infuriatingly mocking.

'You said it was going to court,' she flung at him in panic.

'I did?'

'Stop play-acting! What are you trying to do?' she yelled.

To make matters worse he laughed. She wanted to smack his face because he was goading her into making a fool of herself.

'I simply refuse to allow you to hire a moped, a bicycle or any other vehicle,' he warned. 'I doubt that you'll be capable of pushing a pram when the time comes.'

'I don't think this conversation is getting us anywhere,' she said and turned her back on him. She listened for fading footsteps but there was no sound. She felt his warm breath fanning her cheek as he looked over her shoulder and whispered: 'I'll make your holiday up to you if you promise me you won't drive anywhere?'

'I've had a driving licence since I was eighteen and I've been driving a car round London, and to and from Cheshire without so much as a parking ticket,' she informed him proudly.

'You'd really rather face me in court?'

'If I have to,' she retorted.

He slid his hand caressingly over her hip. 'Think about it, Cora,' he said in a slow, seductive voice and minutes later was gone.

CHAPTER TWO

WHEN she reached the privacy of her own room Cora wondered if she had dreamed the whole conversation. She peeped out through the slats of the venetian blind, watching the traffic go by, but her mind was on other things. If she hadn't already agreed to take her present post she might well have changed her mind about coming to Zenobia's after Mr Delaney had threatened to prosecute. She dreaded the thought of going to court, something she had never done before or even been remotely connected with. The only consolation was that if the system worked similarly to British law it would be ages before it finally came to a show down. She had presumed she would hear from the police, but Darryl Delaney had suggested that he could decide whether to prosecute or not. Did that imply that up to the present time he had not taken action?

She hoped that was what he meant, but no way did she accept that he had a hold over her. Summon me and see if I care, she thought bitterly. But she did care. No one could ever be sure what the outcome of a court case would be and if Darryl Delaney had lived in Bermuda a long while the chances were he was well-known or had contacts. That could surely spell disaster for Cora. A hefty fine, and licence endorsed, which wouldn't look good when she returned to England. She pulled herself up with a jerk and let the blind snap together decisively. What was she thinking about? Going home when she'd only just arrived!

She undressed and prepared for bed, but sat in her comfortable easy chair with her feet up on the end of the bed as she browsed through all the tourist literature. During the fateful Christmas holiday Mandy had guided her to some of the places of interest like the Zoo, Botanical Gardens and Aquarium, but there was so much more to see of historical interest as well as the South Shore beaches to visit where she intended to lie and sunbathe and swim as soon as the temperatures rose to the mid-seventies. A semi-tropical island in close proximity to the Gulf Stream, Bermuda was described in the brochures as rising like a jewel from the mid-Atlantic, with only two seasons, spring and summer. It sounded like Paradise and she meant to take advantage of being able to live and work in such an ideal climate, and to hell with Dr Darryl Delaney!

When she saw the back of him next day walking briskly up to the wards her confidence faded somewhat.

The lovely thing about Bermuda was the timelessness of it all. The lack of pressure, even at Zenobia's. Everywhere a lazy, unhurried attitude slowed people down, enabling them to enjoy life. The day of the storm, and thank goodness they were few, had caused a certain amount of excitement, putting a strain on the normal leisurely working hours, but mostly no one hurried, so seeing the Senior Surgical Registrar full of vibrant energy reminded her that he was unique. He hadn't been influenced by the easy-going attitude, it seemed. She was grateful that he didn't often come to Casualty to work. He had helped out on the day of the storm because Neil Endicott had been off duty and if there were serious cases brought in he would be sent for, but Cora was spared any further needling by him during the subsequent few days.

It was nearing the weekend when she looked forward to having longer off duty periods, and before Sara Kenmore went home on Friday evening she handed over the responsibility for Casualty to Cora.

'Make sure that when Karen Fall comes in tomorrow morning to have her stitches out Mr Delaney gives her a letter to take back to England. A full report will be sent by air-mail later but as the post is none too reliable it might take ages. If he happens to drop in or you need him in an emergency you could remind him,' Sara suggested.

'I hope I don't—need him in an emergency I mean,' Cora admitted.

'Poor old Darryl. It must be a rare experience for him to come up against any opposition. Anyway, Cora, I can't see him for you because he's in Theatre today and getting near to Easter means he'll be working till late, I expect.' She consulted the cards on her desk. 'See that Mr Barrow has an appointment at the Outpatients clinic immediately after Easter, otherwise I think everything's fairly straightforward.'

'Let's hope it stays quiet.'

'It will until just before the holiday, then we shall have more tourists who come to see the fields of lilies growing. They really are a magnificent sight, and the churches will all be beautifully decorated for Easter Sunday.'

'Yes, I've heard about them. I must visit the Cathedral as soon as Easter's over,' Cora said.

'Don't leave it too long or you won't see them at their best. Now, let's see, is that everything?' She looked around her, thinking hard, then stood up. 'A lovely weekend off which coincides with Roy's—oh, that reminds me, we're having a few of our respective colleagues in for drinks tomorrow evening, you and Mandy are welcome.'

'Thanks, but I don't know where you live.'

'Mandy does—better still, talk nicely to Neil and he might give you both a lift.' She raised her voice having noticed Neil pass the door. He came back and stood close behind Cora.

'Perhaps we ought to go off duty now instead of you,' he said. 'I might need a lot of persuading, especially as it's this delectable bird who's going to chat me up in order to get a lift.' He squeezed Cora's waist playfully. 'What do I get in return, blue-eyes?'

'Why do men always think one good turn deserves another?' Cora asked in dismay. 'It's not very flattering, you know. Aren't I worth escorting simply because I'm *me*?'

He pulled her against him, nearly dislodging her cap.

'Meet you outside the nurses' home at eight o'clock,' he whispered.

'Mandy too?'

Neil made a face. 'Spoilsport,' he groaned. 'I had visions of us going off together.'

'You can do that some other time, Dr Endicott,' Sara reprimanded. 'At least our party will give you an excuse to get to know one another better. I'll look forward to seeing you all tomorrow evening then.'

'Sister Longford too?' Neil asked with a less than happy expression.

Sara grinned sheepishly. 'Sister Longford too. She helps to keep order.'

'You can say that again.' Neil carried on to wherever he had been making for, and Sara left.

Cora made the necessary note for Mr Barrow's appointment and just as she was making transport facilities available to take him home the emergency telephone rang.

An ambulance was on its way with a sick woman taken from a cabin cruiser which had come in to Hamilton harbour.

Neil returned as Cora replaced the receiver.

'Emergency,' she explained. 'Suspected perforated ulcer.'

'Mr Delaney will be pleased,' Neil said with a wry smile.

Cora prepared one of the cubicles and a few minutes later the patient was wheeled in on a trolley.

Neil made the first examination after Cora had taken the patient's particulars, and Darryl Delaney was bleeped. He came down to Casualty about ten minutes later, still wearing theatre green, a mask hanging round his neck, his dark hair hidden beneath a cap.

'Sounds like a client for me,' he said as Neil gave him the details. 'Hope you weren't planning to rush off duty at eight o'clock, Staff Nurse.' He looked at his watch, it was very nearly that already. 'If I decide to operate tonight I'll need you to prepare her and we might be glad of your help in Theatre.'

Cora just smiled. She was glad to be of help—to the patient, not Darryl Delaney—though as he spoke to the middle-aged American woman, showing sympathy and understanding, she appreciated that he was a kind, dedicated doctor.

After his examination Cora followed him to the office where he prescribed Mrs Montpelier a premedication drug. Cora stood beside him, recognising a weariness about him.

'Isn't there anyone else who could do it?' Cora asked with concern. 'You've been in Theatre all day.'

'There isn't anyone else, Staff Nurse,' he said sharply. 'I'm there, Theatre One is in use and we have only one more on today's list which will just give you time to prepare Mrs Montpelier. Luckily they took advice from a doctor via radio so we don't have to delay.' He completed his diagnosis and instructions and handed the folder to Cora as he stood up.

'Thank you for your concern, Staff Nurse,' he went on sarcastically, 'but I'm sure I shall cope. I don't tackle things I'm not competent to do, or, like you, I'd expect to land myself in trouble.'

'That was uncalled for, Mr Delaney,' she hissed

angrily at him wishing that she hadn't shown the slightest bit of concern for his welfare.

'Let's see what sort of theatre nurse you are. They've all been working flat out today and one of the girls has just fainted. I'm sure you don't mind.'

He went off with a supercilious air, leaving Cora staring after him with indignation. *She* hadn't been working flat out, she supposed!

'Who does he think he is,' she stormed at Neil Endicott. 'It's not my job to help out in Theatre.'

'Oh dear, is Theatre not one of your favourite places?'

'Ye-es.' She simmered down. 'It is, that's why I don't mind Casualty because you get some Theatre work, but I don't want to assist him!'

'I'll be there to look after you. I'm assisting too. You're right, he's tired, but you were wrong to imply that you'd noticed.' Neil raised his eyebrows as Cora returned to the pupil nurse who was waiting by Mrs Montpelier's trolley to help her with the preparations.

Cora asked her to fetch the theatre gown and cap and then sent her off duty as it was past eight o'clock.

'You staying on?' Night Sister asked.

Cora nodded. 'They appear to have had enough in Theatre for one day so I may as well see Mrs Montpelier through.'

The theatre suite at Zenobia's was very modern and Cora enjoyed working there alongside a friendly Canadian sister. Only once did Darryl Delaney scowl at Cora and that was when she wasn't quick enough to wipe the sweat from his brow and it trickled down his forehead into one eye.

'The other eye, Nurse!' he barked impatiently, then realised that he needed to bend so that she could reach.

As she dabbed his eyes she was aware not only of the vibrant quality of their colour but the intensity of the man. So much of his masculine power seemed to ooze from his eyes, especially as little more of his features were visible.

At last he peeled off his gloves, then turned for her to undo the tapes of his gown.

'Thank you, Staff Nurse, I'm sure Monique is most grateful. Night staff will look after the patient now.'

Cora went to the changing room and disrobed quickly. Anything to get away, though she felt his dark eyes would never stop haunting her. Then she remembered the message concerning Karen Fall; she took a step towards the surgeon's changing room but thought better of it and went off duty. It was too late for him to do anything about it tonight, the clerical staff had all gone home so there was no one to dictate a letter to.

Karen and her mother were early visitors next morning.

'I suppose this has spoilt your holiday,' Cora said as she took them along to a cubicle.

'It has hampered us a bit, but it would have been worse if it had happened in the summer. Karen's been spoilt wherever we've been. She's had special treatment and hasn't really missed out too much, have you, darling?'

'You'll have to come back again won't you, Karen?'

'I'd love to,' she answered Cora eagerly. 'Bermuda is the friendliest place I've ever been to. I want to come back when I can go to the beach every day.'

Cora laughed. 'Then hurry up and get your knee healed up quickly.'

'My husband is an engineer and he's working here for six months so we hope to return later on,' Mrs Fall explained.

'Lucky you. Before I take the stitches out, Mrs Fall, I'll just see if Mr Delaney is anywhere about as you'll need a letter for your own doctor.'

Cora went to find Tod who was checking for broken bones on an accident case just in.

'Don't forget X-rays, Doctor,' Cora quipped light-heartedly as he came from the cubicle.

Tod threw a mock punch at her.

'That's enough from you, honey. I'm not likely ever to forget again, not unless I'm suffering from the after-effects of a night out with a sexy blonde.'

'Just keep your mind on your work.'

'With you around?' he grinned as he washed his hands.

Cora passed him the towel. 'I'm only around until lunch time, and then I'm off for the weekend.'

'Going to Sara's party I bet. Think of me holding the fort here.'

'I'll send Mandy along to keep you company.'

'Then I would be in trouble, she's a cute kid.'

'Tod, any idea if Mr Delaney is about today and where I might find him?'

'Yes, in his office in Outpatients, I expect.'

Cora went to the door marked *Senior Surgical Registrar* and knocked. There was no reply so she opened the door a crack and put her head round just as his mellow voice became apparent.

He was sitting in a swivel chair holding a microphone and as he looked up and saw Cora he snapped off the machine on his desk.

'I didn't invite you in, Staff Nurse, but since you're in what is it?'

'Sister Kenmore asked me to remind you about the letter for Karen Fall's doctor.'

'When is it needed?'

'She's in Casualty now to have the stitches removed and they leave for home later today, that's why they're in early.'

Cora saw Darryl's face darken.

'So why haven't I been asked for a letter before this?'

'Sis—I—could have mentioned it last night, but it was late, and you—were—tired.' Her voice trailed off to a humble whisper as she remembered Neil's caution. The damage was done, she'd antagonised him yet again.

'It's Saturday, Staff Nurse, and we only have a skeleton clerical staff.' He toyed irritably with the microphone in his hand. 'How long have I got?'

'I'm just going to remove the stitches. I did wonder whether you'd like to see her before she goes.'

He eyed her shrewdly. 'Among your many accomplishments—other than trying to perform on a moped—I suppose you've never done any typing?'

'Hm, a long time ago,' Cora said doubtfully.

'A long time ago,' he repeated slowly. 'You're only twenty-four, I think you said, so it can't be all that long ago now, can it?'

'Well,' she shrugged, 'I helped out in an estate agents before I started my training.'

'That sounds safe enough. I suppose you couldn't do much harm to anyone or anything in an office,' he said sarcastically.

'I hadn't better use a hospital typewriter,' she retaliated, 'or I might jam it up.'

She turned to go, but stopped at the door as he said:

'Cora, the patient needs a letter—'

'Then, a handwritten one will have to do,' she replied sweetly.

He stood up and caught up with her at the door. 'Take out the stitches and report back to—no—on second thoughts you'd better stick at what you've been trained to do. I'll do it myself.'

Cora felt mildly pleased with herself as she set about her task and they chatted happily as she did so, then Karen began to giggle and it was an infectious sound, but Cora realised that it must be someone else who was amusing her. She glanced at Karen and then quickly round to find Darryl Delaney behind her. She presumed he'd been making faces or something silly, but now he took a close look at Karen's knee with an innocent expression.

'Coming along fine,' he said. 'It'll be stiff for a while, Karen, so take it easy, but on the other hand a little gentle exercise will help. This is just a brief report to give to your GP, the official one will be sent on by post at a later date.'

He said goodbye to Karen and her mother while Cora took away the dressings tray and when she returned to bandage Karen's leg he had gone.

It wasn't until much later after chuckles and funny remarks from some of the junior nurses which Cora didn't understand that Tod pushed her into the office.

'Where have you been this morning?' he asked with a huge grin on his face.

'Nowhere,' Cora replied testily. 'You know I've been here working.'

Tod turned her round and read aloud: 'No one does anything quite like me.'

'What *are* you on about?'

'Take off your cap,' he ordered.

Cora took out the hair clips which kept it in place and removed the small white cap and there on the back she saw the object of ridicule. A sticky label on which were typed the words Tod had read.

'So that's what Karen was giggling at. Mr Delaney must have put it there. I didn't think he had it in him.'

'Do you really do it better than most?' Tod teased. 'Oh, honey, I don't know how many of the staff have seen it but, wow, is your reputation going to spread.'

'It's only a joke, Tod, don't get excited. No one as yet knows anything about me, not even the great Delaney, him least of all. He's still getting at me because of the accident, which, in case he tries to say different, *was* his fault.'

'I believe you, honey,' Tod said, 'though here the rules might differ from those in Great Britain.'

'What you mean is that Mr Delaney has a set of rules for himself.'

A few minutes later a woman patient was brought in with a suspected fracture. Cora detailed a pupil nurse to take her along to the X-ray department while she attended to some nasty bruises an elderly man had sustained in a fall. He was badly shaken, but Tod could find no serious damage. He lived with his daughter near the old town of St George's so Cora telephoned her and asked her to come and pick him up in an hour's time. She bathed his forehead which he'd cut, took his blood pressure which was slightly raised and later, after a cup of tea, he seemed better. When his daughter arrived Cora tucked his arm through hers and with the aid of his stick he was able to walk to where his daughter had parked her car. Before they reached the door though Darryl Delaney overtook them. He half glanced back at Cora with a sly grin, evidently noticing that his message had been removed from her cap, then he recognised the patient.

'Hullo, Mr Gibbons, not another fall?' His smile was genuine and he touched the old man's arm in a friendly gesture.

'Afraid so, Doctor,' Mr Gibbons said. 'Can't blame me though, can you, sir, when I can come here and have a pretty young nurse to look after me?'

'You be careful of this one, Mr Gibbons,' Darryl said with a wicked smile, 'she's the latest recruit, and I'm not sure Bermuda's quite ready for her.'

'I'm ready for her,' the old man joked. 'Many a good tune played on an old fiddle, you know.'

Cora smiled. He reminded her of her grandfather who had lived with them when she was a child, and this time she couldn't rise to the dynamic doctor's bait.

She wasn't sorry when the morning ended and she could go off to the canteen for lunch where she met up with Mandy.

'What time's this party, then?' her friend asked.

'Eight o'clock. Neil Endicott is going to give us a lift,' Cora explained.

Mandy made a face. 'Oh, is *he* going? That means that Tod won't be able to come.'

'Are you serious about Tod?' Cora asked.

'I might be if I thought it would do me any good, but he chats up every nurse he meets. I bet he's made a pass at you already?'

'No. He prefers blondes,' Cora told her friend drily.

'Just my luck that he's on duty tonight then. Still, Roy's expert at bringing a few of his colleagues along, and there's something to be said for the British police force. Sara's parties are usually pretty good so we'd better get a rest this afternoon.'

Cora decided against telling Mandy about the joke Darryl had played on her. It was the kind of silly prank which might get exaggerated as it was passed on or it just could be totally ignored in which case the fewer who knew about it the better. That Darryl Delaney was taking sufficient notice of Cora to play a joke on her might well instigate a certain amount of envy from any quarter where he was idolised.

As she lay on her bed resting she wondered if the grapevine was spreading the news that the new Staff Nurse in Casualty was the one he had knocked off a moped. But, of course, Cora thought acidly, that wouldn't be the way the story went. The new Staff Nurse would be the crazy idiot who fell off a moped right in the great doctor's path! At least she could look forward to a restful weekend away from such memories.

She slept a little and then, as was the custom in Bermuda, it was time for the traditional afternoon tea at four o'clock, served in the lounge at the nurses' home. She was beginning to feel at home. She'd never had doubts about being happy at Zenobia's—she'd seen enough of it as a patient to verify Mandy's praise of the hospital and its friendly staff—but she was getting to know some of the other girls, and chatting over tea was an excellent way to break down barriers.

Cora had changed out of uniform into a denim skirt and short-sleeved shirt so it wasn't surprising that Monique didn't notice her at once, but after she had been sitting opposite her for a few minutes she said: 'Ah, the new Staff Nurse—Cora—Cora Jordan isn't it?'

Cora nodded. 'That's me, evidently someone's been taking my name in vain.'

'Hardly surprising, Cora, when someone as choosey as Darryl actually trusted *you*, a newcomer, in Theatre.'

Cora smiled in acknowledgement, hesitant to

reply, not knowing whether Monique might be hiding a suspicion of rivalry.

'So you're the one he collided with back around Christmas-time?' she continued, surveying her critically.

'I don't know what you've heard,' Cora said, 'but actually, the truth is Mr Delaney knocked me off a moped, and I was admitted to Zenobia's with concussion.'

'I should think all Bermuda knows that, Cora. For days poor old Darryl went around swearing vengeance on all moped riders. You were lucky it wasn't any worse. Are you quite better?'

'Yes, thanks. As you say, I was lucky.'

'Concussion? Weren't you wearing a crash helmet?'

Cora dropped her gaze to the dainty china cup which she rubbed gently with her thumb. 'Yes, of course, that's the law here the same as it is back home.'

'But you were still concussed? Think how much worse it could have been then without the helmet.'

Cora wished Monique would let it drop. She wanted to forget that she'd been foolish enough not to secure the chin strap and if Darryl Delaney ever found that out her life wouldn't be worth living.

CHAPTER THREE

CORA put all memory of the accident as far to the back of her mind as possible as she changed for the party. Bermuda was the kind of place that warranted pretty colourful clothes, but evenings were cool, the temperatures dropping by ten degrees at night, so over a coral pink silk dress she wore a black velvet jacket and carried a black, fine woollen shawl into which silver and gold threads were woven in the design of a bird in flight. She had bought it in Hamilton during the ill-fated holiday because it bore the hallmark of Bermuda, the graceful Longtail seabird, but this was the first opportunity she'd had to wear it and as Sara Kenmore showed them up to a bedroom on arrival Cora draped the shawl round her shoulders.

The large lounge was dimly lit by pale pink wall lights but cosily warm with a log fire burning in the fireplace, and soft melodies coming from hidden speakers added the final romantic touch to a party atmosphere.

Sara introduced Cora to Roy, her husband, a tall six-footer with a shock of dark blond hair and a boyish face. He paused from serving fruit punch, shook hands, and then dwarfed her by drawing her close and kissing her.

'Must treat you all alike,' he said, having first greeted Mandy in much the same way. 'And how d'you like our island of sunshine?'

'It's all that Mandy said it was, quite enchanting,' Cora said.

'Not working you too hard at the hospital?'

'Careful how you answer that,' Sara rejoindered and went on to enthuse about Cora's shawl.

'All right, Sara darling, I've got the message,' Roy said. 'Perhaps I can get Cora to be careless and leave hers behind. I haven't seen another one like it.'

'It was rather expensive and carried an exclusive ticket,' Cora confessed. 'I have to admit I bought it as a present for one of the family, but in the event my holiday was cut short and I didn't get around to buying other presents so decided to compensate myself with this.'

'I won't make the eternal jokes about Longtails mating in mid-flight, they get a bit stale when you've been here a bit,' Neil said as he took a drink from Roy.

Cora moved aside as the two men conversed and just as Sara was saying: 'Let's see, do you know everyone from Zenobia's,' Cora saw him. She felt her cheek muscles tighten. She hadn't given it a thought, that Darryl Delaney might be among the guests, but he appeared to have made himself at home and was lounging on a sofa, his arm along the back behind Sister Longford.

She was suddenly face to face with them so was obliged to say something.

'Hullo, Sister, Mr Delaney.'

'We're off duty now,' Sara said cheerfully, 'it's Muriel, and Darryl.'

Cora smiled, noticing that Muriel Longford was not quite successful in concealing an expression of disapproval.

Darryl nodded, observing Cora's pink cheeks with a lazy kind of brooding.

'Turn around,' he drawled in a low, roguish tone. 'Let's see the Longtail.'

Cora was surprised that he'd bothered to listen to the conversation but she swivelled round briefly.

'It's very attractive,' Muriel Longford said. 'I don't blame you for not giving it away.'

'I would have preferred to see a large L on your back,' Darryl said, his hooded eyes piercing through her.

Thankfully Neil came to stand beside Cora then and placed his arm around her shoulder protectively.

'We don't yet know that she is a learner, other than riding a moped,' he quipped, but Darryl's smile faded and he clearly disapproved of such a suggestion.

More guests arrived, among them three more off-duty policemen, and Cora and Neil were jostled along into a large conservatory where Mandy was already the centre of attraction.

The food and drink was plentiful, and although Cora was conscious of the fact that Darryl Delaney was present she managed to hang on to Neil Endicott as an escort which helped her to feel more relaxed. He was that kind of man, not outstanding in looks, but his soft blue eyes held a comforting warmth and he made it obvious that he was flattered to be Cora's companion. He was only a couple of inches taller than her so that in spite of the growing noise they could converse easily. His bright ginger hair and freckled complexion gave him an open, youthful appearance and Cora learned that he came from a Devonshire village in England. He had a way of looking into her eyes as he talked with a special absorption as he gave her his undivided attention and later, although a few people started to jig around, disco fashion in the large square hall which had a cool mosaic floor, Neil seemed content to find out as much as Cora was prepared to reveal about herself.

Some time just before midnight, when the laughter became less frivolous and chattering voices softened in accordance with more mellow romantic dance tunes, Neil went to replenish their glasses. As Cora watched him return, through the glass windows which separated the conservatory from the lounge, she saw Darryl Delaney pushing his way through towards her.

Cora instantly panicked, and placing her drink down on a window sill, caught Neil's hand quickly as he reached her.

'Let's dance,' she said enthusiastically, 'or the party will be over.'

'Not Sara's, darling,' Neil said reassuringly, 'it's likely to go on until three o'clock.' He put his drink beside hers but it was Cora who led the way through the narrow side door into the hall. She took off her high-heeled sandals and tossed them into a corner, letting the cold stone floor cool her aching feet. As Neil took her into his arms in a traditional dance-hold she wondered why she had rushed from the conservatory in such indecent haste. By the intense gaze Neil was giving her he had misconstrued her desperate evasion. Now, as she rested her cheek against his, she wondered why she had been so reckless. Her actions gave Neil an excuse for showing some feeling for her when in fact she had been fleeing from Darryl Delaney's attentions. Fool, she rebuked herself silently; whatever made her think that Darryl was pursuing *her*! She couldn't bear to look around in case he was in close proximity, holding someone else close. Neil saw to it that she was soon only aware of his mood, a tender expressive mood of gentle passion, and she felt his fingers caressing her body with increasing warmth.

An antique striking wall clock proclaimed the hour of midnight and a hand came down on Cora's shoulder.

Neil immediately released her and Cora turned to find Darryl dangling her shoes by the dainty straps.

'Sorry I haven't put them on a cushion, princess, but in case the dress changes to rags on the last stroke can I claim a dance?'

He smiled at Neil. 'You can have her back in a few moments as I'm about to leave.'

To Cora's chagrin Neil supported her as Darryl lifted first one ankle then the other in order to replace her shoes.

'I should hate to lift you off the floor,' he said with a smile, and then she was enclosed in an embrace that turned her body to fever heat. Fortunately she was still elfin-like against his superior height so was spared having to meet his powerful gaze. There was nothing tender in his mood, and she very soon realised that all he was doing was testing her skill as a dancer so she put every effort into matching step for step in perfect time. The tempo changed and he released her except for lightly entwining his long fingers among hers, and guided her back to where Neil had perched on the window sill, enjoying his drink.

Darryl handed her back to him.

'In that respect at least she doesn't need to wear learner plates,' he informed Neil drily. 'I'll leave you to test other potentiality. Goodnight.'

Cora excused herself from Neil almost at once and was grateful for the privacy of a tiny cloakroom adjacent to the front door, but after a few moments she realised it was not as secluded as she'd thought, and as familiar voices drifted through the tiny open-louvred window she felt imprisoned and compelled to listen.

'Thank you, Sara darling, for a lovely party.' Darryl's eloquent voice sounded genuine appreciation. Then followed the unmistakable sound of a kiss.

'Glad you could come, Darryl. Give my regards to Mrs Delaney and tell her we were sorry she didn't feel up to coming to the party. Next time perhaps,' Sara returned.

'You don't mind if I leave you youngsters to dance the night away do you, Sara? Darryl's offered me a lift home,' Sister Longford said and Cora found herself pressing her finger-tips to her forehead.

Darryl Delaney was married! It almost took her

breath away but she couldn't comprehend why. He was hateful to her, but evidently had known how to wield enough charm to secure a wife. Yet here he was taking Muriel Longford home. Had gone to her flat before coming on to the party, a notion which conjured up all kinds of mystical madness in Cora's brain. It was only she who didn't seem to be on his wave-length. No one at Zenobia's had denied the fact that they simply worshipped him. She tried to put him from her mind, struggled unsuccessfully to forget the harmony which had knitted them together on the dance floor, and in spite of herself exhilarated her.

Now the thrill died painfully. He had set about trying to make an exhibition of her, hoping to catch her off balance so that he could once more award her a learner's badge. This time though she had proved him wrong. Perhaps now he would let his case rest.

She combed her hair, applied a fresh smear of lipstick, smudged eye-shadow over her lids, brushed up her lashes and went back to the party.

Neil was dancing with Sara in a frivolous manner while Mandy was hardly visible encased as she was by the bulky frame of one of Roy's colleagues.

Cora went into the conservatory and found her drink and a few minutes later Roy came to refill her glass.

'No more,' she protested, 'I'm on duty tomorrow.'

'Not early, I hope,' Roy said grinning. 'You'll soon get used to our Rum Swizzle, the island's speciality drink. It can be quite potent though, so don't say I haven't warned you.'

'You've warned me,' Cora agreed as she took another sip. 'It sort of grows on you, doesn't it? At first I thought there wasn't a great deal of flavour to it, not much more than weak orange squash.'

'It does depend on how much rum, and different varieties at that, goes into it. I purposely make it weak to start off with, then increase the alcoholic strength as we go along, that way we make sure that no one returns to the hospital incapable.'

'Surely that depends on the individual? Some people are affected quicker than others aren't they?' Cora suggested.

'True, and by the sparkle in your blue eyes I'd say you're done to a turn.'

They laughed happily together and Cora was glad of his irrepressible good humour as they joined the dancers in the hall.

The mood became decidedly smoochy. Cora found herself in Neil's arms again as Roy claimed his wife to end the party.

Mandy whispered to Cora that she had a lift home so Neil drove Cora back to the hospital.

'Thanks—for everything,' Cora said, as he pulled up outside the entrance to the nurses' home.

'Hope you've enjoyed yourself, Cora,' he whispered.

Already Cora's hand was searching for the door catch but Neil slid his arm around her shoulders and before she knew it she was responding to his kisses . . .

*

Cora slept late. She was able to because she wasn't due to start work until after lunch. She felt light-headed so decided to walk to the nearest bay as it was a bright sunny day. She knew that there would be a cool breeze coming off the sea and she needed the fresh air to clear her brain. Not because the Rum Swizzle had affected her, but because Neil's advances had caught her unprepared. They were colleagues, she told herself, and at a party everyone lets their hair down. She had thought they were being pleasantly familiar in true party spirit, but as she stood looking out to sea, watching the foaming rollers crashing on to the rocks, she knew all too well that Neil's passion had a seriousness about it. She liked him. He was good to work with and was a genuinely nice type, but she wasn't looking for a serious relationship, not with Neil Endicott. There was a heaviness around her heart, a dull ache which she tried to shrug off, but it simply refused to go away and as the wind gusted round her trousered legs, and dishevelled her tawny hair into wild streamers, she found her memory compelling her to face the truth, however disturbing.

When Darryl Delaney had walked into the small private ward at Zenobia's after the accident, Cora had felt her heartbeats quicken at the charisma which emanated from every part of him. He had smiled gently as he'd introduced himself, placed warm sensuous fingertips at her temples, examined her eyes so that she'd been forced to gaze into his. It had been like straining to see what lay at the bottom of a deep dark pit and as she had blinked she had focussed on his condemning glare. How could she have connected him with Zenobia's? Try as she would she could recall nothing that had suggested he was a hospital doctor—no white coat, no stethoscope, no name tag. In her mind's eye she could see herself, pale and nervous, lying inert, expecting some measure of sympathy and apology. Instead, he had informed her coldly that he would prosecute her for dangerous driving. Her memory played tricks on her now, even though they assured her that no lasting damage had been done. She was lucky, she was told, to be suffering from nothing more serious than concussion.

She supposed now, in retrospect, she had been feeling pleased with herself having just been accepted for the post of Staff Nurse in Casualty. She couldn't remember hearing the approach of any other vehicle, just her own moped engine purring happily along. Stupid as she now knew she had been, she'd laughed to scorn the need for a crash helmet on such a low powered vehicle, knowing the twenty mile per hour speed limit everywhere on the islands.

She wanted to hate Darryl Delaney but she couldn't. He seemed to haunt her. He was determined to make her remember that she had been in the wrong, but she didn't agree with that and there had been no witnesses. Well, not that she knew of, but then she'd been knocked out so how could she know? Instinct—yes, her instincts had told her lots of things, like why she had never received any communication from the police concerning the accident. She had presumed that the hospital authorities had given the police all the relevant details, including the fact that she was shortly to take up a post at Zenobia's.

It was like a black cloud which hovered over her all the while, especially when she was alone, like now. She thought again of Darryl's mocking, but only the two of them, no, only Darryl Delaney, really knew what had happened on that day. Dare she hope that, knowing he was partly, if not wholly to blame, he had not notified the police? Someone must have rescued the moped and crash helmet and returned them to the livery. Mandy had simply assured her that everything had been taken care of when she'd regained consciousness after several hours of total blackout. Had Darryl visited her during that time? At least she had been wearing a decent nightdress when he introduced himself.

She wanted to forget that day and concentrate on the Darryl Delaney she now knew. Did anyone ever get to know a man of his calibre? Dominant, self-assured and, yes, just a tiny bit arrogant. Were those the three vital ingredients which made him attractive? Cora kicked a nearby pebble and turned to walk back the way she had come, remembering their first meeting in Casualty. Did he really not know that she was coming there to work? She saw him again, sitting with Muriel Longford, the latter a tall graceful woman whose Grecian nose seemed to indicate a mean streak, or was it a general look of frustration which spoiled her otherwise pleasant features? But there was a Mrs Delaney and Cora found herself speculating that she would be young and probably very beautiful as well as being versatile. She would need to be to accommodate the handsome doctor's many moods. Cora reproached herself for even thinking about him, yet she was torn between the attention Neil was paying her and attraction which Darryl Delaney drew to himself. How she despised her own wayward emotions for persisting in dwelling on what had passed between them.

After early lunch she reported to Sister Longford who then left to go to the canteen. Neil came on duty and planted a kiss on Cora's cheek.

'Got a hangover?' he asked.

'No—I went for a long walk this morning and let the sea breezes clear the star-dust out of my brain.'

'That sounds a bit cynical. Most girls thrive on a little star-dust.'

Cora laughed good-naturedly. 'All right for parties,' she said, 'but next morning you have to live with reality.'

'Plenty of parties going on all the time. We shall soon start late-night beach parties. Hope you swim—what about water ski-ing and scuba diving?'

'No, I'm just your average sun-worshipper who likes an occasional dip to keep cool. Why else would anyone come to Bermuda?'

'True—but there are plenty of other things to do, tennis, and golf, of course.'

'I'll just be happy to explore for a while,' she said.

'You must let me take you around,' Neil offered. 'I've been here long enough to know how and where to get the best of Bermuda. Perhaps we can get our days off together.'

'That would be nice. Mandy and I mean to get

bicycles so that we can get around more easily.' She hoped that would put him off, but with Neil a little encouragement went a long way and Cora found him difficult to shake off, and during the coming week they spent some off duty together. She enjoyed his company and as fondness for him grew she found Darryl Delaney receding from her foremost thoughts until late one afternoon when an emergency was rushed in to Casualty. A marine engineer from the American naval base, once owned by the British Royal Navy, had been involved in an accident in the engine room of a submarine. In spite of his extensive injuries he remained conscious and it was part of Cora's job to stand by and offer him comfort while Sara Kenmore, Tod, and Neil all worked to remove his greasy overalls and examine his wounds.

He was given a pain-killing injection while they waited for a surgeon to respond to the bleeper, but Sara informed Cora that surgery was already in progress in two of the three theatres.

'They've sent for Darryl,' Sara said, 'let's hope he's in and wasn't doing anything important on his day off.'

Cora was learning fast that once on the staff at Zenobia's you were virtually on duty twenty-four hours a day. It was Easter week so the surgery lists were long, and after today only emergency cases would go to theatre, but now everyone rallied to do what they could to help Bill Palmer, the thirty-year-old engineer from Connecticut. Among other injuries his right foot had been crushed and Cora guessed that there might be a necessity to amputate, though she desperately hoped not. He was determined to stay conscious as long as possible and already had joked with Tod and Neil. His courage impressed everyone.

'Won't be long now, Bill,' she consoled, 'thank goodness you skipped lunch.'

'They going to have to put me out, Nurse?'

'It'll be better for you and easier for them while they determine the extent of the damage, Bill,' Cora explained kindly.

'You don't happen to smoke I s'pose?' he croaked.

'Afraid not.' Cora shook her head sadly. She almost wished she could oblige.

'Gee, you're English. That's one place I'd sure like to go.'

'I'm sure we'd love to have you visit,' she responded eagerly.

'Guess that's out now. I won't be able to carry on with my job if I have to lose my foot.'

'Don't start crossing bridges,' Cora advised. 'Things often seem to be worse than they really are. How is it now? The pain lessened at all?'

He nodded. 'Just numb. I don't feel anything except the need for a fag.'

'Sorry, my friend, that's out for the moment.' Darryl Delaney swished back the curtain and came in with brisk determination.

'Has Theatre Three been prepared?' he asked bluntly.

'I couldn't say,' Cora replied. 'I've remained with the patient. I imagine all the preparations have been made.'

'You coming to the operating room with me, Nurse?' Bill asked grabbing Cora's hand.

Darryl looked from the strained face of the engineer to Cora.

'Of course she is,' Darryl said, 'that's if it'll make you feel better.'

'Who wouldn't with a delightful English girl to hold your hand.'

'Our nurses are the best,' Darryl said positively, and even managed a surreptitious wink as Cora looked at him, considerably surprised at his facetiousness. She realised that the accompanying raised eyebrows implied that he didn't necessarily include her in that statement.

'You know, honey,' Bill said, still grasping Cora's hand, 'you've got the bluest eyes I ever did see.'

'Be careful, Bill, she'll have you anaesthetised without anaesthetic if you aren't careful.' Darryl wasn't smiling now though. In spite of the cheerful conversation to help keep Bill's spirits up the surgeon needed all his skill and judgment to assess the patient's injuries.

It was an hour later before the porters came to wheel Bill away. Cora had sponged him down after the rest of his clothes had been removed and now he was ready in theatre gown and cap covering his light brown hair. He had soft grey eyes and whereas on admission he had been trying to hide a look of intense fear as well as the agony of pain, the pain-killing injection and pre-medication had relaxed his nervous system. He wasn't talking any more but occasionally forced himself to look intently at Cora.

She smiled and squeezed his hand.

'Get me fixed up, honey, and I'll take you out to dinner,' he whispered.

They were in the ante-room now and Bill finally lost consciousness.

Cora turned to go, then heard Darryl's voice calling after her.

'You're going to assist me, Staff Nurse. Sorry I can't spare you to hold his hand as requested, but we'd better make sure you've kept your promise.'

'I didn't promise Bill anything. I thought Sister would be—'

'She said you were free,' he snapped.

She turned and went to the nurses' changing room. She didn't mind, and having been with Bill Palmer for the past few hours felt a personal interest in his condition. Not that she'd ever see him again, she realised, as he would go eventually to Men's Surgical ward after surgery and he'd been specialled in a recovery ward.

As she watched Darryl at work with Neil assisting and she handing the necessary instruments, she found herself intrigued by the dark man opposite her. He spoke very little as he concentrated, and she took care that she gave him no cause for irritation by passing an incorrect instrument. Cora knew that he was doing his utmost to save Bill's foot and the minutes ticked away into hours. Another staff nurse wiped away the sweat caused by the intense heat from the lights, and Darryl paused, straightened up as if he was stiff, and for a long second he stared into Cora's eyes. Then as suddenly he continued with his task, shrugging his shoul-

ders inside his green gown as if angry with himself
for wasting one precious moment. It had been long
enough for Cora to see the man behind the facade.
He was getting weary but he didn't intend her to
notice. Cora wondered how he had been spending
his day off. Sister Longford was off too; was that
significant? She remembered Mrs Delaney and
felt—what did she feel, a speck of envy, or pity?

'Wake up, Staff Nurse!' His tone, sharp but not
really angry, confused her and from then on everything went wrong. The anaesthetist wasn't happy,
the operation was going on too long and shock was
setting in.

Darryl showed remarkable coolness, he kept
right on working, checking every few minutes with
Kenneth, the Bermudan anaesthetist. It seemed to
take for ever, but Bill rallied and when he was
removed at last to the recovery room Cora wondered what his destiny was.

In the ante-room as they removed their gowns
Cora ventured to ask: 'Is there any hope for his
foot, Mr Delaney?'

She had untied the tapes on his gown and he
swung round to face her.

'How can I know that, Cora? We've done our
best haven't we? You must get more theatre practice in.' She started at his rebuke, gentle though it
was. 'Oh, I'm not complaining,' he went on, 'but
you lost your concentration in there. Why?'

It was such a pointed question. How could she
say that it was because she had started to think
about him as a man rather than the competent
surgeon doing a job?

'I'm sorry,' she murmured, lowering her gaze and wishing she still had a mask to cover her guilty crimsoned cheeks.

'You'd better quickly forget Bill Palmer, Cora, he's probably got a wife and kids back in the States.'

She opened her mouth to deny having any private thoughts about the patient when the swing doors opened and Monique walked in.

'Gee, honey,' she said walking up to Darryl quickly, 'why didn't you ring the club, I'd have come back too.'

'No need, we managed,' he replied curtly, and as Cora walked away with leadened feet he called: 'Thanks, Staff Nurse, you did a good job.'

Cora stood in the changing room, thankful that she could have a few moments alone. He had actually thanked her, complimented her, which made a pleasant change. *Don't let it go to your head*, she admonished.

The door burst open aggressively and Monique came in on the pretext of going to her locker.

'Sorry I can't offer to let you have my job, honey,' she said with sarcasm. 'I chose theatre work.'

'And you're welcome,' Cora replied quietly. 'It takes too much concentration for me. I like more activity, and meeting my patients awake.'

'So that you can flirt with the men?'

Cora turned on Monique unable to believe her ears.

'Sister!' she exclaimed deciding to retain some dignity. 'That was unnecessary.'

Monique laughed. 'I'm only kidding, honey. Why not flirt all you want anyway. Men are men—and they love a bit of flattery.'

Cora changed as quickly as she could and returned to Casualty, noticing that Monique went in search of Darryl.

She was hurt, her pride wounded, no one had ever suggested before that she was a flirt. Was that how Darryl Delaney saw her? What had he said to Monique she wondered to cause the other girl's jibes?

There was no question about the doctor's competence and Cora admired him for that, but maybe he was the flirt. Muriel Longford, Monique Galton, she had even felt a slight suspicion about Sara Kenmore, only three of a long list, and what of Mrs Delaney?

He probably boasted at length of his conquests to his male colleagues, Cora decided, but she didn't intend to be one of them. Up to today he had scorned her, spoken seldom without sarcasm, but hadn't he suggested that she might be vulnerable to a little extra attention, some well-timed flattery? Settle out of court, he had suggested, which gave him a slight advantage. No, she resolved positively, he would not break her spirit or connive to win her affections. She would not be a party to intimate friendships under the cover of working relationships. He may have succeeded with others in this way, but Cora vowed she would remain unmoved by his charm. Somehow, someone ought to remind him of his duty to his wife!

When she went off duty she saw the backs of

Darryl Delaney and Monique, who was laughing up at him, her arm tucked possessively through his. She decided to skip supper.

CHAPTER FOUR

ALTHOUGH Cora felt tired she put off going to bed, knowing that her thoughts were too potent to allow her to sleep. She kept herself occupied by taking her smalls to the laundry room, hoping that other colleagues' chatter would lift her from her self-inflicted gloom, but she had the laundry room to herself. The drone of the washing machine only added to the feeling of emptiness, so while she waited for the washing programme to finish she walked to a nearby jetty where the moon reflected a sparkling streamer across the harbour and in the distance visiting cruise ships were gaily illuminated, but even the tree frogs' nocturnal chirping couldn't seem to please her.

Mandy was out on one of her numerous dates. The bubbly, vivacious blonde was seldom free even for one evening so she wouldn't have appreciated Cora's despondency. Was it because of Monique's inferences? Could it be true that she *was* a flirt?

As she put her smalls into the dryer she took stock of herself. It was no use comparing herself with Mandy. They had probably remained friends for the length of time they had because they had different temperaments. Mandy only had to flutter her golden-drenched lashes and laugh at a man from her green-gemmed eyes and she had made a friend. Cora sighed. *She* didn't have the personality which constituted a flirt! All the same she liked men and got on well with them, but she hadn't yet met the man with whom she wanted to live for ever. She sighed again dismally.

Perhaps men could read her emotions. They all openly admitted that Mandy was an attractive, friendly girl. How did they see Cora? Most important of all, was how did Darryl Delaney see her? She flung the last of her smalls in the huge drum and impatiently closed the door with a bang. Why should she care what Darryl Delaney thought of her? But her thoughts were occupied all too frequently with him.

She disliked him intensely, hated him for the jibes he made about her inefficiencies, and yet she knew she was attracted to him because of his attention. Not only the attention paid to her, but she admired the rapport he held with patients, who found him easy to talk to and in consequence wholly trustworthy. She dreamed dreams of those princely black eyes gazing down at her when she had been a patient. Unwittingly she had absorbed every fine detail of his clean-shaven, handsome features with rare, perfectly carved lips. He was just too much of a masterpiece, the sensuous cleft in his chin being the touch of counter-perfection which added to the intrigue of the man.

He seemed not to have left her thoughts for one single second so that when he appeared in Casualty next morning soon after Cora reported for duty, his image was even more impressive, and to her embarrassment she found the blood rushing to her cheeks.

'Good morning, Staff Nurse,' he said brusquely. 'Mrs Steele in cubicle two for X-ray, also Miss Brooks in number four. I'll do my ward round, then see them again later.'

'You're early this morning,' Cora said, rolling up her sleeves and securing her arm bands.

'That's right,' he agreed. 'A speedy and efficient service today so that I can enjoy Easter with a clear conscience.'

'Lucky you,' Cora quipped with a smile.

'Why? Haven't you got a clear conscience?'

After a momentary stare of intense interrogation he left her standing there in complete astonishment. All that she had felt for him just drained away. Was he never going to stop knocking her over that blasted moped accident? She didn't have a clear conscience over the incident but neither could he have!

Sister Longford was tied up with an intestinal obstruction admission so Cora took Mrs Steele, one of the hospital's domestics who had jarred her ankle, and Miss Brooks, a middle-aged shop owner who had tripped and fallen over a dress rack, along to the X-ray department. She left them there and during the next hour assisted Ted and Neil with their respective patients, a young motor-cyclist with leg injuries, and an elderly holiday-maker suffering from severe chest pains.

A porter returned the two ladies from the X-ray department some time later and they were asked to wait in cubicles until Darryl Delaney came down from the wards.

Cora and Sister Longford were snatching a cup of

coffee in the office when Darryl returned.

'Okay, Cora,' he said brightly. 'Are my two ladies back?'

'Yes—'

'And my admission is waiting for confirmation of surgery on ward twenty,' Sister Longford interrupted.

'I've seen him,' Darryl said, 'he's being prepped for surgery at two o'clock. Come on, Staff Nurse, can't waste time drinking coffee.'

Cora replaced her cup on the saucer and followed him out of the office.

'We're supposed to go to the canteen,' she informed him meaningfully, 'but we're too busy this morning.'

'For heaven's sake, don't you get enough off duty for stimulation? There are other ways besides drinking coffee, but you don't need L plates for those, I'm told.'

He looked down at her and grinned at the flash of anger in her eyes, and as they reached the cubicle he chucked her under the chin, adding insult.

Cora put the X-ray up on the screen for Darryl to examine and somehow she got trapped between him and escape. The scent of masculinity invaded her nostrils like a drug. He was in a bright, almost excitable mood now, and she wondered who was responsible. His wife? a patient? or Monique?

She was gazing at the X-ray report in her hand but glanced up to find Darryl staring down at her. She met his stare unflinchingly. What was he reading from her expression, she wondered?

He put a hand on her shoulder and forced her to turn and look at the wall screen.

'Well?' he demanded. 'What do you see?'

'An ankle which is bruised and swollen, but not fractured.'

'What else?' he asked impatiently.

'Fluid—I had noticed that the patient's legs are puffy,' she said in her low, professional voice.

He examined the picture a moment longer, then turned to Mrs Steele.

'Do you have a lot of trouble with your legs swelling, Mrs Steele?'

The patient was a large brown woman who responded instantly to the surgeon.

'I know I'm overweight, Doctor,' she admitted, 'and I know standing doesn't help, but I couldn't work anywhere but at this hospital.'

Darryl smiled. 'We couldn't do without you, Mrs Steele, that's why I'd like you to have some tablets to help the swelling. I'm afraid you'll have to go home and rest for a few days. Your ankle isn't broken, just badly sprained, but that's a painful condition. Staff Nurse will put a crêpe bandage on it and I want you to come back in two days' time.'

'But that's Easter Sunday, Doctor,' Mrs Steele protested.

'We're always open for business, though I shall be off duty. I'll see you one day next week, and meanwhile here's a prescription to get at the pharmacy, and you'll need a certificate.'

'Couldn't I still go on working?' Mrs Steele pleaded.

Darryl shook his head. 'Definitely not for one week. I want you to be sensible now, Mrs Steele, and sit with your feet up on a stool as much as you can for two days until the swelling subsides, then you can exercise it a little more each day.' He turned to Cora. 'When you've bandaged her up see that she takes the certificate I'll leave in the office, and give her an appointment for Sunday.'

They moved on to the next cubicle where Miss Brooks was lying on the couch.

He studied the picture on the wall screen carefully.

'A slightly cracked rib, severe bruising, mm— just as I thought, Miss Brooks, you've cracked a rib so it will be quite painful for a bit, but there's no treatment except common sense. We shan't strap you up. We find that it frequently leads to chest infections so it's better to let nature take its course.'

Miss Brooks looked at Darryl somewhat disdainfully, so he hurried on. 'I'll give you a prescription for some pills to help ease the pain to enable you to get some sleep, but rest is the only cure. I would treat my own wife or mother in exactly the same way, in fact an X-ray has only confirmed what I already diagnosed. Now if you were my mother-in-law . . .'

Miss Brooks smiled. 'I don't think I'll have her treatment,' she said, responding to his joviality.

Darryl laughed. 'I'm sure mother-in-laws are only notoriously vicious from music-hall jokes. You don't have a mother-in-law yet do you, Staff Nurse?'

'No, Mr Delaney, but if and when I do, I sincerely hope we shall be good friends, and prove the comedians wrong.'

He handed her a prescription, his face a grim mask as he said with sarcasm: 'You just keep on working to that end, Staff Nurse, though in my experience mothers of every type do have a tendency to interfere. They've probably brought the jokes upon themselves.'

He hurried away and Cora wondered just what his mother-in-law could be like to evoke such contempt.

For the remainder of the day Cora speculated about Darryl Delaney's private life. Mrs Delaney evidently resided in Bermuda with him. Was it possible that his mother-in-law was here too? Perhaps only for a holiday, but long enough to drive him into Monique's arms, or Muriel Longford's, certainly to Sara Kenmore's party. Perhaps his mother-in-law had genuine cause for interference.

A long queue of patients kept Casualty staff busy until early evening and Cora was glad to see the last patient leave.

'Come for a spin and a drink, Cora?' Neil Endicott asked as they prepared to go off duty.

Tod gave his colleague a playful punch. 'Rotten thing! I was about to ask her for a date,' he said. Cora was on the point of suggesting that she wouldn't dare accept his offer as it was Mandy who had him earmarked when Darryl Delaney breezed into Casualty.

'I can settle that dispute,' he said, evidently having arrived in time to hear what had been said. 'I'll be happy to take Cora off your hands.'

Cora placed her hands on her hips with indignation. 'Well, what d'you know!' she said. 'Three irresistible offers just when I'm all booked up. Sorry, fellas, I shall have to resist the irresistible.'

She went to the office where Sara Kenmore was packing up to go on leave.

'Have a good time, Sister,' Cora said with a smile.

'Oh, I will,' Sara enthused. 'Roy's got his week's leave organised down to the last detail, and I bet we spend most of it in bed.' She winked knowingly as the three doctors came up behind Cora, echoing her good wishes before going off duty.

Cora rolled down her sleeves, put on her cape and picked up her bag.

'Who's the lucky chap?' Sara asked.

'There isn't one.'

'You had three offers—Cora—you must be mad!' Sara exclaimed.

'I'd have liked to go with Neil, but I don't want to encourage him in what can only ever be a good friendship. I didn't want to hurt him; and Mandy would never forgive me if I went out with Tod.'

'So you do really have a secret passion?'

Cora tried to laugh this off but Sara wasn't easily deceived.

'Come on, who?' she implored. 'Tod?'

Cora shook her head. 'Just dreams of my tree frog turning into a prince,' she said. 'A real man might spoil my dream.'

Sara made it obvious that she didn't believe Cora, and Cora realised that she'd sown the seed for a fast-spreading rumour. She parted company with Sara, and the other nurses, wishing that she hadn't been such a fool. She ought to have accepted Neil's offer. She liked him a lot and found him good company, but deep down she was scared of his expectations of a commitment. It wouldn't be fair to go along with him, accepting all that he offered only to turn him down when it became too serious. She needed to be free for a while longer yet. Free to dream these impossible dreams; so what if she had spoilt her chances!

She reached her room and had stripped down to a minimum of underwear when Mandy burst in on her in her usual state of excitement.

'Oh good, you're in at last. Come on, I've booked you on a blind date.'

'Mandy! No! You know that's one thing I do draw the line at,' Cora complained.

'I'm not going to let you back out. It's a nice evening so don't waste it. Duggie is bringing one of his mates along—no—you haven't met him, he wasn't at Sara's party because he was on duty, but Duggie and I met Steve at the diving club.'

'You?—at a diving club?'

'Yes.' Mandy tossed her bouncing curls. 'You don't have to dive, you just go along for the social events and Steve's a nice chap or I wouldn't have dropped you in it. Actually, he isn't keen on making up a foursome either, but he's a bit lonely.'

'Lonely?' Cora was instantly suspicious.

'He's engaged, but she isn't coming out to Bermuda yet so he needs cheering up.'

'Mandy!' Cora protested. 'It's just not on. His

fiancée trusts him. She wouldn't like him being matched up with someone else.'

'He won't fall in love with you, and you mustn't with him,' Mandy warned.

Cora groaned. 'And to think I turned down three dates.'

Mandy's green eyes nearly popped. 'You what?' she shrieked. 'Who with?'

'Neil for one, but I don't want to encourage him, Mandy. Then there was Tod, he saved me from accepting Neil.'

Mandy's expression changed to seriousness.

'It's all right,' Cora explained hurriedly. 'Mr Delaney saved me from both of them.'

'You're going out with Darryl Delaney?'

'And have Monique string me up from the nearest gibbet? No, Mandy. They were only joking so I pretended I had a date,' Cora said.

Mandy sighed with relief. 'Thank goodness for that, so it's okay then, and you weren't telling lies, you have got a date—with Steve.'

'It doesn't sound like a good idea. It's going to be embarrassing because he might think I'm expecting a regular date. I can't very well say "Hi! I'm only here because you're lonely, and I don't want a fella anyway".'

Mandy laughed. 'I'll get you through the evening, Cora, don't worry.'

Cora made a face. 'It's precisely that which worries me.'

'Half an hour to dress, pick me up on the way down.' The door slammed behind the incorrigible Mandy.

As Cora showered and then put on a jump suit in a bright shade of peacock blue she wished she had accepted Neil's offer after all. She didn't want him to get the wrong idea, yet at the same time she'd hate to think that she had upset him. He hadn't *looked* that upset though . . .

The girls crossed to Hamilton harbour on the lower ferry and were met by two tall, casually dressed men. Cora remembered Duggie and by the way he greeted Mandy she noticed that he was more than a little fond of her. Cora hoped her friend knew what she was doing; she usually did even if she did go about things in a reckless kind of way.

'Duggie, you've met Cora,' Mandy said. 'Steve, she's promised not to fall in love with you. She knows all about your fiancée, and anyway she's not up for grabs either.'

Steve smiled pleasantly and looked relieved.

'You engaged too?' he asked.

Cora shook her head. 'No, nothing like that.'

Why wasn't she 'up for grabs' as Mandy put it? She didn't have a male companion, she wasn't in love with anyone—or—? A vision of the senior surgical registrar pushed its way into her mind. It was as if he were constantly taunting her. 'Dare to love me,' he seemed to be saying, 'and then we'll decide whether I shall prosecute, or settle out of court.'

She supposed she had been flattered by his suggestion but now she had to keep reminding herself that there was a Mrs Delaney and in truth, Cora Jordan, staff nurse at Zenobia's hospital, Bermuda, was as free as one of the beautiful Longtail sea-birds. They were seldom seen without a mate in hot pursuit—would that she were so lucky! She came back to reality and realised that Mandy was in full flow with her usual exuberance, gabbling on with hardly a moment to draw breath.

'Mandy's a romantic,' Cora said with a warm smile, 'not to be taken too seriously.'

The men laughed and the evening progressed with mutual light-heartedness until they were sitting at a table in a waterfront inn where English fish and chips were the speciality. It was a favourite haunt of off-duty British policemen and also hospital staff. They were settling themselves at a window table when Cora glanced up at the bar where she was confronted by those haunting black eyes directed straight at her. She looked away quickly, disconcerted that Darryl and Neil were enjoying a drink together at the very same inn. She tried to ignore them, but Mandy was quick to observe her friend's discomfort and whispered something to the effect of it not being Cora's night. After the initial shock though, Cora realised that at least her story had been proven, and she managed to resume some degree of pleasurable interest in her escort.

The evening ended happily. Steve was an easy, friendly person who suggested further meetings merely for companionship, but Cora refused to commit herself.

With Sara Kenmore off duty over the Easter weekend she had limited off duty and was too tired to want to go far. With increasing numbers of holiday-makers visiting Bermuda there were more casualties, and she was kept busy throughout the long weekend. In her quiet moments she knew she ought to feel relieved that the senior surgical registrar was off duty, but deep down she experienced a sense of disappointment at not seeing him.

She saw little of Mandy either, who was spending much of her free time with Duggie, but they met up in the canteen at lunch time on Easter Monday.

'Are you on or off?' Mandy asked.

'Off, thank goodness. Sister Longford is up to her usual nit-picking standard. She's missing our bull-frog friend I imagine.'

'And you wouldn't be?' Mandy quipped.

Cora dropped her gaze to the plate on the table in front of her. Was it so obvious?

'Oh, come on, love, tell Aunt Amanda all about it,' Mandy pleaded. 'It's Darryl Delaney, isn't it? Don't worry, you're not the first and you won't be the last. *Everyone* but *everyone* falls for *him*. You'll get over it. By the way I saw Duggie last night and he said Steve is quite impressed by you and is looking forward to the next time.'

'There isn't going to be a next time,' Cora said flatly. 'And of course I'm not hooked on Mr Delaney.'

'Well, if and when you are my shoulder will be free to cry on. Can't think who else has turned you on but someone has or you'd be glad of Steve's company.'

'Steve's not free, Mandy. It all sounds innocent enough but it's a dangerous game and I'm not going to be guilty of coming between him and his fiancée. Thanks very much but I'll find my own man in my own good time.'

'Okay, okay, but it's fun to make up a foursome sometimes. You're unusually touchy for you, Cora. Whoever this guy is he's got a lot to answer for—ah—*I* know! Of course, it's the engineer who had his foot crushed. Patsy Gillman was telling me that this chap talks of no one but the nurse who looked after him in Casualty. He's been trying to get a message to you. Wants you to visit him, so why don't you? He's still in a room on his own, so Patsy said.'

Cora laughed. 'Mandy, you really are the limit. Just because I happen to hold a patient's hand at a critical time doesn't mean to say I've fallen in love with him. Bill Palmer had a nasty accident. He was really very brave, but I couldn't tell you now what he looks like. For one thing he was covered in grease and oil. We had to cut his overalls off him. Besides that, he's married, if I remember correctly.'

'So what?' Mandy retorted, flashing her green eyes mischievously. 'When did that ever stop anyone falling in love?'

'Well I'm *not*!' Cora denied hotly.

Mandy finished her meal and placed her knife and fork side by side on the plate before gulping down her coffee.

'Must get back to Women's Surgical, I suppose,' she said, wiping her mouth with a paper serviette. 'I'm not off until six and I'm hoping Duggie will ring—that's if Tod doesn't come chasing after me.

If he only knew what he's doing to me, but he isn't even interested.'

'Why should he be when you're always out with someone else? He probably thinks you're not free.'

'Be a pal and enlighten him.'

'Do your own explaining, Mandy Rawson.'

Mandy stood up. 'Maybe you could fix up a foursome with Tod and Neil? No—you're too noble to do a devious thing like that I suppose. What plans have you got for today then?'

'I'm going to the cathedral to see the floral decorations, then,' she shrugged, 'I'll just see what I feel like doing.'

'Maybe you'll bump into Steve.'

'And maybe I won't—see you, Mandy,' she added as her friend returned to duty.

Cora took her time over her coffee, watching as staff came and went, and when Monique entered and went to queue up at the counter Cora got up and left.

She rested on her bed for half an hour and then showered and changed into a pretty cotton dress with short sleeves. The afternoon was sunny and warm, but she took a light Shetland wool cardigan with her which she needed round her shoulders as she went by ferry to Hamilton harbour. Being Bank Holiday most of the shops were closed but business at the ferry terminal was brisk, many holiday-makers making the most of the weather by taking boat cruises round the islands. So far Cora hadn't taken advantage of these opportunities but she promised herself she would as soon as she could.

It was a short walk across the town to the Anglican Cathedral where the beautiful lily decorations almost took her breath away. There were many people admiring the vast show of flowers as well as the unusual Reredos sculptures. Taking a tourist guide book she whiled away an hour reading about the history of the Cathedral and wandering through the aisles. She found the high building cool and peaceful in spite of the throng of tourists and as she rounded a pillar she bumped into an elderly lady who was leaning heavily on a stick.

'I'm so sorry,' Cora apologised in a whisper, 'I'm afraid I wasn't looking where I was going.'

'Are you ever?'

The lady looked aghast at the man who was accompanying her. None other than Darryl Delaney! But at least he was smiling.

'Mother, this is our new—well, not so new now— staff nurse in Accident and Emergency, Cora Jordan, the not-so-expert moped rider.'

Mrs Delaney held out her hand and kept Cora's in her own for several seconds.

'My dear, are you quite all right? Darryl was so worried about you. That was quite a nasty bang on your head.'

'I'm fine,' Cora said, but thought, not my heart which is pounding nineteen to the dozen. She wished desperately that she could quieten the pounding, that she could react rationally, but every movement, every word she uttered sounded magnified and false to her.

'And how are you finding Bermuda?' Mrs Delaney asked.

'It's lovely,' Cora said with a smile, knowing that

her cheeks were flushed and her eyes were brimming with pleasure at this unexpected meeting.

Darryl was standing slightly to one side and behind his mother. They were almost the same height, Mrs Delaney being a tall, elegant woman for her years. Her dark hair was streaked with grey but permed into softly falling waves and curls, and her eyes were as black as her son's. There was no doubt that he had inherited the Latin-American look from his mother. Cora felt her spirits soar. Was this *the* Mrs Delaney she had heard mentioned? Was he unmarried after all?

'I came to see the lilies,' Cora hurried on to explain.

'Easter-time is the beginning of everything for Bermuda,' Mrs Delaney said. 'A true Resurrection. Bermuda is a Paradise, so peaceful, the climate heavenly . . .'

'Mother, I fancy Cora is rapidly finding that out for herself,' Darryl interrupted. 'Are you alone?'

The question was significant, tinged with his usual sarcasm.

Cora nodded and gave him a look of defiance.

'Then do come and have a cup of tea with us, my dear,' Mrs Delaney invited eagerly. 'Darryl should bring his friends home to visit us more often.'

'I . . . I . . .' Cora began, but an excuse just refused to materialise.

'We were just leaving,' Darryl said. 'Have you seen all you want to see?'

'No, actually,' Cora reasserted herself, 'I was going to take a taxi to see the fields of lilies growing.'

'Come and have tea first, then Darryl will drive you to see those, Cora.'

'It's all right, really,' Cora said. 'I can't impose.'

Darryl held her arm and propelled her along to the door.

'You won't be imposing,' he whispered. 'Mother loves visitors and at least you'll be safe in my company. Any designs on mopeds and men you may have had can be forgotten.'

Cora turned to remonstrate but the wicked gleam in his eyes silenced her. She felt like stamping angrily on his foot but somewhere inside her excitement was beginning to bubble.

Hubble, bubble, toil and trouble she thought in a ridiculously childish way. She saw Mrs Delaney as her fairy godmother, Darryl the handsome prince and she knew she must make the most of these precious moments before her bubble burst and Darryl Delaney changed back into a temperamental bull-frog.

CHAPTER FIVE

DARRYL drove back along the coast road to the parish of Paget, past the hospital and on towards the south shore beaches. Turning off into a small side road, he pulled into a large shrub-lined driveway which led to a long, low, white-roofed bungalow. Cora noticed the brass name-plate on the circular archway of stone as they entered. There were moongates everywhere on the island but she was impressed that the Delaneys had one of their own.

A tall, thin man was standing on the lawn looking out to sea in the far distance. He turned when he heard the car and came to open the passenger doors.

'So, we have a visitor. How nice.' He helped Cora out first before Mrs Delaney, and Darryl came round to Cora's side, introducing his father to whom he bore no resemblance at all.

'Cora—that's a good old Irish name,' Mr Delaney said as he went to help his wife.

'Delaney is too, I believe?' Cora countered with a smile.

'That's right, my grandfather emigrated to America, but I was born in England, and so was Darryl.'

'A lot of mixed blood in us, Cora,' Mrs Delaney said, 'but Darryl tells me that it adds something to our charisma, though I can't imagine what.'

'That's what it adds, Mother, intrigue,' Darryl said and taking Cora's arm guided her to the rear of the bungalow. It was set on high ground with a garden of lawns, flowering shrubs and trees which sloped downwards, affording a clear view to the sea about half a mile away.

'Would you like to stay outside and have a cool drink?' Darryl asked.

'Thank you, but I really shouldn't have intruded like this.'

'Why not? Father doesn't see patients on a Bank Holiday, and they're always complaining that I don't bring friends and colleagues home.'

'Your father is a GP here?'

Darryl nodded, helping Cora to settle on a reclining garden chair while he perched on the edge of one by her side. 'You sound surprised.'

Cora shrugged. 'I didn't know,' she said simply. 'I didn't realise your family were here too.'

'We haven't had much opportunity to exchange personal life stories,' Darryl said. 'Mother is the real foreigner, she was born in Brazil but taken to England to live when she was about eight years old. The climate never suited her and in later years she suffered from arthritis, so when they got rid of me to University they came here to start a new life, and it's been most successful. Mother only thinks she needs the walking stick.'

'She walks very well,' Cora observed as Mrs Delaney accompanied her husband to the far end of the garden.

'She had a fall six months ago which has robbed

her of a little confidence when she's out,' Darryl
explained.

A dark brown woman appeared, bearing a tray
of iced drinks, and Doctor and Mrs Delaney joined
Darryl and Cora.

'So you went to admire the artistic decoration in
the Cathedral, Cora?' Dr Delaney asked.

'The lilies—well, they're just *so* gorgeous,' Cora
breathed. 'I've never seen such a beautiful sight
before.'

'I'm going to take her to see the lily fields after
tea,' Darryl said.

'It's kind of you, Darryl,' Cora said, 'but I'm sure
you must have other plans.'

'No, he hasn't,' his mother put in sharply. 'That's
the lovely thing about Bermuda, no one hurries for
anything, though my son finds this peculiarity irk-
some as yet.'

'How long have you been here then?' Cora
asked.

'Long enough,' he replied crisply, and Cora
sensed some dissension between mother and
son.

He went into the bungalow a few moments later
which gave Mrs Delaney the opportunity to find out
all she could about Cora, and the doctor brought up
the subject of her moped accident. She waved this
aside, saying that she had recovered completely.
She desperately needed to know if Darryl was
pursuing the matter, but she was a guest in their
luxurious home so she felt that she couldn't very
well ask, nor could she insist that the fault had been
their son's in these circumstances.

Instead the conversation covered a wide variety of subjects, mostly about Bermuda and the places they assured Cora she should visit.

Cora found the Delaneys pleasant company, the white-haired doctor the type of GP Cora remembered from childhood days, a fatherly family man. He was so unlike Darryl in looks, and in his gentle gallant manner.

Tea was served in a conservatory overlooking the garden and consisted of dainty sandwiches and thin slices of chocolate and fruit cake which went down well with the refreshing tea.

Darryl seemed to be in a hurry afterwards, and as Cora said goodbye Mrs Delaney merely enclosed Cora's outstretched hand between her own. 'You'll be back, my dear. We wouldn't dream of letting you go back to the hospital without supper.'

Darryl put his arm round Cora's waist and almost pulled her away from his mother.

'We'll be back, Mother, about eight,' he said brusquely, and hustled Cora to the car.

As soon as they were out of sight of his parents Cora said: 'Look, you don't have to take me anywhere. I'll get a taxi tour.'

'For heaven's sake, get in the car, girl. Have I made you feel unwelcome?'

Cora paused uncertainly. 'We-ell, yes, a bit,' she admitted softly. 'You're evidently in a hurry to go off somewhere, and I'm messing up your arrangements. It was kind of your parents, but—'

She got no further. His dark eyes penetrated through her so that she stopped mid-sentence. Then, slowly, she watched his mouth coming closer, and in one reckless moment he caught her to him and kissed her with devastating effect. He managed to evaporate every bit of resistance within her, and when he drew back she noticed that he seemed suddenly relaxed.

'I'll remember next time what sort of welcome you expect,' he said, and ushered her into the front passenger seat.

'I didn't mean . . . I wasn't implying . . .' she began in confusion.

'You've had your welcome, now sit still and enjoy the rest of the day,' Darryl said, and as he negotiated the car round to go back down the drive he pulled up sharply and looked across at her, his black brows drawn together quizzically.

'Or am I taking a liberty? Taking you for granted, perhaps? Maybe *you* have a prior engagement this evening?'

Cora shook her head quickly. If only he knew how glad she was that she hadn't made arrangements to see Steve again, or Neil.

'No,' she muttered softly, trying not to let her eagerness show. 'I have no other plans.'

A lengthy silence ensued while Darryl drove through the attractive moongate. He paused long enough for her to see the name-plate more clearly and that it was in fact his father's professional services which were proclaimed.

She used the silence to peruse the Delaney household. His parents seemed pleasant, homely people, but there was some underlying friction between Darryl and his mother. Cora remembered that the invitation to tea and return for supper had

come from Mrs Delaney, and while Darryl hadn't
openly objected he hadn't been pleased either. She
remembered his sarcastic remarks about mothers-
in-law, with an added snipe about mothers in
general. Was Mrs Delaney anxious to see her son
married? Was this her style, to invite any female
member of Zenobia's back to their home?

If so, Cora's chances were slim. Chances of
what? she asked herself. Up to recently she had
admitted nothing but contempt for the man—but
now? She pulled her stomach muscles in and tight-
ened her grip on her embroidered canvas shoulder
bag, glancing across at the masculine hands which
steered the car and directed the gear lever. His left
hand was closest to her and as he changed gear to
descend a hill she noticed the gold ring on his little
finger, attractively set with a black onyx stone
which matched the silky dark hairs on each slender
finger. She felt a sudden urge to roll back his cuffs,
bringing into view the matt of black down which she
knew by instinct covered his arms. Her mind raced
on to envisage his naked torso. He would have firm
but not flabby muscles, a slim waist and narrow hips
and she could visualise his elegance in nothing but
swimming trunks.

'You've gone quiet,' he said, giving her a swift
sidelong glance. 'Does just one kiss knock the
stuffing out of you?'

'Depends who does the kissing,' she replied
tersely, but keeping her tone light.

She knew he instantly smiled, flashing gleaming
white teeth—the whiter for the contrast against his
dark-tanned skin.

Flatter him, her subconscious goaded. He'll lap it up.

'And you have plenty of experience to compare the various brands,' he said in a low voice. She knew by the hint of condemnation that he was referring to Neil and Steve. 'I told you Latin lovers are incomparable,' he continued.

'And conceited,' she retorted.

He laughed spontaneously, a melodious, sensuous sound which reduced her to jelly, but then they came to the fields of lilies and she gasped at the sight. A cool white candlewick bedspread flecked with yellow and green.

'I've never seen anything so beautiful,' she whispered.

He had brought the car to a halt and leaning slightly towards her said: 'Take a look in the mirror, darling. "Fairer than lilies art thou"—where does that come from—the Bible?'

Cora couldn't answer. She was confused by his insincere compliment, and the pure innocence of the fragrant flowers which grew in abundance, each large, curling bloom blending harmoniously with its bed-mate. She didn't feel the need for meaningless conversation, she just wanted to sit and absorb the view.

'It's a shame to pick them,' she said at last, remembering the Easter Day arrangements everywhere.

'It's always a shame to defile beauty,' Darryl agreed. 'But every good thing grows to maturity, and after that—' he shrugged. 'Do you know what makes the Bermuda lily so special?' he asked her, suddenly serious.

'I suppose it's the climate here which makes them thrive,' she said, turning to look at him.

'A century ago a ship put into Bermuda in need of help. On board was a missionary returning to England from Japan with a collection of plants from the Liukiu Islands. The missionary happened to have an old friend here, so when visiting the reverend gentleman he gave him some Japanese lily bulbs which he duly planted and which flourished, becoming *the* Easter lily, fragrant as well as beautiful. Now it's one of Bermuda's main industries. Have you visited the Perfumery?'

'No, not yet.'

'We must rectify that,' he said. 'Every woman must have some Easter lily perfume, though it is a rather sweet scent. Mother doesn't care for it, but there are others, Jasmine, Sweet Pea, Oleander and Passion flower—but you wouldn't need that one.'

'I believe it's so named as a representation of Christ's passion,' Cora reminded him firmly. 'I read about it somewhere.'

'You're well-informed,' Darryl said forgetting his mockery of her. 'It's a rather lovely story, but when we go to the Perfumery you must sample them all and see which one you prefer.'

He leaned across to open her door and seconds later they were following the path which skirted the gently wafting lilies.

The very air was pure and sweet, the breeze from the ocean, which wherever you happened to be in Bermuda was never far away, rippled as if some hidden being was caring personally for each lily. Cora was enchanted and maybe the tranquil scene stirred Darryl's emotions for he caught her hand in his and squeezed it gently. Then in a swift decisive movement he pulled her closer to him so that she looked up questioningly.

'Cora, you are really well now, aren't you? No more headaches or other—?' he began with genuine concern.

'I'm perfectly fit,' she cut in and instead of obeying the urge to fling her arms around his neck she said: 'But I would like to know—?'

'If I'm going to prosecute?' His smile blended well with the laughing lilies. 'And risk having you deported?' he teased. 'Much more fun to settle out of court, don't you think?'

'I don't know what to think,' Cora said solemnly.

He held her quivering chin between warm fingers, sending an electric wave tingling through her veins.

'Don't bother to think at all, then,' he advised gently. 'There'll be time to do that when you've got over the first romantic impression of Bermuda and I don't want to spoil that for you.'

She searched deep into his eyes but could only see a star-studded sparkle. What lay behind his motives? Was this closeness just an off-duty pastime? She suddenly knew that she couldn't bear it if it were, so she swung away out of his grasp and he fell into step beside her to return to the car.

He chatted pleasantly as they returned to his parents' home, but Cora was barely listening. She tried to analyse her feelings. What a fool she was

being to let his attentions affect her. Hadn't everyone warned her against falling for him? Hadn't she
felt this way over men in the past? No! Never so
deeply, never with such powerful urgency. She had
enjoyed many close friendships, but as soon as a
man became amorous with a danger of losing control Cora had called a halt. Such a relationship
would only be with someone very special. Was
Darryl Delaney special enough?

As they reached the entrance to the bungalow
Darryl said: 'I hope he's worth such deep concentration, Cora, and I hope you won't regret letting
him down this evening.'

'I'm not letting anyone down this evening,' she
said quickly, 'well, I hope not,' she added softly to
herself. 'And yes, he is worth such devoted concentration.'

She turned towards him with a smile, but Darryl
put the handbrake on with some aggression, and
before she could add any explanation was out of the
car. How could she tell him that in spite of everything it was he whom she didn't want to let down.
There was no one else, how could there ever
be since that first magical kiss he had given her?
Crazy though she realised she was, her heart was
hooked!

Inside the bungalow air-conditioning kept it
pleasantly cool, and Cora was grateful for the
opportunity to freshen up in the pink and black
bathroom. An aperitif was served in the conservatory before supper which turned out to be a candle-
lit dinner during which Darryl's father was eager to
hear about Cora's training and the changes occur-

ring in British hospitals, as well as medicine generally. Cora relaxed, easily at home with the Delaney
family, even able to converse intelligently with
Darryl, when the telephone rang in the hall.

Darryl began to push back his chair.

'I'll go,' his mother said firmly, and left the room,
closing the door securely behind her.

Cora felt the atmosphere change as it became
charged with tension. Conversation drifted
awkwardly into stony silence and Mrs Delaney
returned, saying in an undercurrent to Darryl: 'I've
explained that you're otherwise engaged.'

Cora watched as Darryl fought for self-control.
His knuckles showed white as he strengthened his
hold on his crisp white table napkin.

'Thank you, Mother,' he said pointedly.

'Now, dear,' Mrs Delaney said to Cora in an all
too eager tone, 'biscuits and cheese?'

'I couldn't manage another thing, Mrs Delaney.
It was a superb meal, thank you'—steak and veget-
ables with a lemon sorbet to follow, washed down
with a delicious red wine. After coffee, which they
took outside on the lawn, she walked through the
garden with Darryl's parents.

Later Darryl joined them and seemed in better
humour again. Who had telephoned him, Cora
wondered, only to be put off by his mother? Could
it have been Monique? and had Darryl telephoned
her back making his peace? Thanks to Mrs Delaney, Darryl was Cora's for tonight, and she didn't
intend to let anyone spoil the evening.

It was late when the strains of Chopin's Polonaise
in A flat died away and Darryl switched off the

music centre. Cora got up to go and while Darryl went to fetch his jacket Cora thanked his parents for having her.

'It's been a pleasure, my dear,' Mrs Delaney said. 'You must come again as soon as you have an evening free.'

'My dear,' Dr Delaney reproached, 'I'm sure Cora has lots of young men eager for her company, and she hasn't had a chance to see Bermuda properly yet. These girls are kept busy at Zenobia's, you know, and like Monique she'll want to spend her free time at the beach or at the golf or diving club.'

'Monique will soon be returning to Canada,' Mrs Delaney remarked gruffly.

'Oh, will she?' Cora said with surprise. 'I had no idea.'

'She's been here over eighteen months and now she's bored with the place.'

'Monique is not bored, or boring, Mother,' Darryl said, coming in on the conversation. 'Her two-year term of duty is up and naturally she'll be quite happy to return home.'

Darryl placed his hands on Cora's waist and practically pushed her on so that she had to plant her feet down firmly long enough to say goodbye to her host and hostess.

Monique seemed to be an important person to Darryl, but Cora refused to dwell on that supposition as they drove off into the moonlit night.

Cora knew that the drive to the nurses' home would take no more than ten minutes, but by the time she realised that they were going in the direction of the sea Darryl was pulling into a south shore beach car park.

'Breath of sea air,' he said, 'to help you sleep.'

'Mm, lovely,' Cora said, and as they stood at the water's edge, watching the rolling waves break over the pink-shelled sand, she knew a moment of heaven. She expected Darryl to kiss her again—after all, wasn't this the perfect setting?—but they strolled along the beach for half an hour before returning to the car.

Cora felt exhilarated, she would sleep, she would dream, oh such dreams . . .

Then she was aware of his arm sliding along the back of her seat and in a few moments she melted into his embrace. His mouth was firm on hers, each kiss more possessive than the one before it, and Cora found herself clutching his arm in case he should let go. She was surprised at her own flood of passion and how quickly she had responded. Her swelling breasts were encased in the gathered bodice of her dress, but she quivered as she felt his sensitive finger-tips cupping one breast and caressing it gently. A slight moan of pleasure escaped from her throat and she heard what sounded like a chuckle from his as he reluctantly drew his mouth from hers.

'Just as well I decided not to defer the good-night kiss until we reached the nurses' home,' he said.

Something in Cora snapped as she rasped out: 'Afraid that Monique might see?'

For a long moment he stared into her eyes and she was thankful that it was dark. She felt his condemnation, sensed his anger as he turned and faced the steering wheel.

'Mother has evidently been talking,' he snarled, and the car sprang to life.

When he drew up outside the nurses' home entrance Cora tried to make amends.

'I . . . I'm sorry, Darryl,' she stammered. 'I don't know what made me say such a stupid thing, especially after you've given me such a very enjoyable time. Please don't blame your mother, though—honestly—she said nothing about Monique or anyone else.'

He left the car engine running, got out and opened the front passenger door. Cora took her time, desperately wanting things to be good between them, yet knowing that she had just poured cold water over a developing situation.

Holding her arm gently he escorted her to the door.

'Goodnight, Cora. I'm glad you've enjoyed yourself,' and the next moment he returned to the car.

Cora stood still, watching as he drove away without wasting a second. All her fever-heat had died down and she shivered with cold. She needed the privacy of her own room and was grateful that no one was around. She crept upstairs, glad that they and the corridors were only dimly lit.

Well, she told her mirrored image, you did a very good job of spoiling your chances.

What chances? she asked. What hope have I got with Monique around? But she was going back to

Canada. Perhaps the situation wasn't as hopeless as it seemed.

When Cora dressed for duty next morning, one glance in the mirror showed up her lack of sleep. She had lain awake for hours, savouring Darryl's every touch, but she was angry with herself for being bitchy. She would have known that Darryl Delaney was not the type of man to make allowances for petty envy. He didn't need to. Didn't he have every blessed female at Zenobia's falling head over heels for him? But it was Monique who was special to him, so, Cora decided, she must be content with her impossible dreams.

As she went to breakfast she even wondered if those magical moments had been real, or were they all part of her dreams?

She was glad when she could escape the noise and bustle of the canteen and report for duty to Sister Longford.

For once there were no patients in the waiting area and Tod who had been on call throughout the night had little to relate to Neil who arrived soon after Cora. But the lull was short-lived; a car accident involving a private car, a delivery van and a cyclist brought in five patients, all suffering from shock, some with bruises and abrasions, but the cyclist was unconscious and had a broken collarbone.

Neil and Sister Longford attended to this patient while Cora and two other nurses dealt with the others. Blood pressure and pulses were checked in accordance with the usual routine, and as one

middle-aged lady was in a more severe state of
shock with very low blood pressure Cora helped
her on to a couch, her feet elevated, and one of the
junior nurses fetched a prepared drip-stand. Cora
cleaned the skin at the site of the injection, placed
the sphygmomanometer cuff round the patient's
arm and blew it up sufficiently to distend the vein,
while Tod, who had been recalled, inserted the
intravenous needle. As soon as the infusion was
started the patient responded well and was encouraged to rest quietly, and as Cora went to check on
the other victims of the multiple accident she heard
the ambulance siren groaning to a low whine outside.

A coronary case was brought in, but before he
could be admitted the ambulance man called: 'He's
arrested, Staff,' and everyone reacted spontaneously as trained. As Tod massaged the forty-
year-old man's heart Cora started mouth-to-mouth
breathing until an oxygen mask was fitted, and Neil
gave an injection to stimulate the heart into action
which thankfully it did within two minutes.

Other patients had to wait until this emergency
was over and the patient sufficiently recovered to
be transferred to the coronary care unit. Everyone
breathed a sigh of relief in the certain knowledge
that only the staff's immediate action and expert
team co-operation had saved his life. It was the one
thing about Casualty which Cora dreaded, as she
guessed everyone did—even the most experienced
doctor or nursing sister. It was on such occasions as
this that every member of the medical staff came to
realise the enormous responsibility they carried,

and for a while the atmosphere in the emergency and accident department was subdued.

But by midday various cases has been redirected for surgical and medical examination, and before Cora went to lunch she accompanied a renal colic case to the men's surgical ward.

Mr Whittingham had been brought in suffering excruciating pain as well as sweating heavily and looking pallid. Neil examined the patient and ordered an injection consisting of a strong pain killer, antispasmodic and sedative, before he was taken to the ward where it was hoped that the stone or gravel causing the pain would be passed.

Patsy Gillman the staff nurse on that ward admitted the patient.

'He's being referred to Mr Delaney, Patsy,' Cora said as she handed her the notes and then looked down at the elderly gentleman. 'You'll be all right now, Mr Whittingham,' she said touching his hand gently. 'This is Staff Nurse Gillman, she'll take good care of you.'

The patient, although still in considerable pain squeezed Cora's hand and whispered his thanks. Cora was at the door when Patsy came after her.

'Cora, have you got a minute?'

'I'm going to lunch,' she said, swivelling round on one heel.

'Be an angel and put your head in to see Bill Palmer. He keeps asking us to give you messages. Didn't Mandy tell you?'

'She did mention something about him, but why me?'

Patsy laughed. 'I know, doesn't say much for the

rest of us, does it? Still, he wants to see you, so, as you're here, try and pacify him—please?'

Cora made a face. 'Can't remember him all that well, still,' she shrugged, 'if it'll help—where is he?'

'In room thirty-two. He's—'

'No,' Cora held up a silencing hand, 'I don't want to know, then I can't be quizzed. It's better if I can be negative, he's your responsibility.'

'I think it's *you* he wants to see. He's quite philosophical about the prospect of losing his foot, maybe even much of his leg.'

Cora raised her eyebrows in despair and followed Patsy's indication to the small one-bedded ward.

She glanced through the circular glass panel in the door as she knocked and opened it.

Bill Palmer was propped up in bed, the sheets and bedspread draped over a cradle protecting his leg from any pressure. He'd been reading a paperback, now he glanced up and as recognition dawned his eyes sparkled with pleasure, his features softening in relaxation.

'Hi, honey!' he drawled in a warm voice.

'I hear you're making a right nuisance of yourself,' Cora said, gently taunting him.

'You bet. They've taken their time finding you.'

'I do get to have some off duty,' she said, tossing her head significantly.

'Come closer, Nurse. I'm not contagious,' he joked, patting the bed beside him.

Cora took a step closer, remembering now the fear she had noticed in his dove-grey eyes, remembering too the dodgy few minutes in the theatre when she had assisted Darryl during the initial and mostly exploratory operation.

'How are you feeling then?' she asked.

He pursed his lips and pulled a face. 'Aw—well—guess you know how it is. I'm bored—and worried.' He put the open book face down on his locker. 'Guess I wish I could offer you a drink, but all I have is iced water.'

'You can worry about drinks when you're on your feet again, Mr Palmer. Is there anything special you wanted me for?'

Cora wished she hadn't asked. He made a grab for her hand and pulled her closer and before she could discourage him he had placed both hands around her trim waist and was holding her fast.

'Just to look at you again, honey, besides a lot of other "special" things. I want to thank you for what you did when I was brought in.'

'But I did nothing, Mr Palmer. It's Mr Delaney you should be thanking, not me.'

'He told me that you went to theatre with me and I'm grateful. I wish you were on this ward.'

Cora tried to push his hands away, and suddenly she felt his hands voluntarily slide down her hips and on to the bed listlessly. She followed his gaze to where Darryl Delaney was standing in the doorway.

CHAPTER SIX

THE registrar's face looked blacker than usual and he didn't even try to hide his inquisitive stare.

'I . . . I was just leaving,' Cora said half-apologetically.

'Um—well—I suppose I can come back later if you're visiting Mr Palmer during your lunch break.' The insinuation was pointed.

'Come again?' Bill Palmer whispered, catching two of Cora's fingers in his own. When Cora didn't answer immediately he added with a naughty wink: 'I'll come and find you as soon as I'm on my good foot if you don't.'

'I think Mr Delaney would like to see you now. I hope all goes well, Mr Palmer.' Cora pulled away and made her exit as swiftly as possible, her cheeks horribly taut and flushed, but she had cooled considerably by the time she reached the canteen.

She queued up and chose an egg salad for her lunch, hoping she would see Mandy, but there was no sign of her. Instead she had only been eating for a few minutes when a shadow fell across her plate and she looked up to find Darryl sitting across from her. He placed his roll, butter and cheese to one side and began to stir his coffee slowly, methodically, his gaze penetrating Cora's.

At last he looked about him, took a sip of coffee

and pushed the cup away to draw his plate in front of him.

'You surprise me, Cora,' he said as he broke open his crusty roll.

She glared at him defiantly. 'That surprises me,' she retorted, 'that anything should surprise *you*!'

'I thought you were different from other girls, but I notice you're playing the field—Neil, Tod, a policeman, and now Bill Palmer. May I remind—'

'You forgot to include yourself, still, I suppose you don't count, but I'm glad you agree with Monique. She thinks I'm a flirt too.'

He regarded her steadily, his lips compressed together tightly as if he dared not speak or he would lose control. Then, between his teeth, he said, 'May I remind you that Bill Palmer has a wife and family at home in the States.'

Cora emptied her mouth, then took extra air into her lungs. She wasn't going to be dictated to by Darryl Delaney, but in her heart of hearts she was hating this confrontation.

'*Mr* Delaney,' she began, 'I'm not the slightest bit interested in Mr Palmer or his private affairs. It has nothing whatsoever to do with you though, but, may *I* remind *you* that I am a staff nurse, and it happens to be my job to see that patients are made comfortable, put at ease as much as possible, have their pain lessened to some degree and generally show an interest in their welfare. So,' she continued adamantly, 'when someone asks to see me I try to comply with that request, and that is all!'

That should have been enough, she thought, but he leaned across the table aggressively.

'It didn't look that innocent to me. You are a flirt; a very expert one with those ravishing blue eyes, knocking every man you meet for six.'

'Don't you mean for sex?'

His dark eyes narrowed so that they were like two black slits glaring at her with nothing but condemnation.

'Possibly,' he growled.

'Can't you go and sit somewhere else?' she asked insolently, feeling that she was losing this battle.

He paused momentarily, then she saw the quiver of a smile at the corners of his mouth while at the same time he clenched his jaw, she noticed, by the tightening muscle.

'I could,' he said slowly, 'but I chose to sit opposite you, and I repeat, you just think carefully, young lady, before you upset a man's marriage.'

'And you think twice before you make such unfounded accusations.'

'Eat your lunch or you'll be in trouble for being late back in Casualty.'

Cora flung her knife and fork down, having eaten very little. 'I don't think I want any more,' she said contemptuously, 'you've put me off my food.'

She got up and stormed out, her feet tapping out each step of bitter rancour which seemed to have knotted every vein in her body. She didn't even take the lift but used corridors and stairs to work off her fury, then as she passed the ground floor lift doors she heard them open as she hurried past and seconds later a hand on her shoulder restrained her progress.

'You left this, Cora,' Darryl said smoothly, holding her shoulder bag out to her, 'and since I'm the cause of your not eating I'd better take you out to dinner tonight. I'll pick you up at eight outside the nurses' home.'

'Oh no you won't,' she said, snatching her bag rudely. 'I'm going out with Neil.'

Darryl's eyes surveyed her critically. Could he see that she was lying?—oh, fool, *fool*, her subconscious wailed, but it was too late now. He believed her; she could tell by the way the anger smouldered in his expression and she hastened on her way before he exploded.

It was late in the afternoon, when Neil and Cora had worked closely together dealing with a middle-aged printer whose fingers had been damaged by being trapped in a machine, that Neil ran a finger lightly up Cora's cheek.

'Are you under the weather today?' he asked kindly.

Cora looked up at him, seeing him as Neil the man now rather than the doctor. She smiled. 'No, I'm okay, just need someone nice to smooth away the day's aggravations.'

'Am I one of those?'

'Of course not, Neil. What makes you say that?'

'I . . . I thought we got on well together. I enjoy your company and I hoped the feeling was mutual.'

'It is, Neil—and—about the other day. I didn't turn you down for another date. I didn't really have one at all, but as I seem to have earned myself the reputation of being a flirt I decided to opt out, then Mandy dragged me off on this blind date. Steve is a friend of Duggie's, the policeman Mandy is using until Tod wakes up. There's nothing in it, Steve is engaged. His fiancée is due to come to Bermuda later on so Duggie was just helping him to have a relaxing evening. I was warned not to fall in love with him.' She smiled, glad of the opportunity to put things right with Neil. At least she felt she owed him an explanation.

'Do you fall in and out of love easily, Cora?' he asked seriously.

'Don't we all? But that's not like really loving someone desperately—*that's* when it hurts.' She was being selfish, thinking only of her wounds, and the admission at last, if only to herself, that she loved Darryl Delaney. It had to be love. Though why, she questioned, when he treated her the way he did? And what point was there in wasting emotion on him when he was evidently attached to Monique in spite of what his mother thought?

'Neil,' she said, looking up at him with the moisture of sadness in her eyes, 'is that offer still open?'

'Of a date?' His tone echoed his delight. 'Of course. Tonight?'

'Mm?' she answered hopefully. The arrangements were made but, Cora realised, only to try to take her mind off Darryl Delaney.

The telephone rang and Sister Longford called to Cora to go to meet the ambulance with Neil to see an elderly man who had been taken ill on the plane coming in from New York.

He was suffering from severe chest pains and looked grey. They made him comfortable in a cubicle and Cora took all his personal details. Neil made an initial examination, finding no cause for his discomfort, but wrote out an X-ray card and a porter took him along the corridor to that department.

Cora was glad that she was working straight through rather than a split shift as it would give her time to get ready for her date with Neil.

After her tea break the porter brought Mr Allen back to Casualty and Cora stayed with him and his anxious wife until Neil returned to see the patient.

Neil looked at the X-rays on which a definite shadow appeared.

'Nurse will take you up to the ward, Mr Allen,' he said at length. 'You have a slight problem in the left lung so we shall need to do more tests. I'm sorry, this seems like a bad start to your holiday.'

'Perhaps we ought to fly straight back to New York,' Mrs Allen suggested with a tremor in her voice.

Neil shook his head. 'That would be most unwise. I'm sure it's nothing that we can't put right with medication, but I must refer you to the medical consultant.'

Neil went to the office and wrote up the notes and later Cora accompanied the patient and his wife to the medical ward.

When she eventually went off duty she felt much less confident about her decision to go out with Neil. She had acted on impulse, momentarily hating Darryl and trying to get back at him by fabricating the date with Neil. Now she was trying to redeem her stupid lie and the fact that she had made the suggestion to Neil meant that he had

probably misconstrued her intentions. She hoped
the evening wouldn't be disastrous.

When Neil met her outside the nurses' home and
suggested going for a meal she readily agreed.
Little did he know the reason for her enthusiasm
which was sheer hunger! He took her to one of the
island's most pleasant hotels and they enjoyed a
long, thoroughly appetising meal and afterwards
they strolled along the hotel's water front.

It was a beautiful evening, a clear starlit sky,
warm with a gentle sea breeze and the inevitable
tree-frogs' chorus. Cora sensed that Neil regarded
this date as a milestone in their friendship. He had
his arm very firmly round her waist and she felt like
screaming when she felt his thumb caressing beneath her breast. Close your eyes and think of
England, was Mandy's advice in such a situation,
but if Cora closed her eyes she would only think of
Darryl. She knew she was wrong to let Neil think
there could ever be anything serious between them,
but she hadn't the heart to turn him off when she
had so clearly led him on.

They came to the garden of the hotel and Neil
suggested sitting down.

'It's not too warm,' she said, quickly thinking up
an excuse. 'Perhaps we could have a last drink?'

He turned her round, hugged her to him, caressing her fondly in an attempt to melt her cast-iron
reserve, but no matter how she tried to make
herself respond it didn't work. Her lips remained
dry and impassive against his eager mouth. She was
amazed that he didn't seem to notice as his hands
roamed purposefully over her cool body. She shud-

dered, partly with the cold and partly with distaste.

She shivered more significantly 'Maybe I ought to have worn something warmer,' she said, trying to quell Neil's passion. 'It really is too cold to stay here.'

He held her at arm's length and she thought how boyish he was with his bright carroty-coloured hair and blue sparkling eyes.

'I can't be doing this very well,' he said, smiling. 'But you've been tense all evening. I'll keep working at it though. I can't forget what a superb body you've got and to think I had to stand by and watch Darryl running his expert fingers all over you.'

Cora pulled away. 'When?' she asked indignantly.

'When he knocked you off your moped. He was in such a state, and wasn't happy until he was sure no bones were broken. But now—' Neil squeezed her affectionately, 'it's my turn to find out your secrets, and I'd rather have you awake and responsive.'

'That's what I'm not tonight, Neil,' Cora whispered, hoping she wasn't, yet knowing she was being utterly cruel.

He kissed her brutally on her mouth and neck, gripped her fiercely and muttered: 'Not even if I keep working at it?'

Cora shook her head and pushed him away.

'Please, Neil—I'm sorry.'

'Going too fast for you, is that it? Well, darling, we are mature people and I'm sure I'm not the first.'

How could she confess that if she allowed him to

continue he would be? For her there were to be no casual affairs. She'd always promised herself that there would only be one really serious relationship and now that she knew it had to be Darryl she couldn't bear this farce.

'Next time, perhaps?' he murmured softly into her hair. 'Who's upset you today?'

Cora shrugged. She had to make up some story but was incapable of telling any more lies, so why not the truth?

'I had a bit of a set-to with Mr Delaney,' she said casually.

Darkness and silence went hand in hand until Neil suggested: 'A last drink then?'

In the hotel's lounge a film was being shown so they took their drinks there and stayed until the end.

Neil was solemn as he drove back towards the hospital and Cora was consumed with guilt, but she managed to give him a cheerful goodnight kiss, and hoped he didn't feel too frustrated.

Alone in her room she could think of little except that she had compensated for her lie to Darryl, but her heart was heavy as she knew she had only added to her reputation of being a flirt in his eyes. She would never look at Darryl now without remembering the Easter Bank Holiday when she had met him and his mother at the Cathedral. They had been pleasant and kind and she had reacted eagerly in the knowledge that he was not married. But soon he might be, there was Monique. His mother had said that Monique would be returning to Canada, but was that wishful thinking?

She stood at the window, watching the twinkling lights in the distant harbour, wishing that indeed Monique would go away and leave Darryl at Zenobia's. But then there would be someone else. Darryl had intimated that he wanted a special kind of girl, not a flirt which, according to him, she was. Best to try to forget him altogether, but how could she when he walked briskly into Casualty without warning early the next morning.

He went straight into Sister Longford's office and then came up softly behind Cora as she prepared dressing trays in the treatment room.

'I heard you ate a hearty dinner last evening,' he said.

'Thank you, yes,' she replied primly, wishing Neil had not imparted this information.

If only her heart would stop pumping so loudly as if it wanted all the world to hear its secret. If nothing else, surely they could be reasonably good friends, she thought, and half-glancing over her shoulder found his handsome face much too close to her own. For no reason that she could think of she remembered Neil telling her that Darryl had examined her after the accident. She experienced the feeling of being turned inside out again and blushed at the thought of him knowing intimate details about her.

'I'm sorry I spoilt your lunch, Cora, but what I said needed to be said. You're a long way from home. This is a romantic island and it's very easy to feel emotional about the friends one makes here. You must know the dangers of getting involved with patients, and I'm sure you'll be sensible. You made quite an impression on my parents so when are you coming to dinner again?'

She turned round to face him.

'When you tell me whether or not I'm being prosecuted for whatever I did wrong,' she said recklessly.

He laughed, his melodious voice echoing in the room, making her feel childish and silly.

He placed one hand on her hip giving it a gentle tap or two, and his lips were only a hair's breadth away from her neck as he said: 'You know very well what you're guilty of, darling, and not only on a moped. Come to dinner soon so that I can tease you some more.'

She felt his lips brush her neck and the next instant he was gone.

Sister Longford took over from the night staff and the day's work began in earnest. There were moments of relative ease, and there were hectic days when one serious emergency followed another. Mrs Steele, the hospital's domestic, had to attend several times for treatment on her sprained ankle before she was allowed to return to work, and then Darryl kept his eye on her.

On one occasion when Cora accompanied a patient to men's surgical ward she looked in on Bill Palmer after receiving more messages from him. He appeared to be depressed following the announcement that he would need to have his leg amputated as treatment had not brought about the desired effect.

'I'm really sorry, Mr Palmer,' she sympathised.

'It won't be easy for you to adjust, and there isn't really anything I can say to help.'

He was out of bed, sitting in a chair near the window. He gazed into her eyes, trying to be flirtatious, but there was just too much at stake for frivolity. But after a few moments he smiled fondly at Cora and took her hand in his.

'If you'll come to visit me, honey, I'll make it,' he said huskily.

Cora looked at him seriously and inclined her head.

'Bill,' she said with a pleading tone, 'you know I can't make a habit of this. Hospital rumours abound like no other variety, and already people are talking.'

'So let them talk. You can take stick can't you?' Now he was the Bill she had expected to find.

'No,' she said solemnly. 'I don't like drawing attention to myself, and it won't be long before you return to the States. Are you staying on here or going home to have the operation?'

His face clouded briefly and he bit on his lip.

'I like the staff here. Mr Delaney has been good to me and I'd feel confident in letting him handle the beastly job. I'd like you to be there too. I should sleep well and dream of those dazzling blue eyes watching over me.'

'When the time comes you can dream whatever dreams you like. I'll come in again one day to see how you are, but, Bill, please don't keep sending messages down to Casualty. It's very embarrassing.'

He grinned triumphantly. 'But you came.'

'Only to shut you up, you monster,' she said in mock anger.

'Promise you'll come again soon?' he begged.

'As soon as I'm able. I have to work, and when I'm off duty—'

'I know, all the doctors get a date in turn.'

'That's not true,' Cora denied indignantly. 'Who told you that?'

'I don't have to be told, honey. They'd be crazy if they didn't want to take out the most attractive girl in Zenobia's.'

Cora laughed with relief. 'I think you ought to be in the main ward and if I were Sister of Men's Surgical that's where you'd be. You're spending too much time alone letting your imagination run away with you.'

'Isn't that what imagination is for?'

She tried to pull her hand free but was not successful before he had pressed his lips desperately against the back of it.

'Now let that spread all over the hospital,' he said with a sudden wicked smile. 'If anyone gets to you, honey, you just refer them to me.'

'You just concentrate on keeping your spirits up,' she recommended and left him staring after her. She knew he was genuine in his attraction for her, and she was flattered, but once the ordeal of amputation was over he would go home to his family and easily forget Zenobia's and her.

When she returned to Casualty she found Mandy there looking for her.

'What are you doing here?' Cora asked in surprise.

'Trying to avoid Sister for one thing as well as desperately trying to get in Tod's way.' She sighed. 'I don't think he'd notice if I staged a fit.'

Cora laughed. 'Would you like me to make you out a card and smuggle you into a cubicle?'

'Mm, please—but he'd just see my body, not the real me.' She giggled as only Mandy could, and Cora tried to silence her.

'Ssh! You'll get me shot—what do you want?'

'Duggie and Steve are going on a dive this evening. I'm on late shift, but Steve wondered if you'd like to go?'

'Late shift too, sorry.'

'You're off this afternoon then? Let's go shopping or to the beach?' Mandy suggested.

'See you at lunch,' Cora whispered, 'now *go*!'

Mandy giggled again childishly and as she walked backwards collided with Darryl Delaney.

'Look where you're going, idiot!' he yelled, then seeing who it was demanded: 'and what are you doing here, Staff Nurse? Your ward is Women's Surgical. This department is too busy to have time for giggling sessions. Nurse Jordan disappeared for half an hour, I suppose you've been catching up on the latest gossip somewhere?'

Mandy disappeared on a cloud of bouncing blonde curls and twirling skirt, her white apron flapping, her cap bobbing dangerously, leaving Cora to face the impatient registrar.

'She'd only been here a minute,' Cora exploded. 'There was no need to hurl abuse at her like that. As usual you weren't looking where you were going.'

'Quite the defensive lioness aren't we?' he said. 'Is that why you came to Bermuda? To watch over our sexy little blonde?'

'Mandy's quite capable of taking care of herself,' Cora retorted.

'The other way round then—you need her to guide you, in matters of the heart at least?'

'Why should I need any guidance?'

'Haven't you just been to Men's Surgical?'

'I took an admission up.'

'Over half an hour ago. Sister Longford has gone to lunch and was expecting you to return to assist me.'

'There's another staff nurse besides me.'

'I was told you were on duty.'

'I am.'

'So let's get on with this aspiration, and keep away from Men's Surgical.'

'I'll go where I like,' she declared vehemently.

He scowled as only Darryl Delaney, the dark handsome lady-killer could, and minutes later they were working closely together, standing side by side in harmony in an effort to free the elderly woman patient of the pain and breathlessness caused by fluid in the lung.

Cora and Mandy spent a lazy afternoon on the beach. The Atlantic ocean whipped up boisterous waves and the water was cold at first, but their bodies soon became acclimatised and Cora announced that from then on she intended to spend every spare minute off-duty on one of the pleasant South Shore beaches.

The sun was gloriously warm, the late April temperature being in the early seventies, and the girls spread out their towels, smothered themselves with sun-oil and relaxed, chatting and catching up on their personal news.

Cora gave only a brief account of her meeting Darryl and his mother at the Cathedral and the ensuing visit to their home, but she enlarged on the date with Neil.

'So what were you doing visiting Men's Surgical and the notorious Bill Palmer?' Mandy asked suspiciously.

'Notorious?' Cora queried.

'Yes, he talks about no one but you, apparently, so much so that even I went along to his room, but I wouldn't do—it's you, honey,' she mimicked, 'and no one else.'

Cora sighed. 'Who starts these blessed rumours?' she said, turning over on to her stomach and peering at Mandy over the top of her sunglasses.

'You did, silly,' Mandy chuckled, 'by visiting him.'

'Only in response to his request,' Cora said. 'I couldn't imagine what he wanted, so to stop the messages I went to see him.'

'It's no good my saying "be warned" is it, Cora? I mean there's probably a wife and kids back home.'

'So he's got a wife and kids,' Cora echoed. 'He means nothing to me except that he's over seven hundred miles of ocean away from home and I'm sorry for him. He's become an embarrassment, and who are you to talk anyway? You're crazy about

Tod yet you let Duggie think you're crazy about him.'

'But that's *me*, and everyone expects a blonde to be unreliable so I don't imagine that any fellow I go out with is serious.'

'Duggie's nice, Mandy, and he is genuinely fond of you,' Cora told her friend.

'If only Tod were here,' Mandy bemoaned. 'Perhaps I should get transferred to Casualty, but what good would that do? He doesn't even notice me when he comes to the ward. He's just polite and agrees with everything I say when he does a round with me, and I'm not myself because I'm secretly idolising him. Oh, heck,' she added ruefully, 'isn't love painful?'

Cora laughed. 'I wouldn't know.'

It was easy to be light-hearted when Mandy was pouring out her soul, but behind the screen of her large dark glasses Cora's expression was misty and nostalgic for the love she knew would never be hers.

Reluctantly a half an hour later they packed up their belongings, put on dresses over their brief bikinis and walked breathlessly to the top of the hill overlooking Horseshoe Bay to catch the bus back to Zenobia's.

'It's criminal to have to work on such a lovely day,' Mandy said as they drank tea in the canteen before going on duty.

'But we're doing a good job,' Cora consoled, 'well, most of the time, and we get better off duty here than back home in England.'

They went their separate ways and after the busy

afternoon clinics, and accident and emergency cases lessened, the hospital became the quiet place it usually was during late evening.

Cora and Tod were dealing with a lady in her early thirties who had a fish bone stuck in her throat when a young nurse came to Cora with a telephone message.

'Alert for a member of the diving club being brought in, Staff Nurse,' she said.

Tod looked across at Cora and made a face.

'Better get all the help we can then. Mr Delaney is an expert in such cases, so bleep him first.'

Fortunately they had succeeded in removing the fish bone, and after giving the patient the necessary advice about not drinking anything too hot and eating soft foods she was allowed to go home.

Darryl came down from one of the wards just as the ambulance brought the emergency in. He was still in his wet-suit but covered in blankets and Cora looked up to see Steve accompanying the patient, also still in a wet-suit.

Then Cora observed the patient more closely and saw that it was Duggie!

CHAPTER SEVEN

THE team of doctors worked together while Cora fetched and carried.

'What happened?' Darryl asked Steve who hovered uncertainly in the vicinity of the treatment room.

'We were exploring an old wreck when some mysterious undercurrent suddenly started to shift everything. It was eerie. Duggie has more guts than me, so he was well inside the hold of the wrecked ship and got trapped by a moving beam. I'd swum clear. It was weird the way the sea-bed seemed to stir up. When I realised Duggie wasn't with me I went back to the wreck, by then everything had calmed again, and I found him unconscious.' Steve covered his face with his hands.

'It's OK,' Darryl said, placing a hand on his shoulder, 'your friend's all right as far as we can tell, apart from a suspected fractured pelvis. Cora, take Steve into a cubicle, get him out of that wet-suit, give him a hot drink, and I'll see you shortly when we've admitted this chap,' he added to Steve.

In the cubicle Cora gave Steve a towelling robe. 'Put this on while I fetch you a cup of tea.'

'I'm fine really,' Steve said. 'It's Duggie I'm concerned for.'

'But you've had a shock too. How did you manage to get him up?'

Steve turned away. 'Just brute force, I suppose. God knows what damage I did to him, but there wasn't much choice.'

Cora left him to go and make tea for everyone. By now it was past time for her to go off duty and the night staff were taking over.

Tod came into the kitchen. 'Friends of yours?' he asked.

'Duggie's a friend of Mandy's.' As soon as Cora had spoken she regretted her honesty, Mandy wouldn't have appreciated it. 'Well, you know, through Sara's husband and all being English we tend to team up. Nothing serious in any of it,' she added. 'They're both policemen.'

Tod took a cup of tea without speaking, and Cora took some to Steve. He was shivering and looked ashen but the tea quickly revived him.

'Suppose I got chilled, coming up and then dashing straight here.'

'You're only human, Steve, but Duggie'll be okay.'

'Will I be able to see him?'

'You'll have to ask the doctors.'

'Ask us what?' Darryl came into the cubicle with Tod.

'About seeing Duggie before he leaves.'

'Let's make sure *you're* fit to leave first.' Darryl glanced at Cora. 'Unethical for you to be here. Shouldn't you be off duty?'

'Yes, and if you don't need me I'll go.'

Darryl arched an eyebrow suggestively so Cora turned to Steve. 'Hope you'll be okay, Steve.'

'Will you tell Mandy about Duggie?' Steve asked.

'Of course. See you, 'bye,' and she left the cubicle hurriedly.

That wasn't going to help Mandy's chances with Tod either, nor hers with Darryl! Unethical indeed, after just one evening in a foursome?

Cora found Mandy with several other girls in the TV lounge at the nurses' home. From the door Cora managed to catch her eye, indicating that she wanted her. Outside in the passage Mandy said: 'What's up?'

'We've just had an emergency.'

'I heard the siren as I came over.'

'It's Duggie, Mandy. Steve came in with him.' Cora went on to explain the brief details as she knew them. 'He's been admitted. I thought you might want to go over there.'

Mandy shrugged. 'Hm,' she mused. 'Not really. I'm terribly sorry, of course, but he's just a fella.'

'Mandy!' Cora reproached. 'That's not very kind. You've been glad to go out with him.'

'That doesn't mean there's anything in it, but I'll go tomorrow perhaps.'

'Steve seemed to think it would be important to you,' Cora said.

'Oh, heck,' Mandy groaned. 'Well, it isn't. Honestly, Cora, the more I go out with other chaps to try to forget Tod the worse it makes it.'

'You shouldn't have let Duggie think you were serious.'

'I didn't, but you know what men are. A kiss and

cuddle and they think they own you.' They sauntered up to Cora's room.

'Don't you think you should at least just say hello to Duggie?' Cora persuaded. 'He was unconscious, but you would have a clear conscience.'

'My conscience is fine, how's yours?'

'Mandy, you're hopeless.'

'I know I exasperate you, Cora, but I'm a big girl now. And anyway, you're not so different, you know. You play Neil along when really you're crazy about a certain senior surgical registrar.'

'Of course I'm not,' Cora denied. 'He has eyes for Monique only.'

'I know,' Mandy sympathised, 'rumours from Theatre are quite graphic, and all under the guise of playing golf.'

Cora was torn between wanting to know more and not wanting to hear things which would inevitably upset her. She decided she had heard enough.

'I think I'm ready for bed, but you really did ought to go to see Duggie, you know, Mandy.'

'Tomorrow, maybe.'

But two days passed and despite Cora's encouragement Mandy stubbornly refused to visit Duggie. Cora realised that she had no feeling for him at all, that Tod filled her waking hours and she was beginning to lose her vivaciousness.

Then Cora bumped into Steve one early evening just as she was going off duty.

'Hullo,' she said. 'How's Duggie?'

'Haven't *you* been to see him either?' His reproach caught Cora unawares.

'No, I haven't, but then I don't know him all that well.'

'He's pretty upset because Mandy hasn't been near him, and she's only on the next ward.'

'I know, Steve, and I have tried to persuade her.'

'You come with me now—please? I'm sure you can think of something to pacify him.'

'The truth usually works best.'

'Which is?'

'Mandy's never short of dates, Steve. What blonde is? But she's hooked on one of the doctors here, only he ignores her. I think she's just woken up to the fact that she's spoiling her chances by always having a man in tow.'

'Duggie is serious about her.'

'I'm sorry, but it's nothing to do with me,' Cora protested.

Steve put an arm around her waist. 'Let's go and console him together. We'll find some way of telling him the score. I doubt if it's the first time he's been jilted, only it's rotten when he's stuck in here and Mandy's within reach.'

Cora couldn't imagine what situation she was getting herself into, but she went willingly with Steve and at the four-bedded ward they came face to face with Darryl Delaney. Cora felt her stomach heave.

'Visitors for you, Duggie,' Darryl said cheerfully. 'We shall have to get some of these girls scuba diving in their spare time.'

Steve looked down at Cora. 'Any good trying to persuade you?'

Cora shook her head. 'No, I don't think so, thanks.'

'Come now, Staff Nurse, that's not the spirit. You've been offered a challenge. Where's your British guts?'

Cora shrugged, then laughed. 'I expect you've got enough for most of us.'

Darryl made a face. 'Ouch! I shan't let you get away with *that*!'

As he passed Cora felt his fingers intertwine with hers meaningfully, then he went on his way. Cora knew that he had been in Theatre for most of the day and guessed that he was in high spirits if he had been working with Monique.

Duggie looked remarkably well. 'So, where's my girl?' he asked Cora pointedly.

'Actually at this moment I don't know, Duggie. I think you mustn't be too possessive of Mandy.'

Duggie sighed. 'No, I'm sure you're right, but we had fun together. I'd have thought the least she'd do was put her head through the door.'

'I did tell her you were here, but that was late the night you came in, and we are kept pretty busy.'

'I know that by watching you girls, but I also know that you have off duty,' Duggie said pointedly.

Cora was at a loss for words, then she said: 'Duggie, sometimes it's harder to visit people you know than the strangers who come under our care.'

'Keep trying, love,' Duggie said with a grin. 'I hope Mandy appreciates what a good friend you are.'

Steve pulled Cora against him. 'She's great,' he

said, 'it's just as well Judith is coming out soon or I might be tempted to forget I'm engaged.'

Duggie laughed. 'We don't stand a chance, mate, not with all these doctors around. Still, there's an awful lot of nurses here.'

'So you aren't really heartbroken about Mandy are you?' Cora said quickly.

Duggie raised his eyebrows. 'I'm wounded,' he admitted, 'but I'll get over it.'

'She will come—even if I have to drag her,' Cora promised. But a week passed before Cora finally persuaded Mandy to visit Duggie and then she insisted that Cora should accompany her.

It was an embarrassing situation as Mandy surprised everyone by dissolving into floods of tears, and only Cora knew that it was her infatuation for Tod that was making her behave in such a way.

Duggie was understanding, in fact he probably understood better than anyone realised, and for the remainder of his stay in Zenobia's it was Cora who visited both him and Bill Palmer in spite of the disapproving glares of Darryl.

'You're getting yourself a shocking reputation,' Mandy told her one evening as they sipped cool drinks in Mandy's room. 'At least I stick to one fellow at a time.'

'Even if you do break their hearts,' Cora quipped. 'The men know my visits are just friendly ones. Like you, I'm saving my affections for the real thing.'

'Love is a painful process,' Mandy bemoaned. 'What more can I do to gain Tod's attention, for heaven's sake?'

'Ignore him,' Cora said. 'I reckon you're trying too hard. Perhaps we could persuade Sara to give another party?'

'And get involved with policemen all over again?'

'I know! Let's have a party of our own? A "Staff Nurse" party. That way everyone who's anyone comes and it sorts out a lot of relationships. Or at least it used to back home.'

'Cora, you're a genius, that's a great idea. I don't know why you should help me to attract Tod's attention though, not after I treated Duggie so badly.'

'At least you admit it. Duggie's a nice man and he was genuinely fond of you, Mandy.'

'I know, that's why I couldn't handle it. Most of them go one step too far and I can get rid of them that way. Still, I don't think he's too angry with me so we'll invite him and Steve.'

Cora sighed. 'Suppose I could invite Bill Palmer. Just to cheer him up, then they could go back to the ward together at ten o'clock. We'll need to get permission, and we'd better make a list of food and drink to get in.'

Permission to use the sitting room at the nurses' home was granted and Cora and Mandy set about making all the arrangements. It was necessary to keep the number to a limit of about twenty-five to thirty so they made personal invitations, Cora to her friends in Casualty which included Sara and Roy, Neil and Tod, and Mandy the colleagues from her ward.

Bill Palmer was due to have his amputation

within the week so the girls set the date for three days prior to his operation. Duggie was making good progress and the two men had become firm friends.

Steve decided he couldn't wait any longer for his fiancée so had bought her a one-way ticket to Bermuda and arrived at the party with an attractive dark-haired girl on his arm.

'This is my Judith,' he introduced to Cora and Mandy, 'and we're getting married at the end of the month.'

The girls were delighted and felt pleased that she had arrived in time to join the party so that she would feel she was among friends, and in this Sara Kenmore eagerly took Judith under her wing.

Mandy was doing her best not to effervesce too much. She had been to the hairdressers and had her lovely blonde hair styled in a more sophisticated way and was wearing a striped flared skirt and silk blouse over her bikini in the hope of impressing Tod.

'Now don't forget to be nice to Duggie as well as Tod,' Cora warned, and she hoped for her friend's sake that Tod would rise to the occasion.

He arrived escorting the two male patients who were soon joining in although they had to remain in wheelchairs.

The party was well under way when Cora realised that Neil hadn't yet arrived. Although she had to circulate with the eats which a local hotel had provided, and the Rum Swizzle, the favourite punch of Bermuda, she was looking to Neil to be her escort for the evening, as well as helping to provide transport to the beach to end the evening.

She was talking to Steve and Judith when she looked up and saw Neil crossing the room towards her. Behind him she saw Darryl Delaney with Mandy of all people firmly in his embrace who was laughing up at the doctor.

It was a forced smile Cora gave Neil as he reached her and kissed her cheek gently.

'Sorry we're late, darling,' Neil said, 'but we had an emergency strangulated hernia to deal with.' He looked down at Cora who was mesmerised by the way Darryl and Mandy seemed to be in close contact with one another. Neil guided her face back to look at him. 'I hope you didn't mind. I brought Darryl with me. After surgery he asked where I was off to in such a hurry, and as he had no prior engagement it seemed the obvious thing to do, to bring him along.'

'I didn't think this would be his scene,' Cora said in dismay. She was thinking that if she had known he was coming she would have dressed differently. A dress over her bikini probably instead of the wrap around skirt made of seersucker cotton in a shade of apple-green with a chiffon tie-at-the-front brief top. As if it mattered, she thought with a touch of irony, he had eyes only for Mandy and now they were dancing together, deep in conversation.

Cora offered Neil a drink, then he took her in his arms and she tried to concentrate on him rather than on Darryl and Mandy. Although her heart had plummetted, she tried to show a spirit of conviviality, pausing occasionally to speak with Duggie and Bill. She wasn't surprised that Steve and Judith had eyes only for each other.

It was a well known fact that everyone would head for the beach eventually and gradually the couples began to drift away, so Neil and Cora took Duggie and Bill back to the ward.

Cora felt desolate inside, especially when Neil said that as he was on call he wouldn't be able to go to the beach, so when she returned alone to the nurses' home she decided to tidy the sitting room, wash up the glasses and go to bed. After all, no one was going to miss her, but as she began stacking the glasses on a tray she discovered that someone had remained behind to help.

'You don't have to,' she said with shock as Darryl took the tray from her.

'If I don't you won't bother to go to the beach.'

'This has to be done,' she said solemnly. 'Why haven't you gone on with Mandy?'

Darryl suddenly leaned across the tray of glasses and kissed her with a rare but bewitching smile in his black eyes.

'Because I managed to get Mandy detailed to Tod who had decided that he would rather eat his heart out than be turned down. We'll do this together. We shan't be missed. I gather all off-duty staff at Zenobia's are going to join in this summer madness.'

Cora wished that she could go too. It was heart-rending to be here with Darryl alone and only to share the washing up! She wanted to ask him what had drawn him and Mandy so closely together. Was

Mandy using him to get to Tod? She really was an incredible manipulator.

The sitting room tidied, the glasses washed, Cora turned to thank Darryl.

'Well,' he said, 'have you got your bikini on?'

Cora looked puzzled. It was nearly midnight, the others would be returning soon, but she nodded.

'Let's go then,' and Darryl pulled her along behind him.

'Where are we going?' she ventured to ask as she sat beside him in his car.

'Not for a moped ride, that's for sure,' he said with amusement.

He drove to the South Shore but instead of following the coast road to one of the more popular beaches he took her to a small inlet banked by trees and shrubs where the water lapped gently at the sandy shore, and not another living thing was visible in the moonlight. Even the Bermudan Longtail seabirds had given up their sensuous mating quest and retired to their cliffside homes.

Darryl produced a rug and towels from the boot of his car and as she stood hesitantly watching he spread the rug out on the sand and then came to stand in front of her. He gripped her waist masterfully, his thumbs caressing her bare skin below her tied top.

'You've done all the work, now it's time to play,' he said provocatively.

She held his arms to restrain him. His appearance had held her captive on his arrival at the party. Light-coloured slacks and a pale blue shirt, the cuffs rolled back a couple of turns exposing his strong forearms and beneath her fingers she could feel the soft silken down which tantalised her so.

Cora felt the tension between them. There was no need for words as he deftly untied her top, then the sash of her skirt, and she felt the cool night breeze waft over her almost naked body.

'You can look or not, just as you please,' he said bluntly. 'My trunks were in the car so I'll have to change here.'

Cora wandered to the water's edge where she allowed the waves to lap and trickle slowly between her toes. She expected it to be cold but it was warm. She expected her companion to come up behind her, but suddenly she was swept up in his arms and carried out into the deep dark sea.

'Now, young lady,' he said severely, 'who was the naughty girl who didn't signal she was going two-thirds of the way round the roundabout?'

'But I did, I know I did,' she protested vehemently.

He plunged her savagely into the water, holding her there as she struggled uselessly against his massive strength before lifting her up again.

'And who was that same naughty girl who hadn't secured the chin strap on her helmet?' he demanded truculently.

'But you couldn't possibly know that,' she said, refusing to admit anything.

He went on taunting her as he dunked her into the sea again and again, splashing, rolling, teasing as she tried to wrestle him off, and all her inhibitions washed out with the tide as they laughed and frolicked together. They swam too, vigorously,

Cora desperately trying to work off the ache which love for Darryl caused.

In the moonlight she saw him go inshore until he could stand. He turned and called her and she savoured this moment as her ace, for no matter what happened between them now she had shared a few precious moments of relaxation alone with her beloved Darryl Delaney.

He looked like a bronzed statue as he waited for her and he put an arm round her shoulder as he guided her back to the secluded spot on the beach. Everything about the setting was just too idyllic. She couldn't bear the thought of having to leave. He threw her a towel, quickly rubbed his own body with another and then turned his full attention on Cora. He placed the towel over her head, gathered it into a handful and drew her head backwards. Laughingly he kissed her, a brief frivolous kiss, the forerunner of many subsequent all-powerful ones which he rained on her mouth and neck. Then he drew the towel over the rest of her body roughly, draping it finally around her slim hips and he drew her hard against him.

Then his kisses became less cruel, his lips moist and warm, searching hers to arouse the desire which flooded every inch of her. His hands became more gentle as he caressed her back, sending a tingling frenzy down her spine. He pressed her body sensuously against his and her head sawm with uncontrollable passion. She wasn't aware of the moment when they collapsed in a heap on the rug, she just knew that she couldn't bear to let him go, and her fingers playing round his neck stirred his emotions until he was caressing every inch of her delicately.

Some little voice of conscience told her that she ought not to allow this to happen. There were other women in his life, Monique especially, but as he roused her sensitivity she arched her body to meet his. She was inflamed with love. What did this mean to him? Just an expression of power? He had teased, taunted, at last revealed that he knew all the details of her accident which apportioned all the blame to her. But she knew she wasn't entirely to blame. He must be prepared to take his share, but right now what they were sharing was too all-consuming to let other thoughts dominate her actions.

'Darryl,' she whispered as she felt his breathing level out, 'we ought to go.'

He nuzzled his mouth into the deep cleft between her breasts and nipped with teasing lips.

'No need, darling,' he whispered. 'Too hot to sleep inside. It's so much more healthy to sleep under the stars. Zenobia's management doesn't make rules and regulations for qualified staff.'

'I'm only a staff nurse, not a sister,' she whispered back.

He snuggled deeper and more possessively, one hand resting sensuously on her hip. 'Go to sleep, there's a good girl.'

'Darryl—no,' she pleaded, yet in spite of her verbal resistance she cradled his head lovingly against her breast.

Suddenly he pulled himself away and slid upwards until his mouth closed over hers, his tongue probing between her lips until she was robbed of all sanity. Her head swam and she had the feeling of being turned inside out again, then she heard him chuckle. He was hateful! Trying her to the point of seduction, making her lose control. It was all only a game to him.

'I was right, Cora darling, no one does it quite like you,' he whispered, 'but, as you so aptly reminded me, you're a staff nurse—hurry up and get promoted to sister, then we'll love the night away.'

Frustration ripped through Cora's senses and with a savage sting she whip-lashed his cheek with her palm.

'Sorry, I'm sure,' she snapped, 'that I didn't remind you before that I'm only a staff nurse.' She pushed him away so that she could stand up, and she dressed quickly.

'Goodnight,' she said angrily, 'I hope you sleep well.'

He was on his feet in a second and gripping her arms tightly.

'Don't be so absurd,' he muttered angrily.

He put on his slacks and shirt. 'What's the matter with you, for heaven's sake? You didn't really think I'd take advantage of you . . . ?'

Cora started to walk up the path to the car. No, of course she didn't expect anything, after all she wasn't Monique. He'd just used her for a little pleasure!

She wished he'd retaliate in some way, abuse her even, but he unlocked the car doors slowly, leisurely, as if he had all the time in the world, and his dark brooding eyes never left her face. She felt humili-

ated. This was the up-and-coming consultant repri-
manding the nurse, only she wasn't too sure what
she had done wrong. He was the one who needed
taking down a peg or two. He was the unfeeling
swine who had manipulated her senses into a state
of utter confusion.

Darryl pulled up outside the nurses' home almost
silently and before Cora could jump out he leaned
across and held her jaw firmly, looking deep into
her liquid eyes.

'You may not be much good on the road, but—'

'I'm as good as you,' she bit out as best she could.
'Why can't you be man enough to admit that you
were as much in the wrong as me? You thought you
were going to overtake and then you saw my wink-
er. Oh, you pulled up, but not in time, not before
you had caught my back wheel. The more I think
about it the clearer it becomes, so the sooner we go
to court and settle it the better.'

'I told you it would be more fun to settle out of
court and *that's* what we're going to do. Tonight
was the first instalment, the first of many, my
sweet.' He crushed his lips so hard on hers that she
cried out from low in her throat.

'No one gets to me quite like you do,' he said as
he released her.

She ran into the nurses' home and up to her
room, only letting the pain of unfulfilled passion
burst into a deluge of weeping when her door was
firmly closed.

CHAPTER EIGHT

CORA idled away the remainder of the next morning after getting up late, and reported for duty to Sara Kenmore at two o'clock in the afternoon.

'Good party, Cora,' Sara said, 'though I didn't see you at the beach?'

'I stayed behind to clear up the mess,' she said, trying to resurrect some party spirit. 'Glad you enjoyed it.'

'I'm sure everyone did. I hear Bill Palmer's going to have his amputation the day after tomorrow?'

'Yes, that's why we invited him to the party. It relieved the boredom of waiting just a little,' Cora said.

'And Duggie's doing fine—bet Steve is too,' Sara said suggestively. 'Oh dear—you hadn't fallen for him, had you?'

'Good lord, no! I'm glad his fiancée has arrived, though. At least his mates can't try to pester him with unwanted female company.'

'I don't think it was altogether unwanted, Cora, but I'm sure Neil is glad he has a free field.'

Tod called at that moment for some help with a young Girl Guide who had cut herself badly on a jagged tin. She was a member of a company of Guides camping out on one of the many small islands which years before had been a prisoners'

island. Now they were clearing the site and re-
novating old buildings, hoping to accommodate
Girl Guides from all over the world. After Tod had
inserted a couple of stitches in her hand Cora
bandaged her up and gave her a tetanus injection
before she was allowed to leave.

Gradually as the day progressed Cora managed
to put the memories of the previous evening out of
her mind. Not that she wanted to forget all of it;
there were parts which she knew she would go on
reliving for ever. She had proved that she could
turn Darryl Delaney on, for one thing, even if the
incident meant nothing to him. He had admitted
that no one affected him quite like she did.

If only he knew just how *he* affected *her*! She'd
never reacted violently to anyone before, and she
was vexed with herself for behaving in such an
irresponsible way, but she loved him to distraction,
so much so that she simply didn't behave like
herself when she was in his company. She understood Mandy's dilemma. This was exactly what she
had tried to explain concerning her relationship
with Tod. At last Cora realised that Mandy must be
genuine about Tod. She keeps saying how painful
love is, thought Cora; at least they were both in
similar situations, and the party should have helped
those situations, but, Cora decided it hadn't helped
her very much, and when she met Mandy at teatime
she didn't look exactly blooming either.

'You look a bit "be kind to staff nurse today"-
ish,' Mandy said, turning her nose up at the sight of
food.

Cora laughed weakly. 'I'd have thought you were

used to that kind of night life. How did it go with Tod?'

What she really wanted to know was why Mandy was enjoying a tête-à-tête with Darryl, but she was too afraid to enquire.

'Ooh, he's so wonderful,' Mandy breathed.

'So?' Cora urged.

Mandy shrugged despondently. 'So, nothing. We had fun at the beach, he brought me home, kissed me goodnight and that's that.'

'It's a start, isn't it?'

Mandy looked gloomily into her cup of tea.

'It was exciting while it lasted, but evidently I didn't impress Tod for all my efforts at sophistication because he didn't suggest another date.'

'He will, Mandy, just give him time, and be yourself,' Cora advised.

Mandy suddenly looked across the small table at her friend. 'And, of course, you're the expert. That's why you didn't come to the beach because Darryl couldn't, I suppose?'

A guilty blush crept into Cora's cheeks, but she was prevented from replying as Mandy hurried on: 'Well, his mother was rushed in late last night. She's on our ward—such a sweet old thing.'

'What's the matter with her?' Cora asked with concern.

'Gall-stones. She's out of pain now, but may have surgery in a day or two if she gets another attack. Apparently Darryl got home just in time, his father was bringing her in.'

'You're right,' Cora agreed trying to hide her

surprise. 'She's a very sweet person. I'll look in and see her if I'm up your way.'

'Come up when you finish tonight, though don't expect to see Darryl. Rumour has it that they don't get on.'

'Just a rumour,' Cora said knowledgeably, 'they seemed all right when I met them at the Cathedral.'

Cora didn't enlighten Mandy that she and Darryl had gone to the beach just when everyone else was returning. She was consumed with guilt now, knowing that Darryl hadn't returned home until the early hours. She consoled herself that Darryl's father, being a doctor, was quite well able to cope but she could just imagine how miserable Darryl must be feeling.

It was almost nine o'clock when she made her way towards Women's Surgical ward and on one of the landings she bumped into Monique Galton.

Cora instantly realised that the theatre sister had been to visit Mrs Delaney. She smiled in passing and would have hurried by but Monique stood in her way.

'Can I have a word?' she asked in a haughty tone which sent the blood draining from Cora's cheeks. 'There are certain codes of conduct we observe at Zenobia's,' she went on, 'namely, that if you invite a person to a party you include their partner, and I'm not amused that Darryl was invited without me.'

'I . . . I didn't invite Darryl,' Cora replied honestly. 'I believe Neil did, believing that Darryl had no other engagements. I'm sorry, but I didn't exactly know that you and he—'

'Well, you know now, honey, so lay off, and don't think you can persuade him not to go to Canada with me because it's all arranged, even to his consultant's post. If you're just off to see his mother don't let her talk you into trying to persuade him either. Darryl's no fool, he can see through his mother, and all her little schemes to keep her darling boy within reach. She may have taken a shine to you, but, believe me, it's only for her own ends, and if Darryl thinks that you and she are conspiring together, well—he'll just explode.'

Monique pushed past Cora and hurried down the stairs, leaving Cora shaken and trembling. Not with fear of the theatre sister, but aghast at the news that Darryl was leaving Zenobia's. So this was what Mrs Delaney was opposing!

Cora felt that she couldn't face Darryl's mother now, she just needed to be alone with her thoughts. She carried on to the floor above and took the lift back down to the ground floor. Her feet seemed to get more leaden with every step of the way to her own room.

For a while she just paced up and down, willing herself to get used to the idea that Darryl and Monique were going to Canada together. The room seemed to swim in hot and cold hazes alternately, even though there was efficient air-conditioning everywhere. At first she could only condemn Darryl for his lack of consideration for his mother, but then she began to despise him for his unfaithfulness to Monique. If he really loved the theatre sister—and surely he must, to be willing to go to Canada with her?—he wouldn't want to pay any attention to Cora. Whether it be just playing around or for real! Cora became even more desolate because now she knew for certain that his kisses were only superficial. However she affected him it was only to satisfy his desire to taunt. It was fairly obvious now that he never intended to prosecute her for dangerous driving. He wouldn't want to get involved in a court case if he was about to leave Bermuda, for such things take time and Darryl Delaney was the type of man to allow nothing to stand in his way.

Bermuda, the pure white lilies, legendary moongates and even the whistling tree-frogs suddenly lost all their attraction. But there was still Neil, and he continued to be kind towards her. But in spite of herself she found his attentions irritating and had to be firm so as not to show her feelings and hurt him.

Cora couldn't decide whether her aching heart was easier to bear when she didn't see Darryl for days at a time or when he assisted in Casualty, nor was it fortuitous when Tod was sent off duty with some bug or other, and within forty-eight hours Mandy was admitted to the nurses' sick quarters with a similar complaint. It meant that Darryl was on duty in Casualty frequently.

After helping one morning when there was a long list of patients with minor ailments he suddenly looked at Cora and smiled. She couldn't explain the smile, she just knew it tore open her own wound to a great gorge of misery and helpless longing for him.

'I suppose you think we should have isolated young Mandy and Tod on one of the smaller wards and let them enjoy the bug together?' he said.

Cora was slow to react.

'You haven't got it too, have you?' he asked with genuine concern. 'You look—wan is the best description I can think of.'

'I'm fine.' She found her voice and knew that her only salvation lay in being as curt as she could. Then on impulse she added: 'How's your mother, Mr Delaney?'

He stared at her as if he hadn't heard correctly, then: 'Why are we behaving like strangers, Cora? And why haven't you been to see for yourself how my mother is?'

We are strangers, she wanted to cry, we have to be. She rallied quickly. 'I didn't like to, I wouldn't like to intrude.'

'You're always worrying about intruding. Lack of confidence and concentration are your trouble. Mother's had her operation and is making excellent progress, but she'd love to see you, I know.'

Cora called the next patient, recognising the familiar tone of sarcasm, but as soon as they were alone again Darryl said:

'How about the next instalment this week? The perfumery as I promised? You look as if you need something to sweeten you.'

How could he be so cruel, she thought, directing fierce blue sparks from her weary eyes, but movement at the door caught her attention and to her astonishment she saw Bill Palmer on crutches, watching her.

'I told you I'd come looking for you, honey,' he called. 'You've deserted me for too long.'

Cora just stared, feeling more than a little guilty that she hadn't been to see him since his operation.

'You're doing well, Bill, but don't overdo it,' Darryl warned, then in an aside to Cora: 'Get him back to his own ward, we don't have time to entertain boyfriends in this department.'

Sara emerged from one of the cubicles and in her usual friendly way exchanged a chatty conversation with Bill, then she came to the cubicle where Cora was cleaning a child's foot wound.

'I'll carry on here, Cora, you have your break now. Take Bill up to the canteen for coffee, then back to his ward.'

'I don't really want to,' Cora whispered. 'I wish you wouldn't drop me into things.'

Sara gave Cora a push. She washed her hands at the basin, knowing that Darryl was talking to Bill but watching her closely at the same time.

'I can have ten minutes for a coffee, Bill,' Cora said coldly as she faced the two men.

'Bill will need that to get there,' Darryl said grinning, 'take twenty.'

'You've only got yourself to blame, honey,' Bill said as they moved slowly through the long corridor to the lift. 'I told you I'd come looking for you. I'm disappointed. I thought you cared about me losing my leg.'

'I do, Bill, but I can't take everyone's problems personally. My heart isn't that large.'

'Cora, I know you don't care a jot about my troubles, but you mean a lot to me. I'm not too proud to admit to being scared as hell on the day I was brought in to Zenobia's, but wherever I go, whenever I think of that name I shall always remember a pair of sky blue eyes that gave me comfort and hope.'

'Oh, Bill, that's a nice thing to say, but I did nothing.'

'You were there, honey, you were patient with me, and I want to take you out to dinner before I leave Bermuda.'

'You don't give up, do you?' Cora said. 'I doubt if they'll let you out. Before you know it you'll be going home.'

'I may have lost a leg but I'm doing well. I have to get to grips with these phantom nerve pains and to do that I need company.'

'You've got Duggie.'

'And he's got Patsy. She's taken over where your friend left off. By the way, I hear she and Doc Freeman have eloped together?' he laughed.

Cora laughed too and as they stepped into the lift Bill put his arm round Cora's shoulder.

'That's better, honey. Now you can relax and let Delaney say or think what he likes.'

Cora tried to ignore the implication as she said: 'I'm sure Mandy would love to elope with Tod, but neither of them are feeling up to it at present.'

'You've been to see them?'

'Of course. Mandy's been pretty rough.'

'You don't look too bright yourself. You're pale and your eyes have lost a bit of their usual sparkle. You don't think you're sickening for something?'

'Strong as an ox, me,' Cora said light-heartedly, but deep inside she knew that she was suffering from a sickness for which there was no known cure.

In the canteen Bill sat down at a table while Cora fetched coffees and doughnuts.

'There's a really good hotel not far from here, honey,' he said eagerly. 'I'm going to ring up and book a table for Sunday. I'll twist Delaney's arm to let me out for a few hours. He'll agree when he knows I'm going out with my own private nurse.'

'I don't know what shift I'm on,' Cora said, anxious to put Bill off.

'You'll be off duty from two o'clock, I've arranged it with Sister Kenmore. I made sure I didn't involve the old dragon.'

'You've got a nerve, Bill Palmer,' Cora admonished. 'Supposing I've got another date?'

'See to it that you haven't.'

Cora escorted him back to Men's Surgical ward where he immediately got a rollicking for not being there when the physiotherapist had called to see him, but Patsy Gillman laughed good-naturedly.

'Incorrigible, this one,' she said. 'There's no keeping him under control. You're welcome to take him off my hands whenever you like, Cora.'

'Sorry, I'm on duty,' Cora said and returned as quickly as she could to Casualty.

She was grateful for the pressures of the emergency and accident department throughout her day's duties, but nothing helped her to decide whether or not she would visit Darryl's mother. She wanted to, if only to hear Mrs Delaney confirm the relationship between Darryl and Monique, but if she did Cora knew that she would feel more wretched than ever.

During her off duty she went to the shops and

bought a pot plant and some biscuits and when she had finished work for the day she took the lift up to the third floor. She was determined to get to Women's Surgical without anyone seeing her; at least Mandy need never know.

Cora was directed to a small side ward where Mrs Delaney was propped up in bed near to the window. As soon as she recognised Cora she opened her arms and it was as much as Cora could do to refrain from rushing into them with a flood of self-pitying tears.

'My dear, I was hoping you'd come. I don't really know why you should want to visit me. Darryl's always telling me how selfish I'm becoming,' Mrs Delaney said.

'I'm sorry I haven't been able to get here before,' Cora said. 'I'm sure you're not the slightest bit selfish.'

Mrs Delaney's lips and chin quivered. 'Is it selfish to want to keep the last of your flock close to you? Is it selfish to want him to meet and marry the nicest girl in the world?'

'It's a rather tall order, Mrs Delaney,' Cora said, smiling through the mist of her own tears. She had wanted confirmation, now she had it irrefutably. 'I know you like pot plants by the lovely ones you have in your conservatory, and I thought you might like some biscuits. They're not too sweet, I hope they'll be all right.'

Mrs Delaney was weeping quietly and Cora went to her, taking her hand in hers.

'I expect you're feeling low,' she comforted as best she could. 'It's post-operative depression, but you really mustn't be depressed on this lovely island.'

Mrs Delaney sniffed and dried her eyes.

'How thoughtful and kind you are, Cora dear. I didn't expect to have to come to Zenobia's as a patient. I've always loved being involved in everything that goes on here though I suppose I'm too old for parties any more.'

'Nonsense,' Cora replied brightly. 'Next time the staff nurses give one you must come and bring Dr Delaney.'

'I've been unwell for some time. My husband said I was fretting over Darryl going to Canada. Well, what did he expect? Darryl's been such a good son to me, until he became friendly with that theatre sister.'

'How many children do you have, Mrs Delaney?' Cora asked, trying to steer clear of further mention of Monique.

'Three more sons and a daughter, all married, and I have seven grandchildren so far, though most of them are scattered all over the world. That's why Darryl has been so special. He's the only one who has followed in his father's footsteps, and isn't the baby special anyhow?' She smiled wistfully.

'I'm sure Darryl wouldn't do anything to upset you intentionally, Mrs Delaney.'

The elderly patient looked doubtful. 'That was true once, my dear, but we're growing ever farther apart since Monique came on the scene. I told Darryl she had her claws out for him, and I was right. Oh, I know I shouldn't interfere, and Monique is—well,' she sniffed and turned away until the tears trickled down her cheeks. 'Darryl could have done better for himself. It isn't only that Canada is a long way away.'

Cora did her best to talk of other things but it was clear that Darryl's mother was against Monique and heartbroken that her son intended to leave Bermuda. Marriage wasn't actually mentioned, but Cora had no doubts that Monique would not settle for less.

She left after about half an hour, having failed to cheer Mrs Delaney up or herself, but on the landing which divided the women's surgical from the men's surgical ward and where the lifts were situated, Cora saw Bill Palmer.

'I thought I saw a familiar figure,' he said, beaming happily.

Cora managed a smile. 'You still chasing me, Bill? You couldn't possibly have recognised me—we all look alike in uniform and why should you have expected me on this floor?'

'You didn't need much persuading and you were really on your way to see me. Still,' he added cheekily, 'I don't mind Delaney's mother having my fruit and flowers as long as I've got you.'

Cora simply shook her head in despair of him.

'Come on in my room,' he added. 'My chums visited me today and brought me some goodies. Now I never knew a girl who could say no to chocolate.'

Cora followed him into his room rather than stay on the landing where everyone could hear his nonsense. He presented her with a huge beribboned box of chocolates and candies.

'Bill, no—they're yours,' she insisted.

'Don't be silly, as if the men would buy me chocolates! Cigarettes and Scotch are more my style, honey. I got one of them to buy these for me to give you, just to say thanks.'

'Bill, this is embarrassing. I did nothing. I'm not even nursing you.'

'You were the first nurse I saw—and it was love at first sight.' He forced the chocolate box into her hands, then leaned forward and kissed her. 'And I still mean to take you out to dinner. I'm not going to say I don't want to go home as soon as possible, but not before I've kept that date with you.'

'Now I know you're crazy,' she said, 'but thanks, and we'll see about the dinner date.'

'I won't take no for an answer, honey.' He held her gently, then she felt him swaying.

'You're trying to do too much,' she scolded. 'You ought to be sitting down.'

'And you need an early night,' he quipped. 'I want to see that sparkle back in your eyes by Sunday. Now I'm going back to my cricket on the box. Come and see me again soon?' he pleaded.

Cora just had to laugh at him. He was so easy to laugh with and in spite of all his insistence she knew he was a nice man who was grateful for Zenobia's care, and who would go willingly home to his wife when the time came.

He was right too, no girl in her right mind ever said no to chocolates. She could go back to her room, wallow in self-pity and gorge herself sick.

Most of the corridors and wards were quiet now

after supper and Cora got out of the lift to find Darryl waiting to go up.

'Hm,' he said, surveying the luxurious gold box she was carrying, 'visitors usually take the chocolates to the patient, not the other way round.'

'Who else but Bill,' she said by way of explanation and because she couldn't think of anything else to say.

His expression darkened and he drew her down a quiet passageway. 'I'm surprised at you for accepting such a gift,' he said impatiently. 'Can't I get it into your thick head that Bill is married with children? In fact, the reason his wife hasn't flown over is because she's recently had a baby. I think you're taking a mean advantage, leading Bill on.'

'Mr Delaney!' Cora was really angry. 'I am not taking a mean advantage of anyone. Bill is grateful for everything that has been done for him here and he merely wanted to show his appreciation.'

'Giving *you* chocolates? Taking *you* out to dinner?'

'It doesn't *mean* anything,' Cora argued hotly.

'No, it doesn't to you. It's all a cheap game of flirting with whoever's willing at the time, isn't it?'

'And your kind of game is permissible I suppose?' Cora raged back at him. 'If you're going to marry Monique then at least be faithful to her!'

She swung round and away as fast as she could. How dared he accuse her of misconduct when he treated his 'partner' so insincerely? Just what definition Monique had meant by 'partner' Cora wasn't sure. Cora had liked Monique Galton in the beginning, now she didn't care if she never saw her again. But, to be fair, she had as much right to try to capture Darryl Delaney as anyone else.

Cora looked blankly at herself in the mirror when she reached her room. Cheeks as pale as porcelain and staring eyes. Yet behind the cold expression her eyes felt as if they were on fire. What had she got, for heaven's sake, that Monique didn't have in much better condition? Of course Darryl was only playing a cheap game of flirting with her, yet he had the cheek to condemn her for the very same thing!

She felt too weary to cry. The pain of unfulfilled love gnawed away inside her and she tried to understand what Mrs Delaney was going through. When she had first met Darryl's parents his mother had seemed fit, but Cora had sensed some friction between them. Now she knew that it was Monique who was the cause and her success in enticing Darryl to Canada. What a weak character he must be, Cora decided, to be so easily led by a woman.

She ran her fingers over her cheeks and wondered why she couldn't devise a plan to keep him in Bermuda if only for his mother's sake.

Gall stones could nag away undetected for years. It was far more likely that Mrs Delaney had aggravated a mild problem with worry.

Cora took off her cap and hung it on the round knob of her wardrobe door. Then she sat on the side of her bed and unbuttoned her uniform dress. She didn't suffer from gall stones but she knew how her love for Darryl was affecting every part of her.

The vanity unit comprising wash basin and dressing table was set against the wall with the wardrobe adjacent and cupboards above. She was lucky to have such a well-fitted room. There was every convenience here at the nurses' home, though she and Mandy had planned that if and when they realised their ambition to become Sisters they would find a flat or cottage to share. Now, all these plans didn't seem so attractive. She'd get over Darryl Delaney—she simply had to—and the sooner he went to Canada the better, she thought bitterly.

Being bitter and angry didn't relieve her anguish. In fact it added to her misery. She tore off the seal on the box of chocolates and proceeded to eat one after the other.

Unlike Mandy, Cora didn't have to watch her figure unduly. She rarely over-ate, and burned off her excess calories by always being on the go, but half a large box of chocolates of varying flavours mixed with candies of marzipan and nuts didn't exactly compliment her emptiness and another look in the mirror warned her that she'd had enough. Why not make herself sick? her image taunted. At least she could go sick for a day and try to get Darryl Delaney out of her system.

She put the lid on the box, must save some for when Mandy was better, then she took some anti-acid pills and drowned them with a glass of bitter-lemon.

Her head began to thump so she went along to the kitchen on her floor and made a pot of tea which she took back to her room and after swallowing two aspirins she crawled beneath the sheets, wishing she could die.

CHAPTER NINE

In her stupor Cora forgot to set her alarm and she surfaced next morning at the moment she should have been reporting for duty. She felt wretched, but hurriedly splashed her face with cold water, dressed and dashed out of the nurses' home.

She only woke properly when Sister Longford began to raise her voice.

'If there's one thing I will not tolerate, Staff Nurse, it's bad time-keeping. There's simply no excuse. More late night parties, I suppose, You must learn to arrange these affairs with suitable off duty.'

Neil attempted to intervene. 'Have you caught this bug off Mandy? You look rotten,' he offered helpfully.

'If you're ill,' Sister Longford snapped, 'you shouldn't have come on duty at all.'

'I'm all right, thanks,' Cora managed weakly.

'Either report sick, Staff Nurse Jordan, or take over reception duties until you're fully awake.'

'I'll do an hour at the desk,' she agreed penitently.

Neil went with her. 'Couldn't you have picked a better morning to oversleep? The dragon's having a go at everyone.'

Cora managed to cope with desk duties after Neil had smuggled her some strong black coffee and as the day wore on she returned to some degree of normality. A long spell of afternoon off duty meant that she could sleep off the effects of over-indulgence, but she knew that her appearance be-lied her true feelings. It was no bug she was suffer-ing from but heartache.

Darryl had careered about in Casualty for a short time before going into Theatre for the remainder of the day, and he seemed to be in about as good humour as Sister Longford, completely ignoring Cora.

No doubt Sister Longford was feeling neglected, Cora realised, and probably felt as miserable as she did about Darryl and Monique. Soon the rumours would be in full sail all over Zenobia's, and quite a few hearts would have taken a battering.

Cora felt better able to cope when she returned to Casualty late afternoon and Sister Longford went off duty. A few minor ailments were waiting to be seen by Neil, the casualty officer, and they worked together amiably.

The evening session was quieter and after a baby of fifteen months suffering from an asthmatic attack had been treated and admitted to the chil-dren's unit Cora checked that everywhere was ready for the night staff to take over.

Neil came down from the ward and removed his white coat.

'I'm on call tonight,' he told Cora, 'so I'm going off to get some sleep if I can. Bleep one of the other housemen if anything urgent comes in. Sorry I can't suggest a drink tonight, Cora, how about tomor-row? I should get off at four, you're off at—' he ran his finger along the duty rota, 'six, let's have a night out?'

Cora didn't know why she exploded, but she rounded on him aggressively.

'Why should I want a night out with you or anybody else? I'm sick of being propositioned all the time. I'm fed up with every darned man in this hospital!'

The look of astonishment on Neil's face brought her to her senses.

'Neil,' she croaked, 'I . . . I'm sorry—' She buried her face in her hands and made for the office. In seconds Neil had his arms round her to comfort her.

'Go on,' he whispered sympathetically, 'get it all out in the open.'

'I didn't mean to be so rude, Neil,' she sobbed. 'I don't know what's come over me.' She blew her nose and dried her eyes, and then looked at him sadly. 'Forgive me,' she whispered. 'You of all people.' She shook her head. 'I had no right to snap at you.'

'Fine Sister you'll turn out to be,' Neil reproached with amusement. 'It must be catching. Well, we all know poor old Moo is a frustrated spinster and had no hope with Darryl, but you?— must admit I thought there were all the signs of something happening, but I didn't realise it was that bad.'

'Heavens,' Cora moaned, 'am I so obvious?'

'Yes, darling. I've known all along that you were infatuated by him,' Neil laughed. 'That's nothing new, every female swoons at the mere sight of him, but I think you're extra mad today because you really love him and he teases you. Isn't that right?'

'Fat lot of good loving him when Monique's already bagged him.'

'I know they belong to the same golf club, but I didn't think it went any deeper. Monique is as crazy as the rest of you women over him, but I had no idea Darryl was flattered enough to submit to her so-called charms.'

'Didn't you know that Darryl is going to Canada with her? He has a consultant's post there,' Cora explained.

'Never! Darryl is devoted to his mother, both his parents come to that, and he loves Bermuda.'

'Monique told me herself and Mrs Delaney confirmed it,' Cora said miserably.

Neil shrugged. 'It's the first I've heard of it. We've been good pals, Darryl and I—funny that he's never talked about Canada. He's only talked about Monique in the same vein as all his other conquests. He knows how women fall over themselves even to be seen talking to him and it just amuses him.'

Cora put her handkerchief away, bitterly regretting her outburst and wishing that she could love Neil in the same way as she did Darryl. It wasn't particularly flattering to have to admit that she might have been rated a conquest along with a string of others. That was Darryl's way, she supposed. Amusing himself watching a woman become besotted over him. It only needed one date, one kiss, one love scene which took his conquest to the edge of surrender and then he tossed her aside like some old sock. And *she'd* been foolish enough to behave as silly as the rest of them. But it didn't matter how much she rebuked herself, the anguish was still there.

'You're not like the others though,' Neil continued. 'At first I thought he goaded you because of the moped incident, then I suspected that he really cared.'

'Only because it was his fault,' Cora said. 'He thought I didn't remember what happened, but the human brain is pretty reliable, and all this Bermudan heat and sunshine has got mine working in top form again.' She pursed her lips thoughtfully. 'I don't suppose I'd go as far as swearing on oath, but I'm pretty certain he caught my rear wheel and sent me flying.'

'Good thing you were wearing a crash helmet,' Neil said.

'Mm—except that I hadn't done the chin-strap up. Stupid, I know, and to my shame Darryl knows that, so even if it had been his fault he would have been exonerated, I expect. Legally I wasn't properly protected, and he being well-known on the island, especially with his father a long-standing resident—well, I wouldn't have stood much chance in court. But I haven't even let him think that I realise that. Still, it makes little difference now. He and Monique are off to Canada in the not too distant future so the accident is best forgotten.'

'As long as you're sure you're okay?' Neil asked compassionately.

Cora sighed deeply. 'I've never felt like this over anyone before. I thought Mandy was just being

Mandy in her passion for Tod, but now I know what it feels like to really be bewitched by someone.'

'There's always me to fall back on, Cora darling,' Neil said with sincerity.

'I regard you as a very loyal friend,' Cora said, her blue eyes meeting his gaze with honesty. 'I've never tried to let you think otherwise, have I, Neil?'

Neil spread his long freckled hands out in a negative gesture. 'I suppose the signs were there, but I only wanted to see every response as ones of mutual affection, or at least interest. We could make a go of it, Cora,' he urged. 'We have a lot in common, we're both British to the core, we're, as you said, genuine friends. A lot of successful marriages have started out with much less.'

'You're very sweet, Neil, but I won't regard that as a genuine proposal. For one thing if you loved me passionately as you'd need to, to make marriage work, you'd be jealous over my feelings for Darryl however useless my love for him is. I'm fond of you, you're so—so—dependable—'

'Steady, now you're trying to soften the blow. I'm no different from the next man, and little do you know it, my sweet Cora, that I'm inwardly dancing with joy that Darryl is going off to Canada with Monique. I shall never give up trying to persuade you that we could be right for each other, and I'm selfish enough to see the probability of promotion when Darryl leaves.'

'The second is natural ambition, the first is just because you're a thoroughly nice guy and feel sorry for me. I hope we'll always be good friends, Neil, and I'll be happy to go places with you on those terms, but,' she shook her head positively. 'nothing more.'

Cora knew he wasn't heartbroken otherwise she might have had to say some very different words, but she was glad to have found the courage to talk frankly, and she knew she could trust Neil not to repeat any of their conversation to anyone else.

When she went off duty she made her way to the section of the medical wards reserved especially for the staff's sick quarters, but was told that Mandy had been discharged and had returned to the nurses' home.

Cora went straight to Mandy's room, found it locked, so she returned to the ground floor expecting to find her in the TV lounge. A few nurses and sisters were watching a film but there was no sign of Mandy.

'Try the sitting room, or the common room,' one of the girls said.

Cora couldn't imagine Mandy wanting to play any active sort of game yet so she looked in the sitting room, but that was empty.

She heard music coming from the common room and supposed someone was running a disco but when she peered in to the dimly lit hall she saw just one couple swaying in time to a romantic melody coming softly from the speakers.

Cora stood spellbound, and watched Mandy and Tod who, despite their sickness bug appeared to be thriving excellently on the love-bug which had bitten both of them with equal tenacity. She crept away, experiencing a chill emptiness in spite of the pleasure seeing their happiness gave her.

Would she ever feel fulfilled as Mandy obviously did? Why must true happiness always elude her? why did she have to want something that was well out of her reach?

Doom and gloom seemed to be swallowing her up so she gave herself a sharp reprimand and went along to the bathroom where she almost fell asleep soaking and dreaming of the man who was responsible for her lethargy.

Mrs Delaney had begged her to visit again, but Cora decided she couldn't bear to. Yet, in the next breath she knew she would in order to hear any personal news of Darryl. She would go on torturing herself today, tomorrow, for always.

Wearing nothing but her cotton dressing-gown Cora drifted wearily back to her room. Mandy was lying on top of the bed, faking a drunken stupor with a half-empty bottle of wine in one hand, a glass in the other.

Cora laughed. 'Evidently you've recovered. I called in to see you and they told me you'd been discharged.'

Mandy opened one eye. 'Have a little drink on me,' she drawled in a slurred voice. Then she sat up unable to hide her excitement.

'We've been celebrating, Tod and me,' she said. 'I saved a drink for you.'

'Do you think you should be drinking?' Cora asked.

'I'm fine, and Tod's *wonderful*,' she breathed in ecstasy. 'Cora, I can't believe it. He's had his eye on me all the time, but thought I was too busily engaged dating everyone else. We're sort of, well, you know, if we could live together, we would.'

'Engaged? Married?' Cora asked raising a quizzical eyebrow.

Mandy shrugged. 'It won't make any difference to us because we're together for keeps. Oh, Cora, I shouldn't be rambling on like this I know. You look *so* defeated. Darling, are *you* ill?'

Mandy slid off the bed and peered at Cora curiously.

'Guess that's just about what I am,' Cora admitted.

'Still no go with Darryl?'

'He's got Monique, and they're going to Canada. His mother is so upset about it.'

'Cheer up, there's Neil, and Bill Palmer, or Sara will always find you a policeman.'

'Just any old man won't do,' Cora said. 'You should know that, Mandy. You're the biggest flirt of all time, but you knew that what you really wanted was Tod, didn't you?'

'True,' Mandy agreed thoughtfully. 'I'm lucky, Tod didn't fall for anyone else. What can I say, Cora? I mean, if Darryl and Monique are serious about each other, there's no point in offering hope.'

'Guess Bermuda is as good a place to dream as anywhere else,' Cora said flatly.

Mandy poured a drink. 'Wish *us* luck, anyway, Cora, then maybe our good fortune will reflect on you.'

Cora raised her glass and drank their good health and wished them well for the future, whilst all she could see ahead for herself was loneliness.

'Dr Slessor signed us off this morning,' Mandy explained. 'Told us to make the most of our convalescing forty-eight hours, and we'd better be back on duty on Sunday or else.'

'Wish Dr Slessor could cure my broken heart,' Cora said wistfully.

'Well, I'll tell you what to do, Cora. Go to the Palm Grove Gardens, pretend Darryl is with you, walk through the long archway of Chinese moongates and wish. You know what the legend says, "Honey-mooners should walk through and make a wish. If you aren't honeymooning, wish anyhow." It's worth a try. It worked for me.'

'Oh, Mandy, you're an incurable romantic; as if any Chinese moongate had anything to do with you and Tod getting together.'

'I'm sure it did. Trouble is,' she said, changing her mood, 'if Darryl's going to Canada there's not much a moongate can do, is there?'

'Don't you think you ought to get to bed, Mandy? You've only got two days to get really fit for work, and I am rather tired myself.'

'Poor old you. I wish—'

'I wish you'd let me get to bed. I'm happy for you, Mandy, and I'll see you when you can tear yourself away from Tod for five minutes.'

'You're a great friend, Cora.' Mandy kissed her friend's cheek affectionately and went off to her own room singing happily.

Cora slept fitfully. She was really pleased for Mandy and Tod, but it didn't help her own dampened spirits.

During a hectic session in Casualty next day

Darryl was called to help. A young motor-cyclist quite extensively injured needed surgery so Cora was detailed to assist in the minor ops theatre.

Monique had come down to take charge, leaving her colleague, Sister Weekes, in the main theatre suite upstairs.

Cora set up the sterile trays and as Darryl repaired and stitched the patient's injuries she handed him the required instruments while Monique worked alongside him. It was an ironical situation, Cora noticed, as she was aware of but tried not to interpret the many glances which passed between surgeon and sister. It was a test of her nerve as she had to keep a clear head and steady hands to anticipate Darryl's requirements, but to have to concentrate opposite the man she loved and watch the silent intimacies exchanged between him and another woman was undeserved punishment. But after the first few traumatic minutes she was able to focus her attention fully on the job. A job which thankfully she loved sufficiently to be able to think about single-mindedly—that of caring for the patient.

Only when she was preparing to take him to the recovery ward did she feel that her legs were giving way beneath her. As Monique untied Darryl's gown tapes Cora heard her say: 'I've ordered a taxi for seven o'clock tomorrow evening, and we fly out at nine.'

The trolley bearing the patient seemed to spin crazily. Cora held on, her own head dazed, her thoughts tightening into cruel comprehension. It wasn't in a week or month that Darryl and Monique were going to Canada, it was tomorrow! That was Sunday and she would be off duty late afternoon to keep her planned dinner date with Bill Palmer. She didn't want to go, hadn't from the start, could she even now get out of it? Only by staging a faint, and that wouldn't be too difficult!

She heard Darryl's superb voice answering Monique but she didn't want to know what he actually said. Soon he would no longer be a doctor at Zenobia's. She wouldn't have to wake each morning and wonder if she might see him during her working period. But she would wake each morning and think of him. Nothing could alter that, no matter how many miles separated them.

For the remainder of the day she tormented herself with the anticipation of Darryl touring each hospital department bidding farewell to his work-mates. She desperately wanted, needed to have a few private moments with him yet she knew that was a futile hope. Monique was certain to accompany him and Cora knew that she couldn't bear the triumph she would see evident in the other girl's expression. She had little doubt now as to how they felt about one another.

During the operation Darryl had avoided looking at Cora. Had he felt guilty, knowing that Mrs Delaney would probably have shared her confidences with Cora? She could even manage to put aside her own dejection in sympathy with the older woman's suffering. How could Darryl be so unfeeling as to go away while his mother was still recovering from surgery? He was an unspeakable brute, she thought, to be so self-centred. Then she remembered Mrs Delaney saying that Darryl was the youngest of her family. Thoroughly spoilt and indulged, Cora assumed, so maybe Darryl wasn't entirely to blame, after all.

Following a spell of off duty she returned to Casualty in time to see Darryl in a natural-coloured lightweight suit accompanied by Monique going in the direction of the stairs. Had she just missed having to say goodbye to them both? She desperately hoped so, but was on tenterhooks at every approaching footstep until she wearily went off duty.

Tomorrow Mrs Delaney would need consoling but that, Cora decided, must be her husband's prerogative and perhaps she could endeavour to enjoy her evening out with Bill.

Cora realised that Darryl was annoyed with her over this date, and he would know all the details because Bill would just love boasting about taking her out. It would no longer matter if Darryl had refused to give Bill permission to leave Zenobia's for three or four hours because now he wouldn't be here to care.

Sunday was usually a relatively quiet day in the accident and emergency department, and Cora was pleased that Sister Longford was on duty so that her presence prevented Neil and Cora from having personal conversation. She wanted to be quiet in her thoughtful mood. She was grateful for a few minor casualties though to occupy her time.

She found Bill waiting for her outside the canteen at lunch time.

'Gee, honey, you aren't going to let me down are you? I've had to plead on bended knee to get Sister to give me permission to go out this evening.'

'Bill, are you sure you really want to? Just because you started all this crazy nonsense about taking me out you don't have to keep it up. Supposing we meet one of your workmates and they tell your wife? Wouldn't she be terribly upset?'

Bill sighed impatiently. 'Cora, my wife and I find a certain excitement in being parted. Our partnership is all the more solid for the getting together every few months. Most important of all is the fact that we trust each other completely, and because I'm taking you out for a thank-you dinner date doesn't mean I'm asking you to smuggle me into your bed. Besides,' he added with a wicked grin, 'Sister made me promise I'd be back in the ward at ten o'clock.'

Cora smiled up at him, appreciating his forthrightness. She would go with Bill and darned well enjoy the evening. It might help to take her mind off the fact that she would probably never see Darryl again.

'Okay then, we ought to book a table at Skye Towers though, they rarely have a spare one on spec, especially on a Sunday when so many other places are closed.'

'All taken care of, honey, even to the taxi ordered for quarter to seven.'

'Don't you think you ought to go in a wheelchair, Bill? It's not that far, I could have pushed you along the coast road. The fresh air would do you good.'

'What's up with you? All the rest of the staff

work overtime in preventing me from thinking that I'm an invalid, and here are you suggesting a wheelchair? No way, honey. I only wish I'd got my artificial leg and foot, but that's going to wait until I get home. I'm getting real attached to these crutches.'

Cora laughed. 'You go steady,' she warned, 'you know what too much confidence can do!'

He walked her to the lift and she experienced a pleasant feeling of *bonhomie*. She may have a bruised heart, but she would be a good companion to Bill, giving him happy memories of Bermuda and Zenobia's to take back to the States with him.

Cora left Bill to return to his own lunch on the ward and she went in search of Mandy, on the same floor. It was an impulsive idea, she knew, but with ten minutes to spare she decided to visit Mrs Delaney. If she waited until tomorrow she guessed that melancholia would have returned and she would be in no fit state to cheer anyone else up, but now she hoped she would find some suitable consolation to pass on to Darryl's unhappy mother.

At once she realised that this was not a suitable moment to visit as the Sister of Women's Surgical ward was serving lunches, but Mandy spotted Cora at the desk and came out to see her.

'I've got a few moments, could I see Mrs Delaney?' Cora asked quietly.

'Mrs Delaney?' Mandy echoed. 'You're too late, she went home this morning.'

'That was quick,' Cora said.

'Apparently she's made an excellent recovery so

her husband wanted her to be at home near the sea. Suppose they have a string of servants anyway, so she won't need to lift a finger.'

Cora changed the subject readily. 'I came as well to see how you're coping?'

'Fine, never felt better.' Then Mandy frowned. 'But I'm not happy about you, Cora. Dark shadows round your eyes and you're as white as a sheet. I think you ought to get a check up.' She paused and looked at her friend suspiciously. 'All this unspent passion for Darryl Delaney isn't making you home-sick—is it?'

Cora created a laugh which she hoped sounded genuine.

'Heavens, no! Whatever gave you such an idea?' She moved away, back into the shadow of the corridor. 'I must go then, see you later perhaps,' and she rushed to the lift.

Home—there was something so attractive about the sound. Was she only deceiving herself into believing she was happy here at Zenobia's? Maybe she had been wrong to follow in Mandy's footsteps after all. They didn't have similar temperaments so what might be right for Mandy wasn't necessarily suitable for Cora. If only she'd never come on that darned holiday, if only she had never set eyes on that wretched tall, dark, handsome Latin-American Don Juan.

In her secret moments of day-dreaming she had believed that Fate had led her to Bermuda and Zenobia's. Who else could have twisted and con-trived to make her the moped rider that he had to bump into, when she was about to join the staff at the very hospital where he was Senior Surgical Registrar?

What else but Fate had arranged the meeting at the Cathedral, and why had there been an instant compatibility with Mrs Delaney?

Fate was cruel, Cora accused and tried to put thoughts of the Delaney family, as well as her own home and family right out of her mind. Of course she wasn't homesick. Tonight she was going to keep that date with Bill Palmer and set out to enjoy herself.

Over the past two days Cora had eaten little as her stomach was still protesting at the quantity of chocolates and candies she had consumed at one sitting. Now she had closed up the box and couldn't bear to be reminded of chocolate.

As she bathed and treated her skin with light body lotion she tried not to dwell on how she was going to get through a large meal such as Skye Towers Hotel was renowned for.

She couldn't decide what to wear. One minute she felt hot, the next cold. She didn't imagine Bill expected evening dress so she finally chose a cream silk dress with elaborate embroidery panels down the front of the bodice. The sleeves were full as was the skirt gathered into an elasticated waistband. It was a simple style rather than provocative, with a neatly frilled mandarin collar at the neck which matched the cuffs at her wrists.

She gazed long and critically at her ghost-like image in the mirror. No man had ever affected her to this extent before and now was the time to pull herself together. She applied a liberal amount of eye-shadow, and brushed her cheek bones lightly with rouge. The effect was immediate and she forgot all her troubles as she clipped dainty pearl earrings to her lobes, and after giving her naturally wavy hair a final brush she put on some fancy leather sandals, slung the matching thonged bag over her shoulder and set off.

There were not the usual comings and goings in Outpatients as she walked through, just a handful of visitors well ahead of her making their way to the wards, and as she covered the distance of long corridor she overtook a young woman of about her own age.

'Oh, excuse me,' the stranger said. 'You look as if you know where you're going. I suppose I am going in the right direction for the men's wards?'

'Yes, that's where I'm going. We can take the lift from the end of the passageway here,' Cora directed as she led the way.

She pressed the button and as they stood side by side in the lift she knew instinctively who the woman was.

She was pale and thin, but her eyes were bright with expectancy. She might even have been a reflection of herself with reddish-brown hair and startling blue eyes.

'Visiting a relative?' Cora ventured to enquire.

The woman nodded and seemed to have difficulty in suppressing a gasp of nervous tension. 'My husband, Bill Palmer, crushed his foot and has had to have it amputated.'

'He's made excellent progress and I'd say he's

just about ready to go home,' Cora said with a smile.

'He doesn't know, but I've come to do just that. I've recently had our third baby so I couldn't come before, but no one's going to look after my Bill but me.'

CHAPTER TEN

CORA smiled, and as the lift reached the surgical floor she allowed Mrs Palmer to go first.

There was a shout and as Cora emerged on the landing she saw Bill enclose his wife in a bear-like hug.

'Gee, honey, I was expecting someone else,' he said with fervour. 'Why didn't you say you were coming today? I've made a date with—'

'Your wife, Bill,' Cora interrupted with a knowing wink. 'We met on the way in.'

Bill kept his wife encircled in his arm as he hopped a step nearer to Cora.

'This, honey, is my favourite nurse in Bermuda, Cora Jordan. She's the only good thing I remember after the accident. Cora, this is Natalie—so, instead of one lovely girl to take out to dinner I've got two.'

'Not on your life, Bill,' Cora said. 'I'm delighted, Natalie, that you could come. I reckon you're due for a celebration dinner, just the two of you.'

'I don't like going back on my word, honey,' Bill began seriously.

'And I really wouldn't mind,' Natalie agreed. 'If Bill was taking you out I guess he had good reason.'

'It was my way of saying thanks,' Bill explained.

'But quite undeserved, Bill,' Cora said. 'After all, Mr Delaney and the others did more than anyone to help you.'

Bill grinned. 'But you're better looking, and you look like Nat here, so I owe you, kid.'

Cora shook her head. 'I wouldn't dream of intruding—' Why was she perpetually saying that? 'The taxi's ordered, the table for two, just make the most of it. Aren't the hospital accommodating you, Natalie?' Cora asked.

'No, though I guess they would have done. I wanted to surprise Bill, so his mates from the base made all the arrangements, and booked me in at the Skye Towers hotel.'

Bill laughed. 'Honey, you got here just in time. Now what would you have said if you'd seen me in the restaurant there with this girl?'

Natalie put her arm round Bill's waist.

'We're special aren't we? Haven't we got it together?'

Bill winked down at her. 'Sure have, honey, and I can't wait to see my new baby daughter.'

'You can, she's at the hotel. I'm feeding her myself so I couldn't leave her behind. Right now she's being guarded by a lovely brown nanny and you've got a week at the Skye Towers to get to know your daughter.'

'What are you calling her?' Cora asked as they stood in the lift and descended once more to ground level.

'Cora,' Bill answered promptly.

'Oh no, not that, it's too old-fashioned,' Cora protested.

'Well, I like it,' Natalie said, 'but I guess our other two will want some say, so Junior's going to end up with about six names.'

At the main entrance Cora went to look for the taxi and saw two, one behind the other at the kerbside: The first one moved off and like a magnet it drew her gaze as she recognised Darryl and Monique sitting together in the back. She wanted to wave, but her hand and arm were like a ton weight, and then the second taxi moved up to where they were standing and she found herself helping Bill in beside the driver which was easier for him.

'Have a marvellous time,' she called, but behind the smiling eyes her heart had crumpled into pieces.

Another taxi pulled in behind the one which took Bill and his wife away. Cora just had to sit down so she got in the back seat and when the driver asked her the destination she almost said 'Airport', instead she heard her own croaking voice say the first thing that came into her head which was: 'Palm Grove Gardens.'

She felt tears begin to prick at the back of her eyes so she opened her bag and took out her sunglasses. She had managed to keep up a good facade and if Natalie hadn't turned up she would right now be enjoying Bill's company. They were a nice couple. Cora knew that Bill would have been capable of helping her to forget Darryl, but now she was alone. Delighted for Bill and Natalie, but misery quickly overtook every other emotion.

The driver pulled in through the gates of a large private estate, and after some minutes stopped at some cages where parrots and other exotic tropical birds surveyed visitors with cool disdain.

The taxi driver made weird noises at the birds in an attempt to make them respond, but they weren't in the mood. He drove on to the main area of the gardens where they could view the luxurious white bungalow. Cora decided to pay him off.

'I can take you on a tour of the islands, Miss,' he offered politely.

'No, thanks, I shall be in Bermuda for a long time. I've got all the time I need to see everything. I can walk back from here.'

She paid the modest fare and walked along a pathway to a beautiful lily pond where the entire plan of the Bermuda islands had been mapped out even to name-tags of towns and places of interest.

The gardens were almost deserted, but the evening was balmy, the sun still shining brightly as Cora walked across the grass. Now she recalled Mandy's advice and knew where the idea of Palm Grove Gardens had come from. Here was the long tunnel of decorative stonework Chinese moongates, covered with fresh green living foliage. At the entrance she silently read the words engraved on the stone plaque: '*Honeymooners should walk through and make a wish: If you are not Honeymooning wish anyhow.*'

Only the romantic type would put any stock in such legends, but she strolled through, feeling a strange mystical power overtake her.

Fate had dealt her a last cruel blow in making her watch Darryl and Monique drive away from Zenobia's, but there was nothing to stop her wishing. At least she could go on dreaming impossible dreams.

How was she ever going to continue working in Casualty, knowing that Darryl would never come stalking across the floor in his officious way? No more would he taunt her about her incompetence, particularly as a moped rider.

She suddenly realised how heavy her head felt, and she began to sway, her legs seeming to crumble. She grabbed a piece of hanging ivy and clung on. This dark archway was claustrophobic so she turned to retrace her steps, but the darkness closed in on her, she was fighting for breath with an overwhelming heat searing her body. It caused her temples to throb and try as she would to hold on to that glimmer of light at the entrance to the tunnel she could bear it no longer, and as if her blood turned to water her knees buckled beneath her, and the light faded. She tried in desperation to clutch at the ivy but the moongates shrouded her and then, nothing . . .

She experienced strange sensations like being transported on a magic carpet, but when at last she opened her eyes she found she was in a strange bed, and the unfamiliar room was in semi-darkness.

Cora closed her eyes against the spinning sensation. Somewhere among the fuzziness in her brain she came to realise that she was really ill. She heard a man's voice softly giving instructions. 'Get her sponged down and into a loose garment. I'll write up something immediately. She's the worst case so far.'

Whispered voices were lost as the owners moved away. Never had her body ached so dreadfully before, or sweated so profusely. She was grateful for the solitude of the room; she wanted to sleep but troubled thoughts aggravated by a roaring temperature prevented her from doing so.

Darryl was lost to her forever. He had gone to Canada with Monique and she simply couldn't bear it. She loved, *adored* him and she would die thinking only of him, but she didn't seem to be able to force that issue, she just tossed and turned, fighting off anyone who came near her, especially the nurse who stripped her of her clothes.

A prick in her arm subdued her at last. She gave up the struggle, irrationally believing that life for her was finished.

She woke several times during what seemed to Cora a week rather than twenty-four hours. She felt hot and clammy, then as suddenly cold and sick. She was only allowed iced drinks and then, after a long deep sleep, she woke to see pale early morning sunlight seeping between the slats of the venetian blinds.

She pulled herself up as she caught sight of a white-coated figure disappearing through the door. She might almost have believed it was Darryl and then as she recalled his departure with Monique she felt totally despondent again. It wasn't all a bad dream, it was all for real.

Night Sister poked her head round the door minutes later.

'So, you're awake!' she said cheerfully. 'How do you feel today?'

'What's been the matter with me?' Cora asked, her mouth dry, her voice husky.

'Some unknown virus. Hit you pretty badly. Here, have a drink?'

The weak orange juice tasted refreshing and Cora lay back on the pillows, aware that she felt physically fragile as well as mentally unhappy.

Sister felt her forehead. 'That's more like it, the fever has lessened considerably. A few more days and you'll be right as ninepence.'

Cora didn't answer. How could she tell the people who were trying to help her that she didn't want to be as 'right as ninepence'. What did that cliché really mean anyway? Was she only worth ninepence? She wasn't even worth *that* much, she thought disconsolately. She didn't want to get better, but the night staff did their best to talk her out of her melancholy and by the time Dr Fraser came to see her mid-morning at least she was washed, clean and fresh in her own nightdress.

'So, young lady,' he greeted in his broad Scottish accent, 'you've decided to shake off that burning heat you were so anxious to torture yourself with.' He studied her temperature and pulse chart, then looked intently at her. 'Nothing to worry about, my dear lassie. We'll have you up and about in no time.'

Cora's lips and chin trembled. Oh, dear, she did hope she wasn't going to weep. It was such a childish thing to do, but she couldn't help herself, and she found she had no voice steady enough with which to hold a conversation.

Dr Fraser sat on the side of her bed and took her hand in his. 'Don't worry, Cora, you're still feeble from the fever, and the strong medication doesn't help either, but you know all about that as well as me.' He smiled suddenly, a big, fatherly comforting smile. 'Now, if it were an affair of the heart that was troubling you I couldn't promise that it would be so easy to cure. As it is you've not been alone, half the hospital staff have been affected to some degree. Maybe you were a wee bit run down, so you got your money's worth out of us.'

Cora tried to create a smile from somewhere, though certainly not from her heart, and finally tears won the battle and spilled from the corners of her eyes. The more she tried to blink them away the more blurred her vision became.

'A couple more days, lassie, and we'll have you on your feet,' he promised and with a tender pat round her cheek Dr Fraser went away with the home Sister.

Cora cried herself to sleep, a sleep which was full of torturous dreams. Darryl came to her, full of love and compassion and then he receded and the next dream was of him standing over her and accusing her all over again of being the cause of her accident.

Hallucinations, mirages, horrible dreams intermingled with more gentle and happy ones persisted throughout the next day and night, but the following morning Cora woke with a feeling of peace at last.

The third-year nurse who tended her was a sweet, good-natured girl but even she hinted at how concerned everyone had been for Cora.

'It was only a forty-eight hour bug for most of us. I'd already had it so it was safe for me to nurse you and the others,' she explained to Cora. 'I reckon it's on the way out now though. Sister thought you might like a bath today. Just a quick one and perhaps tomorrow a hair-do?'

Cora smiled. 'All the necessary things which should make me feel better,' she said flatly.

How could she expect them to understand? How could Dr Fraser ever know how right his words had been? All the medication, the best possible treatment could not make up for her broken heart, her shattered dreams.

She managed a light breakfast of fruit juice and fluffy scrambled eggs on toast, and two cups of tea. She felt so different. At last her heartache could be separated from her physical weakness and she was glad to chat to the domestic who was just finishing cleaning her room when Cora returned from the bathroom.

A nurse brought her a cup of coffee mid-morning, and later the home sister visited her again.

'Do you feel like responding to your visitors today, Cora?' she asked smiling in an unusually friendly way for her.

'You mean I've had some and ignored them?'

'You could say that,' Sister said. 'Your colleagues from Casualty have all been worried about you, but only those who'd had the bug were allowed closer inspection. Mandy and Tod have been in every day.'

'I suppose Mandy brought in all my things which I find mysteriously to hand,' Cora said, glancing towards the bedside locker.

'Yes, that's right. We didn't think you'd want to stay in a hospital gown for long, but it was for the best in the circumstances. It's good to see you looking better. Do you usually get such a high temperature when you're ill?'

'No, but then I'm seldom ill. Only the odd off day all through my training years. Why should this bug hit me more than most?'

'Perhaps you were a bit off colour when you picked it up—or something.' She smoothed the sheets. 'Now, have a rest until after lunch, and then you can get up for a bit, otherwise you'll get weaker.'

That was a hopeful sign, to be allowed up. It meant that her temperature was back to normal. She lay back and closed her eyes, savouring the smell of fresh linen, her clean nightdress and the tangy fragrance of her cologne. She was human again and it felt good, but her brain refused to allow her to forget that she had lost something of great value. It was true what people say about not realising the value of something until it had gone.

Perhaps, if she'd had the courage to tell Darryl how much she loved him—but, no, he didn't love her. Monique had won, and somewhere they were together . . .

She tried to think of other things. She must prepare herself for returning to work and in so doing she dozed.

Some minutes later she woke feeling the presence of someone close. She opened her eyes and at once believed she was hallucinating again. She put a hand to her head. 'Oh, no, it can't be back again.'

'Cora—do you really despise me so much?'

The voice was *his*! She blinked several times. It *was* Darryl Delaney—here—in the flesh.

'W . . . what are you doing here?' she murmured, still not certain if she were dreaming. He was standing close to her bedside and automatically her hand reached out to feel whether he was real. He took her hand and placed it to his lips.

'Darling, you're better at last,' he said. Cora was surprised at the relief in his tone. 'You must have picked up this wretched bug from Mandy—or Tod—and if it was Tod I want to know why,' he added reproachfully.

He was leaning over her, supporting her head and gazing fondly into her eyes. She wanted to touch his dark-tanned cheek, place a finger in the cleft of his chin, but she dared not so she closed her eyes. She *must* stop imagining things. His smile was warm and tender—a real smile—now she knew she was seeing things again. And as if he'd ever call *her* 'darling'! As if he could when he was en route for Canada.

'Are you so filled with guilt that you can't even face me?' he asked in an amused voice.

'Guilt?' She opened her eyes wide. There was no mistaking that it was Darryl Delaney and as usual ready to do battle over her moped again.

'If you picked up the bug from Tod,' he said, gently squeezing her neck.

'What difference would it make to you if I did?' she snapped irritably. 'As it happens Tod and I do work together, and I've been with Mandy as well, so who knows where I picked it up.'

'From both of them probably. You seem to have had a double dose of it.'

'How do you know anything about it and what are you doing here? You went to Canada with Monique.' Aggression was the only safe avenue to take.

'I did?' There was that mischievous familiarity in his voice she loved to hear. 'Pinch me and see if I'm real,' he suggested.

She closed her eyes. No, she would not be party to his frivolity. He was just here to encourage her to surface again. Now, she'd have to go through all the heartache once more. If she kept quiet with her eyes closed he'd go away and she would believe it was all in her mind. It wouldn't be difficult to do, she'd been so confused over the last few days.

She felt his warm breath fanning her lids and then his lips on her forehead in a lingering kiss.

'Wake up, darling,' he said, 'and face the world. It can't be as bad as you think.' She heard him chuckling light-heartedly. 'That must be some wish you made in Palm Grove Gardens.'

'How did you know I was there?'

'Because I found you there.' He sighed and, taking her hands in his, sat on the bed. 'I . . . I realise it must have been upsetting for you to find that Bill's wife had arrived, but I had warned you.'

'There was nothing between me and Bill,' she put in quickly.

Darryl raised his eyebrows in doubt. 'We'll leave that open to question—on his side anyway—unless the man's a fool. However, I decided that it was a pity to waste a good dinner date. Fortunately most of the taxi drivers are radio controlled so it wasn't difficult to trace where Kenneth had taken you.'

There was a long silence while Cora pondered over this, then she said: 'But you went to the airport. You've left Zenobia's. You've taken a consultant's post in Canada.'

Darryl stood up and walked round the bed. He paced up and down before coming to her bedside again.

'Who fed you so much useless information?' he demanded fiercely.

'Monique,' she said softly, 'and your mother seemed so dreadfully upset about you leaving.'

He splayed his hands in a negative gesture. 'I never intended to distress Mother, but I felt I had done my duty by coming to Zenobia's for a year to please my parents. It's only natural that I should have the ambition to become a consultant eventually. Monique happened to have contacts in Montreal. She made it sound very attractive, though I can see now that it was a way of getting me away from my parents' influence, and subsequently to the altar.'

'Isn't that what you wanted?' Cora asked softly.

He took her hand and smoothed it as he considered this carefully. His fingertips caressing the inside of her forearm sent the blood tingling through her veins. He smiled fondly at Cora as he went on: 'Mother didn't like Monique. I thought she was being selfish, that she was opposed to me having a life of my own. Mothers are possessive, Cora. More so over sons, especially the last of a big family. I suppose I felt I owed something to Monique for arranging the interview in Montreal. I was supposed to have flown over with her but when the time came—I mean—well, to be truthful from the moment you arrived here, Canada lost its appeal.'

He bent forward and kissed her cheek. 'I don't suppose I stand much chance, you have so many to choose from. At least Steve's out of the way and Bill will soon be going home, but there's still Neil?'

Darryl looked into her face steadily.

'I know I must have seemed pretty ruthless to you when you first arrived, but I was so worried about you after you fell off that darned moped. Then when you returned here to work all I could remember was the angelic look you had when you were unconscious. This crazy notion came to me then that I'd like to kiss you awake—and I've retained that crazy notion ever since. Do we have to waste any more time?'

His mouth came tantalisingly close to hers but at the last moment Cora turned her head aside.

'If I kiss you,' she whispered, 'I'm afraid you might change into a tree-frog.'

'Try me,' he urged wickedly, 'it might be a change for the better.'

She draped her long, bare arms around his neck and matched her lips to his. It was bliss. Could it last? Was she even at this moment dreaming?

'You gave up the chance of a good job in Canada for me?' Her brain was beginning to sort out the things he'd said.

Darryl nodded as he held her close against his chest.

'Because I love you, darling. We'll go back to

Palm Grove Gardens and walk through the moon-gate as honeymooners, just as soon as it can be arranged. There's just one thing—promise me you'll never ride a moped again?'

Cora held him tightly. Why would there ever be the need to ride a moped when she was to have her own Latin-American lover to transport her to wherever Fate took them?

'Darn you,' she teased, 'why should I promise you anything?' Then with genuine fondness in her eyes she whispered: 'People who love each other don't need to make promises, and I do love you, Darryl, oh, so much!'

He clutched at her shoulders, sending the narrow straps of her flimsy nightdress sliding down her arms, exposing most of the top half of her body. Through his thin shirt she could feel the pounding of his heartbeats and the warmth of his strong, masculine body.

'I shouldn't be doing this,' he murmured. 'You're ill, darling. We have to do tests—'

'I was only ever sick with love, and longing for you,' she admitted, and she showed him how much better she was by the passion in her kiss. 'But how did I get here, and,' she looked down at herself, 'who?'

'Mandy and Home Sister put you to bed. You refused to co-operate, or even wake up properly. Maybe you hadn't become completely acclimatised to Bermuda's invigorating atmosphere. You seemed thoroughly exhausted and yet any attempt to comfort you, by me, was met with forceful opposition.'

Cora smiled, but tears were never far away. Tears of relief, tears of joy but Darryl willingly kissed them away.

Two months later they stood together at the altar in Hamilton Cathedral, impatient to pledge their love and make their solemn vows.

Huge lilies adorned the church, but Cora refused to have them in her bouquet.

'You and your superstitions,' Darryl had teased. 'No lilies because they're bad luck, and no one in their right mind, certainly not doctor and nurse, would put red and white together.' he mimicked, so to complement her white satin gown which was trimmed with exquisite lace Cora carried a white Bible, a present from Darryl, with a simple spray of yellow jasmine and miniature white rosebuds.

To the sound of bells and the cries of well-wishers their shiny limousine drew away from the Cathedral, but not to go immediately to the Delaney home where the reception was to be held.

Only the driver and the newly-weds knew where the first port of call was to be.

Cora held up her billowing skirt and Darryl helped her out of the car to walk across the lush green grass in Palm Grove Gardens, and then with arms entwined they walked through the moongates where each made their silent wish, and then Darryl swung her round and, cupping her face in his hands, his mouth sought hers, sealing their wishes and hopes with the promise of eternal love.

Doctor Nurse Romances

Amongst the intense emotional pressures of modern medical life, doctors and nurses often find romance. Read about their lives and loves in the other three Doctor Nurse titles available this month.

YESTERDAY'S LOVE
by Judith Worthy

Kym Rutherford returns to nurse at St Alphages after seven years' absence to find that the old hospital has been replaced by a gleaming modern building. But nothing can demolish her memories...

NURSE BRYONY
by Rhona Trezise

'I've heard the doctor in charge is a tyrant...' Nurse Bryony Sellers remarks to a handsome stranger. But soon after starting work at the Highfields Nursing Home in Cornwall she finds herself wishing she had never been so indiscreet!

THE FAITHFUL FAILURE
by Kate Norway

Final exams are always an ordeal for the nurses at Middleton Royal, and for Annabel Lake exam tension is not helped by her unhappy love life. Antagonising the new surgeon Simon Dell just about confirms her uncertain future.

Mills & Boon
the rose of romance

A very special gift for Mother's Day

You love Mills & Boon romances. Your mother will love this attractive Mother's Day gift pack. First time in paperback, four superb romances by leading authors. A very special gift for Mother's Day.

United Kingdom £4.40   On sale from 24th Feb 1984

A Grand Illusion   **Sensual Encounter**
Maura McGiveny   Carole Mortimer

Desire in the Desert   **Aquamarine**
Mary Lyons   Madeleine Ker

Look for this gift pack where you buy
Mills & Boon romances.

NEW DO

'*I know exactly what the man must be like—old, pompous, ugly and hidebound.*' With these words Dr Carla Scott is definitely tempting fate, for her new boss Lincoln Falconer is none of these things . . .

NEW DOCTOR AT THE BORONIA

BY
LILIAN DARCY

MILLS & BOON LIMITED
London · Sydney · Toronto

First published in Great Britain 1983
by Mills & Boon Limited, 15–16 Brook's Mews,
London W1A 1DR

ISBN 0 263 74478 7

Set in 10 on 12pt Linotron Times
03/1183

Photoset by Rowland Phototypesetting Ltd
Bury St Edmunds, Suffolk
Made and printed in Great Britain by
Richard Clay (The Chaucer Press) Ltd
Bungay, Suffolk

CHAPTER ONE

'WE'RE going to take you on.' The rather portly middle-aged superintendent of the Boronia Women's Hospital sat back in his chair and took a long look at the young woman seated opposite. He liked what he saw.

Carla Scott was of medium height and slender build, and could almost have appeared gangling but for the fact that she held herself with the poise and grace of a classical dancer. Her hair was a rich brown threaded with coppery lights, and it strengthened the unusual velvet green of her eyes so that in some lights they appeared to be a deep sea-blue. Her skin, too, was beautiful in tone and texture, being creamy and soft without the addition of heavy disguising make-up.

If it wasn't for her too-large mouth, Dr Peter Martin thought, young Dr Scott would be something of a beauty. He wondered what Falconer would make of her . . .

'When will I be able to start?' she was saying.

'Oh . . . er . . . next week.' The superintendent recalled his thoughts quickly and became strictly business-like once more. 'You see, we were caught rather short. Someone left sooner than planned – found that after all his years of training he couldn't actually stick the work!—and we had to find a replacement in a hurry. Is next week all right?'

'It's marvellous,' Carla assured him eagerly. 'I was getting very depressed about not finding anything.'

'Good. I like to hear that sort of enthusiasm, and I think you'll find our Obstetrical wing a pleasant place to be in.'

Dr Martin paused and thought again. Was this last an entirely accurate statement? He recalled Dr Lincoln Falconer's less than enthusiastic reception of the news that Carla Scott, newly qualified at the Granville University Medical School, had been the successful applicant for the internship. Perhaps it might be only fair to warn her that there could be a few problems.

He coughed a little, shifted in his seat, which creaked momentarily under his weight, then groped for words.

'There's just one thing,' he said. 'Your senior obstetrician, Dr Lincoln Falconer. He's a very good man, a brilliant man, actually, but he's strangely old-fashioned in some ways, very down on certain new trends in the profession, and he won't make it easy for you if he decides that you are not up to scratch. You might find that he—how can I phrase it?—puts you on trial a little at first, but he's not a man to hold on to prejudices once he finds that they are unjustified.'

'I see.'

'And I'm sure that in your case he will find they *are* unjustified,' Peter Martin added gallantly, sitting back in his chair. There! he thought. That was done. Nothing too specific or strongly worded. After all, he didn't want Dr Scott to feel frightened of Falconer. Just a little hint, though, so that if there *was* something in Falconer's idea that a Granville graduate would be rather slack and hazy on facts, Dr Scott would have a chance to pull up her socks straight away.

'I certainly hope so,' Carla had said, smiling in response to his words, but inwardly she was suddenly full of misgivings, and some anger too. Dr Martin was called to his outer office at that moment, leaving Carla to mull over what he had just told her.

She might find that Dr Falconer was prejudiced against her, he had said. A good obstetrician, but strangely old-fashioned. Archaic, more likely, she thought, her anger growing. To think that, in this day and age, an intelligent and responsible man should still be opposed to women doctors!—at least, she assumed that that had been the meaning of Dr Martin's rather clumsy and inadequate warning. Had Lincoln Falconer never worked with a woman before? Perhaps he thought that women should do nothing but have babies, so that he could line his pockets with fat consultation fees. He probably didn't care a bit about his patients as people. He sounded like the kind of man who had come across one woman doctor who was not a paragon, and had dismissed the entire sex accordingly.

Whatever the case, Carla determined there and then that Dr Falconer's prejudice would not survive for very much longer.

'I know *exactly* what the man must be like!' she said to her Granville friend and flat-mate Sally Lewis on her return from Sydney that evening. 'Dr Lincoln Falconer: old, pompous, ugly and hide-bound. I suppose that technically he must be a good doctor, since he's done so well, and Dr Martin seems to think a lot of him . . .'

'And I've seen his articles published all over the place,' put in Sally.

'Yes, so have I, now I come to think of it,' Carla nodded. 'But I'm willing to bet that he has very little feeling for his patients, and I'm sure the atmosphere on the wards can't be a happy one when he's around!'

'How old is he, anyway?' Sally asked.

'Oh, fifties I should think from the sound of it,' Carla said. 'Late fifties. Perhaps early sixties, even. Dr Martin didn't actually say. I'm sure he's hideous to look at. I *hope* he is! I do hate him already. I'm determined that he is going to respect me, though.'

'He will,' Sally said soberly. 'You'll make a good doctor, Carla. But it was rather unfair of Dr Martin to tell you what you would be up against with Dr Falconer, don't you think? You'll get all jittery before you've even started.'

'No, I'm glad that he did,' Carla replied, 'Because now I'm prepared, and I know I'll have to work extra hard. Although I would have anyway, of course.'

'But don't you think there's a danger that you are building up too much of a vendetta against him before you've even met him?'

Carla looked at Sally suddenly from her position in the middle of the small sitting-room around which she had been pacing restlessly as she spoke.

'Yes, perhaps you're right. Still, I start next Monday, so I only have five days to wait before I find out if my judgment is correct.'

'Next Monday! As soon as that!'

'Yes, apparently someone left rather suddenly.'

'Hmm, I wonder if that had anything to do with our horrible Dr Falconer!'

'I didn't think of that, but it's possible, isn't it?' Carla mused.

'Oh dear, we're painting him blacker every minute. Perhaps we had better stop. After all, he's a distinguished specialist . . .'

'Which we may be ourselves one day,' countered

Carla. 'Yet that won't turn us miraculously into perfect human beings. No, I think I'm right to distrust Dr Falconer, even though I haven't met him. He has some prejudice against women doctors, and whatever medical skills and personal charms the man may have, nothing can alter the fact that I believe such a prejudice is wrong.'

'Hear, hear! A capital speech!' Sally exclaimed with mock heartiness. 'Now get down off your soap-box and help me with this renal assignment, as you promised to do.'

They settled down to an hour of solid work on the difficult final-year assignment, and then Carla went to bed, leaving Sally still poring over her text-books and notes.

The two girls had been sharing their flat, the lower half of a divided house in one of the quiet tree-lined streets of the coastal town of Granville, for over two years. They got on well together, and the sharing arrangement had not broken up their friendship, as many of their acquaintances had confidently expected it would.

But the little partnership was about to end. Granville was several hours by car from Sydney, and both Sally and Carla would be far too busy this year, one with the grind of her final year of study, the other with her first real job, to make the journey often.

Carla lay in bed that night unable to sleep for a long time as she thought of these things. Her five years at Granville University had been very happy ones. Straight out of school, it had been difficult yet challenging to move away from her home in far-off Perth in order to start her long medical training. The course at Granville was completely new and very different, and she was among the very first batch of students to go through it.

The Granville approach to the study of medicine was unlike anything offered by other medical faculties. To begin with, students were chosen not purely on the strength of their examination results at school, but far more on their fitness to be doctors, assessed through interviews and discussion with the staff of the faculty.

During the course of study itself, students came into contact with patients as early and as often as possible, and it was hoped that it would be this contact which would stimulate their desire to learn, rather than just the fear of stiff examinations looming at the end of each year. Carla had loved the course from start to finish, and had done consistently well in each assignment and project that she had tackled, but she had found herself constantly forced to defend the new course against criticism from outsiders.

'Granville Faculty of Medicine?' someone might say with the hint of a sneer. 'A new course, isn't it? One of those hippy sort of things where you learn all about how to love and care for your patients, and not much about how to actually cure them.'

'It isn't like that at all!' Carla would protest hotly, too sensitive to this criticism to realise that sometimes her tormentors were deliberately taking the role of Devil's Advocate. 'Of course we learn about medicine and disease. Of course we are properly assessed. Do you really think that our professors would be irresponsible enough to let us loose in a hospital without the necessary knowledge? Not to mention the fact that they are distinguished doctors in their own right, every one of them. Some have put their careers on the line by becoming involved in teaching this course, and they would do almost anything to make sure that its graduates succeed.'

Sometimes the critics would then laugh, nod agreement and close the discussion, but sometimes they would keep on for what seemed like hours, asking Carla to explain every little detail of course procedure and assessment until she was heartily sick of the subject. But no-one had succeeded in shaking her belief—her *certainty*!—that she was being well-trained, and she felt confident that she would make a good doctor.

During her last term of study she had begun, along with most others, to apply for internships at various hospitals all over the country, and like her fellows, she had become gradually very disillusioned and rather bitter. It seemed that most people in the medical profession were hanging back, waiting to let other hospitals try out these strange new doctors before they committed themselves to taking one on.

By February Carla, along with many others, had still found nothing, and today's interview with kind yet shrewd Dr Martin had seemed like a miracle. To have found something at last, to be starting so soon, and to be spending her first three months in Obstetrics, an area which had especially interested her all along!

It seemed as though the only fly in the ointment would be Dr Lincoln Falconer, with his 'old-fashioned' prejudice. Carla sketched out a quick scenario of the future, imagining how she would become part of the work so rapidly, and be so accurate in her diagnoses and so popular with her patients, that in a few short weeks the odious Dr Falconer would be eating out of her hand, a changed man.

She knew that the fantasy was childish, but somehow she needed it. There was something about Dr Lincoln Falconer. Was it the name? Was it what she had heard about him? He would simply not get out of her mind.

The next three days were spent in packing, organising and making farewell visits and calls. She had spent five years in Granville, five very formative and important years at that, and it was not going to be easy to leave. She intended to return for holidays, of course, at least as often as she made the long journey to Perth to see her parents and older sister Margaret, but it would not be the same as living here.

To Sally she bestowed, on an indefinite loan, almost all of her household equipment, as she would be living in at the hospital. Nevertheless, there still seemed to be a huge quantity of possessions to transport to her new home, in the tiny second-hand Fiat that her parents had given her for a twenty-first birthday present two years before.

She left the little flat on Sunday morning, giving warm wishes to Lisa, the third-year medical student who was to take over her room immediately, and bidding an almost tearful farewell to Sally. This was the start of a journey which marked, as Carla realised, a huge and permanent change in her life.

For such a symbolic journey, it was completely uneventful, and she arrived mid-afternoon at the hospital, scarcely fatigued. It was the first time she had been able to take stock of the surroundings which would soon become familiar to her, as during her interview, nervousness had relegated them to a blur in the background.

The buildings were modern, tastefully designed and

built in an earthy brown brick that echoed the burnished colours of the Australian landscape. The grounds had been designed with equal care. There were sweeps of tranquil lawn and belts of trees, both Australian species and introduced varieties, that provided a muffler against the harsh disturbing sounds of the busy city.

Staff were accommodated in a cluster of three-storey dwellings, grouped around two tennis courts and a sizeable swimming pool, which in the heat of a February afternoon looked very inviting as Carla stepped from her stuffy car and began to unload the first of her suitcases and boxes.

She had obtained her room key earlier in the week and was able to find Number 314 with no difficulty. It was on the first floor, more private than the ground floor, yet not such a climb up as the second, and her large window commanded a tranquil view of trees and shrubs sloping down to the still-beautiful Jackson's River, which cut its swathe of rocks, greenery and water through the sprawling suburbs of this part of the city.

'You look a little loaded up there,' a pleasant, if rather broadly-accented, Australian voice spoke behind her as she struggled with her second cargo of luggage. 'Can I help?'

Carla turned to meet the frankly interested gaze of a lean and attractive young man, who had obviously been on his way to the pool before seeing her plight, judging from the towel slung across his shoulder and the stylish swimming costume he wore, topped only by a white T-shirt.

'You can, actually,' she said, relieved, allowing him to take the heavy cardboard carton that was balanced precariously on top of its twin. 'I've been a bit overambitious with this load, because I'm so anxious to get everything unpacked . . .'

'So that you can get into the luscious blue of our pool?'

'Right,' she laughed.

'I'll keep on helping you then, and it'll be done in half the time,' the slightly freckled stranger offered.

'Oh, I couldn't let you. There will be at least two more trips even with two of us, and you must be anxious for your swim as much as I am.'

'I can wait,' he said. 'I'll enjoy it more with you to keep me company, in any case. I'm Michael Groom, by the way. Anaesthetist.'

'And I'm . . .'

'Dr Carla Scott,' he finished for her.

'How on earth did you know?' she asked.

'Elementary, my dear Scott. I knew that a certain Dr Scott was starting work in the Obstets. wing tomorrow, I read the titles of the books at the top of this carton— *Diagnostic Indices in Pregnancy*, *Practical Obstetric Problems*, *Medical Care of Newborn Babies* – and I realised that you must be she.'

'I'm impressed.'

'And I must confess I had also had your appearance roughly sketched out to me.'

'Oh really? How is that?'

'Well, you must know what a hospital is like for gossip and news-swapping. One or two people noticed you when you came for your interview, that's all. But may I say that their descriptions of you did not do you justice?' he said with half-teasing, half-serious gallantry.

'Perhaps you may say that,' she returned, 'But not quite yet.'

They made the two remaining trips quickly and

painlessly, chatting easily the whole while, then Michael left Carla to find her swimming costume and beach towel amongst the suitcases and boxes of clothing, saying he would see her down at the pool side.

Carla admitted to herself straight away that she was flattered at his attention, and was looking forward to the swim. Michael was tanned as well as freckled, and his rather untidy sun-bleached hair gave him a boyish air that was far from unattractive. Suddenly she found that she was really relishing the prospect of meeting new people of both sexes, people who were perhaps older, too, than she had been accustomed to spending time with.

Her friendships at Granville University had been satisfying and fun, of course, but in a sense they had been confined to university affairs. In addition, of course, there had been study to occupy her time, and she had passed weeks at a stretch without going out in the evenings at all. Yes, it might be very satisfying to be here in busy Sydney, to be part of the real, vital world of the hospital, with its drama, its poignancy, and even, perhaps, its romance.

Carla lounged by the pool for an hour, amused and entertained by Michael's continuous flow of information, gossip, teasing and banter, and gathered her bathing things very reluctantly when thoughts of her chaotic room finally nagged her into action.

'I'll have to go and sort out my things,' she told Michael. 'I'll feel I've got off to a bad start if I leave it any longer.'

'I might see you at dinner then?' he said, glancing not for the first time at her streamlined slate-blue one-piece costume with its stylish cut and thin neck fastening.

'Yes, perhaps.' Carla left the poolside, and on turning to smile again at Michael when she reached the entrance to her building, she saw that he was already involved in conversation with two young student nurses. They had been dangling their legs in the water at the far end of the pool before he came, talking to each other in giggles and exclamations, but they were happy to turn their attention to him now. The boyish-faced anaesthetist was obviously a bit of a flirt, but he was nice, and pleasant to be with, and Carla knew that she was looking forward to seeing him again.

She settled down with renewed vigour to the task of arranging her room, getting to know it well as she did so. It was quite large, and would have been rectangular but for the tiny private bathroom which occupied one corner. The built in furnishings were of well-finished wood, and the curtains and coverings were a cool dark mulberry. In short, all tastefully done, and she was glad of it, feeling that she was far more likely to be happy here than if she had had to come back to an ugly room each day.

Carla suddenly thought of Lincoln Falconer. She might well need a cheerful room to come home to if what she imagined about the senior obstetrician was true. She had been too busily involved in the task of moving to give much thought to him since the evening of her discussion with Sally, but now she began to wonder about him again, her curiosity heightened by the knowledge that she would be meeting him at last tomorrow.

Or perhaps even tonight at dinner? But no, of course not. He would certainly not live in, and would rarely eat in the dining room, hurrying home as often as possible in order to eat whatever meal his wife had prepared, and to see his children.

Carla's mental image of him grew clearer every minute: Tall, perhaps, but pompously so, balding and slightly overweight, although he would work hard to keep in trim. He would be a dutiful husband and father, but scarcely capable of much demonstrative affection. And at work, too, he would command a certain grudging respect and admiration, but certainly not love.

Really, I ought to be a novelist, creating such a full character out of the little I know about him! Carla thought.

She did not, after all, meet Michael at the meal. She had gone down on the dot of six-thirty, and did not stay long, and it seemed that he preferred eating at a later hour. But she chatted briefly to a fellow intern, Craig Symons, who had started work a month earlier in the gynaecological wing, and felt sure it would not be long before she was an old hand, smiling or talking to almost everyone.

At one especially well laid out table, Carla saw a small group of senior-looking physicians and surgeons, none of whom were under forty, but if one of them was the unpleasant Dr Falconer, she had no idea which.

After the meal she was content to sit and read in the small quiet lounge which served all the residents on her floor, and it was only a few minutes before the hour she had planned to go to bed that Michael Groom found her again.

'So here you are!' he said, as though he had been searching for her a good while. He sat down beside her and she closed her book with a smile.

'Yes. Why? Did you think I would have gone out on the town for my first night in Sydney?'

'No, I thought you'd be already asleep in preparation for your first taste of real medicine tomorrow.'

'Will it be that bad?'

'It won't be bad at all. Unless someone high up takes a dislike to your work, and there's no reason why they should. Falconer's your senior, isn't he?'

'Yes, so I'm told. And I've been warned about him too, by Dr Martin,' Carla said, wanting to find out more about the man, but reluctant to ask directly.

'Warned?' Michael's brow creased, then cleared. 'That's dear old Martin's idea of gallantry. He's a good sort. He's afraid you won't be able to stand up to the old man when he's in a temper, and wants to prepare you in advance.'

'Oh he has a temper, does he?'

'I'm afraid so. He's arrogant as hell, and he cares about his work, and the result is that he doesn't tolerate other people's mistakes easily. Or opinions that differ from his own.'

'I can't imagine that we're going to get on,' Carla said with a slight grimace.

Michael Groom flashed her a quick guarded glance.

'You might. You'd be surprised. He's . . . No, I won't tell you anything more, it's unfair.'

'Do *you* like him?'

'Like him? I don't know. That's the wrong word, really. I admire certain things about him, and I suppose I'm jealous of his success in his work . . . and in other things. Perhaps that's why I can't say honestly that I like him. Anyway, I must be off. I'm working at eleven. I'll see you tomorrow and you can tell me how it all went.'

'I will,' she smiled, and the anaesthetist bounced

jauntily away, leaving Carla to think over what she had learnt about Lincoln Falconer.

Basically, Michael's words had confirmed her own imagined character sketch of the senior obstetrician in an almost uncanny way. Michael had called him 'the old man', had said he was arrogant and possessed a temper, and had not seemed surprised that Dr Martin had thought fit to warn her about him. Probably the doctor's prejudice against women doctors was well known around the hospital.

There was a strange satisfaction in the knowledge that Carla's antipathy would almost certainly turn out to be well-founded, although at the same time, she had misgivings. Her first work as a doctor! She could not afford to be handicapped by personal tensions. Drat Dr Lincoln Falconer. If he was causing her this much worry already, what would it be like when she actually met him?

Carla had been told to be in his waiting room at nine on Monday morning, so in order to leave nothing to chance, she left her room at a quarter to, wearing a cool but smart floral cotton dress and carrying the white coat which would soon cover it.

But she found her way with ease and was obviously going to arrive early. Still, that would by no means create a bad impression. The lift was already waiting when she walked into the main wing of the hospital, and she saw as she entered that it had been kept open by the touch of a button from someone already inside.

He turned away from the lift controls as Carla entered and thanked him briefly for holding the lift, and she gasped unwillingly as she saw his face. It was his proximity, perhaps, for the lift was not large and it seemed almost to be filled by the presence of this tall distinguished stranger whom Carla would have had no hesitation in describing as one of the most dynamically attractive men she had ever seen.

'Which floor?' he asked in a richly timbred voice of unmistakably English origin.

'Fifth, please.' Her own reply came out unusually highly pitched, and she coughed, suddenly full of an absurd confusion.

The stranger carried flowers—roses—that hid his hands with their riot of green leaves and crimson petals. He was obviously a new father, going to visit his wife in the Mothers and Babies ward on the fourth floor, Carla thought, surprised and rather shocked at the sudden pang of envy she felt for the unknown woman who would soon have this lordly man bending over her with a tender word and eyes of love.

Thus far, Carla's life had been a fairly serious one, full of a real dedication to her study that left little time for idle dreaming. But she had had her dreams, nevertheless, as everyone has, and one of them was a dream of romance, and of a man to love and be loved by.

And it was uncanny how closely this stranger, standing so near, corresponded to the shadowy figure that she had always pictured. He was a little older, perhaps, being, she guessed, somewhere in his late thirties, but his bearing, his voice, his grey-green eyes that contained the strong hint of a dry sense of humour, and the turbulent yet well cared for thatch of bronze-brown hair—these things actually seemed familiar, although now that she had seen them in the flesh, her dream image had already faded completely.

They did not speak again, nor catch each other's eye, for after all, the lift journey was a short one, and there was nothing for two strangers to say, but Carla was rather deliciously conscious of the nearness of one sleeve of his expensively-tailored navy blue suit to her own bare arm.

Good heavens, she thought, I am being dreadful, and she quickly imagined out one line of a letter to Sally.

'On my very first morning at the hospital I met the man of my dreams—but he got out at the fourth floor!'

Because she hardly felt that there was any danger in feeling like this. It was even more fleeting than a passing passion for some film star. He would get out at the fourth floor, she would go on to the fifth, and she might see him at most once or twice more, if the hour for visting his wife and child happened to coincide with her own pro-gression around the ward picking up stray pearls of wisdom in the wake of the pompous Dr Falconer as he did his rounds . . .

Actually, however, her one-minute Prince Charming did not get out at the fourth floor, but followed Carla out of the lift at the fifth. In that case, he was probably one of the less relaxed new fathers, and was on his way to give thanks and congratulations, or make a complaint, to one of the staff who had been responsible for his wife's delivery.

He did seem a little tense, Carla thought, listening rather uncomfortably to his footsteps echoing crisply and perhaps impatiently behind her. She could hear the faint swish and rustle of the beautiful roses, too, and was a little surprised that he had not at least popped in to see his no doubt radiant wife before his appointment, whatever it was.

The corridor was long: Carla was passing Room 20, Room 19, and Dr Falconer's office and waiting room were Rooms 4 and 4a. She began to wish that the too-handsome stranger behind her would find whichever room he was looking for and turn off, or overtake her and pass on to the far end of the corridor. She was suddenly apprehensive about meeting Dr Falconer, and would have liked to have been alone in this bright clean sweep of passage, in order to have a few moments to compose herself.

She began to have the uneasy feeling that of late she had allowed her vivid imagination too much rein. Her image of Lincoln Falconer, her pictures of the work she would be doing—perhaps these would interfere with the reality and make it more difficult to adjust.

At last she reached Room 4a. The stranger was still behind her but would now move on and out of her life, unless—horrible thought—he was actually waiting to see Dr Falconer as well! Then they would have to stare uncomfortably across the magazine table at each other until the senior obstetrician put in an appearance.

And in fact the man did turn in behind Carla. There was no receptionist at the desk in the little waiting room. Perhaps it was up to Carla to make the stranger feel at home. If he was a nervous father . . .

She turned to him, trying to appear cool and experienced.

'Can I help you?'

'No,' he replied with a dry smile. 'But I think I can

help you, if you are Carla Scott, and I assume you must be. Welcome to the Boronia, Dr Scott, I am Lincoln Falconer.'

CHAPTER TWO

CARLA gasped. This could not be true! He sensed her disbelief, and said, again drily:

'You seem surprised. Why? Am I so unlike you imagined?'

'Yes.' Carla was still too startled to be anything but blunt. 'I mean, when Dr Martin warn . . . told me that—' she stopped abruptly and looked away, realising that it would be disastrous to go on.

'Yes?'

It was a cool question, and he was very much in control, almost as if he had known what she was going to say. Perhaps he knew of his reputation as a woman hater—or, at least, a woman-doctor hater. Perhaps he knew that Carla would have been warned and was unperturbed by it.

Suddenly a whole lot of things fell into place. Just because the man was attractive didn't mean he was any less prejudiced and arrogant than she had supposed when she had pictured him twenty years older and two hundred percent uglier! Indeed, it was all too likely that a man with his looks, his manner, voice and bearing, would think he had even more right to feel superior to the rest of the human race. Michael Groom's reluctant confessions of admiration and envy made more sense now too.

Oh yes, Carla's original instinct to want to prove herself to this man while at the same time disliking him was going to be right after all, as long as she could manage to dislike the physical manifestation of her ideal!

She turned to him again. He was still obviously waiting for her to answer his questioning 'yes', although he was busy arranging the lovely roses in a vase on his secretary's desk.

'Mrs Fitton's birthday present,' he explained, catching Carla's glance at the flowers.

But his manner still communicated the fact that he wanted an explanation of her stumbled words.

'Dr Martin told me that you . . . er . . . had very high standards,' she said at last, lamely. 'I hope I'll be able to live up to them, and I'm looking forward to working with you very much.'

'Do you know, somehow I don't think you are telling the whole truth there,' was his cool reply. 'But I'll let it go at that. Come into my office.'

She followed his lead, heart racing. He had seemed to be precisely aware of her feelings for him—her dislike, that is. Heaven help her if he ever guessed that her first impression had been one of enormous attraction! And yet this dislike did not seem to ruffle him in the slightest. Carla suddenly wondered if his antipathy towards women extended to include most of the other sex as well. If he was, in short, a bit of a lone wolf.

As she sat down in the chair he had indicated, she looked about quickly for photos of wife and children, but could see none. Perhaps his cool dry tone indicated a cold, unloving and even frigid disposition. But she dismissed the idea at once. She had already seen something in those grey-green eyes, even in her brief acquaintance with them, and in the interesting lines that had begun to crease his mature face, that hinted at a warm and even passionate temperament, not suppressed, but carefully controlled.

'I'm going to throw you in at the deep end,' Dr Falconer said without preamble. 'My morning round starts in fifteen minutes, and I want you to come with me. We probably won't stop the whole morning, and there are some rather difficult problems in Ward B. I'd like to see what you make of them.'

He had opened a drawer and pulled out a sheaf of papers as he spoke, and now put on a pair of reading glasses over which he suddenly gave her a glance of penetrating assessment, which momentarily robbed her of the power of speech.

'I'm sure I shall enjoy it very much,' she said at last.

'And I'm sure you shan't,' Dr Falconer replied at once. 'No-one ever does. It's quite natural to be nervous, and I doubt that you'll be the exception.' Again his tone was so dry that it was impossible to tell exactly what he was feeling as he pronounced the words, and his glasses hid the eyes that might have given her a further clue to his mood.

So there was just a chance that there had been an obscure humour in what he had said, but Carla found she was angry all the same. Was his manner designed to be some kind of test of her toughness? Did he want her to cry, or something, in order to prove whatever theory he had about the unfitness of women doctors? She did not know, and was becoming more confused by her response to him every minute.

'You forget,' she said now, reddening but with the confidence borne of anger, 'that as a graduate of the Granville Faculty, I have had quite a deal of real hospital experience already, far more than the average new intern, and I can assure you that I am not going to fall about in hysterics or diagnose appendicitis instead of . . . of eclampsia, as you seem to expect!'

'Ah, yes, a graduate of Granville,' he murmured as her defiant speech ended. 'So you too feel that you are likely to be different to a graduate of, let us say, Sydney or Melbourne?'

'Yes I do. Different and better, despite the terrible handicap of being a woman,' she retorted with heavy sarcasm.

'I wonder why you say that,' he said, still speaking softly, and pronouncing each word with the perfect clarity of a well-bred Englishman.

'I say it because it seems that you have quite a prejudice against women doctors.'

'You've observed that already, have you?'

Carla could not believe it. He still seemed completely unruffled by her words, and was leading her deeper and deeper into rash replies—replies that she would never before have believed she could be making to a stranger, an older person, and someone who was, moreover, in a position of seniority to her in work.

'Please can we stop this?' she said.

'Yes, I think we should,' was his polite reply. 'We have far too much to get through to be wasting time on this sort of argument. Take this, and look over it thoroughly as soon as you have time.'

He pushed a set of typed and roneo-duplicated notes towards her, and she picked them up.

'We had it made up a year or two ago to give to all our interns. It just maps out this hospital's particular routine, and gives you a guide to your part in it: what is the best time to take Path. tests, where to send them, and with what accompanying data—that sort of thing.'

'Oh good!' Carla exclaimed. 'Because those were the things I was unsure about, although at Granville we . . .'

'Yes, I'm sure you did,' he interrupted, and again his expression was so dry that Carla found it impossible to pinpoint a smile.

He seemed determined to continue their relationship on the bad footing upon which it had begun, but perhaps all doctors were like this, and it was merely the reality of hospital hierarchy, for which the less rigid protocol of Granville had not prepared her. How ironic it would be if the endless criticisms of the course that she had had to parry turned out to be justified!

The senior obstetrician had risen and was putting on a white coat that dazzled with its cleanness.

'You won't always be following me around the wards,' he said. 'In fact, after today I shall expect you to have made a preliminary tour of your section on your own. You'll find most of what I'm saying in those notes, but I'll stress it now anyway. I shall expect to arrive at each bedside and find the complete notes of a case, as well as any specialised equipment I may need when examining the patient. And I shall want to hear your comments, Dr Scott.'

'Yes, of course.'

Carla was at a complete loss with this man, and turned gratefully to the task of putting on her own coat as a chance to escape direct eye-contact with him.

'Obviously, the nursing staff will have made many of those preparations, but you must oversee their work nevertheless.'

Again Carla had to content herself with a nod. Was

there some more intelligent response he was expecting her to make? Perhaps it was his voice that was throwing her off balance. If Dr Falconer had remained the anonymous man in the lift, she might have found the voice almost hypnotic with its deliciously formal and reserved tones, but now! She had to absorb and understand everything that was said, and in addition was determined to maintain her justifiable resentment against him, yet she was conscious all the time of how attractive she could have found him if circumstances had only been different. It seemed unfair.

He was ready now, and they left the office together, Carla standing in the background for a moment while Dr Falconer greeted his secretary and gave his birthday wishes. Then she stepped forward as he introduced her.

'Barbara, this is Dr Carla Scott, who I know you'll help in every way. Dr Scott, my secretary, Mrs Barbara Fitton.'

Carla murmured a greeting and smiled at the motherly looking, middle-aged woman behind the desk. Here at least was one person who might not be too hard to get along with.

'I hope you'll be very happy here, Dr Scott,' Mrs Fitton said.

'I'm sure I shall,' Carla returned cheerfully. But Dr Falconer cut across the tail end of this politeness.

'I wouldn't be too sure if I were you. It's a well-known fact that medical students are worked to death during their internship, and while we don't push you to dangerous levels of exhaustion here at the Boronia, you won't find it as easy as your days at Granville.'

Carla flushed, feeling she had been caught out in the expression of some trite and rather insincere commonplace. She wanted to insist that she really did think she would enjoy getting her teeth into some hard work, but knew that Lincoln Falconer's cynically raised eyebrow would only move even higher. It was ridiculous! Women had been showing for years that they were very equal to the tasks required of a doctor, and conversely, men had collapsed under the pressure of a medical student's life before now. Why was this arrogant obstetrician so determined to shut his eyes to those facts?

He was motioning her towards the door now, and she had just time to catch the half-fond, half-impatient smile that Mrs Fitton gave her employer, before the door of the waiting room had shut off her view. Carla was surprised at the look. It hinted at a warmness between the doctor and his secretary that seemed at odds with the man's outwardly cold personality. Was Mrs Fitton acquainted with the other side to him—if he had one?

There was no time to reflect further on all this, however. The doctor was setting a brisk pace as he strode down the corridor, his shoes cracking smartly on the beige vinyl tiles. Carla noticed that the tiles were literally spotless, and reflected on the advantages of a modern hospital. It must be so much easier here to maintain the level of cleanliness that minimised infection as well as reassuring patients of their well-being.

The cream-painted doors she passed on either side were clearly labelled 'Washroom', 'Store Six', 'Dr Cleland', etc. and she concluded that there were no wards at all on this floor. But it was a pity that Lincoln Falconer himself did not take more time to explain the layout of the Obstetrical Wing to her. Unless becoming familiar with the geography of the place was also a part of the apparently never-ending work that he had been so anxious to stress.

As if to reproach her for this slightly vindictive thought, he slowed at that moment, matched his pace to hers and began to speak.

'This floor is entirely given over to clinics and consultations,' he said. 'You probably know that at the Boronia we try to be involved with a woman's pregnancy from its earliest stages, particularly when there are likely to be problems. Our senior staff are all here on the fifth floor, and we have a sort of Outpatients department in the two-storey wing that runs down towards the staff residences.'

He gestured in that direction and Carla nodded.

'Yes, I had noticed the signs.'

'Women go there for their regular check-ups, and you'll be spending quite a bit of time there. Later, of course, you'll be transferred to theatre work – the gynaecological side of things, if I might put it like that, and of course our Casualty and Emergency sections. You'll spend about three months in my area.'

'Yes, so Dr Martin told me,' Carla nodded, aware of a sudden drop in the pit of her stomach, which she identified with a shock as disappointment. Was she actually sorry that she was only to spend three months working closely with Dr Falconer? What a ludicrous idea! In three months she would have more than proved herself to him and would be able to leave almost triumphantly. She should be looking forward to the day.

They re-entered the lift at that moment, and Carla thought again of her first impression of the doctor, when she had mistakenly believed him to be a new father. She wondered now how she could have reached that conclusion. His frown of concentrated thought, his brisk attitude, these were not the attributes of a man about to visit his wife and new child. It had been the flowers which had confused her.

This time Dr Falconer did press the fourth floor button, and the first as well.

'I've decided to leave you on your own this morning after all. I have quite a bit to attend to on Ward 2, so I'd like you to start straight away on the fourth—which is Mothers and Babies as you probably know. I'm sorry I haven't got time to introduce you to Sister Menzies, but she'll know who you are and will be expecting you. Everything should be routine—anyone with complications isn't in that ward—but I need scarcely point out that you'll still be completely thorough in your examination.'

'Of course,' Carla murmured.

Was she wrong to resent the way he was speaking to her? Perhaps the dry, formal tone was not deliberately designed to intimidate her at all. She was aware that her palms were damp and she was far from cool. Not the best way to feel on her first real round of a real ward, and it was at least partly the fault of this most disconcerting man.

He held back the lift door politely as she fumbled awkwardly with her bag of equipment. Somehow the catch seemed to have fallen open, and it took her several seconds to fasten it, pick up the bag and leave the lift. She was hotter than ever now, and actually blushing, but then as she turned to Dr Falconer with her thanks, a surprising thing happened.

His mouth was folded into a smile, and suddenly, as their eyes met, both laughed.

'Good luck, Dr Scott,' he murmured, still wearing that cool twisted smile, as he leant a casual arm against the lift doors to keep them open.

'Thank you, Dr Falconer,' said Carla.

The moment did not last, because he allowed the doors of the lift to shut between them, but it was enough to restore some of her composure, and she was able to walk into the ward confidently.

'Dr Scott?' Sister Menzies must have been on the look out for Carla's arrival, because she appeared straight away as if from nowhere, exuding efficiency in the white uniform that denoted her seniority.

'Yes, I'm Dr Scott, and I guess that you are Sister Menzies?' Carla said.

'I am. Janet Menzies. Dr Falconer said that you might be making a round by yourself this morning. I think you'll find everything is prepared.'

She was already walking towards her small office as she spoke, and Carla followed, instinctively noting the layout of the ward, and smiling in a general way at three of the nearest patients who were sitting drinking the last mouthfuls of a morning glass of milk.

'I'd like to explain a few things to you first, if I may,' Sister Menzies continued.

'Please do. I want to find out as much about your routine as I can, and as quickly as possible. Dr Falconer didn't seem to have much time . . .'

'He never does, dear, he never does. He takes on far too much work, and he expects everyone else to do the same. I expect you feel as though you've been thrown in at the deep end and left to sink or swim.'

'I do, rather,' Carla admitted.

There was a small silence as the senior nurse gathered

together some papers, then she spoke again, explaining clearly the very things which Carla had felt unsure about, and only a few minutes later she was ready to begin the tour of the ward which would from now on be a regular part of her day.

The place was airy and bright, yet cool—a necessary attribute, as the February day outside was hot and would become humid as the day progressed. Carla was sure that the ward would be a happy place for the forty-eight mothers and their babies who occupied the twelve roomy partitioned cubicles.

At the moment the ward seemed quiet. Carla could hear the tiny cries of two or three babies, and the murmur of conversation between women in several of the cubicles, but there were no visitors at this hour, although hospital policy dictated that visiting times were as flexible as possible.

Nursing staff moved about in side-rooms and passages, preparing equipment or filling in charts, and one or two glanced up with a half-smile as Carla made her way to the far end of the ward with Sister Menzies at her side.

Carla wondered how she would handle her relationship with the nursing staff. She would be younger than many, and yet in a position of authority over them, and the Granville students had been told during their training of the importance of being on good terms with all other staff. She knew that many nurses resented the attitude of some doctors who made no secret of their opinion that nurses were giggling girls seeking early marriage. Of course this was not so, and Carla hoped that she would be able to convey to the nurses the real respect she felt for their profession.

'You should have no problems in here,' Sister Menzies said as they were about to enter the first of the four-bed cubicles. 'Mrs Pearce should have been discharged yesterday, but there are signs of problems at home, so we've asked Jane Kemp, our social worker, to look into things, and meanwhile we're keeping her in for a day or two longer. The other three women and their babies will go tomorrow, unless you think otherwise.'

Carla examined each patient and cast a careful eye over their charts and notes, finding a friendly word for each woman as she did so, and taking genuine delight in the sight of the tiny forms that lay asleep in cribs beside each mother's bed, or cradled softly in her arms.

In fact, the entire round was almost like a textbook chapter, each baby's weight falling within the normal range, each mother's recovery from the painful but unique experience of birth proceeding as it should. Carla had to pause to reassure one mother that her failure to produce milk was in no way her fault and would not harm her child, a task which did demand care and tact, but there was nothing which taxed her medical knowledge at all.

She was quite surprised when she emerged from the last of the cubicles to find that it was already eleven-thirty.

'Do stop for some coffee or tea with us,' Sister Menzies said. 'Mostly you'll find you are too busy, but as it's your first day . . .'

'I'd love a coffee,' Carla admitted gratefully.

The senior nurse bustled round preparing the coffee quickly and served it herself, interrupted only once by a simple-to-answer question from a very junior student nurse. She ushered Carla to a seat in her small but immaculately tidy office, then sat herself. Carla used the opportunity of comparative peace and quiet to clear up one or two details about ward routine that had been puzzling her.

When a third of her drink still remained, Carla glanced at her wrist watch and saw that it was twenty to twelve.

'I'll have to go soon,' she said to Sister Menzies, thinking of several duties that had yet to be attended to before the afternoon clinic in the Outpatients wing.

'Finish your coffee, though,' the older woman advised. 'It isn't healthy to keep on the go all the time. I've seen too many doctors run themselves into the ground not simply because the work is hard and the hours are long, but because they just forget how to take a few minutes in which to really relax. Don't you fall into that pattern too!'

'I'll try not to,' Carla replied.

'Oh dear!' Sister Menzies exclaimed. 'I'm giving you advice like a headmistress, and I have no right to.'

'It's all right,' Carla assured her. 'I'm interested in any and every piece of information or advice that's going at this stage!'

'Don't worry. In a few days you'll wonder how it could ever have seemed strange,' the senior nurse said.

They both laughed, just as Carla became aware of a blurred outline through the frosted glass that formed part of the wall of Sister Menzies' office. A second later Lincoln Falconer appeared in the doorway. He wore the faint hint of a smile that creased the tanned skin of his face into soft lines, but it faded quickly when he saw Carla, and was replaced by a raised eyebrow.

'So here you are, Dr Scott!' he said, deliberately putting surprise into his dry drawling tones. 'I had thought that I would find you had already left, to write up files, collect and assess tests, have your lunch and generally prepare yourself for this afternoon's clinic.'

The criticism in his words was blatant, and Carla flushed, feeling like a schoolgirl who had been caught out in some childish attempt to shirk her studies. Inwardly she was furious. She had used the coffee break almost entirely as a chance to get to know more about her work, and her conscience was clear, but after the way the Senior Obstetrician had worded his reprimand, she was not going to stoop to an explanation, let alone an apology.

She remained silent for a few seconds, searching for a reply, but he spoke again.

'I see that you haven't quite finished your coffee, but I'm afraid you'll have to do without it. I have something to discuss with Sister Menzies.'

'I was just about to leave, actually,' Carla said smoothly, rising to her feet then turning to Sister Menzies. 'Thank you so much for your help this morning— and for your advice just now.'

'That's all right, dear,' the nurse replied, tactfully ignoring the sudden tension that crackled between the two doctors. 'Any time you are unsure of anything, just ask.'

'I will.'

Carla turned to leave the office, deciding to bestow a small smile upon Dr Falconer as a parting gesture. She was already walking along the corridor that led from the ward, head held high and clean chestnut hair bouncing, when Dr Falconer called her back.

'Is Mrs Baker still having excessive trouble with engorgement, Dr Scott?'

'Yes, she is. So I've prescribed an analgesic, as well as plenty of bathing and good support. I hope that is all right, Dr Falconer?'

'Perfectly all right, Dr Scott.'

This seemed to be an indication that she was now free to leave, so she turned again, wondering if his eyes were still upon her as she tried to re-capture the confident walk she had managed before. It was only when she knew that she must be out of his sight that she could relax and begin to think clearly.

The little incident in Janet Menzies office had hardened her resolve to prove herself to her senior, as well as confirming her dislike for him. He certainly must be a bigoted man to be so determined to find fault with her! He had obviously assumed that she had been wasting time in idle chat with Sister Menzies. His reprimand did not seem to have included the nurse, though. Was it a case of favouritism, or did he just expect nurses to be inveterate chatterers, and put up with it?

Whatever the truth, the whole thing was patently unfair!

'So how did it go?' Michael Groom asked Carla with his usual engaging grin as he dropped into a chair opposite her at dinner that night.

'It went well,' she replied, wondering fleetingly if this was the truth.

The afternoon clinic had been busy and interesting. Carla had had no more unpleasant encounters with Dr Falconer, but at the same time she could not feel she had impressed him as she had hoped to do.

'Oh come on,' Michael was saying. 'More detail than that, please! No sticky problems? No brilliant diagnoses? And what do you think of your senior man? Awesome, isn't he?'

So Michael felt the power and attraction of Lincoln Falconer's personality too! Carla found that she wanted to hear what the easy-mannered anaesthetist had to say about the man.

'I suppose he is quite impressive,' she conceded, adding, perhaps rashly, 'But I didn't take to him personally.'

'Oh you didn't? Why? Run into trouble with him, did you?'

The question and the glance that accompanied it were disconcerting. How had Michael pinpointed the matter so accurately? Was it a well-known fact that Dr Lincoln Falconer deliberately antagonised all his junior female colleagues?

'It depends on what you mean by trouble,' Carla replied warily, suddenly unwilling to betray too much to Michael.

'You needn't be afraid to tell me about it, Carla,' he said. 'You wouldn't be the first person to find it difficult to work with him, but at the same time, you'll be a rarity if you don't look back on your months in his area as one of the most enlightening periods of your whole training.'

'That good, is he?'

'Most people think so.'

'Well I'll have to start considering myself a lucky woman then,' Carla commented rather flippantly as she toyed with the last mouthfuls of the beef macaroni dish in front of her.

She could not decide whether she was pleased or otherwise to hear Lincoln Falconer's praises sung in such definite terms. Of course it was gratifying to learn that she was working under someone so highly skilled and well-thought of professionally, but in another way she was disappointed. Somehow it took some of the strength from her principled resolve to dislike the man, and left her strangely up in the air.

'Ninety-nine percent of the unattached female nursing staff would consider you a lucky woman in any case,' Michael Groom was saying now. 'He's the heart-throb of the hospital, but most nurses only see him for a few minutes each day, if that, and know that their love is destined to remain forever unrequited. And probably one or two of the patients are a bit smitten too. They'd give quite a lot to spend hours in intimate consultation with him.'

'It's hardly going to be like that,' Carla protested, annoyed by this reference to the senior obstetrician's undeniable physical charms. 'Since I'm merely an intern, and not some sort of senior consultant, as anyone would assume from the way you are talking! And I wouldn't want to spend hours in consultation with him even if I could,' she said.

If only she had not had that silly fantasy about him in the lift this morning! She decided suddenly that this was the source of her confused feelings about him. It wasn't surprising that many women and girls fancied themselves in love with Lincoln Falconer, but she was utterly determined not to be numbered amongst them, and it was important that Michael realise this.

'Do admit, though,' Michael coaxed, apparently unwilling to let the matter drop. 'He is a good-looking chap. "Magnetically attractive", one of the nurse aides called him when she was confessing her problems to me a few weeks ago. Didn't you feel a sudden sparking of passionate interest when you encountered his dark brooding eyes for the first time across his mahogany desk this morning?'

'They're not dark and brooding, they're greyish-green,' Carla retorted, half-flippant, half-serious. 'And no I did not!'

It was not quite the truth but never mind that, it soon would be. She would school herself relentlessly until she did not even remember her first impression of him.

'Okay, okay,' Michael said. 'Only joking. Perhaps you've got your eye on one of the male nurses, or perhaps, indeed, you're already fixed up back home in Granville.'

'No, I don't have anyone at all like that,' Carla replied absently, but her attention was recalled by the unmistakable glint in the anaesthetist's eye.

'No-one at all like that,' he repeated, apparently casually.

But Carla had the feeling that perhaps this was the piece of information he had been angling for throughout the conversation. She was not perturbed by this. She liked Michael, and if he asked her to go out with him, she wouldn't refuse, but at the same time it was hardly likely to develop into anything serious.

'I hadn't realised that Dr Falconer was English until I met him,' she said now, wanting to change the subject and feeling free to refer to the senior obstetrician again. Everything she could learn about him might make their working relationship easier.

'Oh yes . . . Been out here a few years though, but hasn't lost a particle of that beautiful Cambridge accent,' Michael said. 'Occasionally you get a particularly smitten junior doctor who'll start to imitate it out of sheer admiration, until his life is made unbearable by the teases of the rest of us. You find Falconer's voice attractive, at least then, do you?'

'Oh, I wouldn't say that,' she replied, all too aware that, again, she did indeed. 'I just wondered what he was doing out here, that's all.'

'Likes the climate, I think, for summer sports. He sails, and is a great tennis player of the old school. If he had been twenty years younger, medicine probably wouldn't have had a chance. Someone would have discovered him and he'd be earning a fortune on the international circuit like those American super-brats.'

'Do you think he'll ever go back to England?'

'No, he's doing too well here. The Boronia has a good name, and he's partly the reason. Women with certain problems come from all over Australia to be treated here. And finally, of course, getting back to the subject of England, he's probably a tax-exile. He earns a packet here . . .'

'But he works hard for every cent . . .' It was almost a question.

'As you say. And he's got a private income as well, I believe. Shares or bonds, or something. With no-one to spend it all on, he must just be hoarding it up.'

'No-one to spend it on?'

'Well, he's not married. But of course we hear rumours. A steady girl-friend tucked away somewhere, a different fancy every week, an unfaithful ex-wife back in England.'

'Has he ever been out with anyone from the hospital?' To Carla's own ears, these questions sounded over-inquisitive, but Michael seemed happy to answer them.

'He has taken another doctor out, or a senior nurse, occasionally, but he is very discreet about it, and picks women who are the same, so he could be quite heavily involved with someone now, and it's likely that none of the rest of the staff would know.'

'He doesn't live in, of course?'

'No. Has some flashy little pad over-looking the harbour in one of the Eastern suburbs, I believe. I'm never likely to see it, though.'

There was a small silence, and Carla became aware that the dining hall was emptying and that the day's brightness was fading into evening. She had finished her main course, but had not wanted to interrupt her conversation with Michael to go in search of dessert at the cafeteria-style service bars. There was no time for dessert now. Her evening round was due, and it would hardly improve her standing in the eyes of the man they had been discussing if she were to be late after becoming caught up in conversation.

'I'll have to go,' she said as she rose and smoothed out the skirt of the cotton dress, whose slightly wilted state bore witness to the length and heat of the day.

'Must you? Michael's voice expressed frank disappointment.

'Yes, my evening round . . .'

'Oh-ho! Acquiring the terminology already,' he laughed, evidently not too put out by her unavailability. 'I've got the evening off, I thought we could go out. I was forgetting how hard you interns work. But perhaps another time.'

'Yes, perhaps,' Carla agreed lightly as she began to thread her way amongst the brightly laminated tables to deposit her tray at the counter.

Michael went to the service bar in search of dessert and coffee, and so she left the dining hall alone.

The dying embers of a glorious salmon pink sunset still glowed on the Western horizon as she walked to the Obstetrics wing. She drank in its beauty with pleasure but did not slow her brisk pace. Several cars passed— departing visitors mainly, but staff too, leaving after their day's shift, or arriving for evening duty. Idly she focussed her attention on a particularly beautiful stream-lined dark red sports car that was reversing carefully out of a parking space. The masculine sil- houette in the driver's seat seemed familiar and a moment later, as he turned, she realised why.

It was Lincoln Falconer and he was not alone.

The car swept past Carla as she stood on the grassy footpath waiting to cross the road, and she was able to look quite fully at the occupant of the low-slung passen- ger seat, who glanced briefly across at that moment.

The woman was young, beautifully dressed, and even in the fading light, extremely beautiful, with classical features, lovely colouring and hair of an unusual blonde that seemed almost silver.

The car and its occupants had passed in a moment, leaving only the glow of red tail-lights as Lincoln Falcon- er turned out of the hospital driveway and accelerated smoothly away into the warm summer dusk. He had not seen Carla at all, and the unknown woman's glance had been short and uninterested.

It seemed likely that she was one of the mysterious women in Lincoln's life that Michael Groom had refer- red to, and that she and the Senior Obstetrician were on their way out for some intimate evening together. Carla wondered if she was employed at the hospital or if she had another profession far removed from the world of medicine . . .

Still, of what interest or importance was that to Dr Carla Scott, hurrying off to complete her evening duties? None whatsoever. Why was it then, that the image of the unknown woman, the sleek car, and the dynamic Englishman stayed with her throughout the evening?

CHAPTER THREE

CERTAIN aspects of Carla's work fell into place remarkably quickly, she found. Her room was soon homely and familiar, as was the whole residential block, its dining hall and recreation facilities. Daily rounds lost their threatening newness, and clinics became an opportunity to learn and observe more and more. The experience of helping a woman to give birth had, during her training, been one of the things Carla had found most rewarding, and now that she had the opportunity to be involved in it almost every day, she enjoyed it even more. By the end of her second week, she could look back and know that choosing to be a doctor had been the best decision of her life.

'And fortunately,' Carla wrote in a letter to Sally Lewis, 'I don't see too much of Dr Lincoln Falconer, who is just as bad, if not worse, than we pictured him!'

She was sitting in the grounds, shaded by the huge leafy umbrella of a Moreton Bay fig tree against the rather unpleasant heat of a February Sunday afternoon, and enjoying a few hours of well-earned repose.

Michael Groom had asked her to spend the time with him at Bondi, Sydney's most famous and most crowded beach, but she had politely declined, knowing that she had too many small chores to attend to, and reluctant, in any case, to respond too readily to Michael's evident interest in her. She did like him, but had felt no immediate spark, and though she reminded herself that a 'spark' was by no means a reliable indicator, or a necessary requirement, of love, she was fairly certain that the easy-mannered anaesthetist was not the right kind of man for her . . .

Carla laid aside the letter to Sally for a moment, and the heavy medical textbook on which she was resting it, and gave herself up to thought.

That scathing sentence about Lincoln Falconer: was it the whole truth? She had almost added another phrase to it, something about his incredible good looks, and the frivolous attraction she might have felt for him if he had been anyone other than the man he was. But her pen had stopped, poised above the page, and after several seconds she had added merely a decisive full-stop.

After all, the few moments of attraction were a thing of the past, killed utterly by her growing knowledge of his personality. Because she could not feel that relations were getting less strained between them. His reserve never broke down, it was true, but if anything, this made his disapproval of her even harsher and more difficult to bear.

She thought back on the events of last Thursday night:

Adele Clement's labour had proceeded normally if slowly almost to the end, and it seemed certain that she would be sleeping with the baby safely in a crib beside her by two a.m. Then Carla had discovered with horror that the healthy-sized child's shoulders were severely impacted and that a normal easy delivery would be impossible. Could she handle the situation herself?

'We're going to have to try you in a different position,' she told Mrs Clement, beginning to prepare immediately and running through the procedure in her mind as she did so. Large episiotomy, draw the baby's head back, suprapubic pressure and rotation of the anterior shoulder, symphisiotomy, if necessary . . .

'Call Dr Falconer,' she said to a nurse. 'Or Dr Williams.'

'Dr Williams has an emergency Caesarean,' replied Sister Garland, the Labour ward sister, and a trained mid-wife. 'But I think Dr Falconer is in Pre-term at the moment.'

'Well, call him, please. Right now.' Carla could not help betraying urgency in her voice, although she knew that it was important for Mrs Clement and her husband, sitting anxiously but quietly at his wife's side, to remain calm.

A junior nurse finished placing a pillow beneath the woman's hips then hurried off in search of the doctor, as Roger Clement spoke.

'What's wrong? I thought everything was okay. Isn't it nearly finished?'

'Shall I . . . push harder?' Mrs Clement asked between heavy breaths. She was tired after the long ordeal of her first labour, and it would not be easy for her if the delivery was prolonged..

'No, don't push harder,' Carla replied. 'The baby's shoulders are . . . stuck, and we'll have to move them around before we can go any further.'

'Is it dangerous?' Mr Clement's throat was constricted but he was still calm and squeezing his wife's hand with as much confidence as he could muster.

Carla's thoughts raced before her reply. How much should the couple be told? Should she admit that babies had been known to die if the shoulders were not freed soon enough?

'There is some danger,' she admitted. 'It's a matter of time . . .'

Even as she spoke she was beginning to prepare. She could perform the episiotomy, and then as long as Dr Falconer arrived quickly, there was a good chance. It was the symphisiotomy that was difficult. She remembered the insistence of textbooks and professors that previous experience with this operation was vital in a case of impacted shoulders . . .

And suddenly Lincoln Falconer was there, completely cool but wasting not a fraction of a second.

'I've never done a symphisiotomy, so . . .' Carla began.

'Then you should have sent for me earlier,' he replied, taking in the situation with a calculated glance. The words were spoken too low for anyone else to hear, but Carla flushed.

Only a few minutes had passed before she had decided to call him. But perhaps she should have realised the problem earlier? Yet surely it was something that could not have been predicted? Useless to mull over past actions, though. Dr Falconer gave quick precise instructions to Sister Garland, hovering at his elbow, and completed the operation with precision and speed.

Now they were ready for the task of freeing the baby's shoulder.

'Dr Scott can you provide the suprapubic pressure, please?'

Carla moved to a better position and began the firm pressure with her tired hands.

'Lower down, Doctor.' The hint of irritation in Lincoln Falconer's tone was light but like a steel thread.

She moved her hands as he indicated, thankful that

the action of pressing stilled the trembling which had threatened to take hold of them after this second criticism. The man was insufferable, speaking to her like that in the midst of such a tense scene! What might it do to the morale of the young couple? Not to speak of her own self-confidence.

But no, was she being unfair? After all, what did her own feelings matter in this emergency? She concentrated fully on the present again, as she knew she should have been doing unfailingly already.

Dr Falconer had drawn the baby's head backwards and was now rotating its shoulder with a gentle, firm and steady movement of his well-shaped fingers. His face was set in a heavy frown of concentration, and his knuckles were white with effort.

'We may need general anaesthesia,' he murmured so that only Carla and Sister Garland could hear. Carla felt her heart thump. The shoulder would not free! She knew that as time passed, chances of the baby's death grew higher, and that if Dr Falconer was calling for a general anaesthetic, the situation was very grave.

'Wait a minute . . .' the doctor said a second later. His teeth were clenched in concentration and he was speaking more to himself than aloud. 'It's . . . coming! There!'

Tension eased like the release of a spring, and the rest of the baby's tiny and perfect body was pulled free. Moments later came its first high-pitched cries. It was a healthy girl, and breathing normally.

'I think I can leave the rest to you,' Lincoln Falconer said with his rare cool smile, as he gave a half-glance to Carla. Then, after some words of encouragement and congratulations to Mrs Clement and her husband, he was gone, hurrying back to handle yet another emergency in the Pre-term delivery theatre.

When Carla had finally sunk exhausted into her soft bed that night, her thoughts were not of the young parents' happiness, nor of the satisfaction of a successful night's work, but of Dr Lincoln Falconer. He had made the difficult delivery seem safe, and had acted without hesitation or doubt, but he had certainly not increased her confidence in her own work.

Or was she being over-sensitive? she wondered now, as she picked absently at some blades of the short sweet grass upon which she was sitting. As a doctor, she had to be tough, had to realise that in a crisis, tact and politeness were less than vital. After all, what exactly had the senior obstetrician said to her? Three clipped sentences expressing irritation and impatience, that was all. When she analysed the words themselves, it seemed immature to be so needled by them.

She visualised and almost felt the scene again – the starkly white lights, the tense attention of the nurses, the laboured breathing and occasional cries of Mrs Clement – and again found that she was angered and upset by Dr Falconer's words.

No, not his words, rather his whole manner and mood. The man was so damned reserved, that's what it was: She could feel that he was concealing emotions far stronger and more complex than he allowed himself to express. It was this fact that threw her so completely off balance whenever she thought of him, and whenever she was with him.

No, she would not tell Sally anything more of all this complexity. How could she possibly understand? No-one who had not met Dr Lincoln Falconer could!

'Dr Scott?' a freckled and frizzy-haired student nurse said rather breathlessly behind Carla's left shoulder. She turned, a little startled. She had been too absorbed in thought to hear the girl's approach.

'Yes? Am I wanted?' She began to get to her feet at once, assuming she was needed on the wards, although she was not on call that afternoon. 'I'm sorry, I didn't bring my bleep. Is it urgent?'

'I don't know,' the young nurse replied. 'Apparently Dr Falconer is on the phone for you.'

She pronounced the name almost reverently, and Carla thought briefly of Michael Groom's idea that every unattached female in the hospital had a crush on the senior obstetrician.

'Dr Falconer? On the foyer phone in the residence?'

'Yes, I just happened to answer it on my way through,' the girl explained, following the wake of Carla, who was already hurrying back to the residence buildings. 'And luckily I'm on Ward B so I knew who you were. I've already spent ages looking for you, so I hope it's nothing urgent.'

'I don't know what it can be, actually,' Carla confessed. 'I didn't expect any calls this afternoon.' Much less one from Lincoln Falconer. 'Thank you very much for taking the time to look for me, anyway.'

'Oh, that's all right.' The student nurse ducked away towards the staff car-park as they approached the building, looking relieved at having accomplished her commission at last. She had obviously been on her way somewhere when she had answered the phone.

Carla brushed some wisps of grass from the back of her full-skirted yellow cotton sun-dress, hoping that it had not been creased by her casual sitting position beneath the tree and entered the foyer.

'Hullo?' she said as she picked up the phone. There was no answer at first, and all she could hear was the muffled sound of Lincoln's voice in conversation with someone else. But a moment later he turned his attention to the phone.

'Dr Scott? You've taken a hell of a time!'

'I'm sorry, but I am off duty,' she said, defensive in response to his impatience. 'I was in the grounds and the nurse who took your call couldn't find me. Is it urgent?'

'No, not at all. After all, you're not on call, as you say,' he replied, his tone softening somewhat. 'It's merely that two new members of the Board are having a tour around the hospital and expressed interest in meeting you. You're in no way obliged to come, but if you could . . .'

'I'll be happy to. I'm not doing anything important.' She made her voice sound as cheerful and relaxed as possible, but was conscious that she could never speak and act normally in the company of her senior.

'Good. If you could be in the Board Room as soon as possible then?'

'I'm afraid I don't know . . .'

'Fifth floor,' he interrupted, anticipating her query. 'A few doors down from my office. You should find it easily enough.'

'Right. I'll be there in a few minutes then.'

She hung up and went to her room to put away the unfinished letter to Sally. Should she change? She checked her appearance in the mirror. No, the dress seemed uncreased and clean. She flicked a brush quickly through her glossy hair, fastened a thin gold chain around her creamy throat, and kicked off her leather thongs, replacing them with more formal medium-heeled white sandals. Make-up? Just a touch of mascara, perhaps, and a light application of lipstick.

Dr Falconer's request seemed odd. She knew of the existence of the Board, of course, and if it had recently acquired new members it was logical that they should inspect the facilities of the hospital, but why did they want to meet her, when she was such a junior member of the medical staff? Was the gathering in the Board Room a large one? She started to assume that it must be.

The hospital was comparatively quiet on this hot afternoon as she crossed to the main building, but she was aware that the usual round of hospital life continued on every floor as she passed in the lift on her way to the fifth. She thought that the buzzing of voices might greet her as she approached the Board Room, but in fact she heard only one or two people speaking before knocking on the pale painted door and entering.

'Ah, Dr Scott.' Lincoln Falconer turned immediately to her, as she took in her first impressions of the other occupants of the spacious room.

There were only six: four men and two women. Dr Martin gave her a friendly nod, as did Cynthia Allan, the director of nursing. Carla smiled at Evan Yately, the hospital administrator, too. Then Dr Falconer began a round of introductions. An elderly yet upright gentleman was introduced as Sir Bradley Bedden, chairman of the board, the second woman was Mrs Jane Thomas, treasurer, and Peter Prior, the younger man, was one of the two new members. All held cups of coffee as they stood by a table of light refreshments, and Carla was soon handed a cup.

She was confused. The smallness of the gathering made it even more surprising that she should have been summoned, and she sensed that some of the others felt the same. Where was her place amongst these most exalted members of the hospital community? There was a small silence, broken only by one mundane query from Peter Prior about the administration of the Outpatients department, then Lincoln Falconer spoke.

'I hope Louise isn't too much longer,' he said. 'She must have found her bag by now.'

'Yes,' agreed Dr Martin. 'She was the one who expressed interest in meeting our most junior doctor.'

The door opened at that moment and in walked a woman whom Carla recognised surprisingly well. Strange, actually, how clearly that face was imprinted in her memory when she had only seen it once before, as the woman had swept past in the passenger seat of Dr Falconer's car, nearly two weeks ago now.

'Louise, here is Dr Scott,' Lincoln was saying. 'Carla, this is our second new board member, Louise Clair.'

Both women murmured a commonplace greeting, and Carla hoped that her own face did not reflect the calculated assessment she saw in the features of the other woman.

'I know why she wanted to meet me!' Carla thought, shocked. 'Because she had heard that I was young, unattached, and working quite often with Dr Falconer. She wants to make sure I'm not going to threaten her relationship with him. Well, she need not worry. She's welcome to him as far as I'm concerned, and I'm sure I'm the last person he would be attracted to!'

She studied Louise Clair covertly as the older woman helped herself to a cup of coffee and a couple of the small savoury titbits that were laid out on plates on the side table. She was strikingly attractive, knowing how to make the most of it, too, and it was difficult to imagine her feeling threatened by many other women.

That hair which had glowed out so strongly in Monday's dusk was not blonde but pure grey—or rather, an almost silvery white. Strange, Louise Clair could not be more than thirty-two or thirty-three, yet her hair colour was that of someone thirty years older.

Still, Carla knew that premature greyness existed, and Louise had capitalised on her rarity by enhancing it, instead of trying to cover it up with tint or dye as most women might have done. She was deeply and smoothly tanned in contrast to the silver-grey silk dress she wore, and the lustrous hair which swung like a bell as she tossed her head, completed the striking combination of colours. As for her large eyes, they were of an almost irridescent blue.

'And so what made you decide to come and work at our Boronia Women's?' Louise said, approaching Carla again, coffee in hand.

'It wasn't a matter of deciding, really,' she replied with a light laugh. 'I tried many places, and the Boronia happened to be the one that took me on.'

'Oh . . . I thought perhaps it might have been Lincoln's reputation,' Louise Clair murmured casually, but there was a look of sharp calculation in her eyes which made Carla certain that the remark was not a chance one.

'No, it wasn't that,' she replied, deliberately revealing no further information in her reply. Let Louise Clair draw her own conclusions as to what Carla felt about Lincoln Falconer!

And yet why be so malicious about it? Carla chastised herself inwardly. She knew that she had taken an instant dislike to the woman, but to be fair, it was without rhyme or reason. Miss Clair had a perfect right to be glamour and show personified, and a perfect right to protect her relationship with the very eligible Dr Falconer. If she was brittle and rather shallow, as Carla instinctively felt she was, then this was something to pity rather than dislike.

Conversation had moved on now, to the subject of the proposed new wing, for which plans were already being drawn up, and Carla felt rather left out, standing in the circle of older people and still holding her empty coffee cup. Louise seemed to have satisfied herself that the new intern posed no threat, as she paid no further attention to Carla at all. Finally it was left to Dr Martin to notice her awkwardness and to suggest that she was free to go.

'All this Board business can't be of much interest to you after only two weeks at the Boronia, my dear,' he said. 'Just take yourself off if you've finished that coffee.'

'Yes, I think I will, if you don't mind,' Carla replied very gratefully.

She caught the tail end of an irritated glance from Lincoln Falconer as she spoke and felt anger rising inside her. It was not her fault that she was here in the first place, nor that the discussion on the new wing had been interrupted to allow her to leave. Why did he have to hold her responsible for every little thing that hindered or annoyed him?

When Carla said her goodbyes, she deliberately did not speak to him, and was coldly satisfied when she met his frigid stare, to know that it was reflected by equal iciness in her own deep blue-green eyes.

For a moment it almost seemed as though he was going to say something, restrain her by a cutting phrase, but his eyes moved away, unlocking the fixed gaze between them, and Dr Martin opened the Board Room door for her at that moment.

His heavy gallantry was rather endearing, and she smiled warmly at him as she passed through. Thank goodness not all men left her with a heart pounding in anger, if that was what this unsettling emotion was.

'How was your afternoon?' Michael asked in the dining hall that evening.

'Ruined,' Carla replied unwisely. Somehow the anaesthetist's light, impertinent questions often seemed to trick her out of a normally reserved manner.

'Oh really? By what? Or is it "whom"?'

'Oh, it was nothing, I suppose,' she said, suddenly realising that criticism of Louise Clair, and of Lincoln Falconer, might very easily be spread too far. 'I had to go up and meet the new members of the hospital board. It wasn't terribly interesting, and it chopped my afternoon in half so I didn't do nearly as much as I had intended, and didn't manage to relax either.'

'Told you you should have come to the beach,' Michael crowed.

'I will, next time.'

'Good!' Then he added more seriously: 'Don't make the mistake of staying around the hospital in your time off. Interns get little enough of it anyway, and things have a habit of intruding.'

'You've convinced me.'

But Michael was off on another track.

'New members of the board, hey? That'll be Louise Clair and that other fellow. Forgotten his name.'

'Louise . . . You know her then?'

'Well, the Clair family have been involved with the hospital since the beginning. It's their pet charity. They can afford it, too. They've given thousands over the years.'

'Oh?'

'Haven't you heard of Clair Electronics? Used to be Clair Chem-electric, but old Mr Clair saw which way the wind was blowing and moved into the new technology very early.'

'Yes, I have heard of it. I hadn't connected the names before. They're one of the most successful Australian-owned companies in existence at the moment, aren't they?'

'That's right. But the Clairs are good with their money. They support all sorts of charities and campaigns, but as I say, their pet one is the Boronia. Louise is probably the least charity-minded. I'm quite surprised that she agreed to be on the Board, but she does have brains and she'll probably do a good job if she puts her mind to it . . . Lord! Is that the time?' He had caught sight of the simple silver watch that circled Carla's slim firm wrist.

'Do you have to go?'

'Yes, I'm working, and I'm on the edge of lateness as it is. Otherwise, my love, do not think that I would desert you like this.'

'Well go on, then,' she laughed. 'I don't want to be held responsible if you're not on time. I seem to cop the blame for everything else that goes on around here!'

She regretted the remark as soon as it was out. It was a gross exaggeration of the few minor incidents that had occurred between herself and Dr Falconer, and Michael would be bound to pick up on it. He did.

'More trouble with Dr Falconer?'

Carla tried to back down.

'No, not really. I was thinking of something else. It doesn't matter. Forget I said anything.'

Her clumsy phrasing only made matters worse, and as Michael left, she saw that he was intrigued and curious. How annoying! Why was it that she was always so unwise with her words when she was with him? And why did she have to dwell on those stupid and insignificant exchanges with Lincoln Falconer? Very likely he had no especial grievance against her at all, and it was only her own imagination, fuelled by dislike, that lent importance to his behaviour.

Two of her fellow interns came up at that moment. She had made their acquaintance earlier in the week, and with their common positions in the hospital, it seemed likely that they would become friends. But that evening she declined their invitation to go out for coffee.

'Tired?' Red-haired Janet Jones queried sympathetically. 'So am I. Casualty is just exhausting. But I've got to get out for an hour or two, just for a change of scene.'

'Same here,' agreed Peter Higgins, whose curls were as ruddy as those of his companion. 'Don't you think you should too?'

'In principle, yes,' replied Carla. 'But I'm not in the mood for a café. I thought I'd go for a walk, to "enjoy daylight saving" as my mother always says. I need some new shampoo. That corner shop down the road will be open, won't it?'

'Yes, till nine, I think,' Janet replied.

'Do join us later if you change your mind,' Peter urged, giving her a medical look. He had already confessed that he hoped to specialise in stress conditions and break down therapy, and was comically eager to find signs of over-work and anxiety in his friends and colleagues.

'We'll be at that nice open-air place in Eridge Road,' Janet added.

They left, quickly involved in bantering conversation. It had been nice of them to be so insistent on having her company, when it was fairly evident that they were in that delicious stage of mutual discovery that leads to attraction and love, and would get on far better alone. The two had been at the hospital for a month longer than Carla, and obviously wanted to make her feel welcome and at home.

She stayed only a few minutes longer then went to her room to collect her bag and set off for the shop, taking a round about route that allowed her to enjoy some of the quiet tree-lined streets whose houses faced the skyscrapers of the city a few miles away, and claimed views, if patchy ones, of the harbour, the famous arch of the bridge, and the newer outline of the Opera House 'sails'.

The little corner shop was quite crowded that evening and she had to wait for a few minutes in the queue at the counter after she had found her favourite brand of shampoo in the small beauty and cleanliness products section. At first her thoughts wandered and she was barely aware of the other people who waited, but then her ear caught a familiar name.

'I was up at the Boronia this morning,' a middle-aged woman said to her female companion.

'Were you love? The old trouble?'

'Yes.' She gestured vaguely and discreetly towards her lower abdomen, but did not seem to mind that people might overhear. Her voice was not lowered. 'I saw Mrs Clair turning into the driveway as I was coming out.'

'She's the one that lost her son, isn't she?' the second woman queried, gathering up her brown paper bag full of purchases.

'Yes, tragic, I thought it was. He was such a . . .'

They were through the door now, and had passed out of earshot, and Carla reddened when she found that the check-out girl was waiting for her, with eyes fixed in her direction. Carla had been straining rather too obviously to catch the women's conversation, and she was embarrassed.

But that was the least of her concerns. Far more important was what she had actually overheard. 'Mrs Clair'! Louise Clair was married! And what was more, there was a child!—Or there had been a child, for apparently he had died in tragic circumstances. This put the relationship between Lincoln Falconer and the new board member in a very ugly light.

Carla walked home in a daze, oblivious of the beauty of a summer evening in these well-kept suburban streets. She wondered if it was too strait-laced of her to be so profoundly shocked at the discovery that the highly-regarded obstetrician was having an affair—or at the very least, a dalliance—with a married woman.

Perhaps in this age of free and fluid relationships, such a view was positively puritan. But no, it was not a question of that. For Carla, it all came down to the basic respect and care that human beings should feel for one another, and how could this respect and care exist between three people if two were secretly involved together without the knowledge of the third?

By the time she reached her room her attitude had firmed: If the facts were as they seemed, then she could not approve of what was going on, and she had to add another item to Dr Falconer's growing list of faults.

Arrogant, impatient, woman-hating, prejudiced, and now a trespasser into a marriage.

'Of course there may be "mitigating circumstances",' she said to her reflection in the mirror as she brushed her hair before bed. 'But knowing Lincoln Falconer, I doubt it.'

CHAPTER FOUR

'HAVE a good cry if you need to, Miss Cummings,' Carla said sympathetically to the young and palely pretty woman who sat opposite.

The positive confirmation that she was pregnant had obviously upset her. She was not married. Perhaps there would be trouble at home, or perhaps the prospective father, suspecting what was in the wind, had deserted her.

This was Tuesday afternoon's Outpatients clinic, where patients were seen right from the first diagnosis of pregnancy, until a few days before the birth was due. Many other problems connected with child-bearing were attended to as well.

'I knew it would be positive. I've missed two periods already, and I've been feeling that sick, you wouldn't believe.'

'Yes, you're nearly three months,' Carla murmured. She added, as an encouragement to further confidences: 'And being worried doesn't help, of course . . .'

'I've kept hoping and hoping that Bob would come back. Or at least write, or ring,' Maureen Cummings went on.

Carla sat back ready to listen. There were several other patients waiting, but if this young woman had problems at home, the more that was known about them, the better. Without losing her concentration or her sympathetic manner, Carla jotted a small note on the case file that lay in front of her: 'Refer medical social worker'.

'That's why I left it so long to get the test. I just delayed and delayed. He went off seven weeks ago to try and get work up in the mines in Western Australia, and he said he wouldn't get in touch till he'd got some good news. It was meant to be like a surprise, you know, but now I wish he'd write even if he hasn't found anything, and give an address, just so he'd know about it.'

'How will he feel?' Carla asked gently, wondering in the back of her mind if perhaps this was more the social worker, Jane Kemp's area. Carla's training might have better equipped her for counselling than an ordinary medical course did, but facing a real problem was different from any amount of theory.

'I think he'll be pleased,' Maureen Cummings said. 'Or he would be, if we had more money. We want to get married. We've talked about it.'

She looked at Carla defensively, as though expecting this statement to be challenged. Perhaps the girl's mother had been cynical about the likelihood of Bob's return. Carla glanced down at the case notes again. 'Age: 23.'

'Why, she's almost exactly my age!' Carla thought with slight shock, and began to feel even more interested in the plight of the girl.

'I'm sure if he knew how things were, he'd stand by me. But Mum doesn't think so. I moved back home when he left because I couldn't afford to keep up the flat on my own, and now Mum's at me all the time. She doesn't like him, and doesn't want to like him, and she keeps saying we'll never see or hear from him again.

Normally Mum and I get on really well, but with this . . .'

'It can be a strain, can't it?' said Carla.

'I was wondering if you could give me something for the sickness,' Maureen Cummings asked. 'They call it morning sickness, but mine comes all day, and at night, too, sometimes, and it's exhausting. That's how Mum knew I must be pregnant.'

'I'd strongly advise you against taking anything,' Carla said slowly. 'There are drugs, but we're still not sure that they are completely safe. You're through the worst of it now, anyway. Do try to grin and bear it. Compared to having a retarded child, it's a small price to pay.'

'Oh, I know. I agree really. I was just hoping there was something they'd discovered . . . But I suppose I wouldn't feel safe with any drug.'

'Are you working?'

'Yes, I'm a typist, and I'm going to stay on as long as I can. It'll be so hard to tell the girls at work, though.' Maureen's eyes had almost lost their redness now, and Carla knew she could not afford to spend more time on this one patient.

'We have your address here, don't we? Someone will be round to see you in a couple of days, and she'll help you with anything. She might even be able to help you find your Bob!'

'I hope so—or I hope he just turns up.'

'And we'd like to see you again next week, so if I give you this file, could you see the nurse at the reception desk and make an appointment?'

'Yes, all right.'

Maureen Cummings got up and left the consulting room, touching her abdomen briefly with a sort of

experimental awe. Carla sighed. She looked like someone who might have loved the experience of pregnancy if
she had had the right love and support, but as it was, the
whole thing might be a grim burden, ending with the
pain of giving the baby out for adoption, or the long and
too seldom rewarding task of being a lone parent.

'I'll ring Jane Kemp right away,' Carla thought, but as
her hand rested on the phone, Dr Falconer entered the
clinic.

Up until now he had been on the wards, and there
were quite a few patients waiting to see him, with
complicated problems.

As usual, the sight of him immediately caused Carla's
throat to constrict and her entire body became tense and
ill at ease.

'Any problems, or queries, before I get involved with
my patients?' he asked her.

'No, not really. One rather sad case, though,' Carla
replied. 'I was just going to ring Jane Kemp and ask her
to look into it. A girl—or a woman, really, my age—
unmarried and pregnant and wants to trace the father.'

There! She was speaking normally enough to him
today, and in a bright, intelligent way. It seemed that at
last her fantasy of proving herself decisively to this
disagreeable man might have some chance of coming
true.

'A common enough problem,' Dr Falconer replied,
raising an eyebrow and speaking in his usual dry drawl.
He ran a finger around the inside of his pale blue shirt
collar, as if its stiffness irritated his deeply tanned neck,
and he looked tired and hollow-eyed. He was working
himself too hard, Carla thought, with an unwilling touch
of tenderness.

'And ninety-nine percent of the time, the father never materialises,' he was saying. 'Perhaps she doesn't even know who it is. It seems that women these days often don't.'

'And men these days often don't seem to know how many children they've fathered,' Carla retorted rashly, suddenly angered by his tone, and furious with herself for having allowed that brief moment of sympathy for him to slip through the barrier of her determined dislike. 'But I suppose *that* side of it is all right, according to your morals.'

'I'm surprised that you feel yourself so well-qualified to speak about my morals, considering we have only known each other for a little over two weeks,' he replied.

His eyes brushed down and up, full of scathing lights, as if his dislike encompassed her entire body as well as her personality.

'In fact, I'd be the last person to endorse this current wave of promiscuity, in either sex,' he said. 'Not perhaps for the act itself, but for the heartbreak which it so often causes, when it's indulged in without thought or care for others.'

'I don't think the case I'm talking about involved any promiscuity at all,' Carla said coldly.

'Oh, you're still referring to that are you? Sorry, my mistake. I thought we had got onto a discussion about society's morals in general, and mine in particular!' His tone was marginally less icy. Was he laughing at her behind those learned-looking reading glasses? She felt helplessly angry, as she had before in his presence. The trouble with men who thought they were so superior was that they could almost convince other people of it, too!

'I don't like people like you very much,' she said, in

low passionate tones. 'Just stop trying to squash me, squash my every opinion and idea. I'm trying to be a doctor, a good doctor, but if you keep treating me as though I'm only fit to . . . shine your shoes, then . . . then . . .'

Her words dried up and she was left in hideous silence, so she turned to leave, feeling a strong desire to cry frustrated tears. She would head for a brief refuge in the bathroom before emerging again in complete control.

But he forestalled her, catching her wrist in a capable grasp from which it would have hurt her to break free.

'Just a minute.' His voice was as full of passion as her own had been. 'I don't know where you've got all these ideas about me from, but let me tell you that they are wrong. What is it you think of me? Evidently that I hate women, and that I'm arrogant and judgmental about my patients' morals. I'm not going to defend myself to you. How could I prove that such things were not true? They are *not* true, that's all. I could pull rank and have you dismissed for speaking as you have just done to a senior doctor, but I won't.'

He paused, and she muttered some thanks, not knowing if this was what he expected and wanted, or not.

'I must start my clinic now,' he said. 'Some of those poor women have been waiting for half the afternoon . . .'

'Yes, I've got work to do, too,' Carla murmured.

'But I trust that this little scene will have cleared the air, and that things will work better between us in future?'

'I hope so.'

He rose and took off his glasses, shedding at least five years by the action, and revealing the full cool depth of his grey-green eyes. Carla stood up too, intending to splash her burning cheeks briefly in the tranquil atmosphere of the staff wash-room. Suddenly they were standing very close, their gazes locked.

'For some reason,' Lincoln Falconer said, in a low rolling tone, 'I rather want us to work well together.'

For an incredible moment, Carla thought he was going to kiss her. His eyes softened in a faint smile, and a fine fan of wrinkles formed at their corners. She swayed towards him, wanting it to happen for a few crazy seconds, but then he moved away, and she had a sudden horrible thought. Had he only been testing her willingness to respond, without committing himself in any way? Too late to try to read his mood: he had left the room now, shutting the door softly behind him.

Carla hardened herself again, and already found it incredible that his almost passionate appeal could have broken down her defences to such an extent. She must never think of the moment again, that was certain.

But he was right about some things. She *was* too ready to find fault in everything he said and did, and perhaps she had put meanings into some remarks that were not there, but one hideous fact remained: He might be very critical of modern society's morals, but that did not stop him from having an affair with a married woman. What would his defence have been if she had brought that up? Carla wondered as she returned from the wash-room and called for the next patient.

Dr Falconer had already left the clinic when Carla finished tidying up and completing case notes and file forms later that afternoon. In fact, when she emerged wearily from the consulting room, she found that it was already eight, and the place was deserted, except for one of the receptionist nurses.

'Don't tell me you're still working too!' Carla exclaimed.

'No, I just forgot something. I had to come back to get it,' the matronly Sister Evans replied. 'But I'm surprised to find you here.'

'I'm just leaving now. There's no-one else about, is there? I should check that everything is in order.'

'No, there's no-one. But I'll check things. You get off and have some rest.'

'Oh, I won't be doing that just yet,' laughed Carla. 'I've still got some Path. tests to check and two patients to see on Ward B.'

'Good heavens! You're as bad as Dr Falconer!' the nurse exclaimed. 'He drives himself to the limit, and has been doing so ever since Richard Clair's first heart attack. I've hinted that he shouldn't get involved in Board affairs, but of course a man like Lincoln Falconer makes up his own mind. But perhaps now that Louise Clair has taken over, he'll be able to relax a bit more.'

She bustled off to check that everything was switched off or safely stored for the night, again refusing to listen to Carla's offers of assistance, so Carla made her way back to the main building to attend to the tasks she had sketched out to Sister Evans.

But at first her mind was mainly on Richard Clair. He must be Louise Clair's husband, not her dead child, because Sister Evans had spoken of his 'first heart attack'. Apparently Dr Falconer's involvement in the work of the hospital board had dated from that time, making it seem likely that Richard Clair had been a member of the board until heart trouble had forced him to resign. What was his state of health now?

Carla began to envisage a sickly man, unable to be at all active because of the risk of a further—a third? a fourth?—heart attack. Perhaps he was quite a bit older than Louise Clair, in his forties, or even more. And she started to see Louise as a woman entrapped within a marriage to a much older, sicker, less attractive man, and as a woman stricken by the loss of a child.

It would not be easy, and perhaps this was why Louise had fled into the security and escapism of an affair. Lincoln Falconer might realise that Louise needed such a distraction, and . . .

'I'm making excuses for him,' Carla realised. How stupid!'

It was after nine by the time she finished, and she had not eaten, so when she encountered Michael in the foyer of the residence building, she quickly accepted his suggestion that they go out for a drink or coffee.

'Can we go somewhere where there is food?' she asked.

'Yes, no problem. You do look hungry, now that I look more closely. You have that pinched look.'

'Thanks!'

'Don't mention it!'

'I'll just change then,' Carla said.

'No need. You look great as you are.'

'But I don't *feel* great,' she retorted. 'I've had a long day, and so has this dress. I like to feel clean.'

'I won't stop you then, but you won't take too long, will you? I hate to exhibit any sinister symptoms of professional responsibility, but I'm working tomorrow morning and I want to be on the ball.'

'Don't worry,' Carla replied with a light laugh. 'I'm in the same position. I'll be five minutes, I promise.'

She was as good as her word, and was pleased at the light of approval that flickered briefly in Michael's eyes as he took in the effect of the dark blue-green silk dress she wore. It was short-sleeved, cut full and loose in the bodice, but nipped in sharply at the waist, emphasising the proportioned curves of her figure. And its colour brought out the similar sea-coloured tones in her eyes.

'I approve,' he said, and then led the way to his car, a modest blue Japanese model, but one that was comfortable and entirely adequate for city driving.

'I've picked out a place,' Michael said as they started off. 'I hope that's okay.'

'That's fine. I know nothing of eating out in Sydney.'

'It's a little Italian joint.'

'Lovely!'

'You can eat pasta or pizza to your heart's content and I'll consume modest quantities of gelato icecream and coffee.'

They drove to busy Darling Street and chose a tiny table in the window.

'I love watching people go past,' Michael said. 'It's an endless source of inspiration for conversation, don't you find?'

'Yes I do,' Carla laughed.

'And if it isn't a small world, here comes the Chief and his lady!'

'The Chief?' But she knew who he meant even before the words were out of her mouth.

Lincoln Falconer and Louise Clair strolled slowly past, arm in arm and oblivious of Carla and Michael.

Probably they had just finished a meal in one of the many other restaurants along this road. Louise was laughing, resting her head briefly on Dr Falconer's firm shoulder and then smiling at him with frank desire in her eyes. His own face was less well lit. Carla strained to catch his expression, but before she could, they had passed on. She wondered what poor ill Richard Clair was doing that evening.

'I don't think much of that relationship at all,' Carla said in low decisive tones, suddenly needing to express what she felt.

'What? Not jealous, are we?' Michael teased, watching her carefully.

'Jealous! Of course not,' Carla said, aware that her cheeks had gone pink. The emotion she felt when she thought of the couple *was* strangely akin to jealousy, but it couldn't be. She detested both of them.

There was an awkward silence for a few moments as she searched for her next words. Michael was still watching her, nodding his head slowly as if coming to some new realisation.

'I think it's shocking that Lin . . . that Dr Falconer and Louise Clair are seen together so openly, that's all,' she said.

'Why?'

'Because Louise Clair is married, that's why.'

'Married! She . . . Oh, yes, you're right, I suppose, to feel like that.' There was something odd in his tone, and she looked at him closely.

'Aren't you shocked? Don't you think it's a bad thing?'

'What? As a general rule?'

'Yes. Although I may be old-fashioned to say so.'

'No you're not old-fashioned,' he was suddenly serious, and sighed as he spoke.

'And in this instance in particular,' Carla went on. 'A man in Lincoln's position, and with Mrs Clair a member of the Board! What does it do to the reputation of the hospital?'

'What indeed?' Michael said absently, apparently lost in complex thought. He spoke again briefly. 'Look, Carla, don't say anything about your views around the hospital, will you? I mean, I agree with you whole-heartedly, but . . . it's not any of our business, is it?'

'I disagree. If it affects the hospital, then it is our business. Apparently Richard Clair used to be on the Board before his illness . . .'

'Richard Clair . . .'

'Richard Clair. Louise's husband,' Carla said impatiently. 'You keep repeating everything I say. So with all three of them connected with the hospital so intimately, it's bound to come out. I think the whole thing is weird!'

They did not speak any more about the affair, but Carla's outburst seemed to have altered the atmosphere of the evening. Or was it Michael's mood that had changed? He seemed thoughtful and quiet, and did not suggest that they linger for more coffee when Carla had finished her meal.

He roused himself to adopt his normal lively manner only as they turned into the staff car-park near the residence buildings.

'We must do this more often,' he said with rather forced enthusiasm.

'Yes!' Carla's response was less than sincere, too. She felt she was seeing too much of Michael, but it was hard to refuse his invitations, or to shrug off his company at meals, and he *was* fun to be with.

'Carla?'

His voice was suddenly low and had a questioning intonation. The car was parked, and the engine and lights were off. Carla was about to open the door but he moved closer and laid a hand on her left forearm, not restraining her, but coaxing her to nestle against him.

'No Michael,' she said firmly. She did not want to be kissed tonight. Not by Michael Groom. A fleeting image of Lincoln Falconer's face, close and gazing down at her, crossed her inner vision. His lips had looked firm yet soft, and very capable of tenderness . . .

She pushed the image aside.

'Don't be like that,' Michael was saying, closer still now.

'No, please, I mean it, Michael.'

'Not so fast, hey? All right, I understand. Perhaps I have been pushing it.'

Carla bit her lip. Should she tell him straight out that there was no point in continuing this if he wanted some serious involvement with her? That they could only ever be friends?

Perhaps this was not the truth though. She might one day fall in love with Michael. Carla had always expected that there would have to be an immediate physical attraction between herself and the man she chose to love, but she knew many couples who had come together gradually through friendship and common interests, loving each other physically later on.

So she said nothing. Michael had been gentle in his attempt to make love to her. She would wait a while longer and perhaps the thing would drift apart of its own accord. She suddenly wished she was one of those girls who had been out with dozens of boys, and men, during their university years. She knew so little of the reality of love, and the many forms it could take. She did not even know if she was looking for a serious relationship or not.

Carla wondered suddenly what Lincoln Falconer felt about the fact that the woman he was in love with was married. Probably he did not mind, and perhaps he even preferred it that way. When such a man reached his age without having married, it was obviously out of choice . . .

Michael had stayed in the car, thoughtfully smoking a cigarette after Carla had said an awkward goodnight, so she walked to the residence building alone. She passed another occupied car as she crossed the car-park, and for a second or two, caught sight of two figures locked in a close embrace. Was everyone at the Boronia Women's Hospital in love except herself? Funny, she had never thought so much about such things before.

There was no time to think of them again in the next few days. Work at the hospital began to take more and more of her time, and consumed her thoughts completely. She was tense as she did her morning round on Wednesday, waiting for the moment when Lincoln Falconer would enter. Carla was becoming accustomed to the sudden sight of his tall form in the doorway, and to the odd jerk of her heartbeat as she caught his eye.

The immediate attentiveness and self-conscious activity of the nurses and ward maids was part of the pattern, too, and Carla wondered wryly if there was a single female member of the staff who was completely immune to the attraction of his mature bearing, his rare crinkling and inevitably dry smile, and his eyes that seemed sometimes to be cool and warm at the same moment. She wondered, too, how many people knew of his involvement with Mrs Clair, and what they thought of it.

Today he was later than usual, she thought, as she examined the imperfect healing of an over-weight mother's episiotomy.

'You're right,' she said to Sister Menzies who was hovering nearby. 'There is a slight infection. I don't think the tear will need further repair, though. I'll prescribe a cream and otherwise we'll continue with normal treatment. It's not giving you too much discomfort, is it, Mrs Raye?'

'No, not really,' she replied. 'A bit irritating. But then when I have the sunray lamp on it, it's heaven!'

'Is it? I'm glad,' Carla smiled. 'But I wish more of our methods of treatment could merit that adjective!'

She moved on to the next patient, glancing involuntarily towards the cubicle door as she did so. Still no sign of the senior obstetrician. Of course, he could be working in the other half of the ward . . .

Sister Menzies spoke. Had she noticed Carla's frequent glances and read them correctly?

'I wonder where Dr Cleland is. Dr Falconer isn't usually as late as this.'

'Dr Cleland?' Carla queried. Of course she knew him: he was also an obstetrician, but his work did not generally take him onto this ward during the hours when Carla was there.

'Yes,' Sister Menzies said, surprised. 'Dr Falconer has gone to Melbourne for three days to give some lectures. Didn't you know? Dr Cleland will be taking over, with some help from Dr Smith from Acute Admissions. I'm surprised Dr Falconer didn't tell you . . .'

The senior nurse turned to give an instruction to a first year student, leaving Carla suddenly unaccountably depressed. Lincoln Falconer had not condescended to tell her that he would not be here, merely making arrangements to cover the extra workload and leaving the fact of his absence to be communicated by a casual remark.

Was this a sign of the insignificance of her work in his eyes? No, she thought. Much more likely that he was planning to let her know, but that awful scene of yesterday afternoon had left him no opportunity.

And so it was her own fault really. Anyway, it was a small enough thing. Work would proceed almost as usual without him. She would merely bring any doubts or problems to Robert Cleland or Gordon Smith instead, both of whom were capable men. And surely she was not feeling hurt in a personal sense? Now, more than ever, she and Lincoln Falconer had no personal relationship whatsoever.

Which was exactly how she wanted it.

Once Carla had sorted out these feelings, she was relieved in a way, that she would not see the disturbing doctor for two whole days. In her memory Tuesday's scene had blurred a little in its detail, but its meaning grew stronger all the time. 'I hate you!' Had she really said that? No, wasn't it, 'I hate people like you'? But it amounted to the same thing: an inexcusable way to speak to anyone, let alone a senior doctor, and part of an outburst that was normally quite foreign to her nature.

Why did Dr Falconer so often succeed in rousing her to anger?

She wished she could remember, too, how definite her response to his near-kiss had been. Or rather, she wished she could be back in the scene again, a fly on the wall, able to watch her own actions and judge how they would appear to someone else. In other words, how they would have appeared to him.

Each night of Lincoln Falconer's absence, she lay in bed for a long time, unable to sleep as she replayed the whole scene over in her mind as clearly as she could.

Perhaps she *was* exaggerating it. She had been accused before of having a too-vivid imagination. Perhaps he had forgiven her anger, or was equally ashamed of his own, and perhaps the surge of need within her as he had bent towards her had gone unnoticed.

'Dr Falconer would like to see you before you start work,' the receptionist told Carla as she passed through the main foyer on Friday morning.

'Oh! Yes, of course,' Carla replied, heart racing suddenly.

She knew he was to be back at work today, but had hoped that their first encounter could be in the safe atmosphere of the ward, where any constraint or anger on his part would go unnoticed, and where she might have a chance to prove by her own conduct that Monday's scene was well and truly put behind her.

This summons was unnerving. Carla had not been alone with the doctor in his office since that session on her first morning, less than three weeks ago. That had also been an occasion of flaring emotions, she remembered. Would he bring up Monday's incident again? At the time she had thought he was proposing to forgive and forget, but now, after dwelling on it for so long, she had lost all sense of proportion . . .

She turned to the lift, saw that the door was open, and half-expected as she entered to find Dr Falconer already there, as he had been on the fateful morning of their first meeting. But it was empty.

Carla used the opportunity to check her appearance with special care. Anything to help boost an unusually ailing confidence. Yes, she looked passable. The dress was right – a practical summer suit, as the weather was cooler today than it had been, in a pretty wedgwood blue linen and synthetic blend.

She wore a light touch of make-up, too, and low, thin strapped, sandal-style shoes. Carla found her face less satisfying than her figure. She knew that her mouth was too large, and never saw the subtleties of expression it could communicate. She could only observe the severity it gave her face when she stared at the artificial portrait of the mirror.

The lift arrived. Just time for a final pat of the sleek bobbing waves of her rich brown hair. Why on earth was she making such a thing out of this?

Carla walked through the waiting-room, saw that Mrs Fitton had not yet arrived, and knocked lightly at Dr Falconer's door . . .

CHAPTER FIVE

LINCOLN Falconer sat in his office and gazed unseeingly out of the wide window which overlooked the main driveway of the hospital and the grounds beyond, tapping his pen absently on the expensive teak surface of his large desk. Dr Scott ought to arrive at any minute. He frowned. Why had he left that impulsive message at the reception desk? The cocktail party invitation of course, but he could have issued that some other time.

He had not been thinking of her at all this morning, until he had caught her name spoken by a passing student nurse.

'Yes, I like her too,' the girl's companion, one of the growing number of male nurses at the hospital, had replied. 'One doctor, at least, who doesn't cause instant terror.'

'She's only an intern. She'll probably be as fierce as any in a few years. Look at Dr Cornwell. She's only about thirty, but you'd say that ice ran in her veins . . .'

The two had passed out of hearing, but Lincoln's mind had still been on what they had said about Carla Scott. They liked her. He would like her too, damn her, if she'd let him. If she wasn't so damned impertinent. She had succeeded in making him very angry last Monday, and it had not been a good feeling. Damn her, he thought for the second time. She had done quite a bit to earn his dislike, but on the contrary, he knew he wanted to get to know her better. Perhaps he admired her courage in expressing her opinions. He did like a good argument, but it was more that he wanted to find out what made these Granville graduates tick.

Peter Martin had accused him of prejudice against them, and perhaps he was right. Lincoln knew he was a bit suspicious of anything that smacked of the naive optimism of the sixties flower children.

Some of the phrases from the Granville faculty prospectus came back to him: 'developing the caring skills of our students', 'an integrated approach'. Perhaps it was his British reserve, but some of those phrases really grated. The sort of words that got splashed about everywhere and often meant less than nothing. For Heaven's sake, he believed in caring too, and 'integration', if they meant the same thing by it as he did. But he believed in a thorough and utterly sound knowledge of anatomy and physiology too. And he believed in brains. Nurses were being trained better than ever before, and he did not want to see a doctor's training become sloppy and overburdened with trendy terminology at the same time.

Yes, he would like to talk to Carla . . . Dr Scott, and find out what she really thought about these things. He had a sudden image of sitting alone with her at some intimate little restaurant, watching her hair bob and swing as she talked, using those creamy hands so expressively. All at once this picture made him think of doing the same thing with Helen, it must be, what, ten, eleven years ago now. Before her callous rejection of him and the timely arrival from Australia of the offer of work at the Boronia . . .

He shook his head to clear these thoughts from his mind, although now there was no hurt and anger left, and there had not been for quite a while. He thought of

Louise, depending on him so much now since her brother's death. The family had been such a close one. Old Mrs Clair would never be the same again, and Louise had been more deeply wounded than he had expected, although she hid it well behind that capable and very attractive facade. Hid it too well, he sometimes thought. Would he be able to give her what she needed to recover completely? She loved him, that was clear, or she thought she did. And sometimes—often—he thought he loved her. At other times though, he was less sure . . .

There was a tentative tap at the door.

'Come in,' he called, the authoritative tone giving no hint of the doubts contained in his recent musings.

Carla entered, unable at first to meet his eye for more than a fraction of a second. For some reason, she infinitely preferred to see him wearing his glasses. They seemed to make him less threatening, perhaps because they made him look a few years older. She could relegate him to her father's generation, although he was much closer to her own, and pretend to herself that she did not have any awareness of him as a man at all.

'You wanted to see me?' she murmured, still expecting some reference to last Monday's explosive episode, although now that she dared to look closer, she saw that his manner this morning was comparatively benign. Benign! A ludicrously inappropriate adjective to apply to Dr Lincoln Falconer at any time. Perhaps 'forgiving' or 'merciful' were more suitable.

'Yes, I did,' he was saying, brief and dry as ever, but not hostile. 'Firstly because there is to be a cocktail party at my house on Sunday night at five. Just hospital people—the medical staff and a few senior nurses, as well as one or two people connected with administration. I'd like you to be there if you can.'

It was the last thing she had expected, but of course the invitation could scarcely be considered a personal one. Carla Scott had been included on the list automatically. She wondered why Dr Falconer had not merely tossed out the invitation in the course of their work, or sent a written one through the hospital post, since it obviously amounted to an official hospital affair.

'Yes, I'll be there,' she replied.

'Good.'

There was a small silence and Carla felt that Lincoln's thoughts were far away. And he looked tired and strained too.

'Was there anything else?' she asked, strangely unwilling to break a moment of quiet that for once had no constraint in it.

'Yes, I just wanted to ask you if everything has gone smoothly this week. I'm afraid that in a lot of hospitals interns are usually left to sink or swim, but I don't think that is very good, so if you do have any problems, try to find time to bring them to me—or to any of the other senior doctors.'

'Yes, thank you, I will,' Carla replied a little awkwardly. Again, his words were unexpected, and she did not quite know how he wanted her to reply. 'I'm managing well so far. I'm loving it, and learning more every day.'

'Well, I'll let you get on with it then.'

There was audible relief in his tone and she guessed that he was as glad as she was to terminate the interview, although probably not for the same reasons. Doubtless it was hospital policy to encourage junior members of staff to voice problems or complaints, rather than a gesture Lincoln Falconer had made on his own.

The Boronia prided itself on good staff relations, believing that it led to greater satisfaction for the patients as well. However, she had heard from Peter Higgins that one or two doctors did not even make a token attempt at holding to this policy, so as the senior obstetrician ushered her out of his office and gave her a brief nod and smile of dismissal, she mentally notched up a few good points to him. Or rather, cancelled out some of the black marks he had already earnt in her rigorously principled mind.

The rest of the day was hectic, and so was Saturday, as there was a normal round of duties, a clinic in the afternoon, and a long night of work in the delivery rooms assisting with three complicated births. Carla was still on duty after four a.m.—Sunday morning!—helping with the last stage of a relatively simple birth, but looking forward to tumbling into bed very soon.

Surely nothing could go wrong here now! And Carla did not think she was required in any other part of the hospital this evening—or rather, this morning. She stifled a yawn, as the capable hands of the midwife drew out the baby and Mrs Keens sank back onto the pillows, exhausted but already radiant.

'It's a little girl, Mrs Keens!' Carla said.

'Oh how perfect! Is she healthy? Can I hold her? I wish my husband was here, but I knew he would be too ill. He can't even see a cut finger without feeling sick . . .'

'We'll just make some routine checks on the baby before you hold her, Mrs Keens,' Carla said.

The child was small, only five pounds, but as long as

certain tests gave good results, and the baby was able to feed within two hours, she would be able to lie with Mrs Keens straight away.

Carla's bleep sounded at that moment and she went to the wall-phone installed near the door of the delivery room.

'Reception? Dr Scott speaking. I've just been bleeped, can you tell . . . ?'

'Yes,' replied the tired night receptionist. 'You've got to go to Theatre 2 immediately and scrub up.'

'Right, thank you.'

The receptionist clicked down the receiver at the other end before Carla could ask why she was needed, but she found time to say a few parting words to Mrs Keens before hurrying off.

The corridors seemed long and glaring tonight as she waited for the lift, and she just had time to notice through the end window that the sky was beginning to lighten with the first hint of dawn. She was tired, no use to pretend otherwise, but suddenly she felt a surge of exhilaration. There was something about the hospital this late at night. It kept going while the rest of Sydney was asleep, because its work was vital. Birth, death and illness took little account of the material differences in people's lives, and everyone at some time would come to a doctor in need or pain. It suddenly felt good to be part of such a profession.

Carla reached the maze-like below-ground area where the ultra-modern theatres and their various ante-rooms were situated, still in quite a glow. There was a swing door leading to the ante-room in which patients were wheeled from the big service lift used to transport trolleys and stretchers, and Carla pushed it open unthinkingly, not even seeing the familiar red sign:—'Care when opening!'

'For God's sake, watch what you're doing!'

Lincoln Falconer's furious yet still controlled tones rapped out at the same time as the heavy impact of the door against the patient's trolley. And Carla's small cry of horror overlapped with the prostrate woman's own longer cry of shock and added pain.

Carla's uplift of a few moments before drained away instantly, but she had no time to feel remorse.

'Don't apologise, Doctor,' said the senior obstetrician. 'Just get on with your preparations. I'll speak to you later. This is a cord prolapse and we have to have that baby out by Caesarean in less than fifteen minutes.'

'Yes, Doctor.' Carla's face was burning, and she had to clasp her hands together as she washed them to still their shaking.

A junior nurse stood by holding out a pair of gloves. Lincoln Falconer was already masked, and to Carla it seemed that his face was just a pair of eyes staring in silent condemnation.

She had a few seconds in which to look about, and the room seemed to be full of people who would all have witnessed her painful mistake. Michael stood by his equipment but was too involved in his preparations to give Carla a glance. The senior pediatrician was standing by ready to examine the baby on delivery. The white forms of two nurses were moving about with practical speed, and Dr Falconer was already fully prepared.

'You haven't seen one of these before, Dr Scott?'

'A cord prolapse? No.'

'Then you had better take a good look now.'

It was the only piece of extraneous conversation to take place. The woman was in pain and still conscious. The merciful oblivion of general anaesthesia was not induced until the last minute in order to protect the baby from the effects of the anaesthetising agents.

Carla painted an antiseptic solution onto the abdomen and helped to drape the area, thankful that at least she had stopped shaking and could concentrate on something other than the unfortunate effect of her hasty entry into the theatre.

But her awareness was centred on Dr Falconer throughout the operation. He gave her little to do and she was free to observe each perfectly controlled movement made by his brown hands, scarcely disguised by the modern transparent plastic gloves he wore.

She glanced up only once, to look at his eyes that were more forbidding than ever above the flat green of the mask as they focussed absolutely upon what he was doing. Doubtless his heavy frown, too, was simply a sign of care and concentration, but Carla shivered nonetheless—and caught the tiny gesture of annoyance that Dr Falconer gave as he was disturbed fractionally by the involuntary movement.

The minutes seemed to pass with nightmare slowness, but at last the baby was brought out, alive, though cyanosed and feeble in its movements.

Now attention in the tense atmosphere of the theatre was divided. Dr Fox, the senior pediatrician, was completely involved with the tiny boy, and a nurse hovered close by to give assistance. Dr Falconer was completing the final part of the Caesarean and getting ready to close the incision. Michael stood by with resuscitation equipment.

'The Agpar score is low,' Dr Fox said. 'There's no gasp at all, and muscle tone is limp.'

'It's very blue,' the nurse murmured.

Carla felt tension increase. Perhaps, after all the speed and drama of the operation, and the relief felt when the baby emerged alive, he might still die. She knew that one in a hundred infant deaths in the first week of life were caused by conditions of the umbilical cord.

'Intubation?' Dr Falconer questioned tersely.

'Yes,' Dr Fox replied. 'We'll have to. We can't delay any longer.'

'Watch this, Carla,' said Dr Falconer. 'It's tricky, and you'll be doing it one day.'

'I've practised it on a model,' she murmured in reply, too intent on what was being done to notice his use of her first name.

Dr Fox inserted the endotracheal tube with minute care, and began to rhythmically release oxygen into the baby's lungs at short intervals.

'We've got it!' he said at last. 'Spontaneous respiration! I think it's going to be all right.'

He kept the tube in place for several more minutes but the baby's breathing became stronger all the time, and it began to seem certain that he would be all right, although Carla knew that there were still several more tasks and tests to be performed before they could be sure.

The still-unconscious mother was soon ready to be returned to her bed, the baby was placed in a special crib, and the anxious and still-waiting father could at last receive a first short glimpse of the tiny child who had had to struggle so hard for life.

The tension of the atmosphere began to dissipate. Michael leant across to a junior nurse and made a small joke that brought a flash of a smile to her tired face. Dr Fox was talking to the senior nurse. Dr Falconer had already peeled off gloves, mask and cap, and left only moments later, without having spoken a word to Carla since his instruction to watch the tube insertion carefully.

'I'm not sure what I should be doing,' she said uncertainly to Dr Fox.

'What?' He turned to her, recalling only with difficulty who she was. 'Oh . . . er . . . Dr Scott. Go home, my dear, go home. You've been here longer than you were supposed to anyway, haven't you?'

'Yes, I was due off at one, but things were a bit hectic . . .'

'And then this came up. Well get some rest straight away then!'

'I will,' she said, preparing to go.

She glanced across at Michael. He was still chatting to the little nurse, explaining some part of his complex monitoring equipment to her. Carla decided not to interrupt to say goodnight. Similarly, Sister Gray and the young male nurse who had wheeled in the trolley were cleaning and tidying the theatre.

'I'll just slip out . . .' Carla thought.

This time as she went through the two sets of swing doors the red signs seemed to leap out at her with accusatory brightness. How on earth could she have forgotten them before! Dr Falconer was almost certain to bring up the matter again next time Carla saw him. Which would be at tonight's cocktail party, she suddenly remembered. It seemed impossible that she would have the energy to go. What was the time now? After five. But didn't daylight saving end this weekend? At least that would give her an extra hour's sleep.

She would sleep until lunch time, and then she should spend a bit of time recording some of the details of this morning's operation. The experience could come in useful.

She did not intend to arrive at the cocktail party promptly at five, though. She wanted to be certain that there would already be a good crowd gathered when she made her appearance. Not that she was trying to shirk the likely reprimand from Dr Falconer. She simply wanted to avoid being alone with him until her unfortunate mistake had receded further into the past.

She reached her room and flopped onto the bed, not even able to remove her shoes. For a while she lay there, waiting for the tension that still knotted in her limbs to dissipate, and then she prepared properly for bed, putting her clock and watch back an hour, and setting her alarm for twelve, now seven hours away.

Her thoughts wandered erratically and would not slow down even when she deliberately rolled onto her back and began to talk herself through a relaxation exercise. Eventually she knew that it was futile to chase sleep any longer, and reached for the light novel that lay on her bedside table . . .

It had slipped to the floor, she noticed, hours later when she awoke, but at what point during her heavy slumber she did not know. All she was aware of at first as she took an incredulous look at the clock, was that it was five in the evening, and she must have slept for well over ten hours.

What had happened to her alarm? A closer look told her that she had forgotten to set the bell. Hardly surprising, considering how tired she had been this morning. Even now she was not fully awake and alert. Something nagged at the back of her mind but she could not think what it was. Five o'clock. The time seemed significant for some reason.

The cocktail party at Lincoln Falconer's! She scrambled out of bed, then sat down again quickly. The room was rather stuffy and day-time sleep did not agree with her. Her head was throbbing, and she felt stiff, lifeless and depressed. Perhaps she could skip the party, and give her apologies tomorrow, or later this evening by phone? After all, she was going to be very late now.

The shower beckoned invitingly, and Carla undressed and got under it, pondering the question, but it did not take her long to decide. She would *have* to go to the party, or Dr Falconer would think that she was afraid to face his justifiable reprimand after this morning's incident.

And he would be right of course. It was not that she was reluctant to face up to her own mistakes in general, but in this case, she was afraid of the doctor himself.

The cooling refreshing water splashed over her, streaming through her hair and tingling on her face. If she shampooed her hair quickly, took a pain killer for her head, and put on one of her nicest dresses—perhaps that almost formal black calf-length one—then she would feel healthy and confident enough to face the doubtless rather stiff atmosphere of the hospital gathering.

Aware of the rapid passing of time, she made these

preparations as quickly as possible, and it was only just after six when she was ready to set out, hair only slightly damp after a session with the blow-dryer, and headache almost gone.

A last look in the mirror was re-assuring. The black dress with its satin sheen, thin straps and swirling full skirt below a tight bodice, was all that an after-five dress should be. She had added a dainty bead choker neck-lace, matching earrings and strappy shoes, and carried a cream silk jacket just in case the evening had cooled by the time she left.

Carla picked up the card Dr Falconer had given her and saw his name and profession printed in simple back letters, with the address of the hospital and his private address appearing below. Vaucluse—about half an hour's drive.

As Michael Groom had said, it was one of the most prestigious, as well as most beautiful, suburbs in Sydney. She felt a faint curiosity about the senior obstetrician's private life-style and it overshadowed her nerves. She hoped that Michael would be at the party to satisfy his! Perhaps it might be a pleasant occasion after all—light conversation, a summery drink and perhaps a little food, the chance to get to know a few more of her colleagues and co-workers.

It was twenty-five to seven when she arrived at the house—a detached one with a lush sloping garden, not a town-house or flat. Carla parked her little car, a bit surprised that the street was not more congested with vehicles.

Dr Falconer's car sat in his driveway, and there were a few more up and down the street, but that was all. The party had started an hour and a half ago, of course

Possibly some people had already left, and others had come in groups, several to each car.

There did not seem to be much noise from within either. Was this really the right house? Yes, there was the number '24' in clear figures on the door, and that was certainly Dr Falconer's distinctive dark red car brushed by some low hanging gum leaf clusters from a tall tree that shaded the driveway.

It must simply be a rather quiet party. She rang the doorbell and Dr Falconer answered, his powerful frame blocking her view of the interior.

'I'm sorry I'm late,' Carla faltered. 'I overslept after last night, but I thought that half past six wouldn't be too late to arrive.'

'Half past six!' The doctor exclaimed, stepping aside for her.

She entered, passed through a small entrance hall and came face to face with an empty room. Empty, that is, except for the debris of an obviously ended party.

'My dear girl,' Lincoln Falconer was saying. 'I'm afraid your watch must be a bit out of kilter. It's after half past seven!'

'But I don't understand,' Carla said, flushing to the roots of her hair. 'My alarm said the same. It's not just my watch.'

Suddenly Lincoln Falconer threw back his head and laughed. Carla summoned a cold look.

'I'm afraid I don't quite see the joke.' She tried to pretend that she did not mind his laughing at her expense.

'Well, I'll let you in on it then.' He sobered in response to her tone, but there was still a distinct twinkle in his eye. 'Did you think daylight saving ended last night?'

'Yes. It always ends on this weekend every summer. And my calendar said so, too.'

'You're too clever for your own good. And you have obviously been too busy to listen to the news. Daylight saving has been extended for one month because of the power strikes.'

'Oh yes. I heard a rumour, but I didn't realise it had been decided definitely,' she muttered.

Another time she would have found the occurrence amusing too, of course, but she was too full of the memory of this morning's reprimand now, and too tense in the company of this man.

'Come on, Carla,' Dr Falconer was saying. 'Laugh about it with me, please!'

'I can't.' She broke into a reluctant smile nonetheless. 'It is funny, I suppose. Although if I had been on duty, and had been late for that, would you . . . ?'

'Would I have been furious? Perhaps. But that would have been as much a symptom of my tiredness as the mistake about time was of yours. I'm not that much of an ogre, you know. Like this morning when you opened those doors. Please forgive me for that.'

'No, you had every right to be angry,' Carla said.

He was being so pleasant this evening, she could scarcely believe it, and found that she was warming towards him as a result, more than she would have thought possible. If he had reprimanded her again about her carelessness with the swing doors, she might have defended herself, but now that he was actually apologising for his anger, she wanted to admit her guilt.

'No, I should not have been angry,' he was saying. 'Not when I could see that you were fully aware of what you had done. If you hadn't cared, then, yes, but I could see that you did . . .'

'You could see it?'

'Yes, it was written all over your face. I know you always care about what you do.'

'Oh. Thank you.' She was thrown quite off balance by his praise.

'Don't thank me. I'm only speaking the truth. And now, perhaps I can get you a drink? There are a few hors d'oeuvres left too.'

'No, how can I? The party is over. You would rather be left in peace.'

She was still standing awkwardly near the door of the sitting room, and moved to open it, wanting only to escape from this strangely pleasant interlude, but he spoke, restraining her.

'I would not rather be left in peace! Please stay. In fact, come out to dinner with me.'

'I can't . . .'

'You have a previous engagement?'

'No, it's not that, but . . .'

'Then you *can* come. Please don't say no.' He was quite sincere, and bending quite close to her as he spoke.

'All right.' Carla could only agree, wishing that she had claimed a previous engagement, but it was too late now.

She was sure that the evening could not possibly be a pleasant one, although her old physical awareness of Lincoln Falconer had surged more strongly than ever tonight. He wore the dark trousers of a well-cut suit, but his torso was covered only by a cream shirt, its sleeves rolled to his elbows. The neck was open too, hinting strongly at a chest well-thatched with hair.

This unusual informality made his powerful frame even more attractive than usual, and Carla could not help enjoying the sight of him.

'I should go,' she said again, sensing the danger of her train of thought.

'Afraid I'll ask you to clean up?' he said with a crooked, teasing smile.

'No, of course not!'

'I don't believe you! I saw the glance you gave at my rolled up sleeves, and you're right. I am about to start the washing up. But naturally you will sit down with a drink and listen to some music, while I dispose of all this.' He waved his hand at the jumble of glasses and dirty plates. 'It won't take long.'

'I wouldn't dream of letting you do it all!' Carla retorted, realising at the same time that he had well and truly trapped her now. She could not leave him to clean up this mess after she had first accepted his dinner invitation. 'I'll do my share.'

'You will not. You weren't even at the party.'

The phone rang at that moment, and he moved to answer it. For Carla that settled the matter. The only way to avoid eavesdropping was to busy herself with cleaning up, so she moved to a tray of glasses, ignoring Lincoln's helpless frown.

'Carla, you simply must . . . Hullo? . . . Oh, Louise! How are you? . . . Good!'

Carla could not help overhearing every word on her journeys between kitchen and sitting-room, and again she was sorry that she had accepted the doctor's invitation. Louise Clair was on the phone, probably proposing some outing. The fact of her affair with the senior obstetrician had not entered Carla's head this evening, but now its meaning came back to her in full force. Dr Falconer was still on the phone.

'But dear, I thought you had that drinks party at the Bruces', and then the dinner with those design people . . . You've cancelled the dinner? But why? . . . But Louise I can't. No, something has come up.'

Out of the corner of her eye, as she gathered up a last tray of dirty dishes and crumpled paper napkins, Carla saw him glance across at her. She carried the tray carefully to the kitchen, trying to seem, and be, unaware of his conversation.

'No, it doesn't matter about the cocktails here,' he was saying now. 'Yes, it went well, but I'm actually more worried about you missing that dinner. Your career . . . Yes, I suppose so . . . Peter Prior's phone number? No, not here. Ring the main switchboard of the hospital. Tell them who you are and they will give it to you. But why . . . ? Oh yes, I see.'

Carla shut the kitchen door and began to run hot water into the sink to begin washing up. Lincoln had the right to talk privately to Louise even if their affair was an illicit one.

But the doctor entered only moments later and took the green rubber washing up gloves from Carla just as she was about to put them on.

'I'll tackle this,' he said. 'And you can sit down.'

'No, I'll dry,' Carla insisted.

'I suppose it's no good arguing the point?'

'No use whatsoever. Everyone knows that glasses have to be dried when hot or they look smeary and dirty.'

They completed the task together, chatting more easily than they had ever done before, although only about trivial daily things. He made no mention of the telephone call, and Carla knew she had no right to bring it up. If he felt he had to keep to his promise to take her out, rather than being with Louise, as she had evidently been suggesting, that was his business.

'Now will you have that drink?' he said when the kitchen and sitting-room were both spotless.

'I don't think so,' Carla began.

'You'd rather go out to eat straight away, and get this evening over with?'

'Exactly!'

'We'll assume that neither of those remarks was intended seriously!'

He disappeared into a bedroom at the end of the corridor for a few minutes, leaving Carla alone. It felt strange to be with him like this, alone together in his own house.

It was all that the house of such a man ought to be, too, she thought, her determined dislike of him receding further every minute. The sitting-room was decorated in muted shades of beige and brown, but original paintings added splashes of colour, and an entire wall of books demonstrated Lincoln Falconer's wide reading tastes.

There were medical textbooks and journals, as well as reference books of other kinds, but there were also books of poetry and plays. There were novels, too, ranging from light detective stories to the classics of several centuries, including original French and German works.

Through the open door that led to the dining room, Carla could see side-boards and cabinets containing beautiful sets of old china, glass and cutlery, and realised that these were probably family possessions—heirlooms, some of them—which he had brought out from England.

French windows formed the whole of another wall of Lincoln Falconer's sitting-room, and these led to a terrace which commanded a splendid view of the harbour.

Carla could not resist stepping out there to stand amongst a lush collection of potted plants and take in breaths of the deep blue evening air. The lights of the city were so beautiful from here, reflected in the benign late summer water.

'I'm glad you like it,' Dr Falconer murmured almost in her ear. He had slipped onto the terrace without her hearing, and was standing just behind her.

'It's wonderful,' Carla breathed. 'I wish I could see your garden more clearly, that's all.'

'Yes, I'm quite proud of it – although I can't claim that it's all my own work. I have a gardener who comes in for several hours each week. This lawn below us slopes right down to the water, where I have a small mooring for my boat. You'll have to see all that next time . . . But now shall I show you the rest of the house?'

'Oh, no thank you,' she almost stammered in reply. 'I mean, I think we should go, shouldn't we?'

'If you prefer, yes . . .'

He was looking at her in a way she found disconcerting. And why had she become so flustered at his suggestion that they see the rest of the house? She couldn't quite pinpoint the reason, but it was partly an unwillingness to see too far into his private life. She would go out with him tonight, and might easily enjoy it, but she simply did not want to get to know him too well as a person.

She was afraid of what might happen.

And then Carla thought for the first time of the significance of the first part of Dr Falconer's remark about the garden.

'You'll have to see all that next time,' he had said. When did he think there would be a next time? If it was up to her, there would never be.

'I booked us into a little seafood place,' Lincoln Falconer said as they left the house and walked towards his handsome dark red car parked in the driveway. 'I hope that is all right?'

'It's fine. I love seafood,' Carla replied.

'It's on the waterfront, too, and rather beautiful on a night like this. I think we will have a very pleasant evening.'

'I'm sure we will,' Carla responded politely.

Actually, of course, she was far from sure. Wouldn't the evening be something of a tightrope walk? On one side she was still very wary of Lincoln Falconer, and still disapproved of some of the things she knew about him. But on the other, she found she was actually coming to like him more and more.

This was disturbing. It should be much easier to dislike someone who was. so openly involved with a married woman, and who held such a prejudice against women doctors, even if that prejudice now seemed to be breaking down, in Carla's case at least.

She wondered why he had asked her.

The drive was a very pleasant one in spite of these thoughts, however. The low red sportscar travelled smoothly and Lincoln Falconer was an expert driver, negotiating the city traffic with deceptive ease. He talked easily, too, about general subjects, drawing Carla out and seeming very interested in her replies.

She had put on her pretty cream jacket before they left the house, and she was glad, because when they arrived at the restaurant, a fresh breeze blew from the water, and the walk from the car park would have been cold if she had been wearing only her dress with its flimsy fabric and strap shoulders.

'We're very well matched,' Lincoln said as they entered the restaurant—an old ferry boat permanently anchored and newly decorated with warm colours and glowing lights.

'How do you mean?' Carla was a little flustered by his remark.

'I mean our clothes,' he replied. 'My cream shirt, your cream jacket, my dark suit, and your dress. Even our eyes are similar.'

'Oh no, mine have more blue, and yours more grey,' she said without thinking, then bit her lip.

What would he make of that? Would he be surprised that she had observed his eyes so closely? She was surprised herself. Was it normal to be so aware of the subtleties of a person's eye colour? She thought of Sally Lewis. Now, her eyes were brown, weren't they? No, on second thoughts, blue . . .

But what was he saying now?

'Your eyes are very changeable, I've noticed. Sometimes they are as dark and stormy as the sea, and at others they are a clear, sunny blue-green. The scientist in me says it's the effect of different lights, but it is tempting to believe that it might be a reflection of your mood.'

'I don't know what to say to that,' Carla replied,

deciding that honesty was the only response, given her confusion.

'Well, I suppose my observations amount to a compliment, so please take them as one.'

'In that case, thank you.'

How very odd this conversation was! They were seated now at a window-side table on the upper deck of 'The Old Ferry'—actually the restaurant's name—and could see a large expanse of bay, filled with pleasure boats moored for the night.

A waiter arrived with menus, and Carla turned to hers gratefully. Lincoln Falconer evidently felt that if he was taking a woman out to dinner, he should go the whole way and pay her the sort of compliments that would suggest he was in love with her. It was very fortunate that she knew he was not!

They ordered and ate a delicious meal, tempered with a cool light white wine that made Carla just slightly light-headed, and pulled her out of a reserve she might otherwise have shown towards the senior obstetrician.

He really was very good company, cleverly turning their talk from subject to subject, and being witty yet thoughtful in everything he said. And Carla herself was far from silent, making him laugh on several occasions, and even getting him to concede a point of logic in their one mild disagreement of the evening.

How complicated life could get!

Four hours ago, she would scarcely have imagined that she could be here with him like this. Even less would she have thought that she would be enjoying his company so much. And the idea that she would be fighting a growing attraction to him would have made her laugh aloud.

It was quite late when they finally had no further excuse to linger. Carla was aware of a dreamy lassitude stealing over her—the result of all that good food and wine on top of tiredness, she supposed. Her cheeks felt pink with warmth, and she was not sorry when Lincoln suggested that they leave.

There were only a few tables still occupied, and they were emptying too. A couple walked past on their way out, and the girl smiled at Carla, who nodded back, a little vaguely. She did know that full, rather pouting mouth, and those round sapphire eyes, but . . .

Oh yes, it was a third year nurse from the hospital, Linda Mendoza.

'Don't forget your jacket,' Lincoln Falconer said, as they rose a moment later.

Carla picked up the flimsy shape of cream silk, smoothed it out and put it on, thinking no more of Linda Mendoza.

'Straight back to my place?' Lincoln queried as he started the powerful car.

'Back to *your* pl . . . ! Oh yes, of course,' Carla said, then reddened. For a moment she had forgotten that her car was still parked outside the doctor's house. What on earth would be think of her bitten back exclamation? Would he realise that for a moment she had thought he was assuming she would be spending the night there?

How awful! The fact that she had been able to think such a thing only showed the deep distrust she still held him in, despite the seductive pleasure of their evening together.

She thought of Louise Clair. The unusually lovely woman had figured neither in her thoughts nor in their conversation that evening, but now her image flooded into Carla's inner vision with vengeful clarity.

'I've wanted to forget about her,' Carla admitted to herself, 'because this evening has been so good. I've wanted to believe I was wrong about Lincoln. I'm becoming much too attracted to him, and it has to stop.'

When they pulled smoothly to a stop in his driveway, she moved to leave the car immediately, frightened at how much she was secretly hoping he would ask her in for a hot drink. But he put a hand on her arm.

'Don't go!' he said. 'Not yet. I won't ask you in, because I have a feeling you wouldn't come, but let me say something to you.'

'All right.'

'I want to apologise if I have seemed too harsh on you sometimes in these past three weeks. You said—or let it slip—that Peter Martin had warned you about my . . . prejudices about certain things, and I must tell you that he was right to. I *was* against you because you were a Granville student. I thought you would be full of impressive words but would have little real knowledge, and I must tell you that I have realised I was wrong. I can't speak about all Granville graduates, obviously, but if the others are like you, then they're not bad.'

'Thank you . . .'

'So don't let us start the absurd feud we have been keeping up when we meet again at work this week.'

'I'll be very happy if it is over,' Carla murmured.

So that had been the 'prejudice' Dr Martin had talked about. The familiar and in some ways understandable prejudice against Granville students, not the more deeply ingrained and out-dated one against women doctors that she had imagined. And now he was apologising for it!

'I'll walk you to your car,' he was saying now.

'There's no need. It's that little white one just ten yards away.'

'Nevertheless . . .'

As she stepped out of the car and gathered up her bag, he was beside her, and insisted on staying with her until she reached the car, now almost by itself at the kerb of this quiet street. Carla got the keys from her bag but he was still standing beside her, so she did not open the door. Did he have something more to say?

She looked up at him with a faint questioning lift of her delicately drawn eyebrows, but as she met his glance and looked into his face so close to her own, she found she had no need to ask anything.

What he wanted was suddenly very obvious.

CHAPTER SIX

THEIR kiss lasted far too long.

Carla knew that she should not have let it happen at all, but she had no strength or will to resist. When his firm soft lips had touched her own trembling ones, she had felt a warmth of desire and passion that was completely new to her.

For his was not the brief gentle kiss of a friend, nor the tentative first kiss that follows a first evening out together. It was a physical kiss, the kiss of someone who knew exactly what he wanted, and her own response was equally strong.

The capable arms about her, the press of his long firm body through the thin fabric of her dress, the low, incomprehensible words that he murmured, all these things made a resistance to her own feeling impossible. Carla felt weak, and yet at the same time pulses of intense strength were coursing through her.

But his hands were beginning to seek out the intimate curves of her body, and suddenly she knew it had to stop.

'No!' The word was spoken against the movement of his lips, and she found it very hard to maintain her resolve. 'It's the wine. It means nothing. I don't want this at all.'

She was not fully aware of what she was saying, but found that words helped to create and keep a distance between them, and at last the change in her reached him, and he, too, pulled away, turning from her so that she could not read his expression. The hard set of his shoulders was her only guide to his new mood.

And he was angry, there could be no doubt of that, although his breathing was already almost silent, and fully controlled.

There seemed little left to say. The kiss had happened, and that was all. It was the fault of their too-pleasant evening, and would now be completely forgotten. At least by him.

Carla wondered if she *could* forget it, but knew she had to try. The moment of intimacy had put her into his class now. He was trespassing on the marriage between Louise and Richard Clair, and now Carla in turn was trespassing on Louise's relationship with Lincoln. She felt guilty and ashamed and wanted to put as much distance as possible between herself and Dr Falconer now.

'I'm going home,' she said.

'Yes, you had better,' was all Lincoln Falconer replied, and he did not wait for her to start the car, but strode away into the darkness towards his silent house.

Carla drove without thinking for several minutes, taking turns to left and right from memory, until she came to a dead end and realised that she was lost.

No matter, she had a map, and anyway, wouldn't it be nicer to sit for a while in the dark and anonymous car? She had to sort out her feelings, if that were possible, before she encountered Lincoln Falconer again. The encounter would be much too soon in any case, but if she was still feeling as confused then as she was now, it might easily prove impossible.

The emotions he had roused in her were frightening, and their kiss had not been the only cause of it all. It had been the evening they had spent together as much as anything. And his apology had removed the only one of her original reasons for disliking him that had still remained. Yes, she knew that she could very easily love him if it weren't for Louise Clair.

If Louise Clair wasn't married, Carla would have no reason to think badly of Lincoln Falconer, and if Louise did not exist at all in his life, there might almost be cause for hoping that one day, Lincoln might come to love his most junior colleague . . .

But these 'if's' were pointless. The facts remained, and Carla's only course was really quite clear to her. She might not be able to actually stem the flow of her unwilling attraction to Lincoln Falconer, but it would be very possible to make him hate her and believe that she hated him in return. This was what she would do.

Carla switched on the small interior light of her car and studied the map carefully. From here she could be home in half an hour, and in bed minutes after that. How long before she slept would be another matter, of course.

The next day passed in a kind of numbness in which work was both a comforting distraction and a dangerous reminder. When Carla could become completely involved with her patients and their problems she could forget, but this only made remembrance, when it inevitably came, more difficult to bear.

Lincoln Falconer had not appeared on the ward rounds that morning, at least, not when Carla was there. She did not flatter herself that it was a deliberate avoidance. He had probably found that it fitted better with his schedule if he came later, and would have been relieved to realise that he would escape the sight of Carla at the same time.

Well-meaning Sister Menzies rubbed salt into Carla's wounds, too.

'Finished already?' she said when Carla entered her office to say goodbye. 'You've missed Dr Falconer, then. He said he wouldn't be here for another half an hour.'

'Oh . . .'

'It's a pity, because dear little Mrs Singh in bed 17 is such an interesting case. You'd probably learn something if you stood by while Dr Falconer examined her.'

'Yes, it is a pity,' Carla managed to say. 'But it can't be helped. I have too much else to do.'

'Of course you do. And you're very conscientious. I said so to Dr Falconer, but he said he'd realised the fact himself already. So there you are! A compliment to remember.'

'I will remember it, yes,' Carla nodded, smiling a little blindly at Sister Menzies as she retreated thankfully from the office.

Later at lunch she deliberately sought out one of the most isolated tables, tucked away behind the door and partially hidden from the main dining area by a rectangular pillar.

Any one of a dozen people might bounce up to her in a friendly way, wanting to talk, and she simply needed to spend a little more time alone with her own thoughts today. She did not want to see Michael with his inquisitive questioning, or Peter Higgins and Janet Jones, with the constant evidence of their increasing happiness together.

Actually, she was not very hungry, either, and felt distinctly ill.

Several people had already asked her about her absence from yesterday's cocktail party, which had apparently been enjoyed by all who had pressed into Lincoln Falconer's crowded sitting-room. Carla had lied a little in her reply, saying she had overslept and had then felt too ill to go out.

There was no point in going into the trivial story of her mistake about daylight saving, nor into an account of the beautiful and disastrous evening that had followed.

Images of Lincoln's disturbing kiss came to her again and again. But it was more than just the images. The very feelings he had aroused in her moved meltingly through her body over and over each time she thought of those moments last night.

There was another image that haunted her, too: that of his shoulders set in anger as he turned away from her.

Why should he have felt anger? There was an ugly expression for women who encouraged a man physically and then backed away, but if he thought that the term applied to her, then he was very much mistaken. He had been the one to initiate their kiss, and Carla had pulled away as soon as she was able to.

And for the very best of reasons—Lincoln Falconer was already involved with someone else.

She began to feel angry herself, now, at the injustice of his reaction, and wanted to confront him to demand an explanation and an apology. But she knew she would not. He was senior to her at the hospital, and she should never have accepted his invitation in the first place.

And what was worse, the anger that she should be feeling towards him would not remain hotly within her as it should. Far too often it was replaced with that growing attraction which she had known last night could easily turn to love if only certain things had been different.

Was love this complicated for everyone?

It was after the Monday afternoon clinic that she encountered Dr Falconer at last. He looked tired and strained, and Carla was surprised.

She had expected that he would have put their kiss thoroughly behind him and not dwelt on it sleeplessly as she had. But of course the fact that he seemed tired did not necessarily mean that he had been thinking of it. A man such as Dr Falconer must have many other concerns of great importance pressing upon his mind.

Carla knew that there was a difficult Caesarean birth scheduled any day now. The mother was paralysed after serious injury in a car accident, and the fact that she had been able to conceive at all, and bring her pregnancy to this point, was already something of a miracle. She had come from Brisbane especially to be under Dr Falconer's care, and if the baby was lost at this stage, it would be a tragedy.

'Could I see you alone for a few minutes, Doctor,' Lincoln said to Carla now.

'Yes, if you want to.' Her reply came out grudgingly. After her resolve last night to treat him distantly, she had no wish to be alone with him again so soon.

'Carla . . .' he began, as soon as the door of the silent consulting room had closed between them and the outside world.

He paused, but just the simple speaking of her name—or more, the tone in which he said it—told Carla that as she had feared, he was thinking of yesterday.

'Yes, Dr Falconer,' her own reply, falling into the bland silence of the carpeted room, was deliberately as cool as she could make it.

She had to fob him off. She had to think of Louise Clair, and her own strong principles about extra-marital affairs. She could not condone Lincoln Falconer's behaviour, and she must not allow this awful attraction to keep on breaking through.

'Please . . .' He had crossed the small space that separated them. 'I want to know . . . Oh Carla!'

He tried to take her in his arms, but she resisted with sudden willpower and control. Their struggle was quickly over, as he did not press her, but just that brief contact with his warm, muscular arms, and the closeness of his chest, had stirred Carla to the point where her only response was to be angry.

'You must not touch me,' she burst out in a low vibrant tone. 'You have no right. I know about Louise Clair!'

'Louise Clair is . . .'

'I know what you are going to say, and it makes no difference. Or rather, it makes all the difference. Do you think I could trust a man like you, when you offer that fact as an excuse? I feel cheapened by any involvement in your affairs, and I think we should not speak of this again. May I go now?'

'Yes, I think you have made your meaning quite plain. Thank you for your honesty.'

He had sat down heavily while Carla still stood, almost trembling, in the centre of the clinically bare and hygienic space. He looked strangely exhausted by their encounter, and for a terrible moment, in spite of all her anger. Carla wanted to go to him and cradle his head against her breast.

'Just think of Louise Clair,' she said to herself—the phrase was becoming almost like a charm for her—and turned to leave the room without a backward glance.

'Louise Clair is married.' Did he really think that that would make her fall into his arms for some brief flaming affair? Did the man think he had the right to make love to any woman who captured his fancy, regardless of what loyalties he might owe to someone else?

Richard Clair was no obstacle to his affair with Louise, and now he expected the fact of Louise's marriage to remove any doubts that Carla had. Well, he was very wrong, and now surely after that scene, she would not find it too hard to hate him as she so badly needed to?

He would certainly hate her now.

'Good afternoon, Doctor.' Lincoln's greeting and token smile were formal and distant the next morning when they encountered each other on Ward B, but the familiar cool tone still exercised its power over Carla's senses in spite of everything.

'Yes, good afternoon. I . . . hope you are well,' was her rather stumbled reply.

'I'm very well,' he returned. 'And you?'

'Rather tired, that's all.' Carla smiled faintly, unsure of how much she wanted him to read into her statement.

'Well, I hope you manage to have a restful night tonight then.' He seemed sincere, but did she detect the faintest edge to his remark?

'Thank you,' Carla said. 'I hope so too.'

After this, Dr Falconer entered a cubicle at the far end of the corridor, leaving Carla to wonder what he had been trying to convey beneath the acceptable front of his words.

There had been something, of course. After events such as those of yesterday and Sunday night, no-one could behave in a completely normal way. He must have been as aware of his memories as she was of her own.

It appeared that he was trying to signal that he had put their intimacy completely behind him as she had asked him to. Carla wondered why she was not wholly relieved at this knowledge.

And something happened several days later which showed that it might not be possible to put Sunday evening behind her for a while yet. Carla was on call, and lay with her bleep beside her on a big orange towel by the staff swimming pool.

It was two o'clock on a hot afternoon—as often happened, March had not brought an end to summer, and pools and beaches all over Sydney were still being well used. Carla was trying out a new bikini of a deep golden yellow, and hoped to successfully tread the fine line between acquiring a good tan and getting an unpleasant case of sunburn.

The sun was glorious, and after one quick swim, Carla was quite content to lie and doze. She felt good. Lincoln Falconer was holding scrupulously to his unworded promise to let Sunday and Monday be forgotten, and now that Carla knew she had been wrong about his prejudice against women doctors, she actually found it easier to work with him than she had before.

As long as she kept reminding herself of Lincoln's relationship with Louise Clair, and how much she disapproved of it.

An off-duty student nurse came to the pool and laid

her green towel quite close to Carla's. It was Linda Mendoza. Now where had they seen each other recently? Of course—at The Old Ferry, on the fateful night which she was now so anxious to forget.

'Enjoying life at the Boronia?' the girl asked now, sitting down on her towel and sliding herself to the end of it that was closest to Carla. She had an attractive if rather too short body, and rumpled artificially bleached hair.

'I'm enjoying it very much,' Carla replied politely to Linda's question.

'Yes, I thought you must be. You certainly seemed to be the other night.'

'I don't know what you mean.' Carla flushed and was immediately furious with herself for the betraying colour.

'You'd had a few drinks, I thought,' Linda went on. 'Perhaps you don't remember seeing me. You seemed to be pretty wrapped up in Dr Falconer, too.'

'Of course I remember seeing you!' Carla was goaded into the retort by the ridiculous suggestion that she had been drunk. Two glasses of white wine was scarcely the quantity which would produce the result that Linda had implied!

But Linda did not seem very interested in Carla's replies:

'I must say I wouldn't mind going out with a man like Dr Falconer myself. He's a pretty hot specimen. But of course I've got Damien.' Carla realised that this must be the young man Linda had been with the other night.

'I'd watch out if I were you, though,' Linda continued. 'I mean, I know you are senior to me, but I have been here longer, so I feel I'd better give you this piece of advice—don't let it get around the hospital that you're going out with him.'

'But I'm not going out with him!' Carla said, quite angry now. She did not like Linda Mendoza's manner very much at all. 'That dinner was a single occasion, and was in connection with . . . with work, so I feel I really don't need your advice on how to conduct myself at the Boronia, thank you very much.'

'Oh, all right, sorry. I was mistaken. But all the same, people don't always understand that a dinner for two like that, and at such a quiet and expensive restaurant— Damien and I only went there because it was a very special celebration—can just be about work. You wouldn't want talk about your evening to be spread about.'

'No, I wouldn't. And so I suppose you have kept it a dead secret yourself, since you feel so strongly about it?'

The shot went home. Linda flushed a little.

'Well, I did tell Sandra, my best girlfriend. And of course when I pointed you out to Damien, he recognised you. He's an orderly here, as you might know.'

'That's all right then. I'm relieved,' Carla said, with heavy sarcasm. 'I know Sandra will only tell one friend, and Damien will only tell one, and each of those will only tell another. It won't get far at all. I'm glad the matter is being treated so confidentially!'

Linda looked at Carla closely.

'Oh dear, you really do mind, don't you? Are you afraid that Dr Falconer's girlfriend will find out?'

'No, because there is nothing *to* find out, and I wish you would get that into your head, Nurse Mendoza!'

'Oh, all right. We'll forget the subject. I just thought

you ought to know what this hospital is like for gossip, that's all.'

'I appreciate your concern,' Carla said.

'Well, I'm going in for a dip, so I'll see you later.'

'Yes, goodbye.'

'Bye!'

After Linda Mendoza had dived gracefully into the water and splashed her way to the other end of the pool, Carla picked up her towel and returned to her room. The conversation with the student nurse had not been a pleasant one.

Perhaps the girl had been right to suggest that Carla had drunk too much on Sunday night, because at the time, in her hazy state, the consequences of being seen by Linda at the restaurant had not occurred to her. She had merely smiled at a familiar face and returned her attention to Dr Falconer.

But now she knew that it was very likely that the story of her evening with the senior obstetrician would be all over the hospital very soon, if it wasn't already.

This was depressing, because it would be very hard to scotch rumours with such a strong kernel of truth to them. Linda had said something about 'Dr Falconer's girlfriend'. Did she know that Lincoln Falconer was involved with Louise Clair, or was the remark merely another stab in the dark? Irrespective of the fact that Louise was married herself, Carla did not think that the lovely woman would be very pleased to hear that her Dr Falconer had been seen out with someone else.

Carla thought about the day she had been invited to meet Louise, and remembered the calculation in Mrs Clair's eyes as she assessed the likelihood of Carla being a potential rival.

Still there was little she could do but studiously avoid being seen with Lincoln Falconer, and carry on with her personal life, waiting for the storm to break and hoping that it never did!

Later that week Maureen Cummings came to the Outpatients Clinic again for a routine examination. She looked much happier than she had been on her first visit, and Carla guessed that it might be partly the result of the two private talks Jane Kemp, the hospital social worker, had had with the young woman and her mother.

'How's that morning sickness?' Carla asked.

'Almost gone now,' Maureen said. 'And Mum's being much nicer about everything too, which helps. The sickness was much worse before, just because I couldn't admit that it was happening.'

'But no news of Bob?'

'No, and I just don't know how to start finding him. His Dad died quite a time ago, and Mrs Foster, his Mum, moved to Canada. I don't know if Bob has been writing to her, but even if he is, I don't know her address either, or his sister's. She lives in Queensland.'

'What about advertising in a Western Australian paper?'

'Yes, Mrs Kemp suggested that, so I've started. Just Wednesdays and Saturdays, but I don't even know if he's reading the papers over there.'

'Still, you're looking happier.'

'Oh yes, because the sickness has stopped, and because Mum is being so much nicer. I've got the energy to cope now, and I'm sure that Bob will get in touch soon.'

While they had been talking, Carla had been preparing to do certain routine tests, which she now carried out. Maureen's weight and blood pressure were at expected levels.

'Everything is going along fine with your pregnancy,' Carla announced. 'So no worries on that score, and you are over the danger period of the first three months.'

'That's the stuff about German measles, isn't it?'

'Yes, and there is also a greater likelihood of spontaneous miscarriage. Not that you can stop taking extra care of yourself now—diet is especially important, as you know—but it is a good sign.'

There was one cause for concern, though, but Carla did not mention it yet: Maureen was already rather large, which could suggest twins. Normally, an ultrasound scan would determine the matter quickly and fairly accurately, but with Bob Foster's whereabouts still unknown, Carla was reluctant to do the test straight away. If Maureen was expecting twins, how would she cope with the news?

No, it might be better to wait until her next visit . . .

Carla had consciously tried to avoid Michael Groom since her too-pleasant evening with the disturbing Dr Falconer, and its awful aftermath the following day.

She was afraid of her tendency to talk too freely with the easy mannered anaesthetist. But at the same time, she did not want to hurt him, and found that she could not refuse when he cornered her in the busy dining room on a Wednesday evening and invited her out with him the following Saturday afternoon.

'Don't tell me you are not free,' he said, 'Because I've checked the roster and I know you are.'

'And just how does a humble anaesthetist gain access to the confidential master list of staff hours?' Carla asked with a teasing smile.

'I have a special relationship with the administrator's secretary,' he returned in the same vein.

'Anyway, you're right, I am free,' Carla said. 'But I would like to know exactly what you are proposing before I commit myself to anything.'

She was trying to cover up some moments of obvious hesitation. She needed to go out, to get away from the environment of the hospital, with its constant reminders of Lincoln Falconer and Louise Clair, but was wary of doing anything too intimate with Michael.

'I'm proposing an afternoon on the harbour. A friend has lent me his speed-boat while he is away.'

'It does sound good,' Carla admitted.

'It will be. When are you free exactly?'

'I thought you knew all this!'

'Well . . . I can't remember if it's twelve or one,' Michael grinned.

'It's twelve-thirty.'

'We'll leave straight away then, shall we? We'll have a late picnic lunch, and explore the sights. Have you ever seen the Opera House from the water?'

'No, I haven't, actually . . .'

'Or been under the Bridge?'

'Again, no. I've been meaning to take a ferry ride to do exactly those things, but so far I've been too busy.'

'It'll be nicer doing it under our own steam, anyway,' Michael said.

'Yes, it will. I'll look forward to it.'

'You have been looking strained lately. It'll do you good. Everything is all right, isn't it?'

'Everything is fine,' Carla lied. 'So I'll see you . . . where?' She turned the topic quickly to practical arrangements. Sometimes Michael could be surprisingly perceptive.

'In the foyer here in the residence? At one?'

'Perfect!'

The planned outing started to loom more and more pleasantly on the horizon over the next two days, and by Saturday Carla felt relaxed and happy. Since thinking of Lincoln Falconer was pointless and destructive, and would continue to be so, she might as well begin to think of other things.

The day was sunny though not unpleasantly hot when Carla emerged from her morning clinic to go straight to her room and get ready. She changed into cream cotton jeans and chose a gay candy-striped sailor-style shirt to wear with them. She carried a blue summer jacket as well as a practical but pretty Chinese straw hat, and suntan cream was an important addition to the contents of her bag.

Michael was waiting for her when she ran down to the foyer promptly at one, and he regarded her lithe figure and summery clothing with obvious pleasure.

'We're going to have a great afternoon!' he said, and when they passed Dr Falconer as they slid out of the car park, Michael did not appear to have seen him.

Carla, on the other hand, was acutely aware of his imposing but weary figure as he emerged from the main building and walked towards the dining hall, a stethoscope still hanging forgotten around his tanned neck.

She had allowed herself a brief thought that perhaps they might see him on the harbour today, with his own boat, but it looked as though he was hard at work. Carla did not know if she was disappointed or pleased about this.

As she watched him, he took off the reading glasses he sometimes wore, folded them away into their case and seemed to have to make a conscious effort to relax away the frown that creased his capable brow. Then he worked a finger around his collar as though it was too tight—a gesture Carla had observed before. He noticed the stethoscope now, finally, and she could see him laugh for a moment at his own abstraction in having left it there.

By this time Michael had manoeuvred his car out of the driveway and it became impossible for Carla to look at Dr Falconer any more without craning her neck in a rather obvious way. In any case, he would disappear into the dining hall very soon.

So she turned away and did not see the senior obstetrician glance in her direction, then start and frown as he recognised her and saw who she was with.

Carla was annoyed with herself for finding these unimportant movements of Lincoln Falconer's so interesting and significant. She had resolved to forget the confusing feelings he had aroused in her, and now she found herself reading his every gesture as though she was a loving wife concerned about the pressure of his career!

CHAPTER SEVEN

'WHERE exactly are we going?' she asked Michael brightly, as he began to speed up along the smooth-surfaced road leading away from the hospital.

'We're going to pick up the boat and its trailer from Jim's place then launch it at a jetty near Mosman. I hope you're not too hungry, because it may take a while.'

'That's fine. I managed to snatch two biscuits and a coffee for morning tea, and I had an egg for breakfast. My only worry is that you don't really know how to drive the thing!'

'You just wait and see. I'm almost a professional!'

It was two by the time the small stream-lined motor boat was launched into the crowded waters of a bay which opened off the North side of the harbour. They decided to head directly for a more interesting spot and go ashore for the picnic to which each had contributed their share of ingredients.

'It's no use even trying to find a place where there is no-one,' Michael said. 'Parsley Bay might be nice though. Do you mind wading in to shore a little way?'

'Not at all. I'll roll up my jeans.'

'Good! Then we can find an uncrowded spot on the grass to eat in. I'd like to have you as much to myself as possible!'

Carla did not quite know how to reply to this. She had firmly put behind her all her tormented awareness of

Lincoln Falconer, but did this mean that she was now free and willing to respond to Michael Groom's evident interest instead? He was a dear, but . . .

She laughed at his remark as though she had no idea that he might be serious then began to talk quickly about hospital affairs.

'When do they plan to start building this new wing I hear so much about?' she asked Michael.

'What? Oh! Quite soon, I think, but you must remember that their priorities are somewhat different to yours, Carla.'

Thank goodness! There seemed to be a cheerful teasing note to his voice again.

'Oh really?' she said, encouraging him to go on.

'Yes. You or I might think that the foundations could be put in, at least, before every last detail of protocol is decided on, but not so.'

'How do you mean?'

'I mean the naming of the wing,' Michael replied. 'There's been quite a wrangle over that one. But it has finally been christened at last—The Richard Clair Wing.'

'Richard Clair!' Carla exclaimed. 'I thought they only named buildings after people who had died!'

'He is dead, Carla.'

There was a silence.

'But I thought . . .'

'Oh hell! Yes, I know what you thought. I was a fool to think I could get away with letting you believe it. I should have told you that very first time I realised that you had got the wrong end of the stick about Louise Clair, but I didn't.'

'You're not making sense, Michael.'

'I know . . . I'm a coward, even now I can't bear to tell you, and expose my pathetic character.'

He was silent for a while and Carla was faintly aware of the incongruous sound of soft sea water slapping against the sides of the boat. The harbour was very calm today, and bright and warm from the strong sun in the cloudless sky overhead. A breeze blew very lightly, just enough to move the waving mass of Carla's hair without creating any chill.

Michael had let the boat slow to the point where they were only idling and drifting slowly in the lee of the peninsula which was occupied by the Taronga Park Zoo. Carla could see boats and buses carrying tourists to and from the park, as well as many other pleasure boats like their own, moving through the water. She even heard the trumpeting of an elephant.

It was an absurd setting for a revelation.

'You have to tell me, Michael.'

'All right, I know, I know.'

'Louise Clair's husband is dead,' Carla prompted, quite cold inside. Was she angry with Michael, or afraid of what he was going to say?

'No, not Louise Clair's husband. Her brother.'

'Her brother! Then . . .'

'Louise is not married and never has been. I don't know how you got the idea that she was, but I didn't care about that. When I realised that that was what you thought, and that that was why you were trying to dislike and disapprove of Lincoln Falconer, instead of loving him as you wanted to, I let you go on thinking it.'

'Why?'

'I wanted to have a chance with you myself. I was trying to kill off the competition. Pretty small, wasn't it?

But I let it happen on the spur of the moment, and then it was too late to go back.'

'I wonder if you hadn't made that slip just now, how long it would have been before you would have told me,' Carla said slowly, suddenly aware of a weak-willed side to Michael that she had not fully known about until now.

'I don't know,' he said. 'Someone else would have told you soon. I've been waiting for it, and I've been feeling bad . . . But that's easy to say. Perhaps you don't believe me?'

'Yes, I believe you, but not because I'm in love with you. I never can love you, Michael, you must know that.'

'Yes, all right. I think I knew already.'

'As for how I came to think that Louise was married: I overhead a woman talking about Mrs Clair losing a son, and jumped to the conclusion that it was Louise who had lost an infant child.'

'Whereas in fact it must have been old Mrs Clair they were talking about—Louise's mother.'

'I do let my imagination run away with me, don't I?' Carla managed a smile.

'A little,' Michael smiled back.

'And so how long ago did Richard Clair die?' Carla asked.

'Only last December. He had always had a weak heart, and it was his third attack.'

'And Louise is completely free to marry Lincoln Falconer.'

'Yes, and it does seem rather likely that she will, doesn't it? It has been looking more and more serious lately.'

'Yes.'

'There's nothing more to be said about it, really. Shall

we go ahead with this picnic?' Michael gestured in the direction they had originally decided to take. 'You might rather go home now.'

'No, of course we won't go home!' Carla said.

'Good. Let's eat then. After all that, I'm suddenly very hungry!'

Michael opened the powerful throttle of the small boat and quite soon they had arrived at Parsley Bay, waded ashore with the picnic basket and sat down in the grass with the spread of food before them.

Michael did not seem to be aware that Carla's appetite had completely disappeared, or perhaps he was just being tactful in not mentioning it. His revelations had pulled her emotions in two different directions at once, it seemed to Carla.

On the one hand, she was now free to fall completely in love with Lincoln Falconer: The only obstacle had been her principles about his involvement with a married woman, and now it seemed that he was not and never had been. On the other hand, though, she knew more finally than ever that he could never be hers.

His marriage to Louise Clair might take place any day.

For the first time, she thought about the fact that Michael knew of her attraction to Lincoln Falconer and had known for a long time. Was it this obvious to everyone? She had scarcely been aware of it herself then, or rather, she had continually tried to suppress it.

Carla made herself a rough, picnic-style salad sandwich and nibbled on it slowly, feeling a little sick and utterly without appetite. Michael was silent for a long time, looking out at the sunny bay and harbour beyond, quite crowded with boats of all kinds, as well as swimmers and water-skiers.

Then he spoke out of the blue.

'Apparently you had dinner with him the other night.'

'Yes.' Carla did not need to ask who he was talking about.

'Does Louise know?' he asked.

'I have no idea.'

'Because I hear she can be very jealous,' Michael said.

'I can't help that,' Carla retorted. 'It was after the cocktail party. I don't know if you were there.'

'I was, and I looked for you, but I thought you had decided not to come.'

'I arrived too late, just after everyone had left, and he asked me out to dinner. I did refuse the invitation, but he wouldn't take no for an answer.'

'And in your heart of hearts . . .' he paused.

'Yes, I suppose I did want to be with him.' Carla admitted.

'So what happened?'

'Nothing *happened*, as you put it.'

'Sorry. It was none of my business. I heard about it from Nick Freeman, the radiologist. I daresay the story has probably grown in the telling. You were said to have been draped all over each other.'

'I hate gossip!' Carla exclaimed. 'Why don't people realise how it can hurt.'

'You only realise that when it hurts you,' Michael replied wisely. 'You've probably passed on a few stories of the kind in your time.'

'Yes, that's true. I am being sour today, aren't I?'

'Understandably, I think.'

'You're very good, Michael.'

'In spite of my lapse on the subject of Louise Clair's marital status?'

'In spite of that!' Carla managed a laugh but it was not completely sincere, and she knew that a constraint had sprung up between them that might never disappear.

Could she really completely forgive someone who had lied to her in that way and for those reasons?

'Let's get away from this spot!' Michael exclaimed suddenly. 'I feel like a bit of speed, and a stiff breeze through my hair.'

He jumped up impulsively and then began to pack away the remains of the picnic things. Carla joined in, thinking that she, too, felt like the physical stimulation of a boat ride, rather than the awkwardness of being here with Michael and having nothing much left to say.

She wished that the anaesthetist knew a lot less about herself and Dr Falconer, but sensed thankfully that on this subject, at least, he would be discreet.

The afternoon suddenly became much more pleasant. The water was glorious, and Carla enjoyed the sensation of the fine salt spray stinging coolly on her skin as Michael bounced the little craft over rippling clear green water. They slowed down as they passed the beautiful white edifice of the Opera House, but did not, after all, go beneath the Harbour Bridge. It was a little after four-thirty when they cruised slowly into the quiet shallow waters near the launch ramp.

'Straight back to the hospital?' Michael enquired.

'Yes, I think so,' answered Carla.

'You're not working tonight, are you?'

'No . . .' She hoped that he wasn't going to ask her to dinner as well. Didn't he realise that the revelations of this afternoon made his company rather a strain for her?

'You're lucky! I'm on at seven,' he said, quieting her fears.

They barely spoke again as Michael got the boat onto its trailer and out of the water, and drove to his friend's place to lock it securely in the special boat garage.

It was only when they arrived back at the hospital that he referred again to what he had said over lunch.

'This need not spoil our friendship, Carla?' It was an almost pleading question.

'I . . . I don't know, Michael. I'd like to go on being friends with you, but I'm not sure if it's possible. I think it would be better if we didn't see each other very much for a little while.'

'That's okay . . . I'll deal with these picnic left-overs, then.' He waved a hand at the remains of the picnic things piled in the basket in the back seat of his little car. 'You go in. Have a swim in the pool, or something.'

'Are you sure you don't need help?'

'No, it's fine.'

Carla gathered her things and left the car, wanting to glance back at Michael when she reached the foyer entrance, but making herself resist. But she paused at the stair landing by a window that overlooked the car park, and saw him chatting in his usual easy way to a pretty little ward maid as he carried the picnic basket towards his building. He obviously was not too hurt.

—But what a mess the whole affair had been!

Someone stood outside the door of Carla's room, but after the glare of the day outside, she could not at first see who it was in the comparatively dim corridor. Then the blonde hair and sprightly form of Sally Lewis materialised, and in a moment the younger medical student had enveloped Carla in a warm hug.

'Sally! Oh you darling!' Carla gasped. 'But why didn't you tell me you would be here?'

'My mother's fault,' Sally said. 'I'm invited to a party tonight, but rather typically she thought she had posted the invitation on to me, then came across it the day before yesterday under a pile of Red Cross leaflets. So she rang up the hostess, apologised, found out it was not too late to accept, telephoned me, and here I am!'

'The party is near here?'

'Well . . . Potts Point. But I got here earlier than I thought I would, so I *had* to come and see you. Are you working? Or can we go somewhere?'

'No, I'm not working. Isn't it lucky? I was flat out yesterday, and will be again tomorrow. What about an ice-cream somewhere?'

'Perfect! Then we can talk for ages. I want to hear everything about real hospital life. You have only written once, you naughty thing, and didn't say anything at all!'

'I think that is a testament to the nature of "real hospital life"!' laughed Carla, unbelievably cheered by bright little Sally's unexpected arrival. 'It is very hard work.'

'No matter. You will tell all, down to every last suture, as it were. I *especially* want to hear about the dastardly Doctor F.'

Carla was glad that Sally could not see her face after this remark. She had opened up her room and walked into it, planning to freshen up a little and exchange the large beach bag she carried for a smaller fashion hand-bag. Sally followed her in, apparently not made curious by the silence that had followed her frivolous comment.

'Will you mind if I go dressed like this?' Carla asked.

'No of course not! Look at me! This dress was all right when I started, but after an afternoon in the car it is crumpled, to say the least. I'm having dinner at my parents' place, and I'll change for the party then.'

'They're not serving a meal at the party?'

'No, it's a pretty informal affair, as far as that goes, though huge, I believe. It's an engagement, but I don't even know the couple very well. My parents and the guy's are old friends, live in the same suburb and all that. His father is a doctor, and so is mine, of course. I got asked because I was approximately the right age.'

'Right, I see.'

'I've just had a great idea, actually.'

They were clacking down the stairs in their summery sandals now, as merry as two schoolgirls. Carla had not realised how much she missed the company of a really good friend, someone she had known for a long time, and could be completely open with . . .

'Oh yes?' she said.

'You could come to the party!'

'But . . .'

'Yes! Apparently the invitation says Miss Sally Lewis and friend—obviously designed so that I don't have to leave my current heart-throb at home, but since I haven't got one at the moment, I'm sure they wouldn't mind if I brought you. Is there a phone in the foyer? Shall I ring Mum and find out? Would you like to come?'

'Yes, yes, and yes, in answer to your three questions,' Carla laughed.

Sally rang her mother who seemed certain that Carla would be welcome at the engagement celebration. They ran back upstairs to Carla's room, so that she could choose evening clothes to bring, and go straight to the party after dinner at the Lewises, to which Sally's mother had also invited her.

'I remember this,' Sally said, as they ran down for the second time. 'Going out to a party with you in Granville and having to go back upstairs three times because we had forgotten things.'

'Because *you* forgot them, I seem to remember!' Carla retorted teasingly.

'Oh, now that we're a doctor, we're going to deny that we ever had a rash youth, are we?'

'Shut up!'

'I'll drive, shall I?' asked Sally.

'No, you must be sick of it, after coming all the way from Granville,' Carla replied. 'Let's take my car.'

She found that she was unconsciously looking for Lincoln Falconer as they crossed the car park. Perhaps he would be coming out of the building as he had been at lunch time . . . It was hardly likely at this time of the day, Carla told herself, but this did not stop her looking, and she was glad when Sally agreed to let her drive.

With her mind focussed on that activity, she would not have time to crane her neck about in a vain search for Lincoln.

It was a discipline that would have to be part of her life from now on, she thought resignedly. This would only be the beginning of a long struggle to suppress an attraction for the senior obstetrician which had become frighteningly deep-rooted.

'I noticed you didn't reply when I teased you about your horrible Lincoln Falconer,' Sally said quietly when they were seated in a small gelato bar in Darlinghurst with tall glasses of brightly-coloured ice-cream waiting mouth wateringly in front of them. 'Is he really that bad?'

Carla was silent for a while. Sally was her best friend, and a sensitive and warm-hearted girl beneath her gay manner. Might it not be a comfort to unburden herself to someone who could understand, yet who was completely uninvolved?

'He's not bad at all,' Carla said at last. 'That's my problem.'

'You're in love with him?'

'Yes.' As she said the word, soft and low, she knew it was the first time she had admitted the fact fully, even to herself. She had almost aways used the word 'attraction' before, but Sally's question had made her realise that that word was inaccurate.

And utterly inadequate. It was not simply that Carla was trembling on the brink of a feeling for the senior obstetrician, she was well and truly in it. Or it was in her. It filled her whole being, and it was rather frightening.

'What does he feel about you?' Sally did not make the mistake of continuing the conversation in a frivolous way. Carla's mouth was drawn into a line of dumb pain, and now was not the place for remarks like 'But I thought you loathed him!'

'He doesn't care about me. Not in any way at all.' Carla thought briefly of his kiss but dismissed it. A momentary surge of physical passion provoked by a too-pleasant evening and some very good wine, that was all it had ever been for him.

For the first time since Michael's revelation of the truth about Louise Clair, Carla thought of Lincoln Falconer's unfinished phrase the following day in the consulting room. 'Louise is . . .' Carla had interrupted him, thinking he was about to say that Louise was married, but of course it could not have been that. Still, it did not really make any difference.

'He's practically engaged,' she continued in explanation to Sally. 'In fact, possibly it's official by now. They would keep it a secret for a while because she—Louise Clair is her name—is on the Hospital Board. They probably want to finalise details of the wedding before it is publicly known.'

'So obviously he can't be quite how we pictured him that evening in the flat,' Sally said gently.

'No, not at all. For a start, he is about twenty years younger than we thought. More, probably. And . . . Oh, he is arrogant, I suppose. But he has the right to be. He is such a good and dedicated doctor, and works longer hours than he needs to. Most people in his position would start to rest on their laurels a bit, but he doesn't.'

'And *does* he disapprove of women in medicine?'

'No, I was wrong about that, too. Dr Martin meant something different, and Dr Falconer apologised to me about his own attitude only the other day. He said he had at first had doubts about me because I was from Granville . . .'

'That old thing!'

'Yes, but he said my work had changed his opinion.'

'Good for you! And doesn't that mean that he must think well of you?'

'Yes, as a doctor perhaps, but not as a person. And a few things have happened since then which mean he will never change that opinion.'

'I won't ask you about it. Perhaps it's time we changed the subject altogether.' Sally squeezed Carla's hand quickly across the table. 'Now you eat up your ice-cream while I regale you with harrowing tales about Granville. I eat much too fast if I'm not talking!'

She proceeded to do so, with such a cheerful and witty turn of phrase that Carla was soon laughing quite sincerely, and found herself looking forward to dinner with Sally's family, followed by the party.

She had met Sally's parents twice before in Granville, but had never seen their quiet family home in Potts Point, nor met the two younger children in the family: sister Pauline, who hoped to be a fashion designer, and mischievous little brother Rodney.

They were all as lively as Sally, including Dr Lewis, who seemed to bring his twinkly-eyed bedside manner home with him, and coped admirably with the saucy remarks of his children and their young-hearted mother.

'Upstairs to dress, girls!' exclaimed Mrs Lewis as they finished a home-style meal of chicken casserole and jelly trifle. 'There'll be lots of eligible young men at this party, and with the romance of the engagement in the air, you don't want to lose any opportunities! I wish I was coming too, to help you along.'

'Oh Mother, really! You sound like Mrs Bennet in *Pride and Prejudice*! Won't you be happy unless I walk up the aisle with a title, an estate, and ten thousand a year?'

'Five times that amount, Sally dear. Think of inflation!'

Both laughed, unaware that the silly conversation had sparked off a pang in Carla's heart. She remembered her first conversation with Sally concerning the then-unknown Dr Falconer.

Sally had teasingly suggested that Carla would fall

into the Doctor's arms after finding that she had mis-
judged him.

Well, misjudge him she had, but the rest of the happy
ending was impossibly out of her reach!

Sally was on her way upstairs now, so Carla followed
quickly, trying to drum up her interest in their preparations for the party. Sally had chosen a frilly twenties-
style cocktail dress, and decided to try a glamorously
heavy application of make-up.

'Since I will know barely anyone, I might as well
pretend to be a vamp for once,' she said. 'Why don't you
do the same, Carla? We'll cause a sensation, you in your
gold next to my scarlet.'

'I'm not sure . . .'

'Oh please, just in fun,' Sally begged winningly.

'Oh, all right. As you say, why not?' Carla replied,
reflecting that she had little to lose, although it was not
her usual style. 'It might be fun.'

'It will be. And I'll do your hair, too, in some seductive asymmetrical style.'

'Sounds amazing!'

'Well . . . I must confess, it might not work.'

Carla began to enter whole-heartedly into the dress-
up session, feeling that she was again a carefree teen-
ager, instead of a serious doctor, and when Sally had
finished with her, she scarcely recognised herself.

'I hope the light is a little subdued,' she said a trifle
nervously to Sally.

'Rubbish! Some people will be much dressier than
you, if I know that set. You look fantastic!'

'Yes, I do, rather,' Carla admitted.

The long mirror in Mrs Lewis's bedroom revealed her
new look dramatically. She wore a calf-length dress in

white with a heavy lurex ribbon stripe in gold, that lent colour and sparkle to the whole fabric, and created a rustling frou-frou as she walked.

Sally had lent her a gold and moonstone necklace and matching earrings, which were revealed by the formal upswept arrangement of her glossy chestnut hair. Another touch of gold was added by the combs which kept the style in place.

Carla's wide lips were now a curved bow of red, and Sally's skilful touch with mascara, eyeliner and shadow made her sea-toned eyes look huge and full of alluring secrets. Carla had another moment of misgiving as she took all this in.

'I can't Sally! It's not me!'

'It *is* you. In certain moods. In your mood tonight! You've been working too hard, and spending too much time at the hospital. Dressed like this, you are helping yourself break out a bit, you're doing something a little creative, and you're saying "Damn you, Dr Falconer! I can live and be happy in spite of you". Don't you think?'

'Perhaps.'

'I suppose that will do. Now, what do you think of me?' Sally paraded before the mirror in her turn, with an innocent and obvious pleasure in her appearance. 'Swish, swish. I adore a dress with lots of material in it. My eyes aren't crooked, are they?'

'You're as cross-eyed as a cat!' teased Carla.

'Idiot! I mean the make-up. I'll take that jewellery back if you're not careful . . .'

Mrs Lewis called up to them from the bottom of the stairs at that moment.

'It's after eight-thirty, girls! Are you ready? You really should go.'

'We're just coming, Mother,' Sally called, and clattered cheerfully down the stairs a moment later, followed by Carla.

When they went outside on their way to the car, Carla gave her friend a quick squeeze.

'I'm glad you persuaded me to do this. I did need it. I feel about sixteen, which suddenly seems like a very good feeling.'

'But you mustn't act sixteen, dear, or you'll give away the secret of our success,' Sally replied. 'Remember, we're representing Granville tonight. We must exhibit our enormous intellects subtly but unmistakably.'

They arrived very soon at the house belonging to the engaged man's parents, Dr and Mrs Fisher, as it was only a few blocks from Sally's own place.

'Is Bruce Fisher a doctor too?' Carla asked, referring to the young man whose engagement was to be celebrated that evening.

'No, he's a barrister. But Felicity, his fiancée, is a nurse,' Sally replied, 'So this may well be rather a medical gathering.'

'Oh well, at least that will provide some topics for conversation,' Carla laughed.

There were already many cars lining the normally quiet street, and Carla had to park almost a hundred yards from the house. Sally had been right when she had said it would be a large gathering, she thought.

Carla was concentrating on the cement footpath in front of her—the heels of her shoes were rather flimsy— and so she did not see that amongst the parked cars was one that would have been familiar to her. It was a dark red sportscar of a make that was distinctive and uncommon.

The big wooden door of the house was open a crack, signalling that new arrivals were not expected to knock or ring, and so Sally and Carla walked directly in, the former carrying a fragile and prettily-wrapped box of glassware that was her present to the engaged couple.

'I'll find Mrs Fisher or Bruce and pay my respects,' Sally whispered to Carla. 'But you needn't come. They're probably both frantic at this stage, and we are bound to catch up with them again later, so I'll introduce you then.'

'I can't see a single familiar face,' Carla returned a little anxiously. 'Are you sure it's not better if I come with you?'

'You'll be all right,' Sally replied. 'I can't see anyone I know, either. I don't think that this is the sort of party where it matters.'

She threaded her way through the crowd leaving Carla stranded in the doorway between the small entrance hall and gracefully furnished sitting-room—both equally crowded. She decided to find the drinks and savouries table straight away, although she was neither hungry nor thirsty. It was simply something to make her feel and look occupied in the rather daunting company of all these strangers.

Carla noticed the appreciative glance of more than one male, and realised that Sally's judgment and taste had been good. She did not look out of place, and she did look unusually attractive.

A cassette tape of dance music finished at that moment, and a few people left the centre of the floor in search of a seat, or the greater anonymity of the side of the room, thinning the crowded centre space a little, and allowing Carla to see right across to the door leading to the adjoining dining room.

It was then that she saw Lincoln Falconer

He seemed unaware of her presence, as she was several yards from him, and he was absorbed in conversation with an older man who was probably Dr Fisher, Bruce's father. Carla had not thought for a moment that he might be here. After all, the medical community in Sydney was very large. It was quite a coincidence that Dr Falconer knew Dr Fisher professionally.

Should she turn away, pretending that she had not seen him, and hope to be able to escape his eye for the rest of the evening? Carla wondered. Or should she greet him straight away, get it over with, and then trust that he was as anxious to avoid her as she was to avoid him?

And what of Louise Clair? It was all too likely that she would be here too. What a nightmare!

'Who are you staring at?' Sally asked, coming up to stand by Carla's elbow without her noticing. And before she could stammer a reply, Sally continued to speak. 'That man over there talking to Dr Fisher? He is rather dishy, isn't he? Mature and dependable.'

She noticed Carla's strange expression then, and her interest in the stranger quickened.

'Why, do you know him? You do! It isn't Lincoln Falconer is it?'

'Yes, it is.'

'Oh!'

CHAPTER EIGHT

'SORRY Carla,' Sally was saying.

They had both pushed their way into the safer and quieter atmosphere of the kitchen, and Sally was now looking with concern at her friend's face.

'Don't be sorry,' Carla said. 'You couldn't know that that was him. And you couldn't have known he would be here in the first place.'

'Would you like to leave? I don't mind . . .'

'Of course we won't leave. What would your friends think? And anyway, it's pointless. I can't go on running away from the man. I have to see him every day—or almost—at work, so I might as well learn to cope with it as soon as I can.'

'Yes I suppose so . . .'

At that moment a creamy voice spoke just behind Carla.

'Dr Scott isn't it?'

Carla turned quickly. Yes, it was Louise Clair. She looked gorgeous tonight, as usual, in a crimson crushed velvet dress that hugged her amply curved body closely. And could it be a coincidence that the dress was the exact shade of Dr Falconer's car? Carla doubted it.

'Yes, Mrs . . . Miss Clair,' she corrected herself hastily. It was difficult to accustom herself to the idea that the glamorous board member was a single woman. 'I am Dr Scott. We met during your tour of inspection at the hospital, didn't we?'

'That's right. My friend Dr Falconer introduced us. Lovely to see you here! But I must rush. I've just glimpsed a friend over there whom I haven't seen for months. He'll be hurt if I don't go over. Nice to have met you again anyway.'

She moved away, sliding her closely swathed hips past groups of party minglers, as she murmured smooth apologies.

'He can't possibly be in love with her, Carla,' Sally blurted out in a heavy whisper.

'Shush, please, Sally! Louise will hear, or someone else, and goodness knows how many people here are her friends!'

'It's all right, no-one is listening. And I'm serious about what I said, Carla. If Lincoln Falconer is in love with her, then he isn't worthy of your love.'

'Why? She isn't all that bad,' Carla replied, unexpectedly finding herself defending the sophisticated Louise.

'Yes she is. She's too smooth and too cool. The sort of woman who sees all other women as rivals, and never has a true female friend. I've seen her type before.'

'Don't judge her too harshly, Sally. She is rich, and she has grown up rich. I think she is some kind of designer now. She obviously moves in a fairly brittle world, and she's forced to be like that.'

'Don't tell me! I'm surprised at you, Carla! Where are your fighting instincts? Aren't you even going to make an effort to . . .'

'No, I'm not. You don't understand. It's not some kind of competition or battle. I've never had any right to love him, and I never will have. She has been there right from the start, and . . .'

'And yet he has kissed you, hasn't he?' Sally questioned with persistence and perception.

'Yes. How did you know?'

Carla flushed, unhappy about admitting this fact even to her closest friend.

'There is something about your awareness of him. Something that makes your feelings more than just an infatuation. I guessed that he must have done something more than merely chatting to you over the operating table. He has taken you out, hasn't he?'

'Yes, once. It meant nothing, though,' Carla said in a low voice. 'We had dinner together. It was a lovely evening, and I think the wine must have gone to both our heads. He . . . kissed me just outside his house as I was about to drive home. It meant nothing to him at all.'

'You'll hate me for pestering you like this, won't you?'

'No, of course not. But can we close the subject now? And have no more suggestions of a struggle for possession.'

'If you want to.' Sally gave her friend a quick squeeze and then was grabbed almost straight away by Bruce Fisher who wanted a quick dance with her 'for old times' sake'.

So Carla was left alone once more, feeling ill at ease, suddenly, in her unaccustomed finery. She made her way to the crowded sitting-room again, hoping she would soon be able to dance or talk with someone, but as she pressed through the connecting door from the dining room, she found herself up against, of all people, Lincoln Falconer, who was trying to move in the opposite direction.

'Carla!' He seemed quite pleased to see her. Perhaps he, too, knew only a few people here tonight.

'Dr Falconer! How nice to see you!' She was uncomfortably aware that her dress had become a little twisted and pulled down as she moved through the crowded space, and that the partially exposed curves of her breasts were pushed against his strong chest.

She tried to wriggle her body so that the dress would straighten, but could not move without at least two other people being aware of it. Lincoln would certainly think she was playing the vamp tonight, with all this make-up and piled up hair!

'Please don't call me Dr Falconer when we are away from the hospital like this,' he said. 'My name is Lincoln at parties.'

'Very well, Lincoln,' Carla said hesitantly.

It was the first time she could remember having used his first name to his face, although she knew she had used it often lately in her private thoughts.

'You're looking very lovely tonight!' he said. 'Are you having a good time? Wait! We can't talk like this. There are two seats over in the corner. I'll get you a drink. Punch? And we can relax.'

'Punch would be lovely, but . . .'

'But you'd rather dance?'

Without waiting for a reply, he pulled her back into the sitting-room where people moved about the clearer space in the middle of the floor. At that moment, a slow love song came on and he drew her quite close.

'A party is one of the few places where two people who work together can really relax with each other,' he murmured, his lips almost brushing her ear.

Carla could smell the warm musky scent of his after-shave, and had to fight against a terrible desire to lay her head on his shoulder and surrender completely to these precious moments of contentment in his arms.

But it would be fatal.

'Sometimes I don't think that's a good thing,' she said in reply to his last comment. 'I'd rather keep my colleagues purely as work-mates, and find my friendships—and other relationships—elsewhere.'

'But don't you think that you have the most in common with the people you work with?'

'Perhaps. But that can be confining, since my profession is medicine, which is so involving. And anyway, medicine isn't by any means my only interest. I like music, reading, certain sports . . .'

'So you believe that it's through those interests that you'll meet the man you marry?'

'If I marry, yes.'

Her voice was deliberately as cool and off-putting as she could make it, without being simply rude, and with pain, she felt him stiffen against her and withdraw slightly. Carla's pretence of dislike had been all too successful in repelling him.

'You are fortunate if you can divide your life so clearly into different spheres,' he said, and his voice was now as cool as her own had been. He obviously resented the rebuffal of his attempt at light party flirtation. 'I find that I am just as much myself at work as I am in my private life, so I find people in the world of medicine who share my other interests and I form my relationships accordingly. Perhaps a doctor should not admit that—after all, we are supposed to be inhumanly neutral in our quest to preserve and improve life—but since it is the truth, I can't do otherwise.'

'Of course,' Carla said, and just then the music ended,

to be replaced by a heavy rock song that demanded dancing alone.

Louise Clair was coming towards them, having to fight her way through the bopping bodies.

'Here you are, Lincoln! You told me you would be in the kitchen.' She ignored Carla completely. 'I've got the most awful headache, darling. Do you think we could possibly go? You've done your duty to Dr Fisher, and he won't mind if we leave. I was hoping that Peter might be here . . .' She smiled in a strange enigmatic way at Lincoln, and Carla almost thought she saw a faint flush brighten the woman's already high colour. Then she tossed her head and continued to speak. 'He was invited, but had something else on, and didn't know if he'd manage to find time. And the rest of these people really are not the sort who attract me very much!'

She flicked a strand of her glowing white hair away from a high cheekbone, and smiled very faintly at Carla. It was the merest acknowledgement that she was exempted from Louise's statement, and Carla knew that the woman had really intended the insult to strike home.

She flushed, murmured a commonplace excuse, and moved away, to leave the Doctor and his lovely girl-friend to talk in private. But she could not help catching Dr Falconer's last words.

'Very well, Louise, I don't mind going. I have something rather important to say to you in any case.'

He had weighted the words heavily, and Carla was suddenly sure that this was the night he meant to propose to her. The close dance Lincoln had just had with Carla had been in the nature of a final flirtatious fling. She thought she should hate him for it, but could not. He probably expected her to understand the rules of the game and play them as well as he did.

Perhaps it was not his fault that Carla could not—not with him, anyway.

She could see his tall figure making its way towards the front door, and then he waited there while Louise went to a bedroom to collect the light fur stole she had left there. Carla could not help thinking that such a garment was sheer affectation on a warm night like this, but she could see why Louise had not been able to bear to leave the garment at home.

With its silvery-grey folds draped negligently around her shoulders, the combination of colours she presented was absolutely stunning.

After the couple had left, Carla found that the party mood she had had earlier was utterly gone. If Lincoln Falconer and his fiancée—she might as well get used to calling Louise that—had not been there in the first place it would have been different.

She might have been able to drown all thoughts of them with dancing and conversation. But now all the pain of her feelings was renewed. She dreaded the possibility of hearing the two being discussed by people here who knew them, but fortunately she did not catch the sound of their names again that evening.

Without blaming Sally, Carla wished that she had not been persuaded to dress up in this way. She wanted to be able to merge into the background of this noisy party, but instead she found herself being stared at constantly by male and female eyes. Tonight, hers was hardly the style to suggest that she would rather be a wallflower.

'I must put up a good front though,' Carla thought.

'Or Sally will see I'd rather be home and will be sorry she brought me.'

After this, she put on what she considered a virtuoso performance, captivating more than one young man by the quickness of her repartee, and agreeing to dance with whoever asked her.

She even spent twenty minutes discussing politics with a pretty nurse, who could easily have been, she realised afterwards, Bruce Fisher's fiancée. In fact, she never was introduced to the family who were giving the party!

Sally found her again between eleven and midnight.

'I think I'm going to feel like dancing the whole night away,' she said to Carla, who noticed that a very presentable man was hovering in the background waiting to have her attention again. 'So don't wait. I'll get home somehow.'

'In that case, I might go now,' Carla said quickly. 'I'm working tomorrow, and . . .'

'Fine! I'll fly then, because I know what music is coming up next and it's something I adore dancing to.'

'All right,' Carla laughed, enjoying the sight of her friend so involved in the revelry.

'So goodbye!' Sally gave Carla a quick cuddle. 'I'll be down for holidays soonishly, so I'll see you then.— And look after yourself in the meantime,' she added seriously.

Carla sighed, smiled, went to find her bag, and left.

The night air outside was cool after the heated crush of the party, but she found the slight chill refreshing. Some of the cars that had been parked outside when they arrived had left now, and Carla's little Fiat seemed further away than she had remembered.

An engine started across the road but she did not look in its direction. The car belonged to a couple who had left just seconds before Carla herself. Neither did she look up when another car cruised slowly past in the darkness, so for the second time that evening, she failed to see Lincoln Falconer's dark red sportscar outside the Fisher's house.

But Lincoln, alone now that he had dropped Louise back to her luxurious central-Sydney flat, saw Carla. In fact his entire reason for returning to the party after the rather emotional discussion with Louise had been to see Carla.

Louise had said some harsh things to him, and he in his turn had reproached her. He simply could not understand how she expected him to go on with plans for an engagement when she was quite openly having an affair with Peter Prior.

She had said that he was being ludicrously old fashioned, but he couldn't agree. It was so fortunate for both of them that he had realised some time ago that he did not love her, and had already decided that their engagement was out of the question.

Now he wanted to see Carla, almost as an antidote to Louise, with her confused emotions and brittle beliefs about modern love. Would he, should he, go in to find Carla again?

He had not been able to decide—which was for him rather an unusual problem—and then she had appeared, stunning in that dress, but walking with such preoccupied purpose that he had decided to content himself with looking at her for a few moments before driving slowly back to his house.

Strange how lonely the place had seemed lately.

CHAPTER NINE

'I'M GOING to give you an ultra-sound scan, Maureen,' Carla said with a sigh that she tried unsuccessfully to suppress. In the two weeks since the Fishers' party, she had found this tendency to sigh was growing alarmingly. There were faint lines on her forehead now, too, where no discernible lines had been before.

'An ultra-sound scan?' Maureen Cummings questioned, sounding a little alarmed. Carla realised that her own frown and sigh had probably been misinterpreted by the anxious mother-to-be.

'There is nothing to worry about,' she hastened to say. 'An ultra-sound scan is a harmless technique that can be used to check on the baby's size and position.'

'Why do I need one though? Is the baby not coming along as it should?'

'No . . .' Carla hesitated a little now. It was probably best to tell Maureen straight away what she suspected the test might show. 'You see, it's a test that is also used to check for multiple pregnancy. You've noticed that measurement I take to get an idea of the baby's size?'

'Yes,' Maureen said.

'Well, you're rather large for your time, and I'm afraid you may be expecting twins, although the measurement is not a reliable guide.'

'Twins! I can't even afford one baby!'

'I know,' Carla nodded. 'So let's get that scan done.'

right now, and find out what is going on. As I said, I'm not sure.'

The test was quickly performed and the results emerged with unusual clarity: Not just twins, but triplets! Carla looked into the waiting room and saw that for once there were no women there leafing through magazines or playing with toddlers that they had brought with them.

'Could you bring in two cups of tea, Nurse Francks?' she asked the receptionist nurse who was busy arranging some files.

'Of course, Doctor.'

Carla returned to the consulting room where Maureen Cummings sat crying, as she had done on her first visit when her pregnancy had been confirmed, Carla remembered.

'This changes everything,' the girl sobbed. 'You see, I've been starting to think that perhaps everyone has been right in telling me that Bob won't come back.'

She looked up at Carla through her tears, and Carla nodded but could find no easy words of comfort.

'It's not that I've given up hope,' Maureen went on, 'but I'm just thinking, "what if", you know?'

'Yes . . .'

'And I'd decided that even if I never hear from him again, I'll still bring up this baby on my own. But now that it's three, I can't even envisage it. I think I'm fairly realistic in some ways, and I just know I wouldn't be able to cope.'

'It is a shock,' Carla said. 'Even parents with secure marriages and good incomes find the idea rather too much just at first. But you'll get a lot of help, all through your pregnancy and after the birth.'

She outlined the things that a mother in Maureen's position received as support—supplies for the babies, financial aid, as well as the general Family Allowance. Maureen brightened a little.

'That'd make things bearable if Bob came back,' she said. 'But if he doesn't, Mum says I should put it . . . them . . . up for adoption, and I think I'll have to now.'

'It might be best,' Carla agreed slowly. She did not want to say that even women who were far more firm in their decision found it difficult to keep to once they had actually gone through the experience of birth.

'Would you like to see Jane Kemp again? She'll know a lot more about all the details than I do.'

'The details of adoption?'

'Yes, and of welfare support and that sort of thing, if you decide to keep the babies.'

'I *would* like to see her. She's much nicer than I thought she would be. I had an idea that social workers were all rich do-gooders, but Jane told me some things about her own life that made me feel she actually knew something about unhappiness.'

'Yes, she is good,' Carla smiled. 'The thing I like about her is that she is so full of help that is practical, too. She knows exactly who to ring, what to ask for, and where to go.'

'She'll be a real miracle if she can make this news seem good!' Maureen touched her abdomen with more than a touch of bitterness in her tone, and as she rose to leave, Carla sent up a brief prayer for the return of Bob Foster as soon as possible.

'It does make me realise how comparatively small my own worries are,' she thought after the door had shut behind Maureen.

Nurse Francks tapped on the door and poked her head around it.

'There's still no-one waiting,' she said. 'Dr Falconer just took the last patient. Will you have some more tea?'

'No, thank you. I've still got this.'

'I thought I'd do a bit of cleaning up in the washroom while we're so quiet,' the nurse went on.

'Leave this door open, then,' said Carla. 'That way I'll hear anyone who comes in.'

The woman nodded and went off, leaving Carla alone with her thoughts again. She realised that it was not one jot of comfort to remind herself that others were much worse off than she was.

Oh, it worked in theory, but it seemed that in practice nothing could dissipate the well of pain that filled her.

An image—or many images—of Lincoln Falconer rose in her mind's eye. In the two weeks since the Fishers' party, they had worked together as any two doctors might have done. He seemed to respect her work, and in fact praised it often in that dry English way which never failed to send a pulse of longing through her.

Only two weeks ago! It seemed much longer than that since she had finally allowed herself to admit fully that she loved Dr Falconer. But yes, it was that day—the day of Michael's confession of his deceit about Louise Clair's marriage, and the day of her admission of her love to Sally. She had thought then that she loved him completely, but in fact since then, the longing she felt had only increased.

It might have been easier if he had shown the coldness and dislike that had made her react so strongly against him at first. But this courteous politeness seduced her senses and made it impossible for her to start the process of forgetting him.

Why was he being so nice now? The horrible thought came to her that perhaps he had guessed her secret and was trying to make things easier for her. She wondered what would happen if she burst out to him that she would rather he was rude and unpleasant!

And if only Louise Clair wasn't at the hospital so often! She seemed to be in and out almost every day now—and Carla could not believe that it was just her work on the board that brought her here.

It could not be a coincidence that her increased visits had begun just two days after the Fishers' party. The lovely woman still wore no engagement ring, but that meant nothing. Carla was quite sure that Lincoln Falconer and his fiancée had reached their understanding that night.

Louise's visits were probably a romantic conspiracy between the lovers. Of course they would want to see more of each other than Lincoln Falconer's busy hospital schedule would allow. Someone like Louise Clair would enjoy snatched kisses in the Doctor's quiet fifth floor office.

'Oh, I'm being a bitch!' Carla thought, sick at herself suddenly. 'I'm only thinking of such things with disapproval because *I'd* like to be in Louise's position and I know I never can be.'

She turned to some papers on her desk which needed to be sorted and added to, but before she could become involved in the work, there was a tap at the open door and Lincoln Falconer entered, wearing one of the dark suits in which he looked so dynamic.

Carla knew she had flushed—she almost always did,

now, when she saw him, and she grew uncomfortably hot. He must think that she was horribly gauche!

'Sorry to interrupt,' he said, smiling in his crooked way.

'That's all right.' Her voice came out high-pitched, like a schoolgirl's.

'I had a question to ask you.' He entered and sat down. 'It's about that young woman Maureen Cummings.'

'She has just been in, actually. I did an ultra-sound scan, and she is expecting triplets!'

'Whew! Is she covered by a health fund? How did she react?' He seemed genuinely concerned, and Carla thought how different he actually was from her over-imaginative early portraits of him.

The character she had dreamed up would have been rubbing his hands together in anticipation of the fees he might command with such a potentially complex delivery.

'She was shocked, of course,' Carla replied to his question. 'And the sad thing is, she is beginning to doubt that her Bob will come back. I must say my confidence in him is waning, too.'

'Her Bob! Ah yes! That was what I wanted to ask you.'

'Oh?' Carla was puzzled.

'I couldn't remember his last name. I thought it was Foster, but . . .'

'Yes, it is Foster.'

'And that's spelt in the usual way?'

'Yes.' She was intensely curious about the reason for his unusual interest in this detail of Maureen's case, but because it was Lincoln Falconer, she could not ask.

'And I don't suppose you have any idea of his address?'

'That's exactly the problem.'

'Sorry, how stupid of me! I meant his last address in Sydney.'

Carla shuffled through Maureen's file that still lay on the desk in front of her.

'I have the address of Maureen Cummings' old flat. He was living there too, apparently. Yes, here it is: Flat 6a . . .'

'Just the suburb will do.'

'Merrawa, but . . .'

'Merrawa! Excellent! Thank you.' He stood up and began to walk out.

'But I don't see . . .' Carla began.

Lincoln Falconer waved a vague hand.

'Files . . . like to keep up to date,' he said, not very coherently, and then he was gone.

Carla thought that if they had been lovers, she might have allowed herself to smile fondly after that dear retreating form. There was a facet of his character—it went with the reading glasses he sometimes wore—that was a little like that of an absent-minded professor. It contrasted well with his normal strength and distinction of bearing, Carla thought. It made him more adorably human . . .

She found that she was still standing behind the desk, staring at the open doorway through which he had just disappeared, a soft smile of love and warmth glowing on her face. It was a smile that with no apparent object in view would seem idiotic to anyone who might enter.

She sat down again quickly, and riffled the papers in Maureen's file. As usual five minutes with Lincoln Falconer had succeeded in disturbing her whole afternoon.

He came in again a few hours later, just as she was about to leave, feeling by now very tired. As so often happened, the waiting room had filled rapidly after the earlier lull, and Carla had not spent one more minute alone.

'How was your afternoon?' he asked her, leaning one elbow against the jamb of the door in a characteristic pose that by its very laziness hinted at his great physical strength and fitness.

'Quite good,' Carla forced herself to reply brightly. 'Busy after you left.'

'Yes, busy up my end, too. I saw two paraplegic women who would like to have children—unfortunately for one of them it won't be possible. But it seems likely that this hospital may become a major centre for such cases, drawing patients from the whole of the South Pacific region.'

'That's marvellous! It's a very interesting development . . .'

'Very.' There was a pause, then he went on, 'You're enjoying your work here?'

He still stood in the doorway, while Carla was placed, and felt rather marooned, in the centre of the room, holding a stethoscope awkwardly.

'Yes, I'm very happy at the Boronia,' she replied.

He came into the room now at last, approaching her directly. She wanted to back away but turned the movement into a step towards her desk, intending to lay the stethoscope down on it, but he stopped her with one firm touch of his warm fingers on her bare arm.

'Would you like to have dinner with me again tonight?' he asked in a low voice.

Carla froze. She could not bear to meet his eyes, but guessed what expression she would have found there: a distinct sympathy and pity. She was certain now that he had guessed the secret of her love, and wanted to try to help her over it in some way.

Probably he had Louise's express permission to give this invitation, and would confront Carla with his knowledge over the meal. Perhaps he would tell her that he had arranged for her to move to the Gynaecological Wing of the hospital sooner than planned.

She thought suddenly that it was quite likely this sort of thing had happened before in his career. A colleague had fallen unfortunately in love with him. It was even possible that he had guessed about her unwilling attraction right from the start, and that was why he had been so cold, trying to nip the feeling in the bud . . .

She still could not reply to his question, and the silence between them was growing strained. His fingers still lay on her arm but she was scarcely aware of them until his hand slid upwards, reaching her neck, caressing it gently then moving behind her head to draw her towards him.

'No!' She only mouthed the word, too faint for him to hear, and his relentless yet gentle pressure continued.

Now his other arm was around her, imprisoning her fine-boned shoulders and locking her against his chest in an embrace that she might have wanted to last forever, if things had been different. His lips found hers, and he kissed her with quiet expertise, softly at first, then with increasingly demanding pressure.

But she knew it was only some strange kind of consolation prize. She broke away and stared down, searching for words.

'I don't need this!' she exclaimed at last. 'I don't want it. Please just leave me alone, that's all I ask.'

Lincoln loosened his hold on her immediately and abruptly.

'Very well,' he said. 'I think that will do. You've made your meaning and your feelings clear, and I'll respect them. I had been planning to say something . . . to tell you something today, but your words have made that unnecessary.'

There was a cold finality in his tone, and Carla was goaded into saying something more, since it seemed he resented her rebuffal of his tactful attempt to console her.

'I'm sorry if I've offended you, or . . .'

'Offended me!' He paused, and seemed to become suddenly angry. 'I think you rate your charms a little too highly, my dear!'

Then he turned quickly and left the room, his feet echoing smartly on the hard vinyl tiles of the clinic waiting room. He must already have tidied and locked his consulting room, as Carla heard the main door open and shut decisively, leaving the place in silence.

So her reply had angered him! Well, perhaps it was for the best. It would simply be easier to learn to forget him now, as he would no longer take the trouble to be friendly and warm with her.

Carla was a little surprised at the strength of his reaction though. Perhaps she should have accepted his dinner invitation and gone through the farce of listening to his understanding words and agreeing to whatever proposal for the easing of the situation he might have put to her.

She sighed and completed her last duties in the clinic

before going to the dining hall for a meal which she barely tasted.

'There's a phone call for you downstairs, Dr Scott.'

A second-year student nurse who had a room on the same floor as Carla's own had tapped on her door to deliver this message one evening several days later.

'I'm sorry, I didn't ask who it was,' she added.

'That's all right,' Carla smiled, as she put on a pale grey cardigan and got ready to go down. 'Thanks for bringing the message.'

'She hurried down the stairs, mentally ticking off names on a list of possible callers. Not her parents or Sally—the nurse would have told her if it had been a long-distance call. Someone from the hospital? They would have been more likely to get in touch with her some other way. A friend passing through town?

She had arrived at the perspex-partioned phone booth in the foyer before her deductions had grown any more definite.

'Hullo?'

'Hullo? Dr Scott?' The voice at the other end was female, emotional, and indistinct.

'I'm sorry? Who is it, please?'

'Oh, Dr Scott! It's Maureen Cummings here.'

'Maureen! Is anything wrong? Is it the babies? Come straight away if . . .'

'No, it's not the babies. It's good news, for once in my life. Bob's back!' She stifled a rather hysterical sob, a Carla exclaimed over the news.

'I wanted to ring you,' Maureen was saying now. 'He's only been here two hours. I wanted to thank you for al your support so far, and I wanted to ask if you could thank Dr Falconer.'

'Thank Dr Falconer?'

'Yes, it was him found Bob and told him my troubles. Bob came straight back—he caught the bus all the way from Perth and he's exhausted.'

'That's fabulous, Maureen,' Carla said. 'But I don't understand how . . .'

She stopped. A certain combination of giggling and other playful sounds made it clear that Bob had come up behind Maureen and was catching up on lost time with some teasing kisses.

'Maureen?' Carla tried again.

'Yes, sorry, Dr Scott . . . Oh, Bob! Careful . . .'

'Thanks for telling me your news.' Carla decided to give up. 'I'd better let you go. But don't forget your appointment next week.'

'I won't.'

To the accompaniment of more background noise, she put down the phone, leaving Carla still in the dark about how Lincoln Falconer had traced Bob Foster when neither Maureen, nor her mother, nor the capable hospital social worker had had any success.

Was the man the magician that he seemed? Carla could think of no explanation at all. She remembered that Maureen had asked her to thank him. That would be a difficult and depressing task.

Since his well-meaning attempt to talk about her love for him, and that consoling kiss which had only made things worse, they had not exchanged a single word beyond what working together required. Carla decided to say only a few simple words of thanks to him, and suggest that Maureen herself thank him more fully when she next came to the clinic.

The young mother-to-be looked glowing when she came in the following week, wearing a long loose Indian-style dress of muted blue that hid the growing fullness of her figure.

'I know there isn't really time,' Carla said when she had finished the routine examination. 'As there are one or two patients waiting, but I'm so curious to know how Dr Falconer managed to track Bob down, when no-one else had any success.'

'Oh, hasn't he told you?' Maureen seemed surprised and Carla did not blame her. It did not say much for their working relationship that she had not wanted to ask him and that he had not offered to tell her.

'We've both been rather busy lately,' she explained without conviction.

'Oh yes, I suppose it's like that in a hospital,' Maureen nodded.

'So please do tell me the story.'

'Well, it was quite amazing. Bob had got work for six weeks on a fishing trawler, and one day he managed to catch some huge kind of fish. He told me what sort but I can't remember. Anyway, it turned out that an adventure club had been offering a $1,000 prize for the first catch over a certain weight, and Bob won!'

'That *is* amazing!' Carla exclaimed.

'And the money will come in very handy,' Maureen went on. 'So of course, he had a photo with the fish beside him in the adventure club's magazine, and Dr Falconer saw it and got in contact with him through that. But the first thing I knew of it was when Bob turned up the other evening.'

'What a story!'

'It's not finished yet, though. The article said that Bob wanted to come back from Western Australia and look for permanent work in Sydney, and someone rang two days after the magazine came out offering him a position in a marine business. We're so pleased, because even with the $1,000, he didn't manage to save much over there. And we're going to get married this Saturday.'

'Congratulations!'

'And we'd like you to come.'

Carla was surprised and pleased at the invitation, and accepted it, as she was free that afternoon, before she realised that of course Dr Falconer would have been invited too. Still, it was very likely that he would not be able to come . . .

Michael was sitting by himself in one corner of the noisily echoing dining room that night, and Carla forced herself to go up and speak to him after she had cleared away her tray.

Each had avoided the other fairly carefully since the spoiled picnic, apart from very short chance meetings when the routine of the hospital brought them together. For the whole of last week, though, Carla had not seen him at all, and she wondered if perhaps he had been sick.

He did not see her approaching—he was bent over his food in an unusually pensive attitude, and she had to sit directly in front of him and speak to him before he looked up.

'Hullo, Michael.'

'Carla! Hullo . . .' His instinctive response had been to avoid her eye, but now he visibly forced himself to meet her gaze.

'I haven't seen you for a while. I wondered if you had been sick,' she said.

'No,' he replied. 'Holidays, actually, but only a week. My father was sick so I had to fly home to Coonabarabran.'

'Coonabarabran! I didn't know you were a country boy . . . But is your father better now?'

'Better, yes, but not well. It was his heart, and it will go again, because he never does take any notice of what doctors tell him.'

'It must be a strain for you.'

'More of a strain for Mum. She and Dad should have split up years ago, and it's not easy for her to have to look after him when he is sick, because he makes things so unpleasant for her when he is well. I try to go home as often as I can. It eases things.'

Carla nodded in silence. This was a side to Michael that she had not seen before. She guessed that he did not often reveal it.

'Something else happened while I was up there, too.'

'Oh yes?'

'Yes, I . . . got engaged,' he said sheepishly.

'What!'

'You don't have to sound so surprised.' He looked embarrassed, but beneath it Carla could see that he was quite proud.

'But I *am* surprised,' she said. 'I thought . . .'

'You thought I was cut up over you?'

'Partly. I also thought you had gone back to your old role as hospital flirt!'

'I know. Listen, I'll tell you the whole story.'

Michael had brightened openly now, and Carla knew that even if she could never completely forget the lies he had told her, at least she did not have to have his unhappiness nagging at her.

'You called me a country boy,' he began. 'You don't know how hard I tried to run away from that label!'

'Sorry.'

'No, it doesn't matter . . . You see, I was the success of our street, going away to the city to study and getting to where I am now. Frances has been at home waiting for me practically ever since I first went away, and whenever I go back I fall in love with her all over again. Then I come down to the city and want to run away from my small town personality. So I cool off with her and run after someone else. This doesn't sound very nice, does it?'

'None of us are nice all through,' Carla smiled. 'But go on.'

'This time, though, Frances said she was moving to Adelaide to live with her sister. She even had a job lined up—running a shop, which is what she does in Coonabarabran. I knew she was only going because of me, so I thought hard and finally took the dreaded step.'

'And you're pleased, aren't you?' Carla prodded with a teasing smile.

'I am, actually. Much more than I thought I would be. I suppose it was never Frances I was running away from, more my origins and the town, although even there, deep down, I love the place. Anyway, now Frances is coming down to live in Sydney, so no further obstacles lie in the path of our happiness!'

'And I wish you lots of it, Michael,' Carla said sincerely.

'Thanks. I wish you the same, only more so. How are things with . . . ?'

'It's over,' she made herself say. 'I feel very differently now. It was just an infatuation, that was all, and I've got over it.'

Michael did not notice the tight twisting of Carla's hands in her lap as she told this painful but necessary lie and he believed her completely.

'I'm glad to hear that,' he said. 'Although your chief rival has bowed out of the race,' Michael grinned in his old way.

'I don't know what you mean . . .'

'Haven't you heard the story?'

'No.' To her own ears the word sounded hollow and strange, but Michael noticed nothing.

'Well it appears that we were wrong about Louise and Dr Falconer, that's all. Reliable gossip has it . . .'

'Does such a thing exist?' Carla interrupted with real cynicism.

'Good point, but I do believe this story, actually. It seems Louise is having an affair with Peter Prior. Two or three people have seen them together. And they left the last board meeting in the same car, although they don't live near each other.'

Michael paused, waiting for a response from Carla, but she gave none. She was looking down at the table before her. She knew he wanted her to say something, but her heart was too full. She did not want to hear news like this. A while ago it might have mattered that Louise Clair and Lincoln Falconer were no longer together, but she did not feel that it would make a difference now.

There had been too many awkward and regrettable interchanges between them since that glowing evening at the harbour-side restaurant when she had first become fully immersed in her attraction to him.

Then, if things had been clear and uncomplicated—if there had been no Louise Clair—something might have started and grown between them, but it was too late now. Carla was not even sure if she believed the gossip anyway, remembering the stories that had circulated for a while about her dinner with the senior obstetrician. The only thing that tempted her to believe it at all was the fact that she had twice heard Peter Prior's name come up in conversation between Lincoln and Louise.

'Are you interested in this, Carla?' Michael was demanding impatiently.

'A little,' she replied, looking up at last.

'There's not much else to tell, actually,' Michael went on. 'No-one even knows which of them ditched the other. Some say Lincoln proposed and Louise rejected, but there is a story that he told her it was no go.'

'I can't see how such things can possibly be known,' Carla said sharply.

Michael looked at her for a moment.

'No, you're probably right. Perhaps after all their engagement will be announced.'

'I think that is the most likely possibility,' Carla said steadily as she rose to leave.

CHAPTER TEN

LINCOLN Falconer walked off the tennis courts and slung a fresh white towel around his damp neck.

'Good match, eh, Link?' His partner, a fellow member of the club, said with rather short, laboured breaths.

'Yes, very good,' Lincoln replied a little absently.

They had won, and won well, but that was not an unusual occurrence for Lincoln Falconer. He felt he shed ten years every time he played, and thoroughly relished his twice-weekly opportunity to forget the cares and responsibilities that were part of his working life.

Actually, he usually relished winning too, but somehow lately nothing had seemed terribly important—nothing, that is, except a certain slim-built, chestnut-haired doctor at the Boronia Women's Hospital.

Lincoln let himself and his partner out of the wired enclosure of the tennis court and they entered the club-house, straining to see in the dimness after the contrasting bright light of the outdoor courts.

There had been more than a hint of autumn in the air this afternoon, and the grassy shade beneath the huge trees that surrounded the tennis club had seemed chilly rather than refreshingly cool as it had all summer.

But the day was still cloudlessly sunny, and Lincoln knew that his three fellow players had had a very satisfying afternoon. About the only thing that could be said for his own play, he thought, as he stepped into the shower and felt the refreshing tingle of sharp needles o cool water, was that he had played well enough not to let his partner down.

He stayed in the shower for a long time today, well after he had finished soaping away the film of sweat he had worked up. The water running over him felt soothing, and he had always found it easier to think about difficult things in the shower.

How long was it since he had felt like this? That was easy to answer. Since Helen had rejected him, so many years ago now. He had protected himself against that kind of hurt for a long time, taking out women who made it clear that they were not looking for serious involvement—often for the same reasons as his own.

He had safe-guarded himself in other ways, too: moving his whole life half way around the world, building up a career that was so satisfying he had sometimes felt that marriage would be something of an interference.

And then, of course, he had recovered from Helen's rejection sooner than he would have thought possible when it happened. He could in no way say that it was because of Helen that he had made his life as it now was.

But now he was in the same situation again. Or was it the same? No, it was worse. Strange! He had thought, as most people did, that this sort of thing got easier to bear as one grew older, but, on the contrary, he found that the future seemed blacker now than it had twelve years ago when he was feeling like this.

Was it Carla herself? Partly, perhaps. There had always been a certain element of fantasy about his glittering relationship with Helen, but Carla was so real and warm. Helen and Louise were two of a kind, in many ways, but Carla was different.

She would not have kept trying to coax him back, as Louise had done. He hated the way she had flaunted her presence at the hospital at first, especially when he was quite certain that her only motivation had been pique and hurt pride.

He thought of Helen again. Twelve years ago, he had had more to struggle for in his career. He could not deny that that was important. And he had been able to run away. Now he was too settled, and too important. Too many people depended on him here, and there was his house—that tasteful lonely millstone.

No, he knew that he would be going through the process of slowly recovering his happiness right here in Sydney. He would be working on the difficulties of pregnancy in physically handicapped women, going home to a meal cooked four times a week by Rose, his part-time housekeeper, and the rest of the time by himself, and he would be relaxing with tennis, and, too rarely, in his beloved Snipe class yacht on the harbour.

He stepped out of the shower at last and began to towel himself dry with swift firm movements, turning the operation into a rough massage, as he always liked to do. In the outer cubicle of the shower, a clean suit and shirt hung on a hook in a filmy plastic dry-cleaning bag.

He had been surprised when young Maureen Cummings had invited him to her wedding. A brief bitter laugh broke from his lips as he thought about this. Of course he was glad that Bob Foster had come back, but he had taken the steps to contact him purely because he had been thinking of Carla. She had obviously been worried about the girl—he had seen the numb-looking line that her wide lovely mouth had been set into lately and the frown of tension that too often creased her brow

She would be there this afternoon—that was his main reason for accepting Maureen's shy invitation, rather than smiling gallantly tactful regrets. Not that her presence would afford him anything but pain, because she had made it very clear that nothing could alter her feelings for him.

There had been a time when he had at least believed that she liked him, but her words that day a couple of weeks ago had robbed him of that illusion.

'Leave me alone, that's all I ask,' she had said. A man could scarcely ask for a clearer answer than that! He had felt like a clumsy schoolboy at her words, despising himself for having read her feelings so wrongly. And then when she had perceived something of this, and had apologised for having offended him . . . !

That was when he had made the mistake of getting angry in a vain attempt to save his stupid pride. The words he had used were so false that they were not even original. He had read a very similar phrase somewhere quite a while ago—it was laughable really, if only she knew!—and for some reason it had come to the surface of his turbulent mind at that moment, to be uttered with convincing sincerity.

There! He was dressed and his tie was perfectly adjusted. He left the bathroom with a neat pile of white clothing, and picked up the vinyl sports bag that contained his other tennis things, then stopped at the door of the club-house bar where his fellow players were now enjoying a refreshing glass of beer.

'I'll see you next week, John. Max, Stuart, thank you for the game.'

'Yes, see you, Link!' John Darenth said.

The other two responded in a similar conventional way, and Lincoln left.

Carla drove to the wedding in her little Fiat, hoping that she had timed the journey right. She thought Maureen and Bob had chosen a very pretty way of going through their admittedly hasty ceremony. A civil marriage celebrant would perform the short wedding in Mrs Cummings' well-kept garden, where guests would remain afterwards for a light afternoon tea.

She arrived in time to go up to Maureen's bedroom and give her the present that she and Jane Kemp had chosen between them—an electric food blender which would come in very handy when preparing the triplets' first solid food. The social worker had been invited too, of course, but could not come. Carla admired the final results of Maureen's preparations as she paraded with happy pride before the mirror.

After this, Carla went down into the garden to mingle with the small gathering of close friends and relations who had been invited. Maureen's mother was very pleased to meet 'Doctor Scott' and confided that they were only waiting for three more people before the ceremony would begin: Mrs Llewellyn, the marriage celebrant, who was coming directly from another function, Dr Falconer, and Bob.

'But of course he'll arrive at the last minute, so he is not tempted to see Maureen till she comes down. My brother will be giving her away,' Mrs Cummings said.

'So Dr Falconer accepted his invitation, did he?' Carla asked, trying to make her voice as casual as possible.

'Yes,' Mrs Cummings replied. 'Maureen was very thrilled. I mean, he must be such a busy man with hi work at the hospital. I told her she wasn't to be disappointed if he was suddenly called out on a case, and couldn't get here after all.'

'Yes, that's very possible, actually,' Carla nodded. She knew she would be disappointed if this happened, despite her firm inner determination not to pin her hopes on his presence.

Mrs Cummings turned away to chat to someone else, and at that moment Lincoln Falconer came through the side gate of the little suburban house, and into the pretty back garden full of bright autumn flowers.

Carla flushed as she caught sight of him, and the flush deepened as he came straight to her with a greeting, although it was only natural that he should, and it meant nothing. She was the only other person here that he knew, after all.

Mechanically her hands went to the side seams of the russet autumn-weight dress she wore, and busied themselves with unnecessary straightening.

'Hullo, Carla!'

'Hullo.' Her voice came out weak, high-pitched and husky. It was ridiculous. She saw him virtually every day at the hospital, but there was something different about being here with him like this. And it was a wedding too!

She allowed a weak wave of longing to wash over her. If only she was to be the bride today! Here in this pretty garden, with Lincoln Falconer beside her as the groom!

He looked immaculate as usual. Wasn't that the dark suit he had worn the night when they had eaten out together? He looked confident and assured, too. Why was it that her face reflected her feelings so easily? He would know that she still carried a torch for him. That was a horrible expression, but in fact it did partly describe the burning within her that was her love for Lincoln.

He was talking about tennis now. Apparently he had just come from a game.

'Did you win?' Carla asked conventionally, and gave the proper congratulations when he admitted that he had.

Steady-looking Bob Foster arrived at that moment, followed almost immediately by the marriage celebrant, and two minutes later Maureen came out into the garden on her uncle's arm, looking as radiant as a bride ever did in her frothy eggshell blue dress.

It seemed quite natural that Lincoln and Carla should stand together, but she wondered if he guessed that she was intimately aware of every tiny movement he made during the ceremony. And when it was over, and Bob and Maureen were happily pronounced husband and wife, it again seemed natural that Lincoln should turn to Carla and speak.

'Rather lovely, isn't it?' he said. 'In its own simple way.'

'Yes, I thought so,' Carla replied.

If only she could feel more comfortable! This thirties-style dress was one of her favourites, and she knew it suited her, but today she felt ugly and clumsy.

'You have no marriage plans at all for yourself?' the senior obstetrician was asking now, in cool tones.

'No, I don't think it's wise to make plans for it,' Carla answered. 'I'm sure it's much easier to make the wrong choice, if you are actively on the look out for a marriage partner.'

'Then what is your opinion about how such things

ought to be managed?' he questioned, looking at her rather too intently for her own comfort.

'I think when two people are right for each other, their love will find a path naturally,' Carla said slowly, voicing a belief she had long held, but which, when face to face with Dr Falconer, she became suddenly unsure of. 'And when they are sure about each other, they will both begin to think of marriage.'

'But what if a man falls in love with a woman and she doesn't return it, even when he is quite sure that they would be right for each other? Should he give up and go away, or look for someone else? What should he do?'

'He should do the same as a woman should—he should try to forget.'

'Might it not sometimes be better if he waited for a while and then tried again?'

'If he had the courage to face the possibility of another rejection, he could do that. I'm not sure that I would have that courage,' Carla said.

'What would you think of a man who tried again, if you didn't love him?' Lincoln asked now.

'It would depend on how he went about it. But I would probably admire his courage . . .'

'I'm so glad you could both come,' Maureen interrupted at that moment, breathless but glowing. 'I was terrified you would get called to some important case, Dr Falconer, and I really wanted Bob to meet you.'

Lincoln replied with cheerful politeness and stepped aside a little to include Maureen in a small triangle that would allow conversation to flow easily between them. Carla risked a tiny glance into his eyes, but they were narrowed against the slanting light of the late afternoon sun, and she could not tell if he might have been disappointed by Maureen's chirping interruption.

No! It was absurd of her to even think it. She was disappointed herself, of course, but that was only because she had started to allow herself to read some meaning into his words that was certainly non-existent. After all, what could be more natural than to talk about love and marriage at a wedding?

Carla turned her attention to Maureen's bright voice again and found that the new bride was doing just that.

'Are you married, Dr Falconer? I should have thought to ask you to bring your wife . . .'

'No, I'm not married,' the senior obstetrician replied briefly.

'What a pity!' Maureen exclaimed, then laughed. 'You see, I've already become like all newly-weds. I'm so happy, I simply can't understand why everyone isn't doing the same as me!'

'Perhaps there are some of us who would, if we had the chance,' Lincoln said, and smiled.

'Don't tell me that you haven't got the chance!' Maureen said, her glowing excitement making her a little impertinent. 'I saw you with a very lovely silvery-blonde only a few weeks ago, when I was at the Boronia for a check-up!'

The senior obstetrician smiled again, but not very warmly, and for a moment Carla thought that his reserve would keep him silent. Maureen had gone further in her inquisitiveness than Carla would have done. But then Lincoln seemed, like Carla, to remember that it was Maureen's wedding day, and that perhaps she was entitled to ask impertinent questions.

'I know who you mean,' he said. 'But you mustn't

jump to conclusions as readily as that, just because you want to see everyone in love like yourself. The woman you saw me with is a friend, but she is involved with someone else, and don't suspect that my heart is broken about it, either. Any danger of that comes from quite another quarter!'

'Sorry to interrupt,' Maureen's mother said, having approached in a nervous flurry, too full of worries about the catering arrangements to be aware of the importance of the words she was interrupting. 'Could you help me to bring out the plates of food, Maureen? I've made masses too much. You were right when you told me it would be, but I suppose it'll all get eaten eventually.'

Maureen said that she would go at once, and Carla quickly offered to help too. She knew that her cheeks were burning, and was aware of Lincoln Falconer's tall presence. Was he looking at her as she longed to look at him? And could he see how his words had affected her?

Carla was utterly confused and disturbed now, and was barely aware of the trips she made between the small and rather ugly kitchen, and the cloth-covered trestle tables arranged in a sheltered corner of the garden. How significant had his words been?

She wanted to trust the tiny nuances of his tone, and the soft way he had been leaning towards her as he spoke, but dared not. She was becoming more and more aware of how much the whole of her relationship with him had been complicated and confused by her too-vivid imagination.

From her very first ludicrously inaccurate sketch of his personality, to her mistaken assumption about Louise Clair's marriage, her readiness to jump to conclusions had been the only consistent part of her behaviour!

There had already been too many misunderstandings between them for anything to resolve itself happily now.

As Carla carried two plates of scones to the table she saw that Lincoln was now talking with Bob Foster and another guest. He was being thoroughly polite and charming as usual, but Carla did not think that with his busy schedule he would want to spend much longer at this gathering where he knew so few people.

She told herself that she was glad. It had been nothing but her own beating heart and deep physical awareness of Lincoln Falconer that had lent such importance and such a wealth of hidden meaning to his questions, and his reaction to her own replies. And later, after Maureen's interruption, his response to that last inquisitive enquiry by the new bride: '. . . Don't suspect that my heart is broken about it, either. Any danger of that comes from quite another quarter!' She would not be fool enough to think that that 'other quarter' could be herself. The new Deputy Director of Nursing was very attractive and vivacious, or perhaps he had met some woman at his tennis club who was proving to be a difficult conquest . . .

Carla did not stay for long after she finished helping Mrs Cummings with the trays. She drank a small glass of champagne which had been provided by Maureen's uncle to toast the couple, then said goodbye.

'Has Dr Falconer left yet?' she asked Mrs Cummings, trying to sound casual.

'Yes, he has, love,' she replied. 'He went off nearly a quarter of an hour ago. Did you have something to say to him?'

'No, it can wait,' Carla smiled blindly.

So he had not stayed! Carla was depressed by the news.

despite all her earlier attempts to explain away any significance in Lincoln Falconer's conduct today. Yes! In spite of everything, this wretched heart of hers would not stop hoping.

She felt very lonely as she walked out of the front gate and got into her little car. She knew that she had let herself look forward to this afternoon too much, with its prospect of seeing Lincoln outside the more formal environment of the hospital, and now it was over.

Before, Carla would not have said that she had had any naive hopes about the day, but in retrospect, she knew she had. Somewhere in the unacknowledged background of her dreams, she had had a foolish notion that a wedding atmosphere, with its romance and happiness might . . . What? She did not even know.

Louise Clair might no longer be a rival, but this did not change the fact that Lincoln Falconer had never seen anything more in Carla than the prospect of a mild flirtation. Obviously the strange and admittedly quite searching questions he had asked her this afternoon had meant only that he wanted to know how she was now feeling about him.

A doctor through and through! Carla thought. Checking the progress of healing in the wound he had made in her heart.

She climbed into her little car, thankful to be away from people for a while. And she was on call tonight. With any luck, several women would go into labour, and keep her mind busy with other thoughts. She turned out of the quiet back street in which Mrs Cummings and her daughter had their home, and entered a busier road which contained several sets of traffic lights.

Several blocks ahead, a familiar low dark red car was

stopped at one of them. Not Lincoln surely? Carla
wondered. Mrs Cummings had said that he had left
nearly fifteen minutes before her, and so he should be
almost at the hospital by now. It must be another car of a
similar model and colour.

A minute later she had lost sight of the car in the
traffic, and decided that it had probably turned off on
some other route. Even if it had been Lincoln's, he could
well have been on his way home, and not to the hospital
at all.

Carla felt a stab of pain as she thought of this, pictur-
ing his beautiful house, thinking of his boat, and of his
friends at the tennis club—in short, imagining the whole
life he had, in which she had no share.

How long would it take her to learn to see him and
think of him without this pointless and destructive pain?

Several minutes later she reached the quiet grounds of
the hospital, and slowed to turn into the sweep of the
main driveway which led to the staff car-park between
the residence building and the main wing.

Somewhere inside the engine there was an odd clunk,
but Carla ignored it. The car was old now, and such
sounds were common. She negotiated the driveway
carefully but abstractedly, keeping to the low speed limit
requested by several glaring red and white signs, but her
thoughts still revolved around images of Lincoln.

As she turned into the car-park she pressed the brake
pedal smoothly, and it was only then that her thoughts
returned fully to the here and now, because her foot met
with no resistance at all. She had no brakes!

Fortunately the car's speed was so low that Carla's
sense of panic and danger was short-lived, but nonetheless she could not bring the car to a controlled stop, and

she found herself mounting the kerb with a painful jolt, and then hit a low cement post with a sickening raucous impact.

After this, there was stillness and silence. Carla was not hurt, but felt a wave of deep nausea pass through her, and had to flop her head and arms on to the steering wheel in front of her, and rest there for a few moments with eyes shut. If those brakes had failed just a little earlier when she had been out in the Saturday afternoon traffic, and travelling at a good speed . . .

'Carla!'

Lincoln Falconer spoke at her open window in a voice made strident with anxiety.

Carla looked up slowly, trembling, and still too weak from shock to feel either surprise or pleasure at seeing him standing there. She reached for the handle of the door, suddenly feeling claustrophobic, and needing to breath fresh air, but he anticipated her action and had opened the door and lifted her out before she could gain control of her own movements.

It was wonderful to feel herself in his arms. As he carried her to the nearby grass, she allowed her head to rest for a moment against his shoulder, sorry a few seconds later when he laid her gently down and sat beside her.

The car-park was quiet. At this hour, staff were either on duty or away somewhere enjoying their free time, and only a few figures, mainly the visiting friends and relatives of patients, could be seen in the grounds or near the main entrance.

Lincoln said nothing as Carla lay back on the grass, feeling her strength slowly return. Then she became aware that his gaze was fixed upon her face.

'I'm not hurt,' she said. 'Just shocked. The brakes seem to have failed. I should have had them checked . . .'

She stopped, suddenly self-conscious, and hating the fact that Lincoln, of all people, had been the one to come to her aid. After all, it had been the most minor of accidents. She could have managed by herself and he need never have known it had happened. She was utterly convinced now that Louise's place had already been taken by someone else, and that Lincoln knew of her own love for him and pitied her for it. How could he not know? Her feelings betrayed themselves every minute—the way she had rested her head on his shoulder, and now, lying here in the grass, letting him stay with her instead of insisting that she would be all right.

'I saw the whole thing,' he was saying. 'I'd only just arrived myself . . .'

'Then it *was* your car I saw ahead of me!' Carla exclaimed without thinking. 'I didn't think it could have been, because Mrs Cummings said that you had left fifteen minutes before me . . .'

'I waited for you.'

The words were spoken very low, in a tone that made her look up at him suddenly, but before she could speak or read the expression in his grey-green eyes, he had pulled her towards him in a close embrace that melted the last ounce of resistance she possessed.

He was murmuring her name now and pressing his warm face into her hair.

'I must have finally left just before you did yourself . . . But don't you understand what I was trying to tell you at the wedding?' he said softly.

'I . . . I wasn't sure. I had to go and help Mrs Cummings. I don't know . . .'

'I love you. I want you—I want to have you with me for always, and I'm not going to let you go until I've heard your answer in words of one syllable!'

For a minute, Carla could not answer. Happiness seemed to rise within her like a tide, making her speechless and renewing the trembling that had only just ceased after the shock of the accident.

'Carla?' He loosened his hold a fraction as though suddenly doubtful again of what her answer would be, and she finally found words.

'Of course . . . I love you.'

'Of course?'

'I thought you must have guessed long ago.'

'You credit me with a little too much self-confidence, my darling,' he said, speaking against her ear again as he nuzzled the scented curtain of her hair. 'Most men would give up for good after the third rejection!'

'Three rejections?'

'Yes. That first time I kissed you, you said "I don't want this at all". I've heard those words countless times in my head since. I'll never forget them!' he exclaimed, pausing for a moment as though hearing the words again. 'And then twice more. You seemed to despise me for having been involved with Louise Clair, and you didn't seem to want to know when I tried to tell you that it had been a mistake.'

'For a long time I thought she was married.'

'Married?'

'Yes. I made a stupid mistake. It doesn't matter now.' Carla touched his lips with the tip of an exploring finger as she spoke. 'I thought you were just proposing some affair, carried on at the same time as your relationship with Louise.'

'Did I really seem like that sort of a person?'

'No, you didn't. That was what made it so difficult. Everything I learned about you when I was with you made me love you,' Carla said, tasting every part of this so-important word which she could at last use freely to him. 'And yet the facts seemed to be against you.'

'The facts?'

'My imagination,' she confessed. 'I'll have to learn to curb it.'

'It does seem to have got us into a little trouble—but don't curb it completely, my darling,' he smiled, his voice full of meaning. 'Sometimes I thought I had the same problem. That it was only my imagination that let me believe I saw something in your eyes that belied everything you said to me. Even that last time, when . . . What did I say? Something ridiculous about you "rating your charms too highly". How ludicrous! You said then "Please just leave me alone," but your eyes were so full of fire and warmth . . .'

'You like my eyes, don't you?' she teased. 'You're always noticing them.'

'I adore your eyes,' he returned. 'And as for your charms, I take back what I said. I don't think anyone could rate them too highly!'

'But I still don't completely understand about Louise . . .' Carla began to say.

'I knew quite a while ago that I could never love her,' Lincoln replied. 'But she insisted that we keep seeing each other. "For fun", she said. We went out together, but there was nothing very physical. She's determined to make a success of the new morality, believing that she can be involved with several men at once, without hurting any of them—or herself. I disagreed. She kept coming to the hospital, trying to keep things going, and wanting to be seen with me, even though she and Peter Prior—from the Board—were already seeing each other constantly. I finally put a stop to it though. I tried to tell you the whole story, to gauge your reaction, but you would never let me begin, and I didn't know what to think. Then one day I saw you with Michael Groom, and for a while I thought that you must be in love with him. I thought a dozen different things . . .'

'And so did I, but never the right things,' Carla murmured.

'But it doesn't matter now,' he said.

'Not a bit . . .'

He drew her close again and kissed her slowly, then became his cool, dry self again, releasing her from the happy confinement of his arms as he spoke:

'I think it might be a good idea if we take a look at that car of yours, to see how much it's damaged, then remove ourselves from this compromising position to find a more congenial place. We might have a lot to talk about, don't you think? The details of the wedding, and so forth . . .'

'Yes, Dr Falconer,' Carla began, just as an electronic tone began to sound rhythmically from Lincoln's breast pocket.

They smiled wryly at each other.

'There goes your bleep. Do you think this is going to be typical of our whole married life?' Carla said.

'Probably, my darling.'